A Rebel North

Part Two

of

The Sassana Stone

Pentalogy

JAMES VELLA-BARDON

TEARAWAY PRESS

Copyright

Published by Tearaway Press 2022
PO Box 477, Belrose West, Sydney NSW 2085

Copyright © James Vella-Bardon 2022

James Vella-Bardon asserts the moral right to be identified as the author of this work.

ISBN: 978-0-6451230-2-9

Cover design and typesetting by Rafael Andres

To my friend Pierre Fenech, being an immigrant is indeed a country of its own.

Tributes for
The Sassana Stone
Pentalogy

"Reminds me of works by today's masters such
as Bernard Cornwell, Conn Iggulden and Wilbur Smith"
- The Scotsman

"Has what it takes to become a literary giant"
- Yorkshire Evening Post

"Remember the name of rising author James Vella-Bardon"
- Reader's Digest

"Sheer quality, historical integrity and emotional resonance"
- The London Economic

"This well-plotted story full of adventure, danger
and history is wonderfully told, and Abel is a character
not soon forgotten" – *The US Review Of Books*

Cast of Characters

The MacGlannagh Tribe

Tadhg *Óg* MacGlannagh, Gaelic chieftain of the MacGlannagh tribe

Dervila Bourke, Anglo-Norman wife of Tadhg *Óg*.

Muireann Mac An Bhaird, widow of Tadhg *Óg's* late son Aengus *Cliste*.

Lochlain, only son of Aengus and Muireann.

Cathal *Dubh*, Tadhg *Óg's* marshal (cavalry commander) and nephew.

Donal *Garbh* MacCabe, Scottish constable of the tribe's gallowglass troop

Redmond O'Ronayne, a Jesuit and a qualified physician.

Nial *Dua Claimthe* Ne Dourough, a bondsman in the service of Tadhg *Óg*.

Spaniards

Francisco de Cuéllar, a sea captain shipwrecked in Ireland.

Abelardo de Santiago, a widowed marksman shipwrecked in Ireland.

Sassenachs

George Bingham, English sheriff of Sligo.

John Gilson, an Irish renegade lieutenant in the service of Bingham.

Treasach Burke, an Irish renegade sergeant in the service of Bingham.

The dead

Aengus *Cliste*, only son of Tadhg *Óg* and Dervila, husband of Muireann, father of Lochlain.

Cathal *Óg*, previous chieftain of the MacGlannagh tribe and called *An Faolchù* (The Wolf). Also the elder brother of Tadhg *Óg* and the father of Cathal *Dubh*.

Elsien van der Molen, late wife of Abeldardo de Santiago.

Maerten van der Molen, late brother of Elsien.

Reynier van der Molen, late father of Elsien, Maerten and Pieter.

THE STORY SO FAR...

*I*n 1585, the war between the Spanish crown and Protestant Netherlands is still raging. In the midst of this clash, Abelardo 'Santi' de Santiago, a veteran of the Spanish Army of Flanders, finds himself barracked in the Brabantian village of Willebroek. Santi is renowned for his deadly aim in battle, with his marksmanship earning him the nickname of 'the Lynx of Haarlem'. After briefly courting Elsien, the daughter of local miller Reynier van der Molen, he is quickly married to her when her father discovers that she is with child.

Due to outbreaks of violence in the village that are caused by the ongoing revolt, Reynier decides to hire Santi's Spanish comrades as his bodyguards. These consist of Santi's ruthless sergeant 'Curro' Ramos, corporal 'Salva' Ortiz, Gabriel de Andrés and Tomé 'Cristó' de Cristóbal. Santi warns Reynier not to hire these men but he is ignored by his father-in-law. However Santi's fears are vindicated when Reynier can no longer pay his bodyguards to protect him.

With his comrades fast turning on his father-in-law, Santi decides to join in a surprise raid on a band of Protestant mercenaries in the surrounding woods. Yet he is knocked senseless during the ill-fated ambush and abandoned by his comrades. After recovering consciousness, he makes his way back to Willebroek with the help of his brother-in-law Maerten who was sent *by Elsien to find Santi in the woods. On the way back to Willebroek, Santi and Maerten learn from a local woodcutter that the besieged city of Antwerp has fallen. Santi instantly fears that his unpaid company of soldiers may have been relieved, prompting them to turn on and rob the local Netherlanders before returning home to Spain.*

Upon arriving in Willebroek, Santi's concerns are soon justified. For he and Maerten are horrified to learn that the pregnant Elsien and her father Reynier have died of suffocation after Santi's comrades burned down their house as an act of retaliation against Reynier. In his rage Santiago kills a Spanish officer, then deserts the army and - along with Maerten - abandons Elsien's remaining family to chase her killers all the way to Seville.

After reaching the great city, Santiago and Maerten live clandestinely while they track down Santi's former comrades at night. Santi kills Cristó in cold blood, yet he and Maerten are captured by Ramos after a whore betrays Maerten's whereabouts. Ramos sells Santi and Maerten to a cruel overseer of the Spanish Armada for a small fortune, so that the wretched pair eventually find themselves reduced to galley slaves aboard a hospital ship. They proceed to spend months at sea, suffering every setback and misfortune which is endured by the great navy.

The Armada is eventually defeated by the English fleet at the famous sea battle of Gravelines. During this conflict Santi attacks de Andrés and after a vicious swordfight he manages to somehow fling his former comrade overboard. The battered ships of the Armada attempt to return to Spain by sailing around Scotland and then south along the west coast of Ireland. Santi's hospital ship soon gets cut off from the main fleet and is shipwrecked off the west coast of Ireland. Maerten is tragically lost at sea, while Santi reaches the shore and journeys inland. He soon discovers a country that is oppressed by heartless English troopers that the natives call Sassenachs, which to Santi's Spanish ear sounds like 'Sassanas.'

Santi is hunted by English troopers who have orders from their queen's Viceroy in Dublin to capture and kill all Spanish Armada castaways. He is eventually seized by George Bingham, the brutal English sheriff of Sligo Town, who imprisons Santi and has him tortured. Thanks to an unlikely twist of fate, Santi flees Sligo with an invaluable emerald ring which belongs to a nobleman who sailed with the Spanish Armada. After somehow managing to escape, he rescues a revered Irish bard named Muireann Mac an Bhaird from a Sassana night raid, during which Muireann loses her husband, the Irish prince Aengus MacGlannagh.

Santi and Muireann form an unlikely pairing as they travel north, while seeking to elude their enemies. Along the way Santi also manages to exact his revenge upon Salva and Ramos in an abandoned church. After a desperate last escape from a band of English troopers, Muireann leads Santi deep into her tribe's rebel kingdom of Dartry, where a force of natives repels the pursuing Sassanas. Santi is knocked out cold during the skirmish and later wakes up in an infirmary in MacGlannagh town, alongside the tower house of Rosclogher.

'...these people are generally strong bodied, nimble, bold, haughty, quick-witted, warlike, venturous, inur'd to cold and hunger, lustful, hospitable, constant in their love, implacably malicious, credulous, vain-glorious, resenting; and, according to their old character, violent in all their affections: the bad not to be match'd, the good not to be excell'd...'

- J. Good, a priest, educated at Oxford and Schoolmaster of Limerick, circa 1566

XVI

Rosclogher, Dartry, County Leitrim, Ireland

20 - 26 September 1588

After the chieftain's marshal left my side, the Jesuit muttered something about having to return to the abbey for the night. I tossed about fitfully after O'Ronayne was gone, aching all over due to the many injuries and blows I had endured in Ireland after being shipwrecked. Then I fell at last into a deep sleep, with my mind leading me down the recesses of my memory. Of a sudden there appeared boyhood visions of other children bullying me at the foundling home of the Knights Hospitaller, followed by the sight of my father dying at my feet, during the siege of Saint Michael on the island of Malta.

Then I found myself staring into the face of my late wife Elsien. A face I would never tire of gazing on, despite the slightest of scars on her forehead. It was all that remained of the bruises and cuts she had suffered at Christmastide, when she told me that she had slipped on the ice with her brother Pieter. Her tumble had greatly distressed me at the time, yet it was swiftly forgotten as she drew herself close to me the following night and urged me to partake in the act of love.

I had at first been reluctant to do so, despite the great temptation to claim her honour outside wedlock. Yet at her insistence, our first lovemaking was carried out beneath our Empress tree, although she curiously seemed to derive no pleasure from it. Then my memories shifted and turned into another recollection. I suddenly found myself clutching Elsien's dead form on that ill-starred day in Willebroek, alongside her father's corpse while her brother raged at the other villagers behind us.

The memories ended abruptly when my eyes shot open. I would have woken up in complete darkness were it not for the faint glow of a tallow candle. My cheek brushed against straw as I raised my head, when I noticed that I had fallen out of my bed.

'All dead!' I gasped in disbelief, while I recalled everyone in the vivid nightmare, 'all...dead!'

The realisation was of scant relief, for the ache in my stomach was still all too real. I clutched my belly as it twinged with unease, causing me to suddenly panic.

'No,' I gasped, realising that I could not hold it in, 'no...no...'

There followed an almighty fart, loud and brusque, and for a moment I thought it might rouse the old invalid or the servants. I knew better than to risk losing the ring with the next discharge, so as another rumble left my stomach I tore at the ground and shoved myself forward. I was still too lightheaded to stand, yet no less resolved to reach the pail by the door.

'Whoreson', I hissed at myself, using the old slur sung to me during my childhood, in the foundling home of the knights of Malta. I was instantly overwhelmed by rage and self-loathing at the distant memory of the other orphans laughing out loud, while poking me in the chest as they sang the insult. It instantly had the desired effect, for in my anger I gained enough vigour to crawl forward some more. Upon reaching the foul-smelling pail I rose to one knee and squatted over it while lifting my linen tunic.

'God help me,' I sighed, as the next flatus erupted like a thunderclap.

Yet no one else stirred from sleep despite a low rasp and a groan. To my left, a guard quickly shoved his head through the doorway but instantly withdrew when he realised my business.

'Oh misery,' I whispered to myself between whimpers of unhappiness, sliding my hand through my legs, 'what utter misery...'

Amid these mutterings I engaged in the unpleasant task of searching for the trinket within the ordure, until my fingers closed about hard edges that were swiftly wrapped in my palm. The pail was upended as I clumsily got off it, so that I drew breath through my mouth until I made it back to my bed. Upon reaching it I shoved my besmirched hand between two straw-filled sacks and released the trinket. My exertions were a fiendish struggle due to my head wound, which left me feeling utterly spent. So it was with great effort that I managed to climb back atop my bedding, then fell into a deep, dreamless slumber.

I opened my eyes again late the next morning, to a hearty patting of my cheek. I turned my head and found the Jesuit frowning at me in contempt. His wiry, copper curls were as unruly as ever, with his heavy-lidded green eyes giving him the appearance of one who always lacked sleep. The daylight which streamed through the door behind him revealed that the disgusting mess I had caused during the night was already cleaned up, with sawdust having been scattered around the pail. Some of the servants cast me dark looks from the other side of the cabin.

O'Ronayne's stare was fixed on my right hand, which was still besmirched after my searching for the ring. I coughed uncomfortably, then noticed that O'Ronayne held out a flask of vinegar and a rag, so that I sheepishly withdrew my blanket and allowed him to clean me. When he was finished, he drew a small bell from his cloak and shoved it against my chest. He pushed its lip against my flesh for emphasis, then released it so that it tumbled into my hands.

'The next time,' he uttered between gritted teeth, 'have the servants fetch it for you, if you cannot wait.'

Having served me with this terse reprimand, he turned on his heel and stormed out of the cabin. I sighed aloud at his departure, relieved to be temporarily free of his disapproval. I was also grateful to have found the ring during the night, as I reached out and patted the space between the sacks beneath me, where I had hidden it.

'We'll need to move you somewhere else soon,' I whispered over the edge of my bed, as if the invaluable bauble was not also an inanimate object.

The following days of rest left me feeling revived. The very sight of the Jesuit priest unnerved me, but thankfully his presence at my side became less frequent during my ongoing recovery. Before long he only appeared in the infirmary at dusk, to assess the condition of his older charge and to feed me a curious mixture of beef broth and goat's milk. The protection and care extended by my hosts hastened my healing, and after months of malnourishment, I greedily wolfed down all of the strips of half-cooked cowflesh which were brought to me by the Jesuit's attendants.

I could eventually also rise from my litter and take my first steps, between spells of light headedness caused by my head wound. The guards at the door barred my exit from the infirmary, which confined me to a largely solitary existence. Yet there were days when I could make out eyes peering at me through the boards of the cabin. For a great curiosity had taken hold of the tribesmen in the town, after word quickly spread among them that a Spanish alien was recovering in the infirmary. Because of these rumours, shifting shadows often obscured the daylight that streamed between the boards, as natives outside the cabin tried to spy on me.

One enterprising Dartryman even tried to strike up conversation with me in broken Latin through the boards, until the guards overheard him and drove him away. Another time a portly simpleton, his head bursting with rumours of Spaniards, burst into the cabin while the guards were changing. He proceeded to prod my chest hard with his finger until I woke with a gasp of shock, only to find the gaping fool beaming at me with spittle rolling down his chin. A whole stream of gibberish was howled at me in his frenzied excitement, until he was quickly seized and led back to his family.

When not distracted by the tribesmen's attentions, I often scratched my skin relentlessly because of the vermin in my blanket of sackcloth. Yet I was still grateful for my itchy coverlet, which I held close whenever icy draughts jabbed the cabin's warmth like cold knives shoved between the boards. As I drifted in and out of consciousness, memories of Sergeant Burke's torture chamber and death pit gnawed at my thoughts, as did the overwhelming recollection of his terrifying Spanish spider and the priceless trinket hidden in the sacks beneath me.

These thoughts of the priceless ring also brought to mind the incredible events of previous years, from the heartbreaking discovery of Elsien's body to the hazardous voyage of the Spanish Armada. The wounds and bruises all over my body also reminded me of the many injuries and torments I had been subjected to, ever since I had set foot in Ireland. The death of Ramos and my other former comrades achieved the one overarching objective of my life, yet I felt a deep chasm of emptiness growing within me with each passing day until I even questioned the very meaning of my own existence.

May as well be dead, I thought to myself, as I turned onto my side.

There appeared little left for me to strive towards, for nothing stirred any excitement or passion within me, save for the thought of the ring which I had hidden in the sacks beneath me. At times I was even tempted to search the Jesuit's supplies for a vial of laudanum with which to end it all. Yet while weeping over the recollection of my lost brother-in-law Maerten, I suddenly recalled the vow I had made to him on the rowing benches of the Santa Maria de Visión.

'Promise me,' he had said, during those interminable days spent dawdling along the coast of Ireland, 'promise me that you'll return for him.'

'Of course I will,' I had replied, 'but we shall do it together Marti!'

Of a sudden I felt overwhelmed by a mission which became suddenly apparent to me: to find my youngest brother-in-law Pieter and return him to the New World. I could still remember the sight of the young boy, hiding behind the skirts of his aunt Margareta as I limped away from the corpses of his father and sister to shoot dead the ensign and rescue Maerten. We had not spoken a word to the lad as we rode out of Willebroek, intent on slaying the men who had killed my wife by burning down her house.

It's been so long, I thought to myself, *yet I must return for him if I can. I must find him and take him to the New World.*

The emerald ring in my possession left me resolved to escape from the hell in which I found myself and somehow return to the Continent. It became my primary mission, one that took the edge off the pangs of sorrow which I felt for my late wife and her brother Maerten, which often left me feeling distraught and unnaturally quiet for long periods.

I eventually realised that I had spent almost four days in the infirmary, following the visit paid to me by Dartry's marshal, Cathal the Black. Then on the following morning, my reverie was disturbed by a rumble of hooves belonging to the chieftain Manglana's mounted force. The impending arrival of Dartry's king had already been announced by a scout who appeared in the town earlier that morning, blowing on his horn and causing a stir. Upon receiving this news, O'Ronayne began scuttling about the infirmary in a frenzy, testing the sharpness of his surgeon's knives against his thumbs and inspecting the condition of his implements. All throughout he bellowed orders to his apprentices who unfurled spools of twine, readying it for the stitching of open wounds and the ligature of severed veins.

After checking the Jesuit's medicine chest, the apprentices were swiftly dispatched to the woods, sickle in hand, to fetch more herbs for his poultices. Meanwhile their servants - men they called churls and who were treated little better than slaves – were ordered to bear water from the lake. They immediately did as they were bidden, returning to the cabin with dripping, swaying buckets which hung from their shoulder yokes.

At O'Ronayne's command, some of this water was heated in a lead cauldron and next used to clean all pots, decanters and plates previously used to serve patients. These utensils were scoured with handfuls of straw and sprinkles of potash. The miserable churls were also accorded other menial tasks, which included the collection of firewood and the washing of stained linen which had been used to treat patients.

Having recently been treated like a beast of toil myself, I could not help feeling pity while I observed these efforts. For the churls were clad in filthy rags and their grim-looking faces bore no expression at all. As I was later to discover at great personal cost, these wretches were men who had committed crimes of such severity that the law of my hosts denied them all rights as punishment. They were also prohibited from inheriting property or bearing arms.

Out of the goodness of his own heart, the Jesuit had recruited some of these wretches to assist him in the infirmary. The toil he put them through guaranteed them a meal and nights spent sleeping on the ground like beasts. Before the sun rose again, they would take it in turns to awake and keep the flames going, piling cones upon them to prevent dangerous odours from filling the cabin.

All of their frenzied preparations within the infirmary were instantly abandoned when other blares of the trumpet were heard towards midday. These blasts were instantly followed by the peals of a bell, as Jesuit, attendants and churls alike tore out of the cabin to witness the arrival of the returning host. They left me behind to toss and turn in frustration, for I was also keen to witness the scene of the chieftain's returning militia.

So as the townsfolk's cries grew outside, I pulled myself out of bed and even succeeded in shuffling past the fire alone. Then dizziness seized me again and I tripped over a log and ripped away the fur curtain which hung across the doorway. My arms waved about helplessly, as I almost dislodged the bandaged poultice on my wounded shoulder against one of the doorway's jambs.

'Holy host!'

I groaned in pain, issuing clouds of mist from my mouth until the ache in my shoulder had passed. I next stared from side to side, hardly believing that I had almost succeeded in emerging from the hut unassisted. I had also earned my first glimpse of Manglana town, which had hosted me for at least a week. To my relief the guards outside the infirmary had also abandoned their posts, which allowed me some time to further observe my surrounds.

The infirmary itself stood along the edge of a huge lake which stretched on all sides for as far as the eye could see. A tree-covered tongue of land ran along an opposite bank, which was cloaked in thick forest. Almost a musket shot away from where I lay, a stone tower house rose from an island in the lake. Its clever location fascinated me since it was surrounded by a shield of water on all sides, which made it easily defensible.

'What is this place?' I uttered.

I could make out haycocks, a sawyard and even the inevitable smithy in the town. Then the peals of the bell drew my attention to the sight of a small belfry atop the town's abbey, which rose above the thatched huts before me. Both the infirmary and the abbey were situated at the foot of a gentle rise. At the top of this hillock was a sizeable plot of land which resembled a village green, which was guarded by a manned ringfort that stood to its right.

The rest of the settlement was made up of a cluster of large cabins and smaller huts. It was in truth a village in all but name, with the town surrounded on all sides by distant mountain ranges, which were shrouded by a dense woodland. I took in these environs as I shivered helplessly upon the ground, while hoping that my head would stop spinning. I also felt winded from my exertions, even lacking the strength to cry out to the people who ran out of their huts towards the greensward.

Upon reaching it they joined a great crowd of other townsfolk who milled about the armed host which had appeared. This returning militia mainly consisted of kerns in white tunics who pushed through the gathered crowd. In this way these scarred warriors cleared a path for saffron cavalrymen in long mailshirts, who marched beneath a huge standard which flapped wildly in the breeze, which bore the image of a white shield and two red lions. Like the kerns, these highborn riders had also entered the town on foot, with horseboys close at their backs and leading their masters' steeds by the bridle.

The cries and screams from the townsfolk grew as families were reunited. Yet the widowed women sobbed and shrieked in anguish upon discovering their new status. Their heart wrenching howls were accompanied by the great lowing of those cows which had been captured during Manglana's raid, but through it all I could not catch sight of the chieftain since he was surrounded by tribesmen. After a time spent shivering in the doorway, I made out the grass-stained feet of two of the Jesuit's churls as they returned to the infirmary, after they had witnessed the return of the force which had left the whole town entranced. Their faces were creased by deep scowls when they noticed me on the ground.

'Imeacht gan teacht ort!'

Amid these snarls and dark mutterings, they lifted me to my feet and dragged me back into the cabin, then hurled me onto my bed. Their anger came as little surprise to me, for these servants were treated roughly enough merely for following orders and toiling like beasts. I could not imagine what fate would have befallen them, had the Jesuit found the marshal's charge shivering upon the ground like a herring fallen out of a fisherman's basket.

For the rest of the day, the infirmary was filled with the howling of the wounded. O'Ronayne had not spoken idly when he predicted the storm which would ensue upon the chieftain's return. His travails began when a dozen kerns were hastily borne into the cabin upon their fellows' mantles. A few of them were already in their death throes, so that the loud groaning and the gnashing of teeth left me to plant the palms of my hands over my ears.

Other wounded soldiers were also carried inside the hut, with their white or yellowed tunics covered in red and black blood stains. Injured kerns cried out in the universal plaint of the dying soldier, and the sound often disturbed my slumber. Before long there were over a score of grievously wounded men within the cabin, and O'Ronayne and his apprentices toiled manfully to attend to their needs. The Jesuit wore a constant glare of concentration beneath his knotted brow, as he carried out amputations and treated burns and open wounds.

All throughout these exertions, he revealed a deftness of hand and a stomach for gore to rival the stoutest of skirmishers. With a set jaw he threw himself into the fray of withdrawing musket balls and other missiles from the flesh of the wounded, and more than half would have perished were it not for his valiant efforts and skill. To my great surprise, although the Jesuit did occasionally resort to bloodletting, he did not willingly draw the claret as freely as other surgeons whose work I had witnessed.

I watched him closely with a grudging admiration while his apprentices busied themselves with cleaning and dressing minor wounds and sores. At times they called out to O'Ronayne when a serious injury was discovered which required his attention. Meanwhile the churls busied themselves with delivering generous servings of drink to the grievously wounded, filling their mead horns until the poor wretches were unconscious and bereft of their wits.

No sooner did these invalids produce their first drunken babblings than the Jesuit would stealthily emerge from the shadows, proceeding to tighten a tourniquet about a limb which was beyond saving. His razor-sharp knife was then plunged into their flesh, severing it with great haste. Meanwhile his aides held down the subject of his attentions, who would issue hair-raising screams that sapped one's spirits.

Mercifully only three amputations were required that day. In one case a leg required removal because it had been crushed beneath a horse's hooves. The other two were required to treat arms which had been severed at the shoulder and the forearm by enemy axes. Other sufferers fared worse, with one barely surviving a shot in his chest, as he wheezed horribly besides me, while his comrade had suffered a shrapnel wound in the throat.

The latter perished within an hour of reaching us, despite the Jesuit's best attempts to plug his wound with a linen compress. For the rest, it was the usual removal of arrowheads and balls which took up O'Ronayne's attentions, together with the mending of broken bones, the resetting of dislocated limbs, and other pleasantries which surgeons somehow find it in themselves to attend to.

These tasks busied the Jesuit to such a degree that he had a younger prelate in his tutelage summoned from a nearby village to administer last rites to the dying. When the last of the mead and wine had been served, the churls were charged with keeping the fire raging to dispel the bad smells in the cabin which caused bad humours. Pine cones were also piled upon the flames to keep the overall scent within the cabin healthy.

One of the Jesuit's patients was quite unlike any of the other invalids brought before him. I heard an apprentice gasping the words *galloglaigh* and *Mac Cába* at the sight of this new patient and the two men who bore him into the cabin. These three entrants were as tall and portly as German landsknecht mercenaries and bore huge battle axes. I stared at them in amazement, for all three had broken noses, with their ears disfigured and swollen.

Their cruel expressions, I thought to myself, *make the rugged kerns appear docile by comparison.*

Long quilted coats fluttered about their long shirts of chainmail which reached down to their ankles. Their eyes burned hatefully above their thick moustaches and beards at the sight of anything about them. Their bearing hinted at every evil deed under the sun and they seemed incapable of fear. They possessed an air of great malice and danger, so that the Irish kerns in the hut stepped away from these three new entrants whenever they could.

Yet one of the warriors snatched the Jesuit's attendant by the collar and roared at O'Ronayne's man, all the while pointing at the crossbow bolt which ran through his fellow's thigh. It subsequently took two of these axemen, the two guards from the infirmary door and five churls to hold down the injured warrior while O'Ronayne cut the arrowhead out of his flesh. The Jesuit barely managed to keep his arms from quivering as all manner of curses and oaths were roared at him.

The wounded axeman exhibited fiendish strength during the procedure when he freed one of his arms and punched a poor churl in the chin, knocking him unconscious and sending him rolling over the straw. When at last the bolt was expelled, the brute's grunts were greatly reduced and his two comrades left the hut, buffeting men out of the way with their shoulders. When they were gone O'Ronayne exhaled a huge sigh of relief, then collapsed upon a stool before me. He was winded from his efforts, with his brow coated with beads of sweat while his chest heaved wildly.

'Who were those men?' I asked him.

The Jesuit was still red in the face, when he glared through the doorway and looked disgusted as he turned to face me.

'They are warriors from Scotland, men call gallowglasses: black-hearted and sinful mercenaries in the employ of my lord MacGlannagh. They are our greatest shield and our greatest scourge. A necessary evil we must endure during these terrible times, for they do not know the meaning of fear.'

He paused to take a deep breath, before casting a look over his shoulder and resuming our discourse.

'They are always the last to leave the battlefield, it is said that they saved the day during my Lord's last skirmish. Although few shall grieve the dozen of them who met with death.'

'You need say no more, Father. The manners of mercenaries are generally most loathsome.'

'Alas, grey wolf', said the Jesuit, wiping his brow with the end of his sleeve, 'it is not their manners that are the chief trouble, but their presence. They are often billeted amongst the tribesmen when they are stationed in Rosclogher. Yet they do not respect the innocence of our daughters nor our need to ration for the winter months ahead.'

His laments were not lost on me, for my years of soldiering had often found me lodged with soldiers of fortune. They always preyed on defenceless villagers, often raiding their homes and raping both married and unmarried women. With a sigh I sought to banish these recollections, while seeking to learn more about the chieftain's raid.

'So did Manglana's attack not meet with triumph?'

O'Ronayne stared at the ground for a long while until he answered my question.

'The heads which he rustled shall certainly not go amiss this winter. Yet his attack on Belleek caused more losses than expected. Were it not for the gallowglasses, his force would not even have fled the field.'

'What is this Belleek that you speak of?'

'An enemy garrison, north of Dartry. The attempt to seize it was carried out with other rebel lords who also believe that the Spanish landings will aid our cause. They attempted to take an important garrison from the Sassanas while all eyes were turned to the shipwrecks along the coast. Yet at Belleek they found an enemy which was already prepared for the worst.

The Jesuit's voice was suddenly lowered as he leaned closely towards me.

'It has also been rumoured... that the enemy somehow learned of my Lord's scheme.'

His revelation unnerved me, so that my voice betrayed a note of concern.

'So they did not sack the town?'

'The kerns say they did, but not for long. They were repelled by an unexpected relief force of heretics. The MacGlannagh is to recount what happened to the assembly of freemen today, and he has also requested that you make an appearance in his hall.'

I could not help groaning when I learned that my presence had been requested, which caused the Jesuit to flinch while he cast me a look of concern.

'What ails you, Spaniard?'

I frowned with strain as I lifted myself onto an elbow.

'Can it not wait one more day?'

O'Ronayne grimaced, upon realising that it was my impending meeting with the chieftain which had distressed me.

'You have received enough care, grey wolf. Both the marshal and I agree that your beard is now of respectable length, enough for you to meet with the *dal* - I mean - the assembly of freemen.'

I was too weak to argue. With a loud sigh I rolled onto my back, so that the Jesuit cocked a suspicious eyebrow at me.

'Why are you so reluctant to meet with your protector? Do you fear his questions about the fate which befell the Armada?'

His voice was possessed of a slightly suspicious tone, so that I could deduce that he still suspected me to be a galley slave, one who knew little about what happened above decks during the Spanish Armada's journey. Yet in truth I knew everything, since the endless gossip recounted to us by the one-eared slave Costa had been as plentiful as the weevils we had eaten during the miserable last leg of our journey to Ireland.

'I fear no questions,' was my curt reply.

O'Ronayne frowned, his face twisted in annoyance while he tried to sound calm.

'You should be honoured to have been accorded the free-dom of speech amongst the *dal*. It is usually only allowed to bards or judges.'

At the sight of his obvious annoyance, I tried to explain my reluctance.

''tis indeed a great honour,' I replied, 'yet I do not wish to bear your master tidings of his son's death.'

The Jesuit broke his stare from me then so that I instant-ly berated myself, for fear of having upset him further. O'Ronayne ignored me for a while longer when a loud roar was heard which had us all start in fright. It had been issued by one of the Jesuit's patients, when a bandage was pulled off his scalded thigh by the Jesuit's attendants. After a short pause O'Ronayne addressed me again, his face becoming contorted as he referred once more to the dead tanist.

'The MacGlannagh has already learned of his son's passing. He was told about it after the raid.'

His voice began to quiver as he stared at me with tears forming upon his eyelids.

'It is said that upon receiving the news, my Lord MacGlan-nagh walked over to a handful of the captives seized from Bel-leek. He approached the first of these Sassanas with a bared blade and a hundred sword strokes did not quell his howls of anguish.'

'What?' I asked, profoundly disturbed by this description of my host.

'He next retired to a mountain fastness,' said O'Ronayne, ignoring my question, 'which was the cause of his delayed re-turn. His party were plagued by cold and wolves, and it was a struggle to defend the cattle which they had rustled. Yet he did not emerge for two whole days, and it is said that he has barely uttered a word since.'

'And is that anecdote meant to serve as encouragement?' I asked, hardly relishing the prospect of meeting a king in such a foul mood.

O'Ronayne finally appeared to pick up on my trepidation.

'Do not fear, grey wolf. For hearing of Aengus's bravery from the lips of a Spaniard should serve to fill my Lord Mac-Glannagh with pride. Maybe even dull the pain of his loss. It is also said that his spirits have been raised by other favourable tidings which he has received of late.'

'Oh?' I asked, taken unawares by the unlikely prospect of good news.

'It appears that the English Viceroy in Dublin is beside himself with fear. One of the Sassenachs captured at Belleek has revealed that the Viceroy dreads an uprising by the tribes across Connacht. Even now, he fears that their might will be allied to that of a powerful Spanish force.'

His words left me feeling ill at ease, for each mention of Spain brought back memories of my endless days spent at the oar. Each day I feared that another survivor of the Santa Maria de Visión might appear among my hosts, to reveal that I was a galley slave.

'Hundreds of your countrymen are gathered a few miles north,' said O'Roynane almost joyfully, 'under the command of a great Spanish captain, a certain Antonio de Leiva. Even the Bingham devils are afraid to approach their number. Rumours abound that the MacGlannagh hopes to forge an alliance with them.'

'Why?' I blurted, despite myself, 'do his people not have enough trouble sheltering the Scottish mercenaries?'

The Jesuit's eyebrows were raised at my retort, as an unconscious tribesman started to gibber across the cabin. With a huff the Jesuit rose to his feet, hissing orders at his subordinates in a hoarse voice. For after his exertions of the last two days he was unable to bark commands any longer.

I slumped back on the sackcloth, feeling ill at ease. My exchange with O'Ronayne had left me dreading my meeting Manglana, while realising that Muireann's description of me might decide my fate. It was not uncommon for aliens or commoners to take the blame for the untimely passing of a young aristocrat, which often also meant torture and death. Furthermore, my rough treatment of the ollave when fleeing the lieutenant John Gilson also left me feeling apprehensive.

On the day after the chieftain's return, those patients of the Jesuit who could walk were escorted back to other lodgings by their kinsmen. This left around six wounded kerns in the infirmary, two of whom passed away before the Sabbath. Between the howling of the wind outside and the last throes of the dying, it was impossible to sleep. Dawn had almost broken when my eyes finally closed, so that I did not stir again until my ankle was shaken. I was surprised to hear a low voice that spoke Spanish.

'Greetings, grey wolf. The assembly of freemen await you.'

I immediately assumed that the speaker was the Jesuit, so that I groaned aloud.

'What do they want from me, I wonder?'

There was no reply. Yet when I stirred, I was surprised to discover a blond, raw-boned tribesman standing at the foot of my litter. He wore a wry smile on his strikingly handsome face and did not look much older than me, although he was certainly taller. His beard was trimmed in a way that reminded me of Spain, and beneath his white tunic and embroidered brown jacket he wore trews and boots of Cordovan leather.

His clothing and appearance greatly differed from that of the other tribesmen. Yet the differences did not end there, for the man did not bear a shield and wore a mailed glove upon one hand, with two swords, one hanging from each of his hips. Their grips were ribbed and bound in leather thongs, with the leather frills at the end of their curious scabbards fluttering in the draught. At my obvious surprise at his appearance, the visitor bowed once and deeply while explaining his sudden appearance.

'I am here to escort you to the best hearth in Rosclogher. My Lord MacGlannagh yearns for tidings of the Armada.'

'And where did you learn my tongue?' I asked.

'In Flanders.'

At his back stood two other natives who were haughty of bearing, in the manner of most fighting men. In their left hands they held vicious-looking *skene* daggers, while clutching two spears in their other hand Each of them wore the white tunics I had seen on most natives and their long fringes covered their eyes and reached down to the bridges of their noses. Around their shoulders were woollen jackets of an intricate design and a deep hue of blue. These articles of clothing were most curious, since their hanging oversleeves almost reached their shoes, with thick hanging pleats falling around the waist.

Of greater curiousity were the silver crosses which were emblazoned upon the right breast of these blue-jacketed men. I took them to be symbols of rank, and I later learned that they were borne by a select band of highly trained kerns who formed part of Manglana's bodyguard. They were men charged with defending their chieftain's person at all times, as well as keeping the peace in his territories - not quite unlike the Hermandades back in Seville. I stared back at them in surprise, when the Jesuit appeared through the turf smoke.

'You must pardon our Spanish charge, *dóerfuidir*,' said O'Ronayne as he stood before the kerns, 'for his wits are still dulled by his injury, and he is reluctant to leave the infirmary.'

'What did you call him?' I asked irritably, for I was unfamiliar with the term used by the Jesuit to address the blond swordsman.

O'Ronayne squinted at me as he mulled over the best Spanish translation.

'*Dóerfuidir*...it means bondsman. It means he holds unfree status.'

'Unfree?' I asked in surprise, 'is he a slave?'

'No, not a slave,' said the Jesuit, 'yet he is bound to my lord MacGlannagh and unable to leave his service until he is freed from it.'

The blond bondsman frowned as a hesitant smile played upon his lips.

'Should I relay a message to Lord MacGlannagh that Cathal's hostage is still recovering?'

His mention of the word hostage alarmed me, as O'Ronayne whirled towards me with a glint in his eye.

'Most certainly not! Our grey wolf knows better than to delay our meeting with his protector. Besides, he will be grateful for the warmth of the best hearth in Rosclogher.'

His speaking on my behalf did little to endear him to me, since I was not keen on the prospect of being paraded in front of the highborn Irish like some dancing bear. His reply also left me feeling somewhat belittled, so that I decided to irritate the Jesuit by reaffirming my refusal.

'Can they not hear tidings of the Armada from others? Surely you will succour a Spaniard who is better suited to oratory than me? Maybe some officer of a rank more befitting the chieftain's status? In any event, I am still far too lightheaded.'

At my words O'Ronayne's face turned from scarlet to violet, and his reply was more of an outburst than a resort to reason.

'Nonsense, Spaniard! You cannot hide away in my infirmary for the rest of your days! And would you have us tell your protector that you have refused his invitation?'

His brow darkened in profound annoyance, so that I decided to relent but not before issuing a loud sigh.

'Yet I hardly know these men, good priest. Are they to be my escort?'

The blond bondsman cleared his throat awkwardly as the Jesuit huffed aloud and made a quick introduction.

'Why, how remiss of me. This is Nial Ne Dourough, Spaniard. He is also nicknamed *Dua Claimthe* which means 'two blades', due to the two swords he always carries. Nial is also a highly accomplished two-handed swordsman.'

At his words the bondsman bowed again while O'Ronayne still prattled on at his side.

'After serving in the Army of Flanders, he returned to Ireland years ago and entered the service of the O'Rourke. Nial killed a man and could not pay the fine, so that he was sentenced to death. Yet on the day before his execution, Aengus paid his fine and assigned him to my Lord McGlannagh. Dua Claimthe's Spanish is almost better than mine, for he loyally served Spain in Flanders for years. He often serves as an interpreter on my lord's behalf, during audiences granted to traders and seamen from your land.'

My heart quickened at his mention of meetings between Manglana and other Spanish seamen, who I thought might present me with a way of leaving Ireland.

'I am honoured to meet one who has served Spain so faithfully,' I said, keen to ingratiate myself with him.

'The honour is mine, grey wolf,' replied Nial, 'for I hear that you betrayed no fear in the face of death, when rescuing Lady Mac an Bhaird. And it will be an honour to escort you to my lord MacGlannagh and to serve as your interpreter. However it has been some time now since I last used your tongue, so you might have to pardon my fluency.'

'But did not Father O'Ronayne say that you converse with Spanish traders and seamen on Manglana's behalf?' I asked, barely concealing my sudden disappointment.

Nial raised a regretful eyebrow.

'Alas, the heretic fleet has grown in recent years, and keeps a close watch on our shores. Our old trade and fishing accords with Spain have come to naught, for our dealings with Spaniards had greatly dwindled until the recent landings.'

This news was of great disappointment to me, so that after a few moments I gestured at the flagon in the Jesuit's hand.

'May I have a swig?'

O'Ronayne's mouth hung open and he barely managed a reply.

'No one has ever asked me for any.'

'That is most curious, seeing as you offer it to everyone.'

When he raised the vessel before him, I snatched it from him and swallowed its contents in a single gulp. The bitter brew eased my nerves, while I noticed that Nial was grinning widely, perhaps at my brusque exchange with the Jesuit who beheld me in surprise.

'I am ready,' I said, wishing to be done with the inevitable meeting.

When my hand was extended, the two bluejackets behind Nial stepped forward to help me to my feet. The bondsman's nose twitched when I wobbled before him in an ungainly manner.

'Forgive me grey wolf, but you are in no condition to meet with my Lord MacGlannagh. You smell like a bag of stale turnips. We had best bring you water and vinegar.'

One of the bluejackets stepped forward and threw a folded tunic and mantle on the edge of my bed, then placed two brogues upon the ground. He next reached out his hand, to help me rise from my bed. Yet I waved him away, so that he gave me his back and stepped towards the other natives. They were already talking in their native tongue, without any of them paying me the slightest heed.

As I sat up with a grunt of annoyance, I wondered whether I would be returning to the infirmary after our meeting with the chieftain. It suddenly dawned on me that I might be denied the chance to recover the ring, were I to leave it behind. I was overcome by panic as my mind raced to think of where I could next hide it. The thought was all-consuming as I whipped off my sackcloth tunic and spattered my armpits and chest with vinegar, feeling distressed that there were no pockets in either the tunic or the mantle which the kern had left me to wear.

After the misery of retrieving the ring from the pail, I was not keen on swallowing it again. So I instead hauled off my old tunic and pulled on the new one, then hurled the mantle across my shoulders and rested one arm against the sacks to pull on the brogues. While doing so I pretended to momentarily lose my balance, which won me all the time I needed to slip my hand between the sacks and seize the bauble. With my actions concealed by the woollen cloak which hung off my shoulder, I deftly dropped the ring into a shoe. Then I breathed a low sigh of relief as my feet slipped into both brogues and I stood up to address the natives.

'I am ready.'

I felt reassured as I prodded the trinket in my shoe with my toes, as O'Ronayne turned to observe me. After a few instants, he nodded his approval.

'You look a lot better, grey wolf. You are now ready to return to the world of the living. Let us escort you to the best hearth in Rosclogher!'

I clung to the shoulders of the two bluejackets as we stepped out of the hut, blinking at the glare of daylight. It was a relief to finally be free of the stifling odours in the infirmary. Once outside, countless children and other townsfolk gathered around us to study our party yet stepped away whenever Redmond or Nial raised their arms before me in a protective gesture.

We slowly made past the natives' huts, and I could see that most of them were made from the boughs of trees. We wended our way through the small piles of firewood which were stacked before them, as the bondsman led us towards the banks of the lake to our left. As we gained upon a small pier upon the edge of the lake, I could see that it was constructed of cross-beams supported by stakes.

Two knaves were already on their knees at the waterside, clutching a small ferry built of osier branches and wrapped in animal hide. Its only occupant was a lanky old boatman who stood at the bow clutching a long pole, so that the vessel swayed heavily when we stepped into it. I was grateful for the grip of the bluejackets upon the shoulders of my tunic, as Nial turned and hauled me alongside him by the wrist.

About us the dark water of Lough Melvin was barely rippled by a light breeze while I took in the sight of the dense forest which ran along the distant, opposite bank. A sense of stillness and serenity overcame me despite the bitter cold. The only sounds upon the water were the grunts of the hunched boatman whose punts brought us closer to the rocks and the islets ahead of us and further away from the cluster of huts at our backs.

The keep of Rosclogher loomed over our boat like a raised finger of defiance, surrounded as it was by lake water and small tree clad islands. These islets reminded me of the polders reclaimed from the sea in the Low Countries by the Netherlanders.

'God created the world', I muttered, 'the Dutch created the Netherlands.'

At my words, the stale breath of the Jesuit could be felt against my good ear.

'Yes Spaniard, that island is also created by man. We call it a *crannóg*.'

'Crannog?'

Alongside us, Nial could be seen cringing at my pronunciation as we drew nearer to the keep. It was a rectangular structure of grey bricks bound by lime and gravel, with a smoking chimney on the left side of its roof. Other than the lake water that surrounded it, the tower had no other defences with which to repel the invader, and the least skilled of Italian engineers would have blanched at the sight of its crude, flat walls.

Just when it seemed that we might run into the island itself, our boatman turned the vessel to port so that it slid alongside the wooden platform astride the crannog which was supported by stakes. While our craft was bound to this jetty, the rugged figures of other household guards appeared. They quickly fell to their knees and grabbed the waist of our ferry, helping us onto land with outstretched arms.

After stepping onto the island, the bondsman invited me to lean on his shoulder as six bluejackets instantly shadowed our steps. We followed the Jesuit towards a dome shaped entrance whose door was built of heavy oaken planks. It creaked open to a high-pitched squeal, to reveal a steel gate fitted behind it which the natives called a *yett*. As this second door swung open, I limped up the three steps which lead to it while the ring of kerns about us formed a single file. Meanwhile Nial stepped before me and placed the palms of my hands on his shoulders.

'Now watch your head inside,' he whispered, after we entered the ground floor and he suddenly stood still.

A sharp, overhead creak was heard as a wooden ladder was lowered from the ceiling through a small hatchway. One of the bluejackets seized the end of it and pulled it to the ground, before placing his foot on it.

'*Dreapadh suas.*'

At his order we clambered up the rickety rungs to the next floor and then proceeded to lean down and pass through a low passageway which was half a man's height. This obstacle had been designed to stall the access of any invading enemy, and I cursed in annoyance when my stitched forehead glanced against the edge of its stone lintel.

''pon my oath!'

'I warned you,' whispered Nial over his shoulder.

When I assumed my normal posture, I bumped my head again against a low ceiling so that another curse left my lips. I bit my lip in annoyance and patted my stinging crown, then realised that we had entered a narrow staircase which was carved into the thickness of the fort's wall. It was only wide enough for one man to scale it.

During my ungainly ascent, which was greatly aided by my companions, we passed many slit windows through which I caught glimpses of the lake that surrounded us. Upon reaching the third floor, the bloodcurdling cry of a woman stopped us dead in our tracks. O'Ronayne's eyes widened when he cast a look at Nial, before whispering something in Irish beneath his breath.

'Tá an bhean Dervila fós ag fulaingt go mór as a caillteanas le déanaí.'

'The chieftain's wife?' I whispered fearfully, having recognised the name Dervila.

'Yes Spaniard,' whispered Nial, 'we have reached the women's quarters. Lady Bourke has not yet recovered from news of her son's passing.'

Before I could ask any more questions, the Jesuit gestured to us to follow him up another flight of steps. Our ascent brought us to the topmost quarters of the keep, which were guarded by ten bluejackets. They were the fiercest-looking band of kerns I had yet seen, with a red-haired, stoic faced veteran standing in front of them. He eyed us warily as we approached him, with a scarred hand resting upon the pommel of his sword. After serving us with a low bow, he briefly addressed O'Ronayne while Nial translated the man's words to me over his shoulder.

'We are to wait here until we are summoned. And when we enter, you should keep a few feet distant from the chieftain.'

'I shall keep a respectful distance,' I replied.

'Oh, it's mostly for your own benefit,' said the bondsman with a wry smile, 'to spare you the dragon breath.'

I was not sure what he meant, as a deep voice boomed behind the locked doors ahead of us. Whenever they were slightly jerked towards us, wafts of hot air were released through the space between them, almost as if the doors were a pair of bellows. Each of these drifts felt like gentle caresses upon my face, which had been numbed from the cold outside.

'That is the poet bard,' whispered the bondsman, 'Fearghal O'Dálaigh.'

'What is he saying?'

'He recites a poem that is popular amongst our people, one that is often heard following a raid on the heretics.'

The poet bard could be heard delivering a high-pitched stream of words in the sharp and lilting tongue of the natives, while Nial translated it beneath his breath.

'O man who follows English ways, who cut your thick-clustering hair, graceful hand of my choice, you are not Donnchadh's good son!

If you were, you would not give up your hair for an artificial English mode – the fairest ornament of the land of Fódla! – and your head would not be tonsured!

A man who never loved English ways is Eóghan Bán, beloved of noble ladies!

To English ways he never gave his heart!

A savage life he chose!'

A whole diatribe against the English followed, in which their use of leggings and spurs was mocked. Jeers were heard when Fearghal poured scorn upon the scarfs and rapiers borne by the Sassanas, and he even derided them for sleeping in a feather bed. I could not remember the last time I had slept in a feather bed, and I sighed aloud at the thought of one while Nial still translated the bard's contempt for all things English.

'A troop of horse at the brink of a gap, a fierce fight, a struggle with foot soldiers, these are some of the desires of Donnchadh's son – and seeking battle against the foreigners!

How unlike are you to Eóghan Bán – they laugh at your foot on the stepping-stone! Pity that you have not seen your fault, O man who follows English ways!'

O'Dálaigh's recital ended to loud cheering and what sounded like the fevered thumping of spear butts against the ground. A lump formed in my throat when the guards made way for us, and I clutched the shoulders of both Nial and O'Ronayne for I suddenly felt faint. Upon our entry we were immersed in an overwhelming heat due to the great fire which blazed to our left, leaving me to realise that it was the first time I had felt entirely warm in Ireland. Two knaves stood alongside it to feed it dried logs, with its smoke possessed of the slightest scent of cinnamon. About us, dozens of bearded tribesmen beat their chests to loud cries of Eóghan Bán.

They made for an intimidating sight, so that I was grateful for the presence of the bondsman and the Jesuit alongside me. We walked over the fresh straw scattered across the wooden floor, while the huge hearth cast great, flickering shadows against the whitewashed walls which bore Flemish tapestries and animal hides. Between them hung countless antlers and green leafed branches, which were all trophies from the surrounding wilds beyond the town.

A silence overcame the many tribesmen who turned to stare at their marshal's hostage. I was not surprised to see that they wore great lengths of yellow linen which were possessed of many folds. They also donned collarless coats and jackets, with frieze mantles worn by both the young and the old. Large dogs crunched bones at the tribesmen's feet which were clad in shoes of untanned hide. Many women were also present, who wore brooches of gold and silver on their blouses.

I found myself looking out for Muireann amongst the new faces before me, yet she was nowhere to be seen.

One man was distinguishable from his fellows by a jacket of screaming crimson, and many cheers were still shouted in his direction, which revealed him to be Fearghal, the poet bard. His stare became fixed upon us when we strode before the gathering, with his eyes keen and piercing beneath his shock of white hair. He stood with his feet wide apart and a fist rested upon his waist, stroking his beard with his other hand as he studied us intently.

There stood many clansmen of seniority about him, most of them also silver-headed like him. They huddled closely together and whispered at our approach. Their fringes reached down over their eyes, in a fashion that the natives called the *glibb*. The Jesuit had told me that it was a style of hair which was outlawed by the Sassanas, since it left them confused as to the identity of the natives. This of course only served to encourage its use amongst the rebel tribesmen.

I was unsure how to greet these highborn freemen, so that I bowed to them with as much of a flourish as I could manage. The natives stared back at me impassively. My eyes fell upon a man at the other end of the hall, who was seated upon an oaken throne on an elevated dais. He wore a spade beard which reached down to his waist, being the longest I had yet seen by at least two fists.

Beneath the man's studded jacket, his saffron tunic seemed to possess more folds of linen than all of his assembly put together. Manglana's hands were rested upon his knees while he beheld me almost absently, making hardly any movement at all. About him stood a score of his blue-jacketed household bodyguard, holding their *skene* daggers and with their spears half-raised, so that they resembled a hedgerow of stakes.

Shadows from the fire flickered upon the chieftain's lined face which seemed hewn from flint. There was an almost timeless air about him and the sides of his full head of auburn hair were streaked with silver. To Manglana's left was an empty throne, the seat of power belonging to his queen whose cry we had heard on the lower floors. Dervila's absence did not detract from her husband's awesome presence, and our whole party knelt at his feet before O'Ronayne addressed him in Latin.

'My lord, this is the man rescued at Rossinver.'

Manglana appeared to ignore the Jesuit's presence, with his head shifting slightly sideways as his hawklike gaze fell upon me. The chieftain then asked me a question, which was as sudden as it was unexpected. Manglana's tone was bereft of nuance or warmth, and his deep timbre echoed across the hall.

'Tell us, grey wolf. Of the second coming of the Milesians.'

For a moment I struggled to understand what he meant. Upon noticing my hesitation, Nial hissed a swift instruction.

'Tell them what befell you, grey wolf. Tell them of the Armada.'

Feeling overwhelmed by a great anxiety, the words would not come to me for a painfully long while. My thoughts turned to my many days spent in the crow's nest and chained below decks, with red raw palms wrapped about the end of an oar with only a regretful Brabantian for company. I remembered Maerten's blank stare and in turn the face of his sister. For a moment I fought back the prickle on my eyelids, taking deep breaths to recollect myself and hold back the tears.

Then memories of the one-eared slave named Costa and his relentless gossip returned to my mind. I stuttered once, before turning to the freemen and freely sharing the scraps of hearsay which had spread across the rowers' benches of the Santa Maria de Visión. Nial next translated my words, so that I paused after each phrase to allow him to convey my meaning to the chieftain's hall. Many of the tribesmen stooped forward and strained their ears towards our voices, with dozens of eyes pinned on me while a look of wonder shone from many faces. I started from the very beginning, seeking to embellish my tidings where I could.

'When we set sail from Lisbon, men called us a great and most fortunate navy.'

While I recounted the Armada's troubles, I expected a burst of mocking laughter at my words. Yet my listeners did not stir at Nial's translation, and many appeared desperate for a new tale. Only Fearghal the bard betrayed any scorn as he glowered at me from the shadows at Manglana's elbow, for he appeared greatly discomfited to see his audience transfixed by the tale of a stranger. Although I did not know it then, this was to be an early warning of the future troubles I would endure among the tribe. Yet I pressed on with my tale, knowing that I could ill afford to miss my moment.

'Men arrived from Germany and others from Italy, swelling the Spanish and Portuguese ranks of the Imperial host. Hundreds of Englishmen and Irishmen sang odes of liberation upon the decks, as we set sail on over a hundred ships, armed to the teeth. A hundred and sixty, to be precise.'

My audience was by now held entirely in my grasp, and not a breath was heard when I spoke of the reasons why the great fleet had gathered to deliver England from the English Jezebel.

'For years English pirates had attacked Spanish ships. Drake went as far as to raid Cadiz, afterwards claiming that he had singed the Catholic king's beard. On his part, Philip the second almost choked with rage when word also reached him that the queen of the Scots had been beheaded, after being turned over to the executioner by her heretical cousin Elizabeth Tudor.'

My heart beat wildly when I paused for breath. Not a soul stirred before me and not a single eyelid was batted among my listeners.

'Indeed, the Empire of Spain is the greatest that the world has yet seen, but all too often are the seeds of failure sown in relentless triumph. Which in turn meant that we failed to heed any of the countless bad omens. Before we left Lisbon, our esteemed admiral Alvaro de Bazan, the first Marquis of Santa Cruz and hero of Lepanto, died, to be replaced by the Duke of Medina Sidonia. He was another honourable man, who had spent countless years in faithful service to his king. Yet all tongues wagged about his reluctance to lead the expedition and of his lack of experience. After a slow passage to Corunna, a great storm left us scattered, with three galleys being swept as far as the coast of France. In Corunna the duke ordered that our stocks be replenished, which left us stranded for almost a month. Meanwhile rumours abounded of his pleas to the king in Madrid, begging him to order us to abandon our venture.'

The attentive stare of the tribesmen bore into me, coaxing me to continue.

'We prepared for what should have been the last part of our voyage. Great galleons from Naples and Portugal led the ships of Italy and Germany, which included great Urcas all the way from the Baltic. When we sailed past England, voices were heard about the decks, that our enemy was trapped in harbour by an incoming tide. We could have had them there and then, yet we missed our moment.'

The freemen listened to how our fleet laboured on towards Calais, and quick intakes of breath were drawn when I told of our first skirmishes with the enemy.

'The wind changed, which allowed us to sail towards the enemy ships. Yet this was a foe we had not met before, who sailed shorter but swifter vessels. We were desperate to grapple with them and fight to the death. Yet with their being nimbler and slenderer, the enemy ships slipped away from our hooks all too easily. We spent ourselves in trying to catch a mirage in the desert, and when we at last reached Calais the Spanish troops had not yet arrived. So we waited for them well beyond dusk, with our great galleys bunched tightly together to avoid being picked off by the enemy.'

I briefly paused at the memory of the disaster which followed.

'At midnight great cries were heard on board, when eight balls of flame were seen heading fast towards us. The reserve order was called for our cables and anchors to be cut, and the Armada strayed further east amid great confusion. Dawn found its ships scattered everywhere, with two hundred vessels upon our tail. It was a struggle both frantic and hopeless, as the English raced through us and fired their deadly broadsides. In the time it took us to fire one round, they had already fired three, all delivered at the closest range possible as they slipped through the spaces between us. It was a veritable rain of shot, a bombardment both constant and heavy, and the like of which I have never known at sea.'

For a moment I stuttered, as the memory of my terrible swordfight with Gabri flashed past my mind. Then I remembered the prince's emerald ring, and I stared into space for a few moments until I noticed Nial frowning at me impatiently. One of the eldest tribesmen cleared his throat awkwardly, so that I quickly spoke up again.

'Cannonballs tore through our holds, ripping men apart. At close quarters our galleys were but ungainly giants, which allowed the English to slither through our legs and tear at our heels. Thus was all opportunity lost, of returning England to the one true faith, and of relieving you of your persecution forevermore. After their deathly work was finished our enemy sailed away, leaving us bloodied and broken. Cries of anguish were also heard when two of our galleons vanished beneath the waves.'

A loud sigh was heard at Nial's translation as I pressed on.

'For fear of Dutch pirates, we were ordered to round Scotland and Ireland, a decision that was to be our final undoing. Disease spread while our food and water ran out, and I could not imagine a more miserable journey until the storms struck. The fiercest winds I had ever seen were unleashed, which ripped the sails off our masts and drove our ships apart. Many a man was washed overboard to a watery grave, with those unfortunates still clinging to deck left greener in the face than the waves which battered us. For days thereafter, freezing gales from the north deafened us with unrelenting screams.'

A great sorrow appeared on the faces of those gathered, while they listened to the last words of my account.

'The fleet was scattered and during yet another tempest, my galley was wrecked before the strand you call Streedagh. Many men better than I perished that day upon the beach, killed like wild beasts by the men you call Sassanas. Somehow I fled with my life, cursed to be the bearer of this terrible tale.'

XVII

ROSCLOGHER, DARTRY, COUNTY LEITRIM, IRELAND

26 September 1588

When my account was ended, I was surprised by the haste with which I had summarised the most hazardous year of my life. The highborn freemen stared back at me in silence, with their expectant expressions desirous for more knowledge. Then a rasping snort resounded across the hall, followed by words spoken in a haughty and scornful tone. I was taken aback by the sound, since I had been told by O'Ronayne that only Manglana and the bard Fearghal were accorded the freedom of speech in the chieftain's hall.

The speaker was a swarthy man in a knee-length tunic the colour of brimstone, whose presence I had barely noticed until then. Between his mangled ears and scarred cheeks was a mottled mess of a nose, which looked like it had been chewed by a dog. His eyes held a glimmer of cold steel and his head resembled a tree stump which had been hacked by a blade. Even his eyebrows were streaked with scars. The thick jacket on his shoulders and his huge axe revealed him to be a Scottish gallowglass, and Nial craned his neck towards my good ear again as he hesitantly translated the man's gruff words.

'He says that the rumours are true. That the Spaniards have not come to aid us.'

From the shadows alongside Manglana another man spoke up defiantly, in a deep, resonant voice which was not unfamiliar. A swift glance ahead of me revealed the distinct silhouette of Cathal the Black. The marshal's riposte was spoken in the Irish tongue, which was also swiftly translated by the bondsman.

'But neither are they come to eat our children and take us all slaves, as you previously claimed. I fear that you all too readily lend an ear to the lies which have been spread by the English Viceroy in Dublin'.

My huge Scottish detractor seemed indifferent to the marshal's words, as he walked over and encircled me slowly. He regarded me mistrustfully as yet another snarl left his lips. At my side Nial clenched his two sword pommels while he whispered the Scot's next words.

'They have come to us starving and wounded, to increase the threat that we suffer tenfold. If we harbour these fugitives, a Sassenach army shall march upon us from Dublin before the leaves are out. The desolation inflicted on Desmond shall be as nothing compared to what we will suffer.'

Rumbles of assent and dissent were heard from the highborn freemen around us while Manglana regarded Cathal impassively. On his part the marshal's speech never faltered when he replied to the Scotsman in a low voice.

'That grave threat exists regardless, Donal Garve.'

The Scot named Donal scowled before turning towards my rescuer.

'You speak truth, little lord Cathal. Yet to what end does one tweak a lion's tail further?'

If a slight was intended by Donal's words, then the marshal ignored it as he issued a reply which was laced with irony.

'You should have learned by now, that a furious enemy is also a rash one. And you do ill to compare those base hounds of the Sassenachs to such a noble beast as the lion. For nobility also requires loyalty, a loyalty which does not abandon an ally to a common foe.'

His last remark caused a wave of muffled exchanges to ripple through the gathering, amid a rustle of cloaks and low murmurs of astonishment. Meanwhile I dared not stir, wary that I might worsen the already tense state of affairs. If he felt any shame then the Scot did not show it, as he replied to Cathal with a low growl.

'My only appeal to the assembly is that we do not increase our woes. Throwing our lot in with these castaways shall only draw the attention of Dublin upon us.'

He pointed a finger in my direction, and when he shouted his warning the flesh about his temples and cheeks crinkled like parchment.

'Mark my words, one and all! They shall take what they need and abandon us, before leaving us to face the wrath of our enemies alone! Cruel is fate, which has robbed us of our tanist and instead sent us these aliens who will seal our doom!'

As Nial translated these words, I felt overcome by a great distress, for many a dark look was cast in my direction by members of the assembly. This uncomfortable lull was however soon broken by Cathal's next riposte, which took the edge off the Scot's stark warning.

'Have faith, friend constable, for our Lord works in ways unseen. He has always preserved Dartry. The arrival of these Spaniards is a boon to us in a time of great peril, and I know that they shall not abandon us if we afford them our protection. I wager you a head of your choosing from my herd, for every Spaniard who abandons us after we offer them safe shelter.'

A collective intake of breath was heard at this bold proposal. For it was one that could prove most costly for the marshal and his retainers, in the harsh winter months which lay ahead. Having been momentarily stunned into silence, Donal's look of surprise was soon replaced by a smirk which grew across his face.

'A big wager for a little lord. Yet you must keep to your oath, Marshal. For the Brehon law professes that a blemish shall appear upon the face of he who tells a falsehood.'

Cathal's jaw dropped before it rose again, as he took a step back towards the shadows. He was clearly struggling with the Scot's open slight of his scars, which the smallpox had caused him in his youth. Donal smiled cruelly at his rival's distress, then raised his voice in mockery.

'You are most rash to place your faith in these wretches. They shall deflower our daughters and bring shame upon them. They will hide their trinkets from us and run off with our weapons, without ever affording us the slightest advantage against the Sassenach horde.'

Cathal's reply was immediate, for the scarred marshal had swiftly recovered from the gallowglass' jibe. He instantly delivered a broadside of such vehemence that in that moment I feared for his life, despite his lofty standing within the tribe.

'They sound no worse than you and your men, Donal Garve!'

A burst of laughter was heard at the doors to the hall, which was all too quickly stifled and poorly disguised as a cough. Meanwhile the Scot's face turned violet, as he made towards the marshal who was barely half his height. When the gallowglass constable had covered half the distance between them, the bluejackets in front of Manglana raised their spears, forming a defensive shield around the chieftain and the marshal.

Donal's pace suddenly slackened as he turned away from them. He clenched his sword pommel hard, appearing too angry for words. Cathal's persistence was unflagging as he continued to press for my protection. While he spoke, I assumed as sombre and dignified an expression as I could manage. For I sensed that my fate hung on the conversation between the two unsightly men, so that I was grateful for Nial's translation.

'There are so many of them stranded. Why should we consider them a threat? The reason for their presence among us matters not. All that matters is the faith which they share with us, and their willingness to join our cause. They could teach us all that they know about battle, for we have suffered many a setback upon the open field. And whether or not we accept it, the way everything is done beyond Dartry is changing.'

In that instant I noticed the bard Fearghal also glowering at Cathal *Dubh*, when Donal turned on his heel and directed his own baleful stare at the marshal.

'Be that as it may, little lord Cathal!' bellowed the gallowglass, 'but these beggars are unarmed and worse equipped than us! I say we cast them out of our lands forthwith! Once more do I maintain that they shall unleash the Viceroy's wrath upon us before the feast of Brigid!'

Murmurs of agreement were heard down the hall as Cathal raised his voice in defiance once more and gestured in my direction.

'You underestimate the Imperial troops! The esteem in which they are held precedes them, for they are the best soldiers in the world! The reputation of these Spaniards is based on their courage and valour in the thick of battle, not their weapons alone! It is why they are feared across the world! Only a few days ago did this man stand before a fully armed trooper with just a sword, defending the limp form of our sister Muireann! He risked life and limb to return her to us! Were it not for his gallantry, our ollave would also have perished!'

Donal laughed mockingly at the praise which had been heaped upon me. Then his voice was lower and full of scorn.

'I thought it was your intervention which rescued her, my little lord Cathal. Indeed, you speak as though you witnessed this alien's gallantry with your own eyes. And yet I have heard rumours that our valorous Spaniard turned tail and fled when our tanist was attacked!'

When Nial translated this, my blood boiled at the Scot's assertion. My ears throbbed with rage as I glared at the grinning gallowglass, for I was no longer fearful of his menacing presence. Yet Donal appeared ignorant to my fury, while long moments of unspoken confrontation passed between him and the marshal. No one in the assembly dared to speak, while the Scottish constable turned his gaze away from Cathal and fell to one knee before the chieftain.

'I ask that you grant me your leave. I cannot welcome those who will yet seal our fate'.

Manglana appeared to not even notice him. Then a short, wizened man at the foot of the dais spoke up, after acknowledging the chieftain's nod of approval. I later learned that he was Malachy, the chieftain's detested steward and collector of rents.

'Do as your heart commands, Donal *Garbh*. After all, you have openly disregarded the freedom of speech often enough. But you must return to this hall if you wish to partake of the election. For you shall not be summoned, nor will we await your presence.'

A loud grunt of disgust echoed across the hall when the constable returned to his feet. There followed a swirl of grey hide when he made for the doors, as five gallowglasses in studded jackets followed him out. Each of them grimaced at me when they trudged past, their stares filled with unconcealed hatred. At their exit an awkward silence lingered in the hall, until Manglana spoke. His choice of tongue was a heavily accented Latin, yet of a fluency which ended Nial's whispers.

'It hast been many long days since we were graced by a new tale.'

At the chieftain's words I bowed very deeply, so that my forehead almost glanced my knees. While doing so I caught a glimpse of the bard's face, which had turned as red as his scarlet jacket. This spurred me to swiftly respond to the courteous words of my host, knowing that they might mean the difference between life and death.

'My thanks, noble lord, for delivering me from torment and oblivion. The enemy had all but gained on us when your marshal's men intervened.'

While I spoke, frowns of concentration were seen spreading among Manglana's assembly. Each of the chieftain's lackeys and retainers observed me carefully while I addressed their lord, since I was an alien who bore consequences which they struggled to understand. Manglana appeared satisfied by my reply as he raised his hand and beckoned to my small group to approach him. His blue-jacketed bodyguards warily raised their spears towards us, while they studied our movements for the slightest hint of danger. After the time I had spent standing, my legs were weary and my steps still ungainly, which forced me to cling haplessly to Nial's shoulder once more.

As we drew closer to the raised dais, I could better make out the dour face of the king of Dartry, which was as gnarled as one of the many oaks in his dominion. Once more I beheld the longest beard among the tribe in wonder, as it hung from his bunched jowls in emphasis of his elevated status. There was an air of ruthlessness about him, which lent the deceiving grace of a slow-circling predator to his calm and almost gentle aura. He was evidently a man assured of his power, who looked at me down the long ridge of his nose until I could no longer meet his stare.

'What is thy name, grey wolf?'

I swallowed awkwardly when repeating the name from the distant mists of my childhood, which meant nothing to either Catholic or heretical veterans of Flanders.

'Juan de los Hospitalarios, my lord.'

Manglana mulled over my revelation, while never once relinquishing his severe stare. On my right, his bard still glared at me so that I averted my eyes from his malevolent presence. The chieftain weighed my words without betraying the slightest sentiment. When he addressed me again, it was in a deep and rasping tone, and I thought that my mind might be playing tricks on me when some of his teeth wiggled as he spoke.

'Thou hast my thanks, Spaniard, for sparing my daughter from death. She is worth more than a troop of kerns to me.'

His eyes suddenly glistened, and his voice became possessed of a slight quiver of emotion as he proceeded to refer to his son's passing.

'We have learned that Aengus hath been robbed from us. I have endured much in this life, yet I have never known the pain of such a loss...'

As his voice drifted off, I almost retched when the detestable odour from the chieftain's breath reached us. I suddenly understood the bondsman's earlier warning about dragon breath. It reminded me of my previous exchanges with members of the Spanish nobility, so that I realised that Manglana was being treated with quicksilver since he was afflicted by the French pox. My thoughts were interrupted when the bard spoke abruptly, almost as if to mask his master's momentary weakness.

'Oh Aengus Cliste -
Salmon of wisdom and most worthy tánaiste!

48

Both mac an ri and also beloved by all
Without blemish didst thou grace this world!'

I was surprised by the quality of Fearghal's sudden burst of Latin. Yet his next words were cut short, when Manglana served him with the darkest of stares. A terse silence swiftly returned to the hall as the chieftain addressed me again.

'I prayeth thee to recount the last stand of my son to this assembly, that we may treasure his last moments of life as if we had witnessed it ourselves.'

His request came as no surprise, for O'Ronayne had previously warned me that it would in all likelihood be forthcoming. I had already given much thought to the last fight of the tanist Aengus, both because of the latter's bravery and so that I could try to secure Manglana's favour. So after a moment's hesitation my reply was delivered in an unfaltering voice; one which greatly embellished the last living moments of a man who I had never spoken to, yet whose passing would weigh so heavily upon my future.

'When I saw your son, I did not know who he was. Yet even the ancients could not have shown such a disregard for their life when battling their enemies. That much I know for sure. For verily do I declare to you, my Lord, that I am one who as a boy witnessed Holy martyrdom against the Turk at Fort Saint Elmo upon the rock of Malta. Yet never have I witnessed one so contemptuous of certain death, who sold his life so dearly despite his terrible wounds!'

My voice bristled slightly as it rose, and for a moment I feared that I might have exaggerated my tribute, so that it verged on idle flattery. As my last words were spoken, Manglana beheld me with a look of wonder which was almost reverential, as some of the grief on his face was replaced by awed pride. When I looked away my stare fell upon the pages standing alongside him, as I suddenly made out the features of the chieftain's grandson Lochlain. He was the only son of Aengus and Muireann, who had stormed into the infirmary days earlier to learn of his father's fate.

The princeling's face bore an accusing grimace, and his jaw was set hard as he evidently struggled to hold back his tears. His dismayed expression left me feeling discomfited, so that I looked back towards Manglana. Alongside him the bard could be seen smirking at my sudden hesitation, and this sight coupled with Lochlain's glare left me clenching my fists. My annoyance at my predicament was fast turning into a defiant anger as a blind rage started to well up inside me, which I had often felt in my youth before storming enemy keeps. I channeled the growing fury towards rediscovering my voice, then took one step forward and delivered a stirring tribute to the memory of the late tanist.

'I knew not thy son, but the truth is that he rescued my life. For in seeing the power of his onslaught, I realised there would not be a better moment in which to drag the defenceless ollave away. Yet the honourless Sassanas withdrew their steel to wield guns instead. And even then it seemed that they would not be spared from his deadly skill with the blade, for they fell before him like hay before a scythe. Indeed, nothing would have stopped him other than the fatal shot that no skill could have healed. A great cry of dismay left me then, that there was so little that a starved and beaten wretch like me could do to rescue him, other than to flee the hopeless scene of slaughter with his wife.'

Of course, the motives I bellowed were but barefaced lies. Yet I hoped they might add a shred of dignity to my shameless abandonment of the tanist and his party, when saving my own hide to keep the ring. Manglana observed me intently for what seemed like an age, until he finally broke his severe stare to swiftly wipe a tear from his eyelid. I was overcome by shame as I placed my hand over my eyes to feign sorrow, while staring at the ground and wishing the chieftain would say anything to break the awkward silence. At the sound of a muffled sob, I looked up to find that all heads had been turned towards Aengus' son, Lochlain. His tear-streaked cheeks revealed open sorrow at the account of his father's terrible death. This show of emotion elicited a chilling cry from the chieftain's throne.

'Bí i do phrionsa ciúin! Agus fág mo halla go dtí go n-athróidh tú tú féin! Ní fhulaingeoidh mé an caoineadh íseal atá ag fonnadóirí i mo halla!'

Manglana half rose out of his seat amid his burst of heated words, so that Lochlain instantly fell to one knee before his lord grandfather and trudged out of the hall. His shoulders sagged forwards as a huge bodyguard shadowed his steps with a drawn sword. I could not help feeling a twinge of sorrow when I witnessed the shamed departure of the boy, for it pained me to think that I had been the one to tell him of the manner of his father's death. On his part, the chieftain did not persist with the subject of his own son's passing, and instead referred to his surviving daughter-in-law.

'Thou hast my thanks for sharing these dark tidings, grey wolf, and for rescuing my son's wife who is closer than a daughter to me. For although the wound of Aengus's passing shalt never be healed, her return among us will blunt the pain of his demise.'

Many of the freemen appeared stunned by the tidings of their tanist's passing. I was disturbed by the depth of sorrow on display, while fearing that I might be blamed for Aengus' death. Then the awkward lull was broken when the chieftain nodded at the raised arm of his marshal, Cathal the Black, thereby according to him the freedom of speech.

'Thou also hast my thanks, grey wolf, for having returned to us the *ollamh* Mac an Bhaird. Aengus *mac an ri* and I became closer than blood when we were both fostered in our youth by *Ó Conchobhair Sligigh*. It was during this time that I came to revere Aengus for the great qualities that marked him out from the rest of us. Yet, through his wife and son we have some living memory left of him, which should go some way to soothe the pain which thy tidings have inflicted upon us.'

The marshal barely spoke these words when I realised that he had thrown me a lifeline. One which I could use to enhance my reputation among the highborn members of the tribe. I clasped my hands together as if in prayer and served him with a deep bow.

'It is I that owe thee my thanks, my lord, for your protection and cures which have greatly restored me.'

Cathal received my words with the faintest of nods.

'Speak nothing of it, grey wolf, for we consider hospitality a sacred duty, and more than ever before are we bound to offer aliens a place by the fire. The enemy has destroyed all inns and abbeys which once succoured travellers across the land. But were these still intact, we would still be honoured to host a soldier of Spain, especially one who has rendered us so wondrous a service.'

The marshal paused for effect or to catch his breath, then heaped praise upon Muireann.

'For it was not just any distressed damsel which thou succoured along the banks of Lough Colgagh, grey wolf. Lady Mac an Bhaird is amongst the most learned in our tribe, and there are few better trackers or archers in our number. Despite my most ardent protests she has always ventured forth with the kerns, and many of them would blindly follow her lead into any peril.'

The marshal was interrupted by O'Ronayne, after the Jesuit received a nod from Manglana.

'All too often has she come close to the flame that ultimately consumed her husband. Yet she greatly honours a worthy line, for her father is a revered bard and sub-lord of the MacSweeney *Banagh*. She was sent here to be fostered when only a child, and she has done him prouder than the boldest of sons.'

Cathal raised his voice in agreement.

'Her bond with our late *tánaiste* greatly eased the burden of his duties.'

'That she did,' agreed O'Ronayne, 'yet Aengus was touched by the Divine, and never again will we know his equal.'

All fell silent when the chieftain himself was heard sighing.

'Indeed, he shall be too sorely missed. And Muireann was his foremost aide and student.'

Fevered chatter abounded among the foremost tribesmen, which died down when Manglana raised his voice to address me once more.

'The loss of our *tánaiste* is why we are assembled today, grey wolf. To decide who among the freemen will replace him. For we are encircled by a terrible enemy, the most dangerous tribe that my people have ever faced. Yet for as long as the Lord gives us the strength to resist the Sassenachs, thou art welcome to winter with us.'

After my sufferings at the hands of the Sassanas, Manglana's offer of protection was of great comfort to me. I served my host with a deep bow, before offering him some spirited words in reply.

'I served with many of thy countrymen in the Low Countries, my Lord. They were all brave men, and I am sure you will prevail in your struggle.'

Manglana's stoic features curved into a frown when he replied.

'It shall take some doing. Much that was good has perished because of the enemy. The fields in my allies' lands lie unworked, and many of our sons have left us for the distant shores of alien domains. All we have left to fight for are our traditions.'

O'Ronayne joined in his master's lament, his voice bristling with indignation.

'Our great trade of yore is now but a memory, and the enemy has even destroyed the famous monastic schools. But thirty years ago, they attracted scholars from all over Europe, but today the reputation of our scholars has been eclipsed by the brutality of those who would subdue us. The Bingham butchers are bent on spoiling forest and bog. They people the fields with their own kin, and swan about Connacht as if they were our high kings of yore!'

No sooner did the Jesuit voice this plaint, than many cries of outraged agreement echoed across the hall. Then Fearghal's trained voice pierced the general din like a skewer, while his face turned scarlet once more.

'They know not that we are the children of Conn of the hundred battles! They shall never have peace in our lands! *MacGlannagh Abu'! MacGlannagh Abu'!'*

'MacGlannagh Abu'!' erupted the assembly, so loudly that I thought the rafters might be brought crashing down on our heads, *'MacGlannagh Abu'!'*

These strident war cries were swiftly quelled when the chieftain shot to his feet and raised his arms.

'Peace! Peace my people! Let this meeting not be weighed down with mention of the enemy. Bring forth the usquebaugh, that this grey wolf may not claim that we refused him refreshment.'

He glared at his kinsmen reprovingly, snarling at them in their tongue before resuming his seat. Yet, when I turned to Nial, I could see his eyes twinkling with merriment as he translated Manglana's last words.

'Let us all share in the freedom of speech for the time that the grey wolf is with us, seeing that so few of you observe it at all.'

Highborn youths gathered more closely about me, with some seeming awed to find themselves in the presence of an alien. Others masked their anxiety with a laugh. The younger tribesmen asked me bold questions, since they were ravenous for more stories and new knowledge. In particular they yearned to learn more about Spain, as well as my years of soldiering.

I told them of the great battles in which I had played a part, both as a skirmisher and a sniper. I also added stories which had been whispered to me by various comrades over the years, during the long hours of interminably boring guard duty. My first memories of the siege of Malta were shared, as well as the horrors of Flanders, Lepanto and the Portuguese war of succession. My tales were all well-received, and only brusquely interrupted when a wooden goblet was suddenly held out before me. I was astonished both by its appearance as well as the intricate handiwork of its design. The highborn freemen burst out laughing while I stared at it warily.

'*Usquebaugh!*' they cried, slapping me heartily upon the back. I looked to the Jesuit who gestured at me to drink it.

'Oss-que-baa?' I muttered.

A cup was placed in my hand and a colourless liquid quickly poured into it from a jug. When my mazer was filled, I touched the drink in it with my lips and coughed at the sharpness of its taste.

'What is this?'

Some of the men among the gathering cackled cruelly and flashed knowing winks at each other, as Nial happily translated a yell heard from the back of the throng.

'Our *usquebaugh!* A delicacy from far off Donegal!'

I placed the vessel against my lips again and tipped it backwards. As the brew reached the back of my throat, it instantly set it on fire. I fell forward amid a fit of violent coughing, which only increased the laughter about me. Although the taste was unexpected, it was not entirely unknown to me; for in Flanders I had in my youth been offered a similar brew, which the locals had flavoured with the juniper berry.

Yet it seemed that the Dartrymen were made of sterner stuff and did not need their flaming drink to be sweetened by fruit. I did not want them to brand me as a soft southerner, so I gulped down the cup's remaining contents. As the brew slid down my throat, Nial translated the questions of the grinning youths about us.

'So, grey wolf, what do you make of it?'

I smacked my lips, uncertain how best to reply.

'I thought you only drank the Jesuit's mead,' I croaked.

At Nial's translation the gathering burst into wild chuckles again, with sheer mischief appearing on each delighted face.

'*Usquebaugh!*' they cried again, and I drained more when it was offered.

At the sight of my raised cup the crowd parted as swiftly as the Red Sea before Moses, to allow a knave through them who readily served me with more drink.

'Is that all?' I asked, for I was feeling very light-headed, both from my exertions and from my drinking.

Nial chuckled as another jug was held out towards me.

'Why certainly not! You must also try the king of Spain's daughter! A sweeter nectar does not exist in the whole of this land!'

I smiled grudgingly for the first time in days, since good cheer suddenly seemed so affordable in the safety of Manglana's hall. My cup was once more raised to my lips and my hosts grinned expectantly as I drank the red wine which Nial had poured for me.

'Why, this is excellent!' I exclaimed, after draining the whole cup.

The highborn freemen laughed aloud when Nial translated my words. I realised that the natives about me seemed almost Sicilian in their nature and temperament, being as swift to mirth as they were to anger. The bondsman beckoned to a knave who hurried over towards us with another pitcher.

'Wait till you try this one, grey wolf!' exclaimed Nial, snatching the jug and holding it out towards me, 'it is an excellent Gascoigne red, sold for nine cowskins the hogshead!'

He would later confirm that I was surrounded by many immediate relations of the chieftain. I already suspected this, for many of the freemen resembled Manglana. A few of them also used Latin, with some throwing in the odd word or phrase in Spanish, accompanied by loud chuckles and smiles. The bondsman earned his keep as interpreter that day, for he was assailed by numerous questions that we both endeavoured to answer to the best of our combined abilities.

At one stage the freemen closed in so tightly about us that the household bodyguard were forced to stand before me with raised hands. Eventually even Manglana had to loudly appeal to his kinsmen to take a step back, to prevent us from being crumpled against the wall. I felt a tug at my sleeve and I turned to find O'Ronayne's' green eyes boring into my face.

With a nod of his head, the Jesuit gestured to a boy beside him, who was none other than the princeling Lochlain. Having recovered from his earlier outburst of grief, Muireann's son had silently returned to the hall with his huge bodyguard behind him. As the boy stared at me askance, his lips trembled yet he did not say anything. As I turned away from him the Jesuit tugged at my sleeve.

'Grey wolf! The boy wishes to converse with you!'

With a sigh I turned to face the princeling, while ignoring the other tribesmen. Lochlain's hand trembled upon the hilt of his short sword as he stared at me with shimmering eyes.

'Thou abandoned my father's side,' he said, 'why didst thou not succour him?'

I stared at the princeling's brogues for a few moments, then slowly raised my head to meet his stare.

'Thou art still young, my lord,' I said, 'yet in time thou shall learn that we often regret our actions following the heat of battle. Thou must consider that I was an alien caught in a melee where I knew not friend from foe, while enduring the worst effects of torture, cold and starvation. If thou wouldst learn the whole truth, then thou shouldst know that I did disable one of the enemy. In my wretched state it seemed opportune to rescue your mother. Meanwhile your father exhibited such excellent swordsmanship, that any succour on my part seemed futile. Yet, I erred in judgement, for our honourless enemies drew guns amid a clash of blades and served your father with a mortal wound. Following this tragedy, any engagement of mine would have counted for nothing, except to add two more severed heads to those already hanging from the enemy's garrison walls.'

The princeling appeared dismayed by my reply. As he fumbled for words I turned away and busied myself with replying to the other tribesmen's questions again. Meanwhile my goblet was quickly refilled, so that I drained two more cups until Manglana's voice was heard booming against the walls of his hall.

'There is much that must be discussed and decided this day. The *dál* alone must remain in this hall.'

The chieftain fixed his stare on me following his declaration.

'Thou shalt be quartered in the abbey of Saint Mel, grey wolf.'

I was relieved that I was to be sheltered outside of the infirmary, although for a moment I wondered whether I was to share the same dwelling as the Jesuit. Yet my unease subsided at the chieftain's next words.

'You shall share lodgings with our bondsman. For he is a worthy man and has knowledge of your tongue. No one is to approach you without my command.'

O'Ronayne remained behind when I left the hall, leaning heavily on Nial's shoulder. As we made through the doors and towards the stairwell, I drew my mantle back over both shoulders. Despite the cold outside the hall, I was relieved to get away from the gathering within it. I had not been the subject of so much attention since Alba had honoured me following the bloody mess at Haarlem, or during my early days in the Imperial army when I had to run the gauntlet for napping during sentry duty.

As we walked down the stairs, I found that the exertion required of me was greater than first expected. My light-headedness almost made me miss my step during our descent, so that the tall bondsman used one arm to grip me tightly about the waist. Nial's pace never slackened as he held me, his tone apologetic while he explained the reason for our haste.

'We must away before that beast of Donal MacCabe returns.'

I lifted my head once, then it fell forward again.

This is not good I thought, *the last thing I need is for us to end up face to face with those gallowglasses.*

My concern only grew when I realised that the three kerns who had escorted us to the chieftain had remained in the hall along with O'Ronayne.

'Will he return so soon?' I asked.

'Possibly. The chieftain is to hold what we call a *terchomrac*, a special assembly which has three nights in which to appoint a new *tánaiste*.'

'Tanist? You mean Manglana's heir now Aengus is gone? But why do the freemen need to be involved?'

Nial shook his head briskly, before explaining why my question was wide of the mark.

'The Brehon laws accord no rights of succession to first born sons or close blood relations. The chieftain's heir must always be elected by the assembly of freemen.'

'What?' I replied, 'so Aengus was elected as tanist??'

'Yes,' replied the bondsman, 'his being Manglana's son did not make him tanist.'

As we descended the next flight of steps, his words left me puzzled. How could a society function without the right of primogeniture, a cardinal rule which had existed since time immemorial?

When we reached the next level of the tower-house, we found ourselves back on the floor where the tribe's high-born womenfolk resided. I could see recesses in the walls for sleeping places and clothes of different colours neatly folded alongside them. A loud drip drop was heard from the other side of the floor, when Nial grabbed my sleeve and pulled me towards him. He was possessed of a beetle-browed stare as he studied my face.

'Are you well, friend Juan? You are very pale.'

In truth a great light-headedness had seized me, after the flood of emotions I had experienced during our encounter with the assembly of freemen. Yet despite my weariness I gritted my teeth, resolved to make it back to the town before the Scots reappeared.

'I should endure for a while longer,' I whispered.

The bondsman's lips slightly parted as he made to reply. Yet before he could utter anything, a violent howl was heard behind him, and we turned to find a woman racing towards us. Her greying auburn hair was unfurled over her shoulders, and other women hurried after her, their faces white with shock. Tears streamed from the woman's red raw eyes and over her cheeks as another cry of agony left her lips.

'Coward!' she shrieked at me in Latin.

Her high cheekbones trembled in the ageing beauty of her face, her hawklike glare filled with fury. Her handsome features greatly differed from the other Irish women I had seen, for they reminded me of the Flemish. Her figure was slender beneath the linen gown that fluttered behind her, as she bore down on us like a maddened mare. My jaw dropped when she shoved Nial's outstretched arm aside and slashed at my forehead with her fingernails.

With a gasp, the bondsman – who had also turned as white as a sheet – hesitated but a moment before attempting to shield me from her approach with his body. As he fended off her flailing arms, he yelled what sounded like protests in Irish, often shouting the word 'Dervila'. The woman's breath reeked of wine as she next proceeded to attack him too with her talons, crying out words in Latin while he attempted to seize her wrists. I realised to my horror that blood was already streaming down his face from three scratches across his forehead.

'Beggar!' cried Manglana's wife, 'coward! My son died to protect a cowardly beggar! My fine son!'

The tormented queen somehow managed to get past the bondsman again, as he bellowed in protest. I grabbed her wrists while her clawing hands scraped my forehead again, and it was all I could do to prevent her from gouging my eyes out. I heard the cry of another woman as Dartry's queen tore at my cheeks and nose, while my surrounds seemed to swirl about me.

Feeling utterly spent, my hands fell to my sides and my legs gave way beneath me as I collapsed onto my knees, with my bloodied face smacking the ground. As I drifted in and out of a swoon, I glimpsed a maroon boot as someone turned me onto my back. The tear-streaked face of Muireann appeared in the haze, issuing orders that sounded ever more distant.

XVIII

ROSCLOGHER TO THE DARTRY MOUNTAINS, DARTRY, COUNTY LEITRIM

26 - 28 September 1588

When I opened my eyes, I thought that I was back in the infirmary. Then I heard the sound of chickens as I regained consciousness. The light in the hut was poor, and the fire alongside me had long died out, so that my limbs were cold. My slumber had been dreamless but also fitful, for a thick blanket of grey sheep's wool was bunched up at my feet.

I could still feel a great light-headedness, so that the room seemed to rise and fall. Then a distant, low voice was heard, in a tongue and cadence which was both sombre and somewhat familiar. As I turned my head towards it, a flap of cloth fell over my right eye. The sudden blindness made me start, until I realised that it was part of a bandage bound around the gashes on my forehead. In that instant I recalled the attack of the chieftain's wife, so that a great unease overcame me. I sat up with a grunt and a gasp, leaning heavily upon the edge of my bed which was a converted trough filled with dried rushes.

A glow through the doorway revealed the entrance to my new quarters, while I half considered escaping from the town. I struggled over the edge of the trough to return to my feet, when I suddenly realised that I was barefooted. A great fright seized me when I saw the brogues against my makeshift bed, for I quickly remembered the ring inside them. I reached over and snatched up the shoes, being instantly relieved to find the gem still wedged inside one of them. Before anyone could see me, I slipped the brogues on again.

I next rose to my feet and staggered towards the doorway. The distant voice could still be heard, rising and falling like a siren's serenade. In my addled state of mind, I left my mantle behind me, so that it was in a greyish white tunic that I stepped into the wind outside. As I shuffled out of the wood and wattle outhouse, I noticed that many others like it were scattered above and below the gentle hillock that rose before me, which was surmounted at its crest by the silhouette of far-off mountaintops. I was stunned by the relative tranquillity, while the livestock issued the odd bellow from the pens and barns.

Then a great wind sent the grass swishing about me like rippling water. It caught me in its swirl, chilling me to the bone as my hair and tunic fluttered wildly. For a moment the great lowing of cattle and the screech of fowl were temporarily drowned out, as well as the distant voice I sought out. I shielded my eyes from the bright sun which reigned alone in a cloudless sky, yet it took them at least a minute to become adjusted to the glare. I next noticed that two byres flanked the small hut from which I had emerged. These structures housed livestock at the foot of the small hillock, being flanked by a low rubble wall which was the confine of gardens and hives.

I quickly realised that the outbuilding was at the southern end of the abbey behind me. When I turned towards it, I could see the lake shimmering along its northern side. Two finely pruned trees of the sycamore bordered the abbey's small doorway in its west wall. A large group of tribesmen thronged about this doorway and a small window, taking in the sound of the voice which had roused me. It rose and fell while reciting a prayer in Latin, a Requiem which I had often heard after battle.

O God, whose property is ever to have mercy and to spare,
we humbly entreat Thee on behalf of the soul of Thy servant
whom Thou hast bidden to pass out of this world:

that Thou wouldst not deliver him into the hands of the enemy
nor forget him for ever, but command him to be taken up by the holy Angels,
and to be borne to our home in paradise,

that as he had put his faith and hope in Thee
he may not undergo the pains of hell
but may possess everlasting joys.

These words were intended to be soothing, yet I felt deeply disturbed when I caught sight of a handful of men who were huddled together some distance away from the group of

Dartrymen. For their long, padded jackets instantly revealed them to be gallowglass mercenaries, those same fearsome Scots I had seen in the infirmary and in Manglana's hall. As they leant on their great two-headed axes and stamped their feet in the chill, I instantly fell in a heap upon the grass when one of them produced a sound like muffled laughter.

'Christ's bones', I muttered to myself, as I crawled back towards my new lodging.

While the sonorous words emerged from inside the chapel, I looked over my shoulder towards the mercenaries, which confirmed that none of them had noticed me. I crept past our hut and around the abbey on hands and knees, overcome by curiosity and keen to see what lay along its eastern side-wall. I quickly found that a large wooden structure had been constructed against it. There were no sounds of either cattle or fowl within this structure, which led me to suspect that it served some residential purpose. While I observed it carefully, the words in Latin grew louder because of my proximity to the chapel.

Day of wrath and doom impending,
heaven and earth in ashes ending

Oh what fear man's bosom rendenth,
when from heaven the judge decendeth,
on whose sentence all dependeth.

I staggered away as quickly as my legs would bear me, through the open door of the wooden structure. As I entered it I stared about me in wonder, for a broad table and benches stood before me, and the ground was covered in fresh straw. A small fire still smouldered in the fireplace, so that I approached it with raised fingers, to warm them near the semi-lit embers. I cast my head about me while the deep voice of the priest resonated in my ears.

Christ our Lord, in whom the hope of blessed resurrection has shone on us,
so that those who are saddened by the certainty of dying
may be consoled by the promise of a future deathless life.

For to thy faithful people, Oh Lord,
life is changed, not taken away,
and when the home of this earthly sojourn is dissolved,
an eternal dwelling place is being prepared in the heavens.

I could not help feeling at ease within the building, for it was the homeliest place I had stepped into since I had resided in Reynier's house in Willebroek. Pewter cups and wooden plates were laid upon the table, as well as iron candleholders of an intricate design. Many other trinkets and pieces of furniture also caught my eye, not least of all a wooden shelf which was filled with books. My jaw dropped at the sight of them, since there was little I prized more in the world than leafing through a volume and poring over its pages.

I started when a stifled cough was heard behind me, then turned to find two people in a corner of the room. They were a couple of O'Ronayne's attendants from the infirmary, who beckoned to me to approach them. As I shuffled over towards them, I could not help wondering what they were doing crouching against the cold, grey sandstone wall. Yet I soon saw that in its bricks there was fashioned a low window, through which one could see the inside of the chapel.

I quietly observed the little church's nave which was filled with folk from the town. Those natives wearing white tunics were gathered tightly just in front of us, with the saffron-clad highborn further ahead and closer to the chancel and altar. Two rows of blue-jacketed bodyguards stood along the aisles, who had entered the church fully armed. To a man they could be seen keeping a close eye on their master, Manglana, who stood on the left of the front row of benches. Of greater interest were the distant feet of a corpse which lay upon a trestle table before the altar. O'Ronayne solemnly stood over it, still delivering a sermon in his best Latin.

'Indeed, there can be no greater love, nor sacrifice, than giving one's life up for his fellow man.'

No sooner were these words spoken than a loud cry was heard across the chapel, issued by a woman in a russet farthingale who fell to her feet beside the trestle table. She frantically grasped the corpse's hand while she wailed, which dislodged the body from the bench upon which it lay. It collapsed to the ground beside her, as most of the tribesmen in saffron issued loud exclamations of concern. As they closed in about her, I realised to my horror that the corpse which the woman held to her breast was headless, with her next cry further confirming her identity.

'Aengus *mac an ri!*'

Upon hearing Dervila scream again, I recalled her recent attack on me in the tower house. I shuddered and fell to one knee, with my hands trembling before me. One of O'Ronayne's apprentices proceeded to gently rest his hand upon my shoulder.

'Thou looketh distraught, grey wolf,' he said in fluent Latin, 'perhaps thou shouldst not expose yourself to further sorrows. Allow me to escort thee back to thy lodgings.'

In my anguish I could not reply, nor did I protest as the youth pulled my arm over his shoulder and heaved me back onto my feet. After we stepped outside he led me to the outhouse, where he helped me back onto the trough and laid the blanket upon me. Meanwhile my shivering had not yet abated. I was uncertain whether it was caused by fear of Dervila or the haunting sight of Aengus's corpse, or both. Yet even after the apprentice left my side, sleep did not come easily. It was only when the funeral mass was delivered in its entirety and the distant wailing of keeners had long passed, that I fell into a deep slumber.

Some time later, I stirred at the sound of a shuffle against the wall. Whoever it was that had entered my lodgings was watching me and spoke at my movement.

'Are you revived, grey wolf? You have now slept for nearly two whole days.'

The loud hiss of rainfall was heard in the darkness outside and such blackness had gathered about me that the person who spoke was barely discernible. I was blurry-eyed as I raised my head at the sharp rasp of a tinderbox being struck. The glow of a candle filled most of the room, revealing the grinning features of Nial who squatted besides it. After lighting the taper he picked it up in his gauntleted right hand and put its flame upon the kindling which he had placed upon the hearth.

Within moments there was a sweet smell of turf smoke in the hut, while the bondsman proceeded to light other candles in stone sconces. The scent of their beeswax soon mingled with that of the fire, and I sighed contentedly at the comforting heady scent and the growing warmth. The light revealed the second trough to my right, which was also filled with rushes. The bondsman proceeded to peel the soggy arms of his jacket off his elbows and squeezed it tightly. He next rolled up his garment on his chest and laid it along the edge of his bed as a pillow.

'Is this your home?' I asked.

Nial's ready smile turned into a grimace while he undid his sword belt.

'I fled my home when I was still a whiskerless lad. I was already both a rebel and an outlaw, before enlisting with the king of Spain's army. It has since vanished from the face of this world, as have all of my kin.'

He rested his hands on the sword pommels that lay on either side of his waist and grimaced ruefully.

'These two are now the only kinsmen I have left, grey wolf.'

In the glowing firelight I could tell that one was a fine Castilian blade of Toledo steel, with a cup-hilt on its pommel that shielded his bare hand. His other hand was gauntleted and rested upon a cleaver that I had often seen among the Irish. It appeared to be much heavier than its Iberian counterpart for it was a double handed slaughter sword and sheathed in a broad scabbard. Its grip was made of wood and bound with a leather tong while the ends of the crossguard were twisted with one pointed upwards and the other one pointing down.

'For indeed', he added, rattling his blades in their scabbards for emphasis, 'I would not have gone far in this world without these two, and each represent the two worlds in which I have walked. For this is *Tizona*,' he said, drawing the Spanish rapier from its sheath and holding its length out before him, 'which may yet skewer as many heretics as El Cid slew infidels. And this is *Caladcholg*,' he added, as the Irish blade rang from his side and clashed against the Spanish steel held before him, 'which is named after the famed blade of Fergus mac Róich, which was possessed of such power that it could sever the tops from hills.'

'Does that explain the flat-topped mountains around here?' I asked.

The bondsman laughed aloud as he sheathed the weapons. He then walked over towards me, removing the steel gauntlet from his right hand and unbuckling his two sword belts.

'You jest, grey wolf, but you could not imagine how many of your arrogant countrymen fell before these blades. For many an insolent Spaniard dared to call me an Irish beggar during my time spent in Flanders, as did many men of other nations. Upon returning to Ireland, I hired my swords out as a *bonnaught* - a mercenary. One day I was insulted by a saffron-clad fop, who dared to challenge me to a duel. He lay dead at my feet moments later, only for his spiteful relatives to accuse me of murder. They claimed my life since I could not pay the fine. Fortunately, Aengus was travelling through our settlement on his way to a bardic contest. He paid the fine on my behalf and I was reduced to the status of bondsman and gifted to his father.'

His brow darkened as he scowled at the memory and he gazed into nothingness for a while. Then he raised his head and stared about him, as if suddenly recalling my presence.

'These days my only kin are my blades, and my home is wherever my master chooses to send me. As for this hut, it was a shelter for pilgrims in happier days, since there are now all too few of them left. The roads lie unused and the paths are choked with brigands and Sassenachs, who each present the same peril to an innocent traveller that belongs to the faith.'

He turned on his heel with his swords half raised.

'Nowadays it is but a shelter for knaves, who tend the Jesuit's flock in winter months.'

He stared at the straw upon the ground, as he voiced an afterthought.

'Although tomorrow I suspect that it shall house all too many travellers from across Dartry.'

'What travellers?' I asked nervously, fearing that I might be discovered by any surviving crew members of the Santa Maria de Visión.

Upon noting the irritation in my voice, Nial cast me a curious look as he lay his swords against the end of his trough bed. While his back was turned I quickly shoved my fingers through the brogues near my bed, feeling instantly relieved to find the ring within one of them.

'You have slumbered for far too long since your last fall, grey wolf,' said Nial, as I swiftly withdrew my hand from my shoes, 'in which time I never saw so many goings-on among the tribe. They shall be the town gossip for years to come. Which is to say nothing of the great ceremony which is to be held tomorrow, and which shall draw the leaders of all of the *tuatha* across the country, who swear fealty to my lord Mac-Glannagh.'

At his words I propped myself up on an elbow, watching him closely as he dropped himself onto his bed. Nial's fair locks fell upon his folded jacket while he crossed his long legs before him. As he slid his hands behind his head, he almost resembled a carefree young farmhand sprawled across the hay in a rick. He rested a leg across one knee when he spoke again, staring at a leak in the roof's sheathing as if he had not a care in the world.

'How do you feel, friend Juan?'

'Better, not as light-headed as before.'

'I am glad to hear it, for we were distressed by your tumble. The ollave Mac an Bhaird berated us soundly, for fear that we had roused you too early from your rest in the infirmary. Indeed, you have slept for a long time since Lady Dervila drew her talons and swooped on us.'

Of a sudden I recalled the attack of Manglana's queen, and the scene in the abbey that morning, where she had dropped the corpse of her son from the trestle table. I also realised that some of the marks on the bondsman's face were not shadows, but scratches from the queen's assault.

'You have spoken with Lady Mac an Bhaird?' I asked.

'Hardly, for it was her that spoke to me, and in a great fury too. For she had somehow hauled herself away from her mourning to join the assembly of freemen, when she found me fending off Lady Bourke. Which was a true act of Providence, since I feared that I was going to have to draw steel to keep my lord's wife at bay. Yet I doubt I would be here now if I had done so. For the ollave had hardly intervened to calm

Dervila that the constable MacCabe and his guard of gallow-glasses appeared upon the steps before us.'

'Why did the ollave join the assembly? Was she summoned there by Manglana?'

'Lady Mac an Bhaird was on her way to vote for the new tánaiste. A grim task for the previous incumbent's spouse, only recently widowed. Yet a more gruesome task awaited her the following day.'

'What?' I asked, my voice filled with concern.

With another sigh the bondsman sat up and reached out for a decanter on a stool at his shoulder. He next got out of bed and walked over to a corner of the hut, returning with two horns which he had filled to the brim. I hesitantly took the one which he offered to me as Nial spoke in a reassuring tone.

'Drink up, grey wolf. 'tis but brandy.'

The taste of the brew was less sharp than the usquebaugh, although still strong. It filled my chest with a warm glow which proceeded to reach all of my joints. I was careful not to spill a drop, feeling grateful for my sudden change of circumstances and for a brew that did not taste like gravel. My ears pricked up when the bondsman returned to his bed, for there were many tidings which he wanted to share with me.

'The day after the new *tánaiste* was elected, a troop of horsemen appeared along the confines of Dartry. They were men of the O'Connor Sligo, who wanted to return a corpse to the MacGlannagh for which they dared not ask a price.'

When he said this, I nearly choked on my drink.

'Aengus?!'

Nial swallowed a mouthful of brandy before he spoke again.

'Yes. The headless corpse of Aengus. Its size and the great reddish-brown torso were at once both recognisable, as was the empty scabbard of his great sword *Tintreach*.'

The deep lowing of a cow was heard outside and a dog yelped. I could not help thinking about the Requiem mass when the bondsman spoke again.

'Today we laid him to rest by his ancestors, in our loftiest heights. May he rest in peace and be forever blessed, for we shall never see his like again. If ever someone's candle was blown out too quickly, then it was his.'

A muffled sound was next heard from the bondsman. I was not sure if he had restrained a sob or helped himself to his drink, when he spoke again with a steely resolve.

'We shall return hence tomorrow, to appoint his successor, the man elected by the *derbfine* itself. Our sorrow shall always hang heavier than a millstone about us, yet despair will be abandoned when new blood rekindles our hopes anew.'

'Who was elected tanist?' I asked, feeling highly curious about the outcome of the election and the potential consequences it would have for me.

Nial's reply was accompanied by a satisfied grin, which only stoked my curiousity further.

'It was a very close affair. The marshal Cathal the Black was said to be my lord's favourite, but Donal MacCabe wields a great influence among the tribe, and had the gall to partake of both the election and the voting. He was also said to be Dervila's preferred choice.'

A snort of contempt was heard from the bondsman following these words. His mention of the gallowglass constable caused me great distress, for it seemed odd that a mercenary might occupy so lofty a position among the tribe.

'So can anyone become tanist? Even an alien?'

Nial wagged a lean forefinger in the air.

'No. Only those descended from my lord chieftain's great-grandfather. They are what we call the *derbfine*.'

'Then how can a common soldier of fortune be elected second in command?'

'Donal MacCabe is not descended by blood, yet he is wed to my lord's sister. This would not usually render one eligible for membership of the *derbfine*, less an election for *tánaiste*. Yet MacCabe holds great sway, for he is a very wealthy man. Our lord chieftain is deep in his debt, for the cost of our fight with the enemy is most steep. Which in turn means that little can be denied to our gallowglass constable, who even paid the chieftain's whole army during the last fighting season.'

'Zwounds!' I exclaimed.

Nial sighed aloud.

'The MacGlannagh has given up all that he can to offset his debts, granting priceless privileges to pay off his loans. Donal's membership of the *derbfine* is but one of these payments in kind, and our lord chieftain has also had to offer him lands and allowed him to build a keep at our southern borders. He will doubtless soon demand recognition as the leader of a *tuath* and then begin to strengthen his authority across Dartry, in the manner of other gallowglass constables in other lands. Some have even risen to the post of chieftain, as has Manus MacSweeney in Banagh. For Donal is an audacious fox and will no doubt seek to court Lady Mac an Bhaird, what with her now becoming the wealthiest widow in Dartry.'

'Truly?' I asked, with my jaw dropping open.

''tis hardly my habit to tell lies!' snorted the bondsman, 'anyone in the town can tell you that! She has regained the right to her dowry and a third of her late husband's estate. Which is not to mention the remainder that she holds, until her heirs are of an age to claim it.'

'But is the constable not already married?'

'That he is. But we have divorce in our tribe. And it is not unknown for men to marry more than once.'

'I see,' I replied faintly, finding myself wholly surprised by this revelation so that I was not sure what else to say about it.

We sipped at our horns deep into the night, striking up more conversation like a pair of old friends. I took a liking to the bondsman, finding a strange comfort in his frank disposition and honesty. I was keen to learn more about the tribe, so that for a time I even forgot about the irritating itch of lice in my bed blanket. Most of our talk centred on the gallowglass constable, Donal 'Garve' MacCabe, the grizzled warrior who had openly opposed the hosting of Spaniards in Manglana's hall. Nial's voice was lowered whenever the Scot was mentioned.

'Take heed, for the constable is armed with fiendish strength and a dangerous guile. He is not one to run afoul of, for he commands many men: a battle of fierce redshanks who are a strong bulwark against those who would seek to encroach on our borders. They have partaken of many skirmishes against other tribes, leading away many of their best heads.'

A piercing unease had grown within me at Nial's description of my powerful detractor, which I sought to counter with a contemptuous retort.

'In other words, he is nothing more than a cattle thief!'

The bondsman chuckled aloud while he shook his head at my impudence.

'Not quite. You forget that the chief currency in this part of Ireland is livestock. Mainly heads of cattle. For we get no food from enemy plantations, and cows are our only certainty of making it through winter. Starvation has long been our enemy's greatest weapon, which is why the Sassenachs constantly seek to discover which tribes possess the most heads of cattle. It is what draws them forth from their garrison towns, when they unleash merry hell amongst us with raids of their own.'

'All of which would make Muireann a prized asset?'

Nial nodded and got back to his feet, then swiftly drained his horn and placed it upon a large chest of his belongings.

'A prized asset for a very rich man. Who is not poor in allies either, like the chieftain's wife.'

He looked about him even more carefully before whispering his next words.

'Indeed an idle rumour still persists of an affair between Donal and Dervila. I think it is untrue, but they are close enough to warrant it. On her part, the Norman witch does little to deny it.'

At his irreverent reference to Manglana's wife, Nial cleared his throat awkwardly and paced back towards his bedstead, speaking once more about the constable.

'He is a defiant and brutish sort, his way is that of force alone. He often acts in defiance of orders from Duncarbery, where the chief stronghold of our lord chieftain lies. The assembly wants less skirmishes with other tribes, yet Donal refuses to break with tradition. He believes that neighbouring tribes who deal with the Sassenachs should be attacked at every opportunity. The O'Reillys are his favourite victims.'

'And what does the chieftain think of this behaviour?' I asked, hoping that Manglana might at least have a rein on the Scot's seemingly unfettered power.

A few moments of silence passed before the bondsman spoke again. In the flickering light of the fire, I was uncertain whether his eyes were open or closed.

'My Lord MacGlannagh would all too readily draw his sword against anyone who he considers to be an enemy of our overlord, Brian O'Rourke. The only person who kept his impulses in check was his son Aengus. I dread to think what might happen now that our *tánaiste* is dead.'

'You fear that Donal might urge him to take up arms unnecessarily?'

Nial sighed wearily.

'Donal is not alone in observing tradition, for he has an unlikely ally in the bard Fearghal, who also rejects anything resembling progress among the tribe. I can only hope that my lord Cathal and Lady Muireann might restrain the chieftain from further acts of rashness. Our losses at Ballymote could have been more significant were there not other rebels who got the worst of it.'

I squinted at the ceiling, mulling over the bondsman's revelations.

'Well, he does indeed sound like a double-dyed villain and a true soldier of fortune. But can he and his men not be replaced by others?'

Nial folded his arms behind his head and hummed thoughtfully to himself.

'You are not alone in thinking this. Most *galloglaigh* are usually recruited three months a year, during the fighting season of summer. They are thereafter disbanded, when they return home. Yet one is not so easily rid of Donal. For he and his battle formed part of the dowry which our lady Dervila Bourke's father gifted our lord chieftain on his daughter's wedding day. The gifts of chieftains are not so easily refused, and I need not warn you of the ire that the chieftain might endure at the hands of his wife.'

My heart sank at his words as I asked the question which had most plagued my mind.

'So Donal has the protection of Manglana's queen?'

'Yes, friend Juan. And he has her ear too, for it was certainly him who filled Lady Bourke's head with vile rumours about your fleeing the enemy and abandoning the *tánaiste* to his fate. But fear not, grey wolf, for you have been defended by someone she holds dear.'

He smiled as he said this and I instantly thought of the ollave.

'After we were attacked upon the stairs, the Jesuit prevailed upon our lady – when her wits were restored – that she had heard false tidings about your involvement in the death of her son, which were confirmed by the *ollamh* Mac an Bhaird. And Lochlain *mac an ri* also spoke up on your behalf.'

'Muireann's son?' I exclaimed, recalling the red-headed youth who had endlessly queried the cause of his father's demise, 'but what cause did he have to intercede on my behalf?!'

'Well,' replied the bondsman thoughtfully, 'clearly he is taken by you, for it seems that he also made his grandmother pledge your safety to him. It is most fortunate for you to have a young princeling as an ally, it seems that his late father's high esteem of Spanish soldiers was imparted to him.'

I was somewhat relieved to hear this news as I sagged back against my pillow and sipped at the last of my brandy.

'Of a certainty, one always has more use for friends than for enemies.'

'True,' replied Nial, as he swirled the contents of his horn and turned slowly onto his side with a grunt, 'and the outcome of the election has also been good for you, I believe.'

'You mean Cathal was elected?' I exclaimed, feeling greatly heartened by these tidings.

Nial paused to refill our horns with the decanter in his outstretched hand, then fell back onto his rolled jacket. He wore a huge grin of satisfaction on his face as he took a long swig of brandy.

'Yes friend Juan, Cathal the Black will be our next lord tánaiste. Hardly a mean feat, for one often considered the runt of his father's litter. For he was but a whiskerless boy when he caught the red plague, when the best surgeons predicted that he would not see out the year. Besides marking his flesh, the disease also cursed him with a short stature. It was expected that he would become a scholar, yet he instead became our champion cattle raider. That has always been the way of Cathal the Black: sailing close to the winds of setback but always scraping through in triumph.'

The bondsman grinned.

'Indeed, it is said that it was but the difference of a single vote that secured him this lofty post. To think that he once barely fled Dartry with his life.'

'He once fled Dartry?'

The bondsman rested his forefinger upon his lips and proceeded with a cautious whisper.

'Do not raise your voice, grey wolf, for you never know who might be eavesdropping. The marshal's late father, Cathal *Óg*, was formerly the lord chieftain of the MacGlannaghs. It is said that a more ruthless man never lived. He is reputed to have had a heart of ice and a penchant for exerting his power at every opportunity. He did this against both the weak and the strong, earning him the nickname *An Faolchù*, which in our tongue means 'the wolf.' His acts of violence were random and often senseless, so that it was rumoured that he was not right in the head.'

Nial paused to drink, before he further described the former king of Dartry.

'Many were those among the assembly whose wives and daughters were forced to submit to his violent advances, and he encouraged his sons to follow his ways, so that the tribe and our neighbouring allies feared them almost more than the enemy. Most also feared that they would spell the ruin of the tribe, and it was only his younger brother, our lord chieftain Tadhg *Óg*, who dared to openly stand up to them. It is rumoured that Tadhg *Óg* came up with the plan for Cathal the Black to slay *An Faolchù*. Yet when this attempt was foiled, he and Tadhg *Óg* barely fled Dartry with Aengus and their fellow conspirators, to be hidden away by the O'Rourkes of Breifne.'

'You're saying Cathal tried to kill his own father?'

'Yes Spaniard. The crime of kin-slaying called *fingal*, considered by my people to be one of the most terrible offences.'

'And what became of *An Faolchù?*'

'It is said that the attempt on his life drove him mad. His acts of inhumanity only increased, until one day he perished in the woods during a hunting expedition. It is commonly believed that the O'Reillys sprang a trap for him and his eldest sons, who perished along with him. Although the O'Reillys have always hotly denied this.'

'That is truly a tall tale,' I exclaimed, 'that Cathal is believed to have conspired with his uncle to kill his own father.'

The bondsman looked about him as he leant towards me.

'It is also commonly rumoured and believed, that Cathal is the issue of an affair between *An Faolchù* and a mysterious Spanish concubine.'

'So the new tanist is a bastard?' I exclaimed, feeling overwhelmed by all the revelations.

Nial's jaw dropped as he stared at me aghast, until his mouth was closed again in an awkward half-smile.

'We consider all of our children to be legitimate, grey wolf.'

A cough was followed by a splutter as I nearly choked on my drink.

'You are not serious?'

The bondsman stared at me for a few moments until a glimmer of recollection was seen in his eyes.

'It is God's own truth. Among the Gaels, the children born outside marriage are not branded as bastards. It is different here to how it is in Spain.'

For a few moments I was left dumbstruck by his revelation, and I wondered if I would ever become accustomed to the ways of my hosts.

'From a fugitive to a second-in-command,' I finally managed, 'this Cathal is indeed a master of returning from the brink.'

'Aye, that he is. Being our champion cattle raider, he also owns many heads of cattle and enjoys great popularity among the tribe. For although he keeps his distance from most Dartrymen, it is said that his agents often extend gifts of cowflesh and white meats to those in need.'

'Why is he so aloof?'

'There is an unfortunate superstition which lingers among the Gaels, that blemishes to one's face are the mark of a liar. As you heard in my lord MacGlannagh's hall, it is a condition that is all too often exploited by less honourable men like Donal MacCabe. Indeed, it will be interesting to see how Cathal will appear before the tribesmen at his election ceremony tomorrow. But his looks are not the only cause of certain tribesmen's misgivings. For Cathal is also the only surviving son of *An Faolchù*, so that the admiration of the members of the assembly is partly grudging and tainted with fear, that he might be a man who could turn mad like his father.

'So these fears persist, despite the rumours of his attempted *fingal*?'

'Yes,' replied the bondsman, 'yet these fears are unfounded, for he is one that is noble in spirit, and no man has more respect amongst the tribe, now that Aengus is gone. And hardly was his father found dead and his exiled uncle pronounced chieftain, that he was immediately declared captain of the MacGlannagh's horse, since few better riders have been seen among the sons of Dartry. The bond between him and the chieftain is strong, and happy is the news of his election.

For the rivalry between a chieftain and his *tánaiste* has often proved the undoing of many a tribe.'

'So the only threat to the tribe's future is the constable Mac-Cabe?'

Nial took another long sip from his horn before replying.

'That remains to be seen.'

'Yet surely Cathal's appointment to the post of tanist should bridle the constable's influence?'

'I doubt there is any hope of that. For although the constable is not often in Rosclogher, and is mostly stationed at Duncarbery, the whole of Dartry is not large enough to accommodate the ambitions of three powerful men.'

The bondsman's words of foreboding lingered with me as our conversation dwindled and he drifted off to sleep. Yet my own repose was uneasy that night, for our talk had left me feeling anxious that I might never leave this strange land where everything was different. At last my thoughts strayed to the memory of the emerald, and I wondered when I might find the time to look at it, if indeed I would find the time at all. Shadows flickered against the walls when slumber claimed me, with the last sound I heard being a crackle from the hearth.

When I awoke, bright light bathed the straw strewn across the ground. I sat up swiftly and drew a deep breath, feeling clear headed and vigorous for the first time in days. My left shoulder ached less too, so that it was my ears that throbbed instead, filled as they were with the peals of the abbey's bell. From beside the hearth, the beaming face of the bondsman greeted me while he held his brown jacket over the smoke from the dying flames, to rid it of fleas.

'Good day, grey wolf.'

'How long have I slept for?'

The bondsman grinned while he adjusted his sword belt.

'Most of the morning. Perhaps it would be best if you got some fresh air. The sun is long risen.'

At his words a chill wind blew through the hut, and he swiftly threw his jacket over his shoulders.

'Good Lord! 'tis a cold, Protestant wind that blows no one any good!'

I smiled faintly as he spoke again.

'How are you feeling?'

'Much better. That brandy from last night has left me feeling restored.'

Nial laughed, then nodded to a pimpled knave who entered our hut, carrying a fresh pail of water as well as a vial of vinegar and a sword. He also bore a fresh mantle and tunic, which he placed at the end of my bed with the sword before hurrying out of the hut. When he was gone the bondsman strode over towards me, studying me carefully.

'Do you feel well enough to ride?'

'Ride? Where?'

'Cathal *Dubh* has requested your presence at the rite of his appointment.'

I nodded slowly to him, then stood up to wash and change my garments. When I took off my old tunic, I noticed Nial quailing at the sight of my naked back, which I knew was lined with scars and lacerations. As I proceeded to take a wet rag out of the pail to wash myself, he made for the doorway with an awkward frown.

'I shall go and fetch the horses. Meet me outside when you are ready.'

'My thanks for all of your aid, friend Nial.'

He nodded with a smile, seeming almost embarrassed.

'Speak nothing of it. It is an honour for me to assist a soldier of Spain.'

After he was gone, I stuck my head through the doorway, relishing the sight of him trudging off towards a distant stable wherefrom there emerged a high-pitched neigh.

I rushed back inside and swiftly washed my face, eyes and ears with water from the bucket. Yet I refrained from saying my morning prayers, for I needed to attend to a greater priority. I realised that a more private moment would not soon be forthcoming, so I took off one of my brogues and put my fingers in it. I felt a flood of relief as I fished the gem out of the shoe and proceeded to wipe it with the cloth. I next fell on my haunches and crouched in a corner of the hut, with my face to its wall of wattle as I held the unworldly gem in the palms of my shaking hands.

The ring's casing was yellow gold, which was of a high value although not enough to be life-altering. Yet the bud that sparkled atop it was a pure verdant ecstasy. I happily admired the emerald which was the size of a finger's knuckle, the reward for all the anguish I had suffered from the day I had been betrayed by the Morisco whore in Seville. It would also serve as a passport to the New World, a place where all my ills and misfortunes would be restored.

So much had happened since my flight from Sligo, that it seemed almost impossible that I held the same ring which I had found in the bowels of the sheriff's keep. The events which led me to possess such a priceless trinket seemed far-fetched while I beheld its sparkle. The unlikelihood of my situation also meant a few more moments of wordless awe before I could bring myself to wrench my stare away from the stone, muttering to myself in disbelief.

'Perhaps you were meant to come to me. Maybe that is why I spent all those days at the oar.'

The utter absurdity of my words was lost on me then, and I already glimpsed images of myself within the verdant gleam of the stone, sailing across the Atlantic beneath sails of blue damask with richly clad retainers who laughed and sang with beautiful, savage women upon their arms. The droves of cattle I would own appeared in imaginary, rolling plains before my eyes, as did other visions of what I would do with my new-found riches once the gem was sold to some wealthy hidalgo. This comprehension of the impossible fortune in my hand filled me with a great resolve, for my path to the Indies suddenly lay wide open before me.

'But first,' I said with a deep resolve, 'I must fetch Pieter.'

I had often questioned the reason for my sufferings aboard the Santa Maria de Visión, but now the answer lay directly before me. I knew that if I played my cards right and somehow spirited the trinket back to the Continent, that I might use it to return to the Province of Brabant. Where I would find Elsien's brother and aunt and take them with me to Spain and then the Indies.

'And upon my return to Seville,' I growled, 'I will track down that harlot of *La Lechera* and teach her a lesson she shan't forget.'

I wrapped my fingers about the stone and held it in a tight grip, hiding its sparkle from view.

'I will get revenge on every last whoreson who helped consign me and Maerten to the oar,' I whispered, 'I shall purchase the title of hidalgo and be exempt from tax, secure a line of credit from some fat Genoese banker to seize my chances in the Indies.'

I also resolved to be patient and not share my secret with anyone, regardless of how many months I spent among the tribe in Dartry. For patience was no stranger to me, since it had been my companion in countless skirmishes which found me waiting in a trench or a tree for hours on end.

As I held the bauble between my fingers, the ring glinted wordlessly in the morning brightness, as if gently torturing me by stoking up my hopes and aspirations. Then the sunlight revealed a mark on the inside of the golden band which I first took to be a scratch. With a gasp, I suddenly realised that it was in fact an inscription. I held the golden band up, slowly turning it in the light as I made out the words scrawled within it.

'to my Eufrasia, with all my love for you and our child - F.R.'

I mouthed the words in bafflement, until the whinny of a horse outside the hut suddenly made me come to. I quickly placed the ring back in the shoe and spattered my armpits with vinegar, then wore the clothes on my bed. I next wrapped my hand about the wooden grip of my blade, which was ribbed and bound with a leather thong. I pulled the weapon out of its scabbard and raised its steel in front of my face, recalling that the sword was the symbol of all Spanish troops who fought for God and king. It also reminded me of all the atrocities I had witnessed by the Imperial troops, which were committed in the name of the one true faith.

I observed the unfamiliar symbol of an Irish swordsmith above its hilt, then lifted the blade and swung it before me from left to right a few times, which only served to show that my sword arm had weakened considerably. With a sigh of resignation, I realised that even wielding a sword the way I once did would require weeks of practice. When my fingertips touched the blade's edges, they flinched at the razor-sharp touch.

It was a weapon fashioned for both slashing and hacking, which possessed a blade that was remarkably straight. I returned it to the sheath bound to my hip, then walked to the doorway and curiously studied my environs. I found that the constant billow of wind had abated, so that it felt like a calming stillness lay across the town of Manglana. The day was cold yet clear, since the gales from the previous night had swept all cloud over the mountains.

Amid the silence about me I felt grateful to be healed and armed by new allies, with a full belly beneath new clothes and a fortune in my shoe. The distant dark outline of mountains rising beyond the hillock felt somehow reassuring, as if it were a stout fortress wall. Upon beholding it, I worded the realisation which suddenly struck me after all I had been through.

'I am alive.'

I walked out of the cabin with a spring in my step and my hand rested on my sword pommel. The peals of the abbey's bell had long dwindled, with the huts and cabins about me appearing emptier than a butcher's shop at Lent. From among them there appeared a solitary and familiar figure who waved at me, so that I made towards him. When I reached him, the bondsman twitched his nose.

'That was a fair dose of vinegar.'

'Is it not a special occasion?'

He grinned back at me as we next proceeded to make our way through the town, where I squinted at the huts about me in wonder.

'What do you call this place?'

'It is called the MacGlannagh's town.'

As I looked over my shoulder, I noticed that the huts along the lake's edge consisted of large and sturdily built cabins, unlike the infirmary where I had first resided. As we moved away from the water, the huts like the one I shared with the bondsman became more common, except that they were even smaller and not built of wooden panels. They were instead circular shelters which were no steadier than wickerwork built of hurdles and long turf, with its gaps filled with earth and moss. Some were guarded from the wind by rude boardings, which confirmed my suspicions that their construction was not the most secure.

Pens and the odd barn stood among them, with the smell of fresh sods being very thick. When we got closer to the stone ringfort that guarded the settlement, the bondsman stopped before the doors of a wooden enclosure, wherefrom there emerged the odd neigh and whinny. An aged groom emerged from inside it and led two horses to us.

As Nial patted their muzzles, he caught me staring at the black mount. It was a stallion that whinnied nervously and blew up sizeable clouds of mist. As the bondsman handed its reins to me, I recognised the steed which I had stolen from the Sassana lieutenant Gilson, when I had rescued the ollave. I had not seen the horse since the ambush on Treasach Burke, and was surprised to find that it had survived the ambush un-scathed. It was a robust creature with full quarters and of a handsome size, a stallion possessed of great power.

'Am I to ride him again?'

'Of course. He is yours.'

In the absence of stirrups, I imitated Nial by hauling myself onto my steed after grabbing its ear, which caused the horse to shake its back and kick the air a bit. The strange pillow-like saddle upon its back left me feeling perplexed, with my feet left kicking at thin air as I tried to find stirrups. One of the horseboys smiled as he passed me a rod, then gestured to the bondsman who used a similar stick to goad his mount into a canter.

After I used my rod in the same way, Gilson's stallion quick-ly caught up with Nial's steed as we approached a small range of outbuildings in the shadow of the long ringfort. I finally noticed the presence of other townsfolk, as elders and wives with young children peered at us from the doorways of their huts. These town dwellers at the edge of the settlement ap-peared a more desperate people, scrawnier and less privileged than the other tribesmen I had seen. They regarded us with awe and curiousity, although some of them also hid away with a scowl.

'They seem afraid of us,' I said to Nial.

'Perhaps, although I think that they are mostly curious. They are mostly afraid whenever they are forced to billet the gallowglasses, when the Scots warriors appear in the town. They also endure difficulty during Easter, Christmas, Whitsuntide and Michaelmas.

'Why?'

'Well,' said Nial with a shrug, 'because it is at these times of the year that the tribe's chief families leave their large cabins along the lake to feast in whichever house they choose and to take whatever they wish.'

'How is that allowed?' I asked in bafflement.

'It is the tradition of the tribe,' replied the bondsman, 'the freemen are lords of the land, the men under whose protection the lesser tribesmen live. Which in turn means that no oats and barley can be spared for the tribesmen or the churls, if they are needed to feed the cavalry horses. Especially not during these troubled times.'

'Times are troubled indeed when kings must take food from the mouths of the very people they should protect.'

Nial frowned knowingly before he shrugged.

'I need not teach you the ways of men, grey wolf. You know that even in your world, each rank of society also owes duties to the rank above it.'

As we passed over the last tamped down avenues between the wickerwork huts, I noted that even the old women were armed. The bondsman acknowledged my remark.

'At any moment they are ready to answer a call to arms. We have a great tradition of fighting women, like the Queen Maeve of yore. The foremost woman of our day is *Gráinne Ní Mháille*, a veritable pirate queen who terrorises ships on the coast. She has built herself a fearsome reputation.'

'They sound like a handful,' I said, but the bondsman's lips remained pursed.

'It is a tough life outside the walls of Rosclogher, grey wolf. And one which has only become harder. There was a time when a ceremony guaranteed peace, yet these days we must defend ourselves at all times.'

'Is it the same throughout the land?'

Nial shrugged.

'In those districts held by the enemy, one may not bear weapons. Yet beyond the Pale nearly all go armed.'

A last hut was occupied by dishevelled women, some of whom bore smiles that were as suggestive as they were toothless. They were evidently also women of fortune, just like those found on the edge of every other town in the world. A red-haired specimen among them even blew me a kiss, while I realised that some things in Ireland were not all that different from Spain.

The odd chicken scurried away as we passed the last dwellings of the underprivileged, when there appeared a small gathering of men in chainmail. Their brawny arms rested upon slender battle axes, with their faces a portrait of dourness as we rode past them. They were the Scots mercenaries who were billeted in the town, and my eyes fell upon the muskets they carried. The V springs and curved cocks on these guns revealed them to be snaphaunces.

'A cheerful lot, are they not?' I asked.

Nial shrugged once more.

'Men of the constable MacCabe. To be trusted as far as you can throw them.'

As I observed their dress and the menace which they exuded, one of them stepped forward. A glare of hate was stamped on his face and his axe was half raised as Nial reached over to tug at my sleeve.

'Do not hold their gaze for too long, grey wolf. Those warriors are born killers, as hard as the rocky crags they were born in.'

We next found ourselves in the shadow of the ringfort. As I stared at its stone wall, there emerged from its entrance a guard of ten wood-kerns. They wordlessly encircled us, forming an armed escort as we made towards our destination. We covered the turf between the fort and the brush at the town's edge, when the unmistakable raw stench of middens greeted us.

A small rustle was heard from one of the pits that were filled with rubbish from the tribe. I turned my head in shock when I noticed that the sound came not from a creature but from an aged crone in rags, whose silver hair hung down in mad tangles. My horse pulled up in fright when she crept out of the hole with the carcass of a dead hare held in her gnarled fist. Her bent finger was smeared with filth and held out before me, as her eyes widened in madness behind her crooked nose.

'Thosaigh eachtrannach! Éalaigh leat ó na tailte seo! Déanfaidh an mac tíre liath litriú ar ár mbolg agus fiú é a bheith istigh ann! Caith amach é Tugaim rabhadh duit!'

I started at her shrieks of rage, when one of the kerns ran up to me and jerked the reins of my mount, so that it trotted on after Nial's.

'Who was that?' I gasped, feeling rocked by the sight of a creature so ragged and tormented.

'That is mad Orla,' replied the bondsman, 'long reduced to depending upon alms from the town. Her husband was once a proud warrior, and she was respected among the tribesmen. But our constant fighting with the enemy widowed her and claimed the lives of all her sons and the greater part of her family. Some say that she went mad from grief, before she also proceeded to lose her sight. O'Ronayne has managed to restore some of her vision, although I suspect it has done her more harm than good, for she has since been able to walk again unassisted. The children often have to be stopped from taunting her and no one is bound by law to be responsible for her deeds. Apart from the *druth* Brian, we have no other fools in the tribe. But the two that we do have make up for thrice their number in the amount of trouble they cause.'

'But what was she saying?' I insisted, still feeling troubled by the woman's angry stares in my direction.

'Just the ramblings of a crazed crone, grey wolf, nothing to be concerned with. She claimed to have seen the doom of the tribe, while pointing at a poor Spanish castaway rescued from the brink of death.'

I shifted awkwardly in my saddle at his words, as the bondsman looked at me over his shoulder and issued a small chuckle.

'You are still not faring any better with the local women, grey wolf.'

After we passed the round fort, another ring of protection appeared. It consisted of a shield of bog which encircled the town for over a league, forming another layer of defence. The kerns formed a single file and skipped over the rocks hidden in it which were known only to them. Nial urged me to also dismount after jumping off his saddle, then led me over the hidden track of rocks which were embedded in an irregular manner. We wended our way through the stinking mud while I stared about me in awe.

'It is impossible to drag artillery through here.'

The bondsman ignored my words as he gestured to me frantically.

'Stay close behind me, do not stray off the path!'

Once the ling-covered bog was traversed, Nial and I climbed back on our mounts. We next followed a narrow track which was barely two feet wide and led up towards the great heights which loomed over the town. As we climbed higher the horses faltered, yet the wood-kerns never relinquished their step. With a set jaw, they each hurried up the incline which our mounts struggled to scale. I could see other riders further ahead, also keeping to the hidden tracks as they made towards a leftward crest in the mountains.

I was surprised to see the women riding ahead of their men, all the while spurring their steeds forward. The female fashion of sitting sideways atop a horse had not yet reached Ireland, or else went ignored. Furthermore, none of the natives used a saddle while riding, since they also used rods with hooked goads on their ends to spur on their horses. On the final rise, ferns and violet pansies grew along our track, with a cold wind blowing over the heights of the last accessible hills.

This reduced the heat of the sun's glare, which tore through a clear sky that was smudged by wisps of cloud. We soon abandoned the track of the mountain to dismount from our horses, then led our mounts over a grassy path that glistened with dew. When I looked beyond the slopes below us, Rosclogher resembled a rook on a chessboard.

Two horseboys hastened over to us and took the bridles from our hands, then made towards their fellows who guarded their masters' mounts. The mountain air was much fresher than that by the marsh and all about us the rise was a rippling sea of green. I hurried after the bondsman in the direction of a large pile of white stones and together we made our way over the grass towards the gaunt, wind-whipped figures who stood alongside the white mound of rubble. It was a stirring and glorious sight, which filled me with awe as I took in the sweeping magnificence of our environs.

'An *oenach*, a gathering summoned by the chieftain,' said Nial in explanation, with a clink heard from his gauntlet as he gripped one of his sword pommels.

There were natives standing close together at the back of the throng, wearing kilts or tunics which reached down to their knees. They also wore woollen coats which they clasped tightly about their shoulders, with their capes pulled down low over their long fringes which were ruffled by the strong draughts of wind that howled about us. The large gathering also appeared to be divided according to rank, as the bondsman whispered a description of the natives on the outside of the ring.

'They are the *tuatha*, bands of herdsmen who pay tribute to the MacGlannagh.'

'Are they not cold up here?' I asked, since some of them were scantily clad in a tunic and mantle.

'It matters not', he replied. 'Every able tribesman is expected to ascend to the burial places where the *tánaiste* is to be appointed.'

As we stepped past them, I recognised some of the freemen who were richly attired in silk capes and mantles. Their hair was worn crisped and long, hanging down their shoulders and back, for it had been washed and combed for the occasion. Many tribesmen had ventured forth hatless, with their long hair and beards rippling in the wind as they waited with serious expressions. The throng parted before the savage wood kerne that guarded us as we strode towards the front of the gathering where Nial saluted O'Ronayne. The Jesuit was surrounded by a group of his own retainers, which included fellow priests, kerns and apprentices. He grunted his approval when the bondsman praised the election outcome.

'A choice both wise and inevitable. He is as virtuous as his late foster brother, if not as gifted.'

O'Ronayne next returned his gaze to the mound of white stones in front of us, which stood alongside an aged, quivering whitethorn. Manglana and his nephew Cathal were closest to the pile of rocks, both swathed in their mantles and bearing tall, conical hats with broad brims in the crook of their arms. The marshal's skin was an extraordinarily pale white, and his blemishes appeared, as if by a miracle, to have disappeared. The newfound texture of his skin was due to a daubing with ceruse pigment which contrasted greatly with his raven black hair.

As he stood by his uncle, I could not help thinking how similar they appeared, despite the freakish colour of the marshal's skin. I also remembered Nial's words from the night previous when he said that the chieftain and the newly elected tanist were rumoured to be father and son. Both men were clad in rough frieze jackets and tight trousers under their broad mantles. They were encircled by almost a hundred knaves with freshly braided hair, who stood still as statues when Cathal walked through them. While the elected tanist approached the bone-coloured pile behind him, Nial leaned towards my ear and pronounced the slightest of whispers.

'That is the burial cairn of his ancestors.'

Not a soul stirred, so that only the shrill whistle of the mountain breeze was heard. A middle-aged woman with an air of great authority strode past the bodyguards who shied away from her with their heads bowed in reverence. I could see that she bore thick scrolls of vellum, and fixed Cathal with a hawklike gaze while he struggled to ascend the revered stones and pebbles. Some rattled against each other when I nudged the bondsman and pointed towards the woman.

'Echna' he whispered, 'the Brehon Judge.'

The Jesuit whirled upon us with a huff, and I picked up a whiff of barley beer when he shushed us with his forefinger pressed against his lips. Nobody noticed him, for the Dartrymen's attentions were fixed on the Judge who administered oaths in a tone both solemn and high-pitched. Cathal attempted to remain as still as he could against the buffeting gale, while trying to keep his balance atop the cairn. He shouted parts of what she said, although his voice was barely audible because of the wind. All of those present beheld him in awe, yet my eyes were fixed on a woman who suddenly appeared at the shoulder of the Brehon Judge and who was flanked by two great wolfhounds.

Her slender hand emerged from the sleeve of a dark kirtle, as she held her dark mantle which was wrapped over her head and across her face to avoid it becoming undone by the wind. This garment reached down to her shoes where it met the end of a saffron tunic. I realized that it was the first time I had seen Muireann without mud and grime, outside the darkness of the keep. Her eyes sparkled with a keen awareness, and her face shone with a bold haughtiness that I found strongly compelling.

With the rod held before him, the marshal maintained a stoic expression, turning three times from left to right and again from right to left. When he was finished O'Ronayne walked over towards Manglana's side, while Nial described what happened.

'The wand represents the conduct of a tanist. It is straight and without stain.'

'And what of his movements?'

'Three times either way, done in honour of the Holy Trinity.'

The tanist surveyed the view of the lake below us, turning his head in all directions as he beheld as much of the Dartry as possible. He pronounced the tribe's name which was repeated by O'Roynane, then also echoed by all those present who yelled out in unison.

'The MacGlannagh!

To my great discomfort, I realised that other Scottish mercenaries were also present among the crowd as they raised their axes towards Cathal. Yet their constable Donal McCabe was nowhere to be seen, and I also realised that I could not see Lady Dervila anywhere either. Cathal leapt in triumph off the stones, an act which sparked fevered chatter among those assembled. Nial smiled openly, seemingly satisfied by the outcome of the ceremony.

'From now on, we must refer to him as the MacGlannagh, as if we were addressing the chieftain himself.'

Cathal's chest swelled with pride as he saluted Manglana who regarded him with an austere expression. The chieftain then wrapped Cathal in a big hug, leaving the new tanist to grab the sides of his burly uncle to keep from falling. Once he had freed himself from Manglana's embrace, the marshal turned tanist fell to one knee, as a score of rugged tribesmen approached him and proceeded to each remove a brogue from one foot.

With a cry of his new title they hurled the shoes over his head, which I took to be an absurd gesture. Upon noticing my bemusement, Nial explained that the shoe throwers were leaders of tuaths who swore fealty to the chieftain, and who had just demonstrated their support of his subordinate. After this strange ritual was completed, Cathal next proceeded to embrace O'Ronayne, before bowing deeply to Echna and Muireann and turning to the cheering gathering. The chieftain's new second-in-command had a daring glint in his eye when he spoke, with the bondsman swiftly translating his words.

'Let the games begin.'

XIX

The Dartry mountains to Rosclogher, Dartry, County Leitrim

28 September 1588

When the ceremony was over, the crowd readied to disperse. It parted like the Red Sea to allow the chieftain through it, followed by the bard and the new tanist who walked with his head held high. I noticed that Cathal no longer appeared fearful of being seen closely in broad daylight. Thanks to the few handfuls of the ceruse pigment which had been used to colour his face, the contours of his scars were barely visible and his features reflected the sun's brilliance. The rest of the gathering turned to follow him downhill according to their rank.

We made after them until the grassy path lost its steepness, then reached a gentler slope where many mounts were hitched, grazing peacefully under the watchful eye of scrawny horseboys. Thereafter the rest of the descent was tackled on horseback, while the lower born freemen streamed downhill on foot along courses known to them alone. Their progress was remarkably swift, so that the bondsman and I quickly lost sight of them as we led our steeds downhill at a cautious trot and rounded the first ridge. I shuffled madly to keep from tumbling off my horse's back, with the downhill journey proving both lengthy and laborious.

'We should have walked.'

Nial nodded his agreement.

'It may well have proved swifter. But the horse is a mark of status that one should not lightly forego.'

When the remaining slopes became steeper, we only spoke in short gasps, with our thighs tightly squeezed against our mounts' flanks like talons. When at last we reached the foot of the great rise we covered the remaining stretches of ground at a bold canter, until we came to the shield of marshland. Once the treacherous path through it was crossed, we were met by the pungent odour of middens and laystalls along the periphery of the town.

Beyond them a group of tribesmen could be seen gathered on the sward of grass between the ringfort and bog, which was to serve as a green for their impending contests. An excited hubbub had overcome the tribe, while Nial explained that the funeral games which should have followed the burial of Aengus had been delayed until after Cathal *Dubh's* election ceremony. Around us folk laughed and shouted in excited voices, while the sun shone down on proceedings.

When we rode towards the stable, I noticed that the grass about us was possessed of an even surface. I noted that many churls must have cleared it during the ceremony upon the mountain, for all of the stones and pebbles which had previously hindered my steed had been cleared from the face of the tract of land. A small pavilion had also been pitched near the ringfort, with scores of blue jackets standing before it. Their spearheads gleamed with sunlight as Manglana slumped upon a raised throne behind them, wearing a dismissive frown upon his face. One of his household servants was already filling his cup while I noticed the empty throne alongside the chieftain.

'Where is the queen, Dervila?'

Nial cast me a disdainful stare over his shoulder.

'I do not know. Perhaps she is still in the keep, refusing to show her face in support of the new *tánaiste*. She has never been able to stand the sight of him. For it is said that he reminds her of his late father *An Faolchù*, whom she always despised.'

I nodded slowly while feeling relieved that I would not have to worry about another attack by Manglana's wife.

'And what of the Scottish constable? Donal MacCabe?'

'He is most likely still recovering from the outcome of the election, for the reek of loss is still too thick in his nostrils. But he shall not miss out on the great cattle raid, you can bet your finest stud bull on that.'

'What cattle-raid?' I asked, while wondering if I might be asked to bear arms in the service of the natives.

'Our traditions demand that a new tanist marks his election by raiding the herd of a neighbouring tribe. There will be much sport and feasting today, yet before the week is out Cathal will have claimed his new title in blood.'

His grim prediction caused me to restrain a shiver, when a loud cry was heard in the direction of the pavilion. We jerked our heads towards the sound and kept our horses from bolting, trying to make out the cause of the sudden cries and gasps that could be heard about us. In the day's brightness, it did not take long for me to recognize the figure of Manglana's wife approaching the green through the main thoroughfare of the town. Lady Dervila had decided to make an appearance after all, and a score of gallowglass mercenaries encircled her. I also spotted the fearsome sight of Donal MacCabe amongst them, and his stern expression appeared unaffected by his narrow loss at the election.

The gallowglass constable's drab clothing contrasted greatly with that of Dervila, since Manglana's queen had donned a red gown that was lined with marten fur, giving her an appearance which was both stunning and regal. It also left me wondering how so much red dye had been obtained or afforded. Atop her head a small scarlet hat was borne over the cap which held her hair tightly against the back of her head, so that it could barely be seen at all.

Her dress was lavish in the extreme when compared to the frayed smocks worn by most female natives, including those I had noticed in Sligo. The radiance of her stunning countenance brought a lump to my throat, for it entirely eclipsed the grubby faces of most women about me. I was certainly not alone in being impressed, for every matron and her daughter called out in wonder at the sight of her.

Five female companions also surrounded Dartry's queen. Although they were not as richly attired as their mistress, their clothes were both sober and presentable, consisting of black petticoats and bodices. These ladies-in-waiting were maidens of great beauty whose hair flowed freely about their shoulders, and I later discovered that three of them were Manglana's younger relations. The other two wore the linen headdresses of married women, with one masking her face with a sheer veil. Despite this, I could still recognize the figure of the ollave Muireann Mac an Bhaird. Her two great dogs still shadowed her steps, and I nudged the bondsman and pointed at them.

'The two great dogs, do they belong to the ollave?'

'Yes,' he replied, 'they are her faithful hounds Roe and Branan, who never leave her side, except when they are locked away in the keep. God help the man who tries to lay a hand on the ollave when they are around.'

I felt a twinge of annoyance when Muireann was obscured by the surrounding guard of Scotsmen, who turned towards the vacant throne within the pavilion. Dervila paid no heed to the bluejackets or the highborn Irishmen who regaled her with flourishing bows. As she strode up to her seat, Manglana did not betray any awareness of her, nor did he even stand up to greet her.

I then noticed something about the chieftain which briefly captured my attention. For upon closer inspection I saw that he did not carry a staff in his hands, as I had first thought, but something very much resembling an old friend from battles past. I realised that he had in his possession a wheellock, although I was not close enough to Manglana to be able to recognise the gun's maker or its quality.

'Is that a rifle?' I asked, as I pointed in its direction.

Nial shrugged.

'It is a recent acquisition of my lord, borne to him from the beaches by some of his men. It is but a trophy, for the Dartrymen mistrust firearms and mostly use bows.'

'Why?'

'Why not?' replied the blond bondsman, throwing himself off his horse to a loud jingle from his scabbards, 'they can fit six arrows to our bow in the time it takes to load a gun.'

Not the way I load it, I thought, as I beheld Manglana, who still regarded the preparations upon the green with an impassive eye. He had not yet uttered a single word to his wife. Dervila looked forlorn, as if she would have preferred to be anywhere else, rather than by his side. An exalted company were gathered before Dartry's king and queen, which included the bard, O'Ronayne and the ollave Muireann. As I reined my horse in and dismounted, a great peat pyre burst into flame before the ringfort. I regarded the blaze in awe as a knave appeared to take our horses back to the barn. Before they were led away, I patted Gilson's stallion behind its ear, prompting it to buck its head nervously.

'Do not be troubled,' I whispered to my fellow alien, as it nervously twitched its ear, 'we shall get through this together.'

As the horses were returned to the stables, the bondsman dropped to one knee and bowed. I quickly followed suit, upon realizing that the new tanist had just appeared behind us, approaching us with a haunting grin on his pallid face. After acknowledging our gesture, he beckoned to us to follow him and his score of blue-jacketed kerns. Together we walked towards the tent, where Cathal's bodyguard pushed aside the fast-gathering tribesmen who loudly saluted the tanist as their lord MacGlannagh. Upon approaching the exalted company within the pavilion, the new tanist bowed to them once, then returned to observing the tournament preparations.

After casting his eyes over the turf, he barked commands to his knaves and servants, so that the broiling of cows in their own hide was soon underway, to provide those present with beef. The gathered throng were next served by an inauguration ode from Fearghal, who stood before the pavilion and delivered the recital in a deep, unflattering voice, to the strumming of a crippled harpist who sat alongside him.

'Need I translate again?' asked Nial wearily.

'No, thank you,' was my reply, since I did not deem it necessary.

As we looked on, the bard skilfully refrained from uttering certain vowel sounds, to create an internal rhyming within phrases. All hung on his every last word, delivered in the sharp and lilting tongue of the natives, which was possessed of a timeless timbre. Although I could not yet understand the words, I tried to comprehend their meaning. For I knew that learning the tongue would greatly aid me in my flight when the time was right.

When Fearghal's recital was delivered, the crowd broke into cheers and clapping. Yet the bard resumed his seat alongside Manglana without ever once acknowledging the acclamation. I recalled my conversation with Nial the night before, when I was told about the exalted role held by the bard among the tribe. For to them Fearghal was one of the *fili*, who held the power of wording the memory and spirit of their ancestors' achievements and those in their own lifetime. It was an esteemed role which the bard had inherited from his own father, a role possessed of greater import than that of a mere poet or orator.

The Dartrymen's attentions next turned to less exalted yet more popular diversions as a number of activities commenced in an arena of sorts: a large square of the green which was cordoned off by stout ropes that were bound to wooden posts at each of its four corners. Proceedings were initiated with a tug of war, which was a hotly contested tussle among groups of men from the *tuatha* across Dartry, to great peals of laughter from onlookers. There followed a variety of sports which included both long and high jumps, as well as races between fleet-footed tribesmen and the very popular wrestling matches. During this last event I watched on as huge natives stripped down to the waist before locking grips, as they attempted to drop their adversaries to the ground and hold them there.

Following each trial, the tanist would summon the victors before the pavilion, where he rewarded them with praise and generous gifts which ranged from articles of clothing to livestock. No such prize was awarded after the horse races held about the square ring, for the new tanist was undefeated due to his skill at riding. The contests then turned increasingly martial, since more weapons were brandished by the tribe than could be found in a Basque foundry.

Archery preceded spear throws and sword fighting, and the sight of combat stirred me deeply. I admired the relish with which my hosts took to fighting, and it was evident that the onlooking natives prized a contestant's skill as much as victory itself. The more aged among the tribesmen could be seen nodding in approval at the sight of a deft parry or counter thrust. Throughout this contest, I stood upon the edge of the pavilion and quietly ignored all of the natives' attempts to coax me to take part.

Indeed I only stirred to join Nial when he approached the fresh beef being broiled above the large fires which raged about the greensward. The scent of freshly roasted meat made my heart thud with excitement, after having lived off scraps and sea biscuit for so long. I buried my teeth into the fare on offer like a ravenous wolf ripping up the softest venison, as Nial smiled sympathetically at the sight.

''tis indeed a great feast', I gasped between mouthfuls.

'Aye', he replied, helping himself to a cutting of cowflesh, 'times are tough but the *tánaiste* shall not deny the people a good feast. Securing the loyalty of the *tuatha* is of the greatest importance during these treacherous times.'

While we ate our fill, we watched the tribesmen's endeavours upon the green. Their encounters were sharp and fierce, so that O'Ronayne often hurried from Manglana's side to attend to bruised limbs or a cracked bone. One young upstart even had to be carried off to the infirmary. When a tribesman collapsed during the boxing, a loud screech of frenzied laughter was heard to our left, since mad Orla had suddenly appeared among the crowd.

Most of the MacGlannaghs shied away from her stinking and wretched presence, while I felt relieved that she had not seen me, absorbed as she was by the sight of the sparring contestants. As the cries of the crowd rose and waned with the progress of the encounters, she howled at each sickening thud of knuckles against bared flesh, even throwing punches of her own at thin air. After a time her presence went ignored, for everyone was excited about the ensuing activities and the weather still held as the wind died down further.

Whenever my attentions strayed towards Muireann, a great roar drew my attention back to the proceedings. I realised that a number of targets had been erected on the green, with archery replacing boxing as a herdsman struck a bullseye to earn himself a goat. When it came to the swordfighting, Nial left my side and strode onto the turf with his hands rested upon his sword pommels. Loud cheers were heard when he approached a blue jacketed bodyguard. After saluting his adversary, his blades rang from their scabbards as the bondsman instantly set upon the blue jacket and overpowered him within minutes. I beheld Nial in wonder, for he was highly skilled at wielding blades with both hands, so that his assault seemed to come from two swordsmen not one.

Between bouts he withdrew to a corner of the field away from the rest of us, regaining his breath as he studied those contestants who would next face him. Yet none could dispossess him of his steels, for his sword pommels seemed joined to him at the wrist, and one by one he drove his opponents to distraction with his Spanish rapier Tizona, which they attempted to fend off with their shield, until a perfectly timed blow from his Irish cleaver Caladcholg whacked their swords clean out of their hands, swiftly ending their encounters.

He was that rarest of swordsmen, the master of an art which I had never witnessed before. His reactions seemed impossibly quick, always leaving him not one but many steps ahead of his opponents' manoeuvres. Indeed, his mind and movements were as sharp as a Basque pike, as he lithely skipped away whenever his adversaries attempted to butt him with

either shoulders or shields, to great snorts of frustration. By
the end of the contest none overcame him or lasted longer
than a few minutes as they tried to parry his blows. Nial received praise from the new tanist amid the great cries of *Dua
Claimthe* from the crowd, then walked away from the pavilion leading the prize of a heifer behind him.

'Impressive skill *Senor* Ne Dourough,' I acknowledged with
a nod of my head.

The bondsman used his forearm to wipe away the few beads
of sweat which had gathered upon his brow.

'Hardly so. It was far easier for me without Aengus. He
alone could give me some trouble, for he was my best student.'

With a sigh he beckoned to a knave who led the heifer away
by its halter. He next returned his attentions to the events of
the green as he rested his hands on his sword pommels.

'So you are not a mere bondsman but also a fencing master?' I asked.

'I am,' he replied, 'the foremost fencing master in Dartry.'

'Then Dartry is fortunate to have you,' I replied, 'for I have
never witnessed such a display of dual wielding.'

Nial shrugged.

'The Lord decreed that my arms be equal in strength and
dexterity. My father would be proud of me today, for he was
my teacher. Munster could not boast of a greater swordsman
during his day.'

Our discourse was interrupted by the roars of outrage
about us, when the Dartrymen of Rosclogher shook their
fists in rage at a large, oaken statue which was dragged onto
the green by a band of churls. The howls of outrage and anger
doubled at its approach, and I saw that it was the figure of a

woman bearing a sceptre and an orb. The oaken effigy was held in such contempt that some of the onlookers ran up and spat on it, while others shook their fists at it. I was about to ask who the statue represented, when Nial growled beneath his breath.

'That bitch of the Jezebel hellwhore, Elizabeth Tudor. If only the Sassenach devil-queen were before us in the flesh.'

As two bodyguards hurled a large rock to the ground on the other side of the green, I could see that the raised effigy of the English queen was to be used as a target to raise morale and encourage rebellious sentiment. An awed silence descended when Cathal walked onto the sward. He wore a triumphant grin as he held up two skinned badgers before his fellow tribesmen. I was enthralled by the scene, so that I pulled the bondsman's sleeve and asked him to translate the marshal's words.

'I hold before you the prize of excellence. For whoever can strike the Sassenach hellwhore.'

Fevered talk overcame the crowd at the sight of the gifts which were proffered by their newly elected tanist. Upon noticing my puzzlement, the bondsman proceeded to explain the excitement.

'We consider the brock to be a great delicacy, grey wolf.'

Many members of the gathering were already brandishing all manner of darts to hurl at the target, while the tanist shouted the rules of the contest.

'He who strikes the queen shall be beaten by he who pierces her heart! Both lose to whoever can topple the heretic witch!'

Nervous chuckles were heard among the throng of contestants, while some pointed at one of Cathal's knaves who scraped a large cross upon the queen's breast to mark out her heart.

'Whoever wins get these two badgers!' shouted Cathal, 'all weapons may be used in the attempt!'

Many tribesmen barged past us as they hurried onto the field to take on the challenge. Scuffles broke out while men pushed at each other to be first in line. The tanist's knaves struggled to keep them in file, so as to ensure that none took turns at the same time. Meanwhile Cathal still bellowed commands from beside the rock, which had been cast onto the green to serve as a marker.

'One at a time! Not a single foot must go before the stone!'

Scores of attempts were made to hit the target but neither man or woman struck the cross. A few of the spears fell short, and others flew over the target. The attempts grew more frenzied, as a few tribesmen even wiped their hands on a rag before hurling their spear. All of the attempts fell short, so that many contestants tried their luck again.

Some of the Scottish mercenaries stood by and laughed at the Dartrymen's efforts. Eventually a few of them decided to take part. Some of the surer throws bounced off the statue's shoulder or arms, as the wooden eyes of the English queen stared back mockingly at the contestants. Nial cursed aloud when his javelin bounced off the statue's shoulder, and a great cheer was heard when Cathal threw off his cloak. The bondsman leant towards me when he returned to my side, observing the tanist who readied to take the next throw.

'This should be worth watching.'

Cathal resembled a raging bull as his great exhalation caused a cloud of mist to gather before his face. He next snatched up his spear, then pushed his long *glibb* fringe to the side of his forehead while he stepped some distance away from the stone boundary. He expertly began his run with his right foot, lifting the dart over his head and stopping less than a yard away from the rock in front of him when he turned his palm towards the sky.

The iron tip of the javelin dipped slightly when Cathal's arm swung across his body. He landed on his other foot as his spear revolved in the air in a slightly curved arc. Gasps of amazement were heard as it flew across the green. When it seemed that it might fall short of the armour before us, it pierced the cross on the breast to a loud cry. Yet just as the spear point became embedded in its target, the haft shuddered twice before the javelin collapsed to the ground. Amid the loud groan which ensued, the tanist turned to the crowd with a smile.

'Can anyone better that?'

Heads were shaken while men slapped their thighs in annoyance, with none daring to meet Cathal's questioning stare. Upon realising that no one would take up his challenge, the tanist turned towards the dignitaries in the pavilion. He next amazed all present by falling to one knee, with his right arm outstretched towards the ladies in Dervila's company as Nial translated his words again.

'Dear sister and revered ollave, I have shared the suffering of your loss over past days. But would you not honour us with one attempt on the day of my ascension? So that no doubt shall linger that I am indeed worthy of my own badgers?'

All attention turned to Muireann who remained rooted to her seat. She did not seem to betray any movement, except for a slight twitch of her shoulders. After a few awkward moments, Dervila bent forward and whispered some words to Muireann. This spurred the ollave to slowly rise to her feet and bow to the company of the chieftain who regarded her from beneath the pavilion.

I watched her in wonder as she stepped onto the green, taking up the bow which was brought to her by a knave and inspecting its string as if it were the chord of a harp. She next examined the arrows picked from a quiver and raised the bow, swiftly pulling the fletching back against the bowstring. Her lip trembled slightly as she held the drawn haft between thumb and forefinger.

'Come on,' I found myself whispering. 'I know you can do it.'

Silence reigned across the greensward before the arrow was released from her grasp, causing sharp intakes of breath when it struck the cross marked upon the trembling statue. A great roar was heard from an onlooker behind us, followed by an eruption of strident cries at the best bowshot which had been seen that day. The ollave slowly turned on her heel and walked off to resume her place in front of Manglana's wife, seemingly deaf to the cheers which erupted about her.

'That was a fair shot,' I whispered to Nial.

The bondsman nodded slowly, his gaze full of admiration at the fine display of archery which had just been witnessed.

'There was only ever one archer better than Aengus. That woman was born to shoot the bolt.'

'How many things can she do?'

Nial grinned, betraying an ill-concealed admiration.

'Whatever the ollave does, she does well.'

'Indeed,' I replied, recalling the Parthian shot that she had managed upon a galloping horse, when we were chased by the evil sergeant Burke. I suddenly realised that I was the object of the chieftain's stare, as he observed me with his bearded chin rested upon his right fist. When the general clamour died down he called to me from his seat.

'Wilt thou not partake of our contest, grey wolf?'

I politely declined, telling him that I could not match the ability of his kinsmen. The chieftain nodded once, then seemed to ponder my words while he studied me. A smirk flickered at the edge of his lips when he spoke again, nodding his head in the direction of the ollave.

'Thou cannot best a woman in the use of arms?'

I was overcome by a hot flush of embarrassment as a couple of the younger natives laughed aloud. With the gauntlet thrown at my feet, I was left with little choice but to take up the challenge. I approached the greensward with a slight limp, as murmurs and snatched whispers grew about me. Then I turned to the pavilion and raised a curled forefinger, as I pretended to pull an unseen trigger in the direction of the chieftain.

Manglana's bluejacket bodyguards instantly drew closely about him, perhaps fearful of some foreign magic as they raised their spears in my direction. Yet Cathal the Black quickly stepped forward with a raised hand, while summoning one of his knaves to hand me a musket. When the weapon was brought to me, I immediately refused it, gesturing instead to the rifle which was held by the chieftain. The audacity of my request seemed to shock his retainers, who beheld me with wide-eyed expressions. Behind them Manglana gently stroked his beard while he observed me with an air of amusement.

'Thou knowest how to use this gun?'

'I could load it in my sleep, Sire.'

Manglana slowly rose to his feet and lifted the rifle off the ground. He balanced it upon the palms of his hands for a few moments during which he fixed me with a level gaze. Then when I least expected it, he threw it into the air towards me, leaving me to madly fumble for it. Manglana's yellowed, loose teeth were bared when he proceeded to laugh at me, with his subsequent cry echoing across the green while the rest of the tribe stared on in bemusement.

'Then load it now, grey wolf.'

As my trembling fingers passed over the weapon, I felt relieved by its tubular, metallic feel. Its craftsmanship was superb, for it was one of those countless sturdy contraptions made in Germany, possessed of a stock that was inlaid with stag-horn. The ingenuity of its extendible butt took my breath away, for it was a prized hunting weapon, which suggested that its owner had been one of the many highborn adventurers who had embarked upon the Armada expedition.

The Imperial emblem of the double-headed eagle adorned its ingenious base, with the sickle mark of the master gunsmith Simon Marquart the Elder visible upon its upper breech, further marking it out as a princely possession. A mud encrusted signature of the famous Bavarian gunsmith Pech was scrawled across the rifle's barrel, which had a spanner attached to it that rendered the gun that rarest of self-loading devices.

After days spent toiling at the oar and fleeing in the wilderness, my reunion with the rifle made me feel like any artisan reunited with the tools of his trade. The weapon brought a strange peace to the depths of my soul, since it provided some familiarity in a land where everything was so different. My trance was broken by a mocking laugh which I took to have been issued by mad Orla, yet when I looked up I realised that it had been produced by the chieftain's wife. I started at this, for I was still wary of Lady Dervila after her recent attack upon me in the tower house. Yet she posed no immediate threat as she called out to me in Latin.

'Thou shalt have much luck with a musket if thou knowest not the use of the spear.'

I restrained a look of disgust at her ignorance, instead managing to engage in a flourishing bow as I sought to ingratiate myself with her.

"'tis a rifle, Your Majesty,' I said.

The mirth upon Dervila's face faded away as her husband beheld me with growing severity, with his smirk having already vanished from his lips. Meanwhile Cathal turned to address Muireann, who had been following our exchange with a keen interest.

'Revered *ollamh*, wilt thou accept the challenge of a firearm?'

Muireann's voice was possessed of an alluring cadence when she replied in the Irish tongue, with Nial being swift to translate her words.

'She says that the hackbut cannot pierce armour from such a distance, but that you are free to persist with your obstinacy.'

I was irked by this remark, for she had witnessed my marksmanship firsthand, with the memory of Ramos toppling from his horse being a recent one. A hurt, betrayed look must have flashed over my face but the ollave maintained an impassive gaze. So I decided to put her remark down to the kick in the head which she had received from Gilson's horse, while choosing to focus on the challenge at hand. I gently knocked the gun's muzzle upon the ground, ignoring the dark stares from some of the tribe's more distinguished spearmen.

Tell-tale sand fell out of its barrel, which implied that the weapon had not been used. I raised it off the ground and turned it about, then peered through its bore. Some specks of sand appeared, which would serve as good wadding after a few thrusts of the scouring stick. Whoever had carried it to Dartry had used it as a crutch or a walking stick, due to ignorance of its huge value or in their haste to flee the Sassanas.

For a moment I considered abandoning the challenge, because I was uncertain if the gun was still up to the task. Then I thought better of it, for its handiwork appeared sturdy enough and the expectant eyes of the surrounding tribesmen persuaded me to take a punt on the weapon. I looked about the pavilion inquiringly and held out my right hand.

'The device shall not load itself. I need powder, balls and a scouring stick.'

Cathal barked at his serving boys who fetched what I needed. In his enthusiasm to assist the tribe's revered guest, one of the striplings also brought me a length of slow match doused in vinegar which I refused. Some of the powder in a priming flask was poured into the palm of my hand, which I had already wiped hard against the front of my tunic. I felt the granules with my fingertips and found them to be slightly damp, which was swiftly pointed out to the tanist.

'This powder is moist. I need it to be dry.'

With a severe expression, Cathal spread his hands out before me.

'The rest of the powder is not yet corned.'

'No matter, bring it to me anyway.'

When my request was met, I took a handful of the powder out of the fresh sack and poured it onto a pewter plate, then ground down the thick granules with the pommel of a dagger handed to me by Nial. The tanist looked on in wonder as I pinched the right quantities of powder on instinct, letting them trickle from between my thumb and forefinger into the priming pan which I had jerked open. When this was done, I flicked the small wheel of steel grooved by cross cuts with my thumb, to test the edge of the pyrite which was attached to the doghead. A surge of relief passed through me when I felt their undamaged edge. I also felt appeased by the sharpness of the serrations as I carefully scraped the remaining chunk of powder from the dish into the breech.

I next retrieved the scouring stick from between my knees and used it to jam a lead ball down the muzzle until it felt like my elbow might snap. The scrape of the stick's end against the grooves filled me with renewed optimism, for I suddenly realized that they were spiral and would greatly improve the gun's aim. I withdrew the rod and dropped it to the ground, then wound the spanner like a clockwork toy.

My fingers danced lithely across the length of the weapon. Although their movement had somewhat slowed through lack of practice, hard rowing and blows of the enemy, I knew that they were still quick enough to make an impression on those gathered about me. On a hunch, I slipped some more gunpowder into the priming pan and gave the spring a quarter turn with the spanner. This proved harder than first expected, yet reassured me that there was still a strong mainspring on the inside. When the gun was loaded, I jerked my head at the tanist to signal my readiness.

'Thou shouldst step up to the mark,' said Cathal, gesturing to the rock which stood a few feet ahead of me.

'I can hit her from here.'

At my claim, the clamour from the onlookers decreased, when Manglana called out to me.

'To the face?'

My right hand left the bottom of the bore and I stuck my thumb out before me. Closing one eye, I held the tip of my finger just below the effigy and attempted to fathom the steps the statue would have needed to cover the distance of my thumbnail, based on my previous observation that it was the height of a tall man. Upon surmising that there were about fifty yards between myself and the queen of the Sassanas, I turned to Manglana and nodded my head in the affirmative.

The chieftain met my gesture with a bemused grin. Snatches of laughter were heard about me, with numbers appearing on the fingers of the tribesmen as they placed their last bets. Behind me I heard the scrape of soles upon grass when Nial rested his hand gently upon my shoulder and he leaned over towards me.

'Are you sure, grey wolf? One should not make idle boasts amongst fighting men.'

With a grunt, I shrugged his hand off my shoulder as he stepped away from me with a muffled gasp of surprise. After stretching my arms and rolling my shoulders to loosen them up, I brought down the doghead and raised the gun's butt to my shoulder. My scarred cheek rested against a barrel which was heavily built to reduce the gun's recoil and I peered through the silver sights at the tiny wooden head in the distance.

Despite my years of experience spent wielding the firearm, the old fears returned when the rifle butt was brought to rest on my shoulder. Had I loaded enough powder? Was the wadding blocking the ball? And would the powder in the pan reach that in the barrel? I promptly dispelled these concerns from my mind and whispered some lines selected from the Old Testament. They were taken from the first book of Samuel, which recounted how a heroic young David slew the giant Goliath with a single stone perfectly hurled from his sling.

This day will the Lord deliver thee into mine hand;
and I will smite thee,
and take thy head from thee

The words steadied my nerves as a dead silence reigned across the green, and titters of nervous laughter died away. I was reassured by the ease with which my old posture returned, so that a renewed resolution steadied my hand. The moments before firing were when I was at my most formidable, with my excitement at the impending explosion causing my heart to beat fast and hard.

My marksmanship had defined the entire span of my life, ever since I was a barefooted boy in Malta. From the days I had first seen a Hospitaller knight wielding a musket along the wharves, to my years in the army of Flanders which I had joined as a fugitive. The gun had been my close companion during the dark days after the Iron Duke had saved my life, and after I had joined the wretched fellowship of Curro Ramos.

The prayer had its desired effect, and with a grimace I shook off my sense of foreboding. My body bristled once more in anticipation as I focused only on the distant effigy. My palm rested against the barrel, my fingers uncurling but once before they were placed about the hair trigger. As I readied to take my shot, the wood carved face of Elizabeth Tudor beheld me silently with an unspoken challenge.

A billow of wind made me hesitate, yet a moment later a touch of the hair trigger produced a slight spark and a slight trail of smoke. The main charge was fired an instant later and shrouded my head and shoulders in a rotten fog. The muzzle was thrown up into the air and the gun's thrust all but spun me onto my knees. My ears were pounded by the sound of the weapon; the kick of its stock against my shoulder was as strong as that of a maddened plough horse.

After a few moments my hearing returned, as my ears were filled with the snorts of Dartrymen and the odd mocking laugh. Then a cry of surprise followed, and a score of tribesmen could be seen running across the green to inspect the effigy. Someone pushed me out of the way and ran after them, while another tribesmen jumped up and down and madly tapped at the space between his eyes. I was surrounded by his fellows and led up to the statue with hearty slaps upon the back. Upon reaching the statue I could see that the ball from my rifle had punctured the space between its brows and fore-head.

Mad Orla jumped about me screeching 'boom! boom!', while mimicking a rifleman and feigning shots in the air. She was roughly shoved aside as a tribesmen pushed me back to the great marker-stone, where I saw that both the chieftain and his wife had risen to their feet in amazement. Manglana was soon bellowing at his tanist to bring me more balls and powder. I knew that these were expensive items which were used sparingly during training practice. Yet no balls and powder were denied me that day, as many of those present urged me to attempt one shot after another.

Two more shots went close while three others hit the effigy's head again. They each left me grimacing from the blows of the gun to my shoulder which was still tender. Yet each time it took me half the time to load the wheellock than it would have taken me to ready a matchlock for firing. This was not lost on the tribesmen who were greatly impressed by the device and went wild whenever I hit the mark. I waved my hand at them when I finally decided to rest at the foot of the pavilion, as Lady Dervila rose to her feet and addressed me with bulging eyes and a loud voice.

'Is marcóir breá tú, mac tíre liath! Ionat tá léargas againn ar ár dtodhchaí. Éilím leis seo go gcuirfeá oiliúint orm féin agus ar mo mhná conas gunna a chaitheamh!'

I looked at her nervously, then stared at Nial who reappeared at my side.

'What did she say?'

'She wants you to teach her and her ladies-in-waiting the use of the rifle.'

I was uncertain what to say and loud roars of laughter were heard from the chieftain who addressed her dismissively. Dervila glared at him while her face reddened with rage. She next raised her skirts and left the pavilion to make towards the lake, with the scowling Scottish mercenaries closely gathered behind her. Yet few heeded her departure as they beheld me in disbelief, while the tanist seized me by the shoulders and laughed out loud.

'Thou art indeed a good shot, grey wolf! By the hesitant way in which you declared your weapon, I thought thou were but a common musketeer!'

He next held out the gifts of excellence towards me, yet I thought it was best to be chivalrous in glory while I regaled the tanist with a curt bow.

'My thanks, my lord MacGlannagh. Yet I request that thou gifts them to the ollave instead. Archers of her skill should be greatly prized.'

A slight hiss was heard from Muireann when she was offered the skinned badgers in my stead. She swiftly rose to her feet and strode off towards the keep after the chieftain's wife, with her huge dogs bounding after her. Nial barely restrained a low chuckle when he spoke.

'You still seem to be attracting the ire of women, grey wolf.'

With the games having ended, Manglana rose to his feet and stepped before me, serving me with a deep and lingering stare. I could not meet his gaze for long and I flinched when he wrapped his hand about the rifle, causing a wide smile to appear beneath his cavernous eyes. After releasing his grip from the gun, he exchanged words with the bondsman, who slightly baulked before the dragon breath while nodding his understanding.

Manglana then made his way back to the lake, beckoning to the leaders of the *tuatha* who were clustered about his protective guard of bluejackets. They swiftly made after him to seek his counsel, since news of the Armada landings had raced through Dartry like wildfire. After the Sassanas' outrages which I had witnessed in person, I had no doubt that the Irish had many concerns to share with their protector to whom they paid tribute.

As they trudged off, I addressed Nial again, with the rifle still held gratefully in my grasp.

'Is it a gift?'

'No grey wolf, it is a bond. We are no longer that different, you and I. You are now bound to my lord MacGlannagh for the duration of your stay with us. He has also ordered you to teach his bodyguards marksmanship.'

'When?' I stuttered, hardly believing the chieftain's request.

'Tomorrow,' said the bondsman, 'so you had best get some practice. Lord MacGlannagh cannot believe what he witnessed today. He cannot wait to test your aim after you have had time to practice it.

XX

Rosclogher and surrounds in Dartry, County Leitrim

28 September – 2 October 1588

After the contests were ended, most of the tribesmen did not leave the greensward. They chose instead to take advantage of its cleared surface, as they engaged in a strange pastime which I had not previously witnessed. It was played with curved wooden sticks which were used to strike a ball of leather. The game was contested by two great gatherings of men, which consisted of the town dwellers and men of the visiting tuatha. Nial instantly left my side to take part in it, with the sport stirring my interest for at least an hour. It was a violent game, with the blows of the sticks striking other men as often as they hit the ball. Brawls often broke out between the players, with a band of blue jacketed kerns from the ring-fort having to also intervene to restore order.

By the time a third scuffle broke out, my interest in the contest had waned, with my mind turning to my latest exchange with the ollave Muireann and her rejection of my badgers. The princely gift of Manglana also occupied my thoughts and I yearned to fire it a few times more and further regain my old sharpness. Before doing so I called out to a few of the tribesmen and handed them the tanist's gift of badgers, leaving them cheering in delight and thanking me in their own tongue.

Having rid myself of these skinned creatures, I proceeded to the edge of the ring of bog. I tested my aim with the rifle on a stump along its border, on which I hewed a deep cross with the point of my sword. My aim was true more often than not, yet the roar of the rifle soon drew the unwanted attention of mad Orla, who had returned to picking rubbish in the middens but a stone's throw away from me.

My heart sank when I saw her wrinkled face appearing above the edge of a pit, with her reddened eyes bulging madly as she ran over and danced about me, all the while making the sign of the rifle and shouting at the top of her voice. Her crazed antics and flailing arms blocked my line of sight, but she skipped away frightfully when I lost my temper and attempted to seize her by the arm. Yet shortly after withdrawing she would return the moment I took aim again, so that I spent more time attempting to fend her off rather than shooting.

I was greatly relieved when one of her daughters appeared. The maiden was dressed in a tunic that was both worn and browned, and she flashed me a snaggle-toothed grin as she dragged her mother away. By the time dusk had set in and the cries from the green dwindled, the bole of the stump was riddled with three dozen shots. Over half of them had met their mark, which left me feeling half-satisfied with my efforts.

I rested the smoking rifle on my shoulder and trudged back towards the greensward. In the deepening dusk I found Nial, streaked with sweat and breathing heavily following his exertions during the game. Yet the players and their sticks had been swiftly replaced by large cooking fires and long rows of trestle tables, about which there bustled a literal army of knaves and servants. At the centre of the sward sat Manglana between his bard Fearghal and the new tanist Cathal, who were themselves surrounded by other highborn MacGlannaghs and O'Ronayne. This exalted group was in turn flanked by the herdsmen from the *tuatha*, who awaited a fine feast beneath a clear, starlit sky.

The bondsman and I sat upon benches placed between the MacGlannaghs and the visiting tribesmen, our nostrils full of the mouth-watering scent of braised cowflesh mingled with peat smoke. My horn was refilled with usquebaugh whenever my head was turned, for the churls who waited upon us were swift to ensure that we never went without food and drink. A loud chant rocked the tables as men banged upon them to great peals of laughter. Meanwhile the Dartrymen banished any fears of their bitter struggle with the Sassenachs through loud and defiant songs.

As the night progressed, I also came to realise that my exploits with the rifle had captured the popular imagination. Many of the tribesmen called out to me by the name *An Spáinn*, which I knew to be their word for Spain, while making gestures at the rifle which still hung from my shoulder. Each time I nodded back at them they would laugh out loudly and defiantly, to a great banging of tables while their long glibb fringes swung before their faces.

Their attentions strayed elsewhere when Cathal *Dubh* finally urged them to leave me be, for he could read the undisguised annoyance in my face after an hour spent being treated like some circus attraction. Yet as the feasting continued, it was clear that not all were pleased by my skills with the rifle. For I often caught the bard's dark stares in my direction, since he no doubt felt threatened anew by the popularity I had gained through my marksmanship at the tanist's contests.

His glances were not heeded for long as my thoughts were soon clouded by the many goblets of wine and usquebaugh. Eventually the only memory of the night was of my stumbling back to the hut, aided by the visiting herdsmen who still sang songs into the darkness with no regard for the slumbering townsfolk about them. Upon entering through the door of the outhouse, we fell into a heap by the small fire.

I was claimed by a dreamless sleep until late the following morning, when daylight cast a sheen against the wattle walls of my abode and my ears were filled with the sound of rumbling hooves. Although it had been many days since the Sassanas had captured me, the noise woke me with a start, until I remembered where I was. There was no sign of the visiting herdsmen, save for their abandoned blankets. Nial was squinting into a piece of mirror near the doorway, while shaving the sides of his beard with a blade. He turned towards me and smiled broadly when I bade him a good morning. I next gestured inquiringly at the blankets on the floor about us, as Nial nodded his understanding.

'The *tuatha* have returned to their grazing lands, for what remains of the pasturing season.'

My head was jerked at the doorway as we heard the din of the horsemen outside.

'I did not know that they also rode here'.

Nial smiled again.

'That is not them. It is the sound of Cathal *Dubh* and our cavalry, who are leaving Dartry to raid Breifne O'Reilly. Last night the bard stirred up many passions, long after you toppled off your stool, when he called on our *tánaiste* to prove his strength in battle. So Cathal has met the call, as was expected of him. I suspect that he will be gone a few days, so in the meantime we should try to keep out of trouble and steer clear of the *galloglaigh*.'

I tried to recall the bard's addresses at the dinner banquet, yet the attempt was swiftly abandoned, for my head still spun from too much drink.

'Are you not joining him?'

'Nay,' replied the bondsman, 'I am but my lord MacGlannagh's humble fencing master, tasked with increasing good swordsmanship across Dartry.'

He proceeded to shear one wayward hair upon the end of his chin, before addressing me again.

'How are you feeling today?'

'Better, much better.'

'That is heartening news, for the chieftain awaits your appearance at the tower house, to be instructed in the use of the rifle. It seems that your little display has been the only thing he has talked about since yesterday. You have made a good impression on him, grey wolf.'

I was not sure what to say. Upon noting my hesitation, the bondsman spoke again.

'Lord MacGlannagh has also provided you with the indefinite use of these quarters, and you are to receive a meal every evening. Your sword, gear and horse are also yours to keep, for they are his gifts to you. The rifle is also yours, for as long as you remain in Dartry, and a knave has brought you a bandolier, priming flask and other supplies which you need for the gun.'

Manglana's allowances were indeed generous, although I restrained the urge to argue that Gilson's horse was already my war spoil and not the chieftain's property to be given back to me. For a moment I also thought of telling Nial that I intended to eventually leave Ireland to return to the Continent. Yet I quickly surmised that sharing this goal too soon might compromise the hospitality extended to me in Dartry: a hospitality which was a far better fate than rotting upon a grappling hook in the dungeons of Sligo. So I instead chose to hold my tongue and ready my gear until the bondsman left the hut to relieve himself. While he was gone, I also chose to quietly remove the ring from my brogue and slip it into one of the bandolier's ampoules which hung around my chest.

No sooner was this accomplished, than I inspected my shot and priming flask until Nial reappeared to escort me towards the lakeside jetty. As we stepped outside I noticed that the skies were flecked by snatches of cloud which had been blown inland from the sea overnight, which resembled grey and white bales of hay in the heavens above. Yet there was still no rain and the sun cast a glow upon the crests of the surrounding mountains whose grassy sides appeared to shimmer in the light. It was a sight that left me rubbing my eyes upon the ferry, all the way to the crannog.

Upon reaching the islet, we found Manglana puffing up cold mist like a wary bullock, surrounded by his knaves and a dozen of his bodyguards. The chieftain wore long, flowing, saffron robes, as well as a solemn expression while he wordlessly awaited my arrival. His small band stood upon a small stretch of brown earth, which was the only surface of the island which was not bounded by the keep of Rosclogher. I stepped before them into the shadow of the fort's precincts, although the daylight had grown enough for us to see each other. After I had explained the range of the priceless wheellock and shown him how to load it, Manglana's face assumed a stare which bordered upon astonishment.

'tis swiftest loading that I have ever beheld,' he told me, releasing a waft of breath so rancid that it left me blinking in disbelief.

'Indeed it is my lord,' I replied tersely, 'for the absence of the cord wins precious time, yet this is a device that is not hardy like the musket. It must be constantly cleaned and inspected before being used in battle.'

I reloaded the weapon while we took it in turns to take aim at a boar's head mounted upon a stake on the westward side of the islet. My first shot bounced off our target's forehead as the chieftain stared on in wonderment, speaking to me in Latin while I squirmed before his dragon breath.

'If I had but a score of riflemen, I would drive Bingham and his devils back into the river Shannon.'

Manglana's next attempts also went wide and only served to disturb the swans on the lake. The chieftain withstood the recoil well enough, but years using a musket had done nothing to steady his aim. Across the water some tribesmen stood upon the lake's edge to study the cause of the din, with a number of freemen gathering in the tower house doorway behind us to watch the spectacle.

That morning Manglana proved himself a student who was keen to the point of impatience. Whenever he snatched the weapon back from me, he frowned with concentration as he tried to load it himself, grimacing irately when it took him thrice the time it took me to ready it for firing. Having assumed the role of his instructor, I could learn more about his nature from the way in which he responded to my teachings. Like many others I had encountered in positions of rank, I found him to be impulsive and ill-disposed to listening fully to my instructions. Eventually I held back from teaching him all that I knew, instead helping him to reload the gun whenever he looked at me askance.

I often squirmed at the sight of him wrestling with the sophisticated weapon, as with scarred hands he tried to bend its mechanism to his brutish will, ignorant and unwilling to comprehend its subtleties. After a time, he managed a steady loading, but when I armed the weapon within a minute, he beheld me almost resentfully as he leant over towards me.

'Where didst thou learn thy handling of it?'

It was the closest I had come to Manglana's person, and although I was well used to the gunsmoke's stink of rotten eggs, I almost gagged at his words for his breath smelt worse than horse manure, and I would have retched were it not for the seaward breeze. I regathered myself while trying not to breathe in too deeply, extending a reply to my host who observed me carefully.

'Ah, it takes time and practice, sire. A certain dexterity of the limbs is required, and thou must shoot until thy shoulders - indeed thy whole body - becomes hard yet soft, just like a spring.'

For over an hour Manglana resisted the harsh kick of the wheellock, since he had endured the same when firing matchlocks for years. Yet its blows eventually wearied him, and he could not help betraying a wince during his last two attempts. Besides displaying a steely-minded determination, he had also shown an open contempt for those of his subjects who slept late into the morning, with many more bleary-eyed freemen gathering outside the door of the keep, while feigning an interest in their lord's efforts.

Whenever their cheers became too loud, he cast them a dark look which silenced the lot of them. He next asked me how the ramrod could be used more effectively, and why the doghead had to be flicked forward after and not before the rifle was loaded. His mind was still keen to comprehend the extent of the wheellock's uses. At one point his eyes narrowed like the slit windows in his keep and he pointed to a passing duck flying over the lake.

'Shoot it.'

When I duly met his request, he smacked his fist in excitement when he saw the feathered form fluttering down towards the water, and he instantly beckoned to his knaves to head out in a small skiff and retrieve it. When he asked me when I had first used a wheellock. I recalled how the Duke of Alba had entrusted me and a party of marksmen with a highly perilous task during the great struggle against the heretics in the Low Countries.

'I was picked to form part of an elite squadron charged with guarding munitions which were transported along the Spanish Road. We were the first Spanish troops to be given a self-igniting rifle, for they were safer to use around gunpowder provisions than the musket with its flaming match cord.'

Manglana nodded at my explanation and remained silent, perhaps because he was impressed by my mentioning the Iron Duke. With a swirl of his beard, he beckoned to his blue jackets as he took his leave of me.

'My thanks grey wolf, for teaching me the use of this unholy device. I shall summon thee again in coming days, but now I must attend to other matters.'

Nial and I stared after him as he walked back towards his keep, and in the doorway I could make out the striking features of his wife Lady Dervila, as well as the beautiful ollave Muireann. Yet I did not observe them for long, since the moment the chieftain vanished into his towerhouse, all of his relatives and retainers disappeared after him.

Two days later, the tanist had still not returned from his cattle raiding. All kinds of rumours spread among the tribe, which told of Cathal having landed himself in great peril. Other more malicious tongues whispered that his good fortune had finally run out, since this was the fate of all scarred liars. After Nial bore me these snatches of gossip, he remained unfazed when I expressed some concern.

'It is but the usual gossip and idle chatter of old crones and cowards. Cathal is our champion cattle raider and he will return. The land of the O'Reillys is a fair few miles from here, and their *túatha* will be more watchful before winter sets in.'

Apart from my morning instruction of Manglana in fire-arms, my time in the town was otherwise uneventful, so that I often found myself resting in the outhouse outside the abbey. Throughout this time the bondsman was excellent company, when he was not training the bluejackets who were stationed in the ringfort. I was enthralled by the technique of Nial's swordsmanship, and readily accepted his invitation to a sparring session on the greensward before dusk set in.

Although my ability with the blade had not entirely abandoned me, the bondsman's skill and speed were uncanny. Each time we crossed steels, he was at least always two steps ahead of me, leaving me on the back foot. So it came as little surprise when my blade flew out of my hand in our last bout of fencing. I had been bested throughout by a seasoned duelling master, and I was thankful to count on him as an ally amongst the tribesmen.

As for my relations with the suspicious Jesuit, it seemed that my early misgivings about being hosted by him had proved unfounded. O'Ronayne was a man of such industry that I never ran into him, for his many roles included those of physician, apothecary, priest and teacher of Latin. The means at his disposal were also significant, rendering him a figure of great import among the tribe. His infirmary was supported by Lady Dervila, with Manglana also fully backing his initiatives. Which meant that the abbey and its chapel were well maintained, with the Jesuit also afforded the command a whole bevy of attendants and servants who supported him with his various responsibilities, which included novices and barber surgeons.

Upon realising that O'Ronayne was unlikely to be encountered again, I even dared to venture into the church of Saint Mel, falling to my knees in prayer of thanks at my unlikely delivery from both the sea and the Sassanas. In truth I was not a man of great faith, yet my unlikely escape from the storms and from Sligo – not to mention my acquisition of the priceless ring - had filled me with the perhaps illusory belief that there might be some justice in the world. My sense of gratitude was at times also overwhelmed by a great anger which flared up in me whenever I thought of Elsien's passing.

In the meantime, other concerns reinforced my desire to flee Dartry at the earliest opportunity. It was not the first time that the stories of other Spaniards roaming in the wild had reached my ears. Some spoke of shadows seen crawling along Dartry's borders, while other tribesmen said that men were seen wandering beneath the waxing moon, who fled into the forest when one called out to them.

The leaves of the great sycamores outside *Doire Mel* were browning when yet another Armada survivor also found his way to Rosclogher, more dead than alive. His ribs were visible beneath his chest, and his legs were so thin that they could hardly bear him. One of Cathal's kerns had been despatched by his master to escort the wretch to Manglana's town, where he was hastened away to the infirmary. He was placed under the watchful care of O'Ronayne, and in the days that followed I heard that four more of the wretches were taken in. Manglana's powerful overlord O'Rourke also sent another five castaways to Dartry to be hosted by his neighbouring sub-lord.

Thereafter fresh gossip reached all four corners of Dartry, which told of a great Spanish force gathered in a fort north of the coast, in a place that the natives called *Na Cealla Beaga*. Some spoke of a host of hundreds of Spaniards, a force so great that even the Sassanas were afraid to approach them. It was also claimed that their leader was none other than Don Alonso de Leiva, who had served as second admiral during the doomed expedition of the Armada. The presence of this force had stirred the passions of his host the MacSweeney, and those other rebel tribes which surrounded his camp.

Each of them hoped to strike an alliance with these castaways, for it was common knowledge that there were only two thousand troopers in the English Viceroy's garrison in Dublin, half of whom were Irish. It was not lost on the northern rebel chieftains that an alliance with the Spaniards – renowned for being the best soldiers in the world – would stem the incursions of the Sassanas, if not liberate the whole of Ireland. Nial also told me that Dartry's overlord, the mighty O'Rourke of Breifne, was readying to send five hundred cows to de Leiva's men on the western coast.

On the fourth day of my instruction, Manglana received me with the closest thing resembling a smile which I had seen on his long face. He was bursting with satisfaction, for his overlord O'Rourke had requested that the great drove of cattle be allowed to traverse the safe passages which Manglana held in Dartry. O'Rourke had also asked that the Spaniards in Manglana's territory sign a letter which he had addressed to de Leiva, asking the Armada's second admiral to ally himself with the northern rebels.

After the chieftain's rifle shots of the day were fired, we were beset by a light rainfall from the grey heavens. Manglana was undeterred by the weather, as he immediately entrusted the

errand to me and the bondsman. He requested us to bear the
O'Rourke's letter to the recovering Spaniards. Although I was
reluctant to acquiesce to this demand, it was not in my interest to decline it either, leaving me with little choice but to
bow deeply to my protector and gracefully accept his request.

When the lake was crossed and the jetty on the lake's edge
reached, Nial and I were met by some of the townsfolk who
grinned at us and pretended to fire an invisible weapon. With
the slightest of nods in their direction, we made towards
the guards at the infirmary's entrance where the bondsman
stopped by the doorway.

'I shall wait for you here.'

My brows were knotted in puzzlement when I turned towards him.

'Will you not join me?'

Nial shook his head.

'They are only recently arrived in Dartry and have already
experienced too much that is different. Perhaps it would be
best for them to be addressed by one of their own.'

With a shrug of the shoulders, I feigned indifference as
I left Nial outside in the rain and entered the cabin. Upon
passing through the guards and the rude boardings, I was met
by the familiar smell of moss and sods. The Spaniards within
were haggard men in piteous condition, and days of hunger
and toil had rendered them literal bags of skin and bone.

To a man they were black around the eyes from days without
sleep, and their sallow expressions were more akin to those of
abandoned dogs than of people. Two of them even bore the
scars of a wolf attack, and only three of them sat upright in
their litters. Despite their poor condition I regarded the men

warily, for I was already dreading the haughty arrogance of lowborn Spaniards. Men who thought that the indomitable strength of their Empire made them superior to men of other nations, whom they could treat with either contempt or cruelty.

Indeed, the sight of them filled me with a deep unease, for I could already foretell the shock that would seize the tribe once the men they had rescued made their recovery. I dreaded the thought, while also recalling the enthusiasm with which I had flung myself into the Spanish army in my youth, when I still believed it to be a force bursting with honourable and valorous men. Only to find that it was in truth a force abounding with scores of ragged ruffians, who would join a mutiny at the drop of a hat and were capable of the most despicable of crimes. Crimes that all too often went unpunished by incompetent officers of Ramos's ilk.

As my eyes became accustomed to the poor light, I could better make out the men's faces. The sight of them left no doubt in my mind that once the Spaniards were recovered enough to leave the infirmary, that there would be many an Irish tribesman cuckolded and swindled at dice or cards. They were also men in whose company I had been forced to sharpen my wits and often relinquish my humanity just to stay alive. I could already envisage the duels that would break out in the passageways between the huts in the town, whenever a native refused to make way for an armed Spaniard.

Yet upon recalling my protector's errand, I dispelled these thoughts, as I did my best to engage in a cordial address. For despite my general low opinion of Spanish soldiers, I thought I should at least give the castaways the benefit of the doubt, while praying that their recent sufferings might had tempered their hubris. I felt somewhat relieved when a pair of the younger ones nodded to me in greeting. I later discovered that they were unfortunate peasant boys from the Canary Islands, who had been press-ganged into joining the Grand Armada against their will.

The two boys were so shaken from their recent ordeals that not a peep was heard out of them, not even to sound a line of *silbo gomero*: that famous whistling tongue for which the shepherds of their country were famous. As I studied the other stowaways to ensure that I knew none of them, one of the rescued men rose to his feet. He was a stocky specimen and possessed the ugliest sneer of the lot.

'Who are you?'

His overbearing tone was a timely reminder of a Spanish soldier's arrogance. I cleared my throat awkwardly at his abrupt question, while resting my hand upon my sword pommel to assume some air of authority. Given my Irish clothing it was a gesture both futile and piteous, although I did my best to match the man's haughty voice.

'My name is Juan de los Hospitalarios. I am a survivor of the Santa Maria de Visión.'

The man eyed my blade without betraying any fear, then spoke again in a thick Basque accent.

'You look none the worse for wear, Juan de los Hospitalarios.'

He uttered my name slowly and contemptuously. I also caught a proud glint in his eye as he stepped before the hut's entrance and rested his hands upon his hips, with his legs spread wide apart as if to bar my way. I ignored his words and grimaced as I tried in vain to sidestep any unnecessary confrontation.

'I was the first to reach Dartry.'

A lanky castaway squinted at me from his bed of rushes, with his Milanese accent betraying his Lombard origins.

'Tell us, Juan. What do these savages have in mind for us?'

His crude reference to the natives left me feeling taken aback, so that it took a few moments for me to regain my composure.

'They want nothing more than to be our allies.'

'Ally themselves with Spaniards?' exclaimed another, before feigning to choke with shock, 'does not everyone hate us?'

His jest drew some nervous chuckling from his fellows while another squinted at me suspiciously.

'How did you reach these people so quickly?'

I sighed aloud. For although I hoped that the truth might placate them, I could already predict the direction in which our conversation would flow.

'I was escorted here by the natives. After I rescued Manglana's daughter.'

Two of the men instantly whistled to each other before one of them called out to me with a wink and a broad grin.

'Helped yourself to their women already? You are quick off the mark Juanito!'

Before I could object, another held his crotch with both hands and pulled a face.

'Better find me a hussy before they burst!'

Raucous laughter erupted as men slapped their hands against their thighs and the crude boardings, wrapt in their mirth and vulgarity. When the loudest hoots subsided, a few of the fools could still be heard tittering from their beds. Without waiting for their chortling to subside, my arm shot out towards them as I held O'Rourke's letter aloft.

'Never mind that', I snapped, 'for we have another, more pressing priority. Our protector has asked that we sign this billet.'

As the chieftain's parchment was waved before them, the Basque raised his pudgy nose towards it, almost as if I had just presented him with a turd. He then sneered wickedly, hissing a riposte from the corner of his mouth.

'How do we know that this message is what you claim it to be? And besides, I never sign anything on anyone's behalf.'

I rolled my eyes as I often did when confronted by mulish, Spanish stubbornness, knowing full well that my attempts at reason would be of no use. For the haughtiness of the men was such that they were known to fight twice their number in battle, without even batting an eyelid. They would also approach the gallows with a spring in their step, if it meant preserving the slightest bit of their misplaced pride.

'I swear to you that I do not speak false. I have signed it myself.'

The Basque chuckled.

'And is that meant to provide us with comfort? In any event I do not know my letters.'

'It matters not,' I growled, 'for I expected as much. Yet if you but scrawl a little cross on this note, I will write your name alongside it.'

The men cast me dark glances as they drew closely together and mulled over my offer in muffled whispers. Meanwhile the fattest one among them could be heard asking if I had just mocked the Basque.

'What does the letter say?!' they shouted at last, 'read it to us word for word! And the devil take you if you speak false or omit anything!'

At their request, I read them the contents of the message. In it the O'Rourke sought to reassure Don Alonso de Leiva that he was a faithful subject of the king of Spain and was sheltering Spanish soldiers at great personal risk. The overlord also informed the Armada's second admiral that the troops of the English crown in Dublin numbered only two thousand men, of whom half were Irish. He also strongly encouraged de Leiva to join the northern rebels in their struggle, to form a force that could drive the heretics out of Ireland and into the sea. Silence reigned when my reading ended, and after a few moments I noticed one of my listeners peering at me in suspicion.

'How do we know you haven't recited all this from your head?'

I exhaled loudly, since my patience had reached its lowest ebb.

'Are there truly none among you who can read?'

The Basque strode up to me, his chest puffed out in defiance.

'Yet even if you speak the truth, why the hell should we fight with these barefoot yokels?! Let us instead ready ourselves to flee this hellish backwater!'

His last word was barely uttered when I grabbed him by the throat and flung him onto the ground like a straw doll. He glared back at me with bared teeth, desperately trying to remove my tightening fingers from around his throat. I snarled back at the miscreant, my face only inches away from his.

'Have some respect for our host, tosspot...do not slap the hand of friendship in hell...'

A great rage had seized me at the thought that my stay among the Dartrymen was to be threatened by the tosspots gathered about me. For in recent days I had earned a grudging, growing respect from the natives. Manglana himself had seemed impressed during our long discourses, often questioning me about strategy and battle tactics. I resented how the eventual behaviour of these Spaniards was set to embarrass me with the highborn tribesmen. For although I was world-weary and tired of life, it would take a lot more setback for me to forget my manners. In my anger I had all but throttled the Basque I had assaulted, when an elderly specimen piped up as he stepped behind me, resting his palm upon my tensed shoulder.

'Peace, friend Juan', he said, 'remember that we are all in the same boat.'

I released the man's throat from my grip, leaving him to cough and splutter upon the ground. When his breath was regained, he issued blasphemy of the blackest pitch, since men could swear better in Spanish than in any other tongue, save for the one used by Maltese dockers. I ignored his words while shoving the piece of paper at the man behind me, whose accent sounded distinctly Catalan.

'What is your name?'

The short man squinted at me suspiciously while he studied my expression. He looked away and replied to me beneath his breath.

'Men call me Valdo.'

Without relinquishing my hard stare, I tightened my grip about the sword given to me by the natives and held up the billet before him again. At my feet the Basque still wheezed hoarsely as he sought to regain his breath.

'Then all of you sign the letter, good Valdo, and I shall be gone before you know it.'

The Catalan's eyes fell to the hand on my sword pommel before they met my stare, which was still fixed on his sallow face. With a slight nod of agreement, he took the document and asked one of the Jesuit's attendants for quill and ink.

When I finally emerged from the cabin, the rain had subsided, although the skies seemed to have darkened from light blue to dark grey. In the gathering gloom I made out the approaching figure of the bondsman, who led two horses by the bridle. When he drew closer Nial regarded me with a look of concern, for I was still flustered after my encounter with the hard-headed Iberians.

'Do you feel well, friend Juan? You are red in the face.'

'I am worried about the quality of these Spaniards.'

'Why am I not surprised. Did they sign the letter?'

I held the billet out to him, its smudged, yellowed surface filled with inky scrawls. The bondsman nodded at the signatures on the document.

'Did you also sign the letter and write your name down on it, as I instructed? Together with those of the illiterate Spaniards?'

'Yes.'

'Excellent. I shall have it delivered to Banagh in all haste.'

'Should I take it there?' I asked, half hoping that I might join de Leiva's force and somehow return to Spain with them.

The bondsman frowned at me.

'You? Why would you need to take it? Are you not Lord MacGlannagh's guest? No, grey wolf, you will remain with us. I shall have a runner deliver it.'

He took the document from my hand and passed me the reins of one of the horses behind him, which was the black destrier I had stolen from Lieutenant Gilson.

'Are we to ride?' I asked him, as I looked at the greyness which had gathered in the sky above.

'That we are,' replied the bondsman, 'and you should bring your rifle, although it seems to not even leave your side at night. My lord MacGlannagh has asked us to join his company, who are readying to collect some outstanding *duabarach*.'

I frowned at this latest Irish word which was unknown to me.

'Collecting what?'

He chuckled at my question before grabbing his mount by its left ear and effortlessly heaving himself onto its back.

'The black rent!' he declared loudly, 'surely a veteran of Flanders knows the meaning of that?'

The moment he said this I was instantly reminded of Elsien's burned out house and her corpse. It was a memory which left me staring aghast into space.

'Grey wolf!' said Nial in a concerned tone, so that I instantly regained my focus.

'From whom?' I asked, as I regained my composure, 'have the tuatha not paid tribute to our lord already?'

'I said it was *black*,' said the bondsman, 'for there is a tuath that has been sighted travelling through our lands, whose leader was not at the election ceremony. He has yet to render any tribute to my Lord MacGlannagh. His folk are said to have found new pastures in the very shadow of *Sliabh Aradh* itself, with their livestock last seen grazing upon the edge of moorland at its back. Our lord therefore intends to pay them a visit, to ensure that his protection - which they presently enjoy - does not go unpaid.'

'And what part am I to play in all of this?'

Nial flashed me a wink and a grin.

'Your reputation precedes you, friend Juan. Rumour of your skill with the firearm has spread to all corners of Dartry. Many tribesmen have heard tell of your magic spear, which can even strike clouds and far off mountaintops amid a thunderous flash and a great puff of smoke.'

I groaned at this exaggeration while I wordlessly hauled myself upon my English mount, which did not take kindly to me using its ear as a handgrip. I next clutched at its mane, clinging to the beast's back in a manner which lacked both dignity and grace. I secretly cursed the ollave Muireann for having rid it of its saddle and stirrups, then thumped my ankles into its flanks. My mount trotted after the bondsman's steed, which had already reached the western side of the town. I had to jerk the reins a few times to finally get the cursed horse to break into a canter, which drew chuckles and mocking laughter from a few onlooking tribesmen.

Together we passed the last hut upon the edge of the town, which belonged to mad Orla and her daughters who were notable by their absence. The bondsman next veered towards the ringfort which rose to our right, then reined in his mount and issued a shrill whistle. In instants a dozen guards emerged from inside it, along with a youth.

Beneath the rim of the youth's tunic, his knees and thighs were spattered with mud, with his grass-stained feet also marking him out as a message-bearer. Nial leant over his steed to issue stern commands to the runner in the Irish tongue, before passing him the letter which had been signed by the Spaniards in Dartry. The whiskerless stripling snatched it and darted off towards the ring of bog, with his hair fluttering about his fast-shrinking head.

I was stunned by the fleetness of the barefooted messenger, while staring on at the rustling grass ahead of us and wondering if I had seen him at all. Meanwhile the dozen kerns gathered about us and shadowed our progress when we set off again for the marsh. Once past the ring of bog, we kept to a beaten path scarcely visible beneath the cover of trees. I silently remembered that we had previously struck it when climbing the peak of *Sliabh Arad* to attend Cathal *Dubh's* inauguration.

When the cover of thick foliage thinned out, two of our guards ran ahead to scout the terrain which lay between us and the mountains ahead. The land in between was covered with stunted trees that were as crooked as old widows, along with rushes which were bunched together in scattered clumps across the uneven grassland. For less than half an hour we crossed this terrain and drew nearer to the growing grey-green mound ahead of us, which was possessed of an eerie cast. We next took up the path through the rising upland, which led to the great mound of rocks where Cathal had claimed his recent lordship. After wending our way through a cluster of peat hags, our party climbed along the edge of a deep, clefted gully.

The town and lake behind us grew ever more distant as the breathing of our mounts and guards became louder. I could not but marvel at the imposing height of Truskmore to our right, its head crowned by an immense wreath of grey cloud. The mountain towered imperiously over the great heights about it, rendering them little hillocks which were gathered about the mighty feet of a lord among mountains. From time to time the bondsman gestured to the land behind us, as he described it to me.

'There, beyond *Cionn Locha*, is the border between our lands and *Tír Chonaill*. It is territory of the *Ó Gallchobhair*.'

He also picked out the distant ridge of mountains to the north of the lake in which the keep was located, and the glint of a river could be seen shimmering between them.

'They are a powerful tribe and hold two keeps along the fords of the *Éirne* called *Béal Leice* and *Béal Átha Seanaidh*. To the northeast lie the lands of *Machaire Buí*, which are claimed by *Mac Uidhir,* the lord of *Fir Manach*'.

'Are they our friends or our foes?'

My guide frowned as his lip was curled in contempt.

'As with most of our neighbours, their allegiance shifts like the wind.'

'And which way does the wind presently blow?'

He frowned at me, then returned his attentions to our path. When the first drops of rain were felt upon our heads, we pulled up the hoods of our capes and rode on in silence, while I picked out deer that grazed on the distant heights.

- XX -

We climbed another knoll which was covered by small bushes and the odd rowan tree. My attention turned to the narrow ridge which we had previously scaled and to the sheer cliffs on the north side of *Sliabh Aradh*. When the pace of Nial's mount slowed, I pulled the reins of my steed and readied to dismount, having assumed that we were to proceed to its peak on foot.

Yet the bondsman had no intention of dismounting, only slowing his progress long enough to direct his mount down a gentle descent. In so doing, he led us towards a brownish rise along a grassy land which was firm underfoot, but which soon became more arid and marshier as we reached the stretch between the two heights.

Below us the land was covered with short, sharp peaks, and following our descent past these small hillocks we kept to a short stony track. It climbed northwards in the direction of the jagged green teeth that crested another, lesser height. The rocks on the path made for a jolty ride on the last descent towards a steep, grassy gully which cut through the cliff face and ran south. Its firmness afforded us an easier progress, although we kept away from the low stretch of muddied ground.

There followed a large tract of undulating moorland over an uneven upland. After the marshy earth was crossed, the bondsman made for the edge of the rise, bringing us at last to a stone corbelled structure around seven feet wide and about as high as the bondsman. Its low lintelled doorway was closed with sods, and no steam rose from its chimney flue. The bondsman referred to it as a sweat-house, with scores of Manglana's bodyguards sitting cross-legged about it or standing guard. They were jacketed in blue and seemingly waiting on some idle errand. I stared at them in confusion, attempting to understand why they were gathered there.

Our appearance did not cause any of them to raise an eyebrow towards us. The bondsman also appeared ignorant to their presence, pausing only to greet two of the gathering who I recognised as Manglana's steward Malachy and Echna the old Brehon Judge. As I rode alongside him, Nial pointed at the other heights which met the heavens to the east.

'The land of *Bréifne* lies yonder, a territory that is divided in two. Men call the western side *Bréifne O'Ruairc*, and it is the domain of our overlord. The other half is *Bréifne Ó Raghallaigh*.'

'Is that not the name of the O'Reilly tribe that the tanist intends to raid?'

Nial nodded his head with a rueful smile.

'Aye, it is. They are traitors and Royalists who often support the crown. Further south is Carbury, held by the O'Harts. To the north lie the lands of the O'Donnell, and west of them is the lordship of Banagh, ruled by the O'Donnell's sub-lord, the worthy MacSweeny. It is a rugged land which hosts the army of de Leiva, and it is also the birthplace of our *ollamh* Muireann Mac an Bhaird.'

I noted the mention of her full name with a confused frown.

'Is she not MacGlannagh?'

The bondsman grimaced before addressing my error.

'No, grey wolf. Did the chieftain not tell you that he fostered her? Do not forget it when you address her. Our women do not lose their name upon marriage, and in this land the pride of one's clan is not to be slighted.'

I nodded slowly, suddenly remembering how the Jesuit had explained to me that Irish women always retained the name of their sept, even after marriage. I next wondered why we had not yet dismounted and was about to ask what we were waiting for, when a high-pitched squeal was heard behind us. As we turned towards the stone sweathouse at our backs, I gasped when its wooden door was kicked open, releasing a cloud of steam and a scent of burned bracken. Two young maidens ran through it, as naked as Eve in the garden of Eden, shielding both their breasts and crotches as best they could.

Their moist hair was stuck to their faces and necks, while they bore hesitant grins and had the narrowed eyes of newly corrupted women. At the steward Malachy's order a tribesman approached them with fresh linen tunics, which the two damsels snatched from him and swirled about their bare forms. Although I strained my neck to catch a glimpse of these women, none of the bluejackets stirred or turned their head towards the damsels.

One of these beauties burst into a nervous giggle when the armed escort who had accompanied Nial and me formed a defensive ring about the women. These armed men escorted the cackling girls away from us, back towards the height of *Sliabh Aradh*. The bondsman seemed not to notice their disappearance, yet we could not ignore the other naked person who emerged from the sweathouse, as calmly as if he were on a morning walk along the banks of Lough Melvin.

In an instant our backs turned bolt upright, with everyone holding their breath as the chieftain himself, Tadhg *Óg* Mac-Glannagh, stepped out onto the heather. His form was a sight to behold, for his muscles were as taut as bowstrings and the two sides of his breast looked like square shields. His biceps glistened and throbbed in the early morning sunlight, with his green eyes gleaming in a stern-looking face. Steam wafted off him as if he were some deity who had forayed into the hellish depths of Hades, only to emerge unscathed.

He projected a defiant air when he walked towards us, as we all beheld his appearance with an awed reverence. His legs, too, were muscular, with the only blemish on his body being the red rawness along his groin which spread like a spider's web almost to his knees and navel. The French pox had left its indelible mark on his formidable body, so that it was widely known that O'Ronayne often administered servings of quicksilver to Manglana. These ministrations were the cause of the chieftain's infamous 'dragon breath' and why some of his teeth wiggled loosely on the rare occasions when he smiled.

Following his steamy dalliance with the two maidens, Manglana raised his face towards the gentle drops of rain which still doused his company. I beheld Dartry's king in awe, as he breathed out big puffs of mist, with thick tendrils of steam rising off his body. Manglana never once betrayed the pain that these sores caused him, as he next scratched at his long beard and turned his head towards us. He broke into a grin when he caught me gaping at the sores around his groin, and I was not sure what to say when I met his stare.

'No pleasure without pain, grey wolf,' he croaked softly, 'although of late the pain has by far exceeded the pleasure.'

He raised his right arm, extending the palm of his hand as a bodyguard ran towards him holding a saffron tunic made up of many ells of linen, as well as a fur mantle. When I turned to face Nial, the bondsman served me with a long stare of foreboding which I well understood, since I had spent many years amongst soldiers. It was obvious from his expression that I was not to breathe a word of what I had just witnessed.

When his horse was brought to him, Manglana climbed atop it and set off at a gentle canter, flanked by his steward and the mounted Judge. The size of Manglana's company indicated that the chieftain intended to make a full account of the tribute that was owed to him at law. A tribute which was to also be enforced by the many blades he had at hand, as well as a smoke-belching rifle if necessary. We descended a tamped down track, and it was less than an hour before we were at the bottom of the southward descent, having reached the river at the feet of the great mountain, which ran both west and east for as far as the eye could see.

We made our way along it in silence, with the bluejackets running alongside us until we came upon a cluster of makeshift huts. They were but a dozen small structures built out of sods and wattle, with a score of herdsmen gathered about them. These men were possessed of a wild caste, who silently watched their grazing black sheep and scrawny cows which speckled the brown bank of the watercourse which ran past us.

Our company rode through the settlement as furious glares were directed at us. I reached for the rifle on my back, yet none of the hostile herders dared to raise their arms against Manglana's bodyguards who carefully watched them with raised spears. The chieftain appeared ignorant to these happenings, with his brisk canter never faltering until he reined his steed in near a low peat fire in the middle of the huts.

We dismounted after him beside the flames, where there were gathered six hooded figures. I was alerted to their high rank by their flowing tunics of many folds and the tips of their lengthy beards which rested over their chests. I had not seen any of them at the tanist's inauguration. Their faces were the picture of disquiet when Manglana approached them. Half of them quickly shot to their feet as he walked towards them, with their hands falling upon their sword hilts.

As I looked about us, I caught sight of the muddied faces of women and children, who fearfully stared at us from within their small homes. I was overcome by pity at the sight of the frightened little faces but instantly cast the feeling aside. For years I had myself ransacked the homes of innocents to find food, since the king of Spain's soldiers were always paid months if not years late. My face mirrored Nial's grim expression as I brandished my rifle and made after the chieftain. Without so much as a nod at the tuath's elders, Manglana seated himself on a log which lay across them, then raised his hands to their burning peat fire. The chieftain next gestured to his steward Malachy and his Judge Echna to sit astride him, just as they had done on horseback.

As the bondsman and I stepped behind the eminent three-some, Manglana cleared his throat and spoke. At his words the elders in front of him looked a man among their number whose beard was plain white and whose tunic was possessed of numerous ells of linen. After a moment of hesitation, this elder called out across the huts to a herdsman who minded the cows upon the edge of the settlement. The herdsman silently drew his long *skene* dagger from his belt upon receiving this command, then walked up to one of the scrawnier cows.

With a deft movement he severed the animal's windpipe, so that it did not produce a sound when it collapsed to the ground.

Blood spurted from the beast's neck when other herders fell to their knees and repeatedly shoved the dying beast's forelegs forwards, as if they were manning a pump. This hastened the bleeding from its throat, while its hind legs lashed out wildly in its final death throes. Meanwhile, my attentions were torn between these efforts and the first tense words of the men who sat before me. They cast dark stares at the surrounding bluejackets as they paused to listen to Manglana's address. After the chieftain spoke, his steward next took up the exchange with the elderly herders, often pausing from his discourse to purse his lips in thought.

The sense of loathing and hostility from the *tuath*'s elders was evident in their tone. I gently primed the doghead on my rifle, with my eyes shifting from left to right as I tried to pick out any threats to the chieftain's person. To add to my unease, the words between the steward Malachy and the eldest herdsman suddenly turned heated. Finally Manglana himself piped up, gesturing to Echna who drew an old book from her satchel, then shuffled through its pages before reading one of them in a solemn voice.

At her words one of the tuath's elders rose to his feet, shaking his fists in fury and yelling in her direction. My ears were filled with a sharp ring when Nial's blades left their scabbards, and my rifle was instantly raised, with its sights set upon the ranting man. As our weapons were readied, most of Manglana's bodyguards outside the settlement came crashing into the camp to join their fellows, so that the elders before us were soon surrounded by a veritable hedgerow of spearpoints held by the snarling bluejackets.

This instantly stemmed the dissenter's protests, as he fell back among his seated fellows who were suddenly overwhelmed by fear. A great silence fell over the camp anew, until the chieftain raised his hand and commanded his bodyguards to lower their spears. Then the aged jurist on his left resumed her explanation, while the elders beheld her hatefully while never daring to raise their voices again.

I sighed with relief as my attention returned to the herders who were dragging the slain cow's carcass by its hindquarters towards us, after removing its head, front legs and offal. I watched on curiously as they proceeded to rip the hide off the dead creature with their blades, then hacked off its back legs and chopped it up on the grass. The hide was then stretched above a peat fire, with three of its sides secured by stout chord to stakes around the flames. More fuel was thrown onto the growing fire and the raw beef on the grass was hurled into the hide which served as a sort of cauldron, with the braised cowflesh within it soon seething and spitting.

Meanwhile Echna had finished speaking, with Manglana's steward Malachy resuming his discussion with the elderly herders. Another hour of conversation followed, which only ended when wooden plates filled with choice cuttings of the braised meat were laid out before the chieftain and the exalted members of his retinue,. Cups of milk were also handed to Manglana and his guests as the last talks with the tuath's leaders were concluded.

At the end of this discussion one of their number rose to his feet, to engage in what sounded like a rhyme. At his last words

Manglana rose to his feet and walked back to his mount, with his face still betraying no emotion as his steward and jurist closely trailed his footsteps. Nial and I hurried after them, surrounded by a ring of bluejackets as we returned to our horses. As we readied to ride off, I could make out a party of Manglana's bodyguards leading away over half of the tuath's livestock.

Having collected the chieftain's lawful dues, our party made back upland. A great westward wind had picked up, while I looked over my shoulder at the tuath which had reluctantly hosted us. Their faces were the picture of dismay and hatred, which was understandable, given that winter was so close. The sudden loss of their livestock meant that many of them would go hungry for days in the months ahead. I cleared my throat awkwardly as I glimpsed two scrawny children, a boy and a girl, who stared at us forlornly through a hut's doorway.

This land, I thought to myself, so *different in so many ways, yet I suppose that some things are the same the world over.*

'We brought a large force to a very small camp,' I remarked to Nial.

'Hardly, friend Juan. Connacht has become a lawless land, so one can never have a large enough escort. You never know when you might run into an enemy troop.'

It was obvious from his dark stare that something rankled him, so I kept my silence for the rest of our climb. Our party returned to the path we had struck to reach the river, yet our progress was slower because of the cattle which had to be escorted to new pastures. Every so often, a kern would break away from the main body to retrieve a wayward sheep, or prod a cow with a spear butt to return it to our path.

For the rest, it was the chieftain's great wolfhounds which kept the main body of livestock in step with Manglana's band. The odd bark was issued from their froth-lined lips, as our party silently crossed the upland and tackled the descent of *Sliabh Aradh*. Upon reaching its foot and the windswept foliage about it, Nial veered towards the direction of Lough Melvin as Manglana's party rumbled on away from us.

'Are we not to journey on with the chieftain?' I called out in bafflement, as Manglana's men proceeded in the direction of Truskmore.

'No!' yelled the bondsman, barely audible in the wind, 'he is guiding his new heads towards his chief seat in Dartry, along the coast at Tullaghan! We have played the part that was requested of us and must now hasten back to Rosclogher. For the watchers in the mountains keep a constant vigil on the passes into this land, yet nightfall oft cloaks the trespass of our enemies.'

I kicked my horse after him, just as the last kerns of the chieftain's armed band disappeared over a distant slope. The sky was darker and the light cover of trees barely shielded us from the new onset of rain, so that we pulled our hoods on once more. Ahead of us, the sun's glow was reduced to a shimmer upon the lake. As we rode down towards the distant body of water, I asked Nial about Manglana's other seat of power.

'It is located in Carbury,' he replied, 'and commands the roads from Ballyshannon to Sligo. Donal MacCabe is often stationed there, along with his force of *galloglaigh*. We call it a *dun*, for it is the chief seat of the MacGlannagh's power, and for this reason its name is Duncarbery. The large fortress there exceeds the tower house in Rosclogher for strength and size; it has always been the chief seat of the MacGlannaghs' power.'

Nial and I covered the stretch of uneven lowland at a swift canter, next making for the great cover of trees which bordered the marsh. Our great haste disturbed me, yet I still called out to my companion. I was eager to learn more about Dartry, in the hope that this knowledge might help facilitate my eventual departure.

'That old man seemed upset by the judge Echna's words...'

Nial snorted in frustration.

'Aye. There are those who think that our lord rules by title alone, that the vigilance of these lands is achieved solely through favour and duty. That they would slip past one border and then the next, claiming to swear fealty to the chieftain whose land they trespass, without honouring any oaths to any lord.'

The sight of Lough Melvin ahead of us vanished when we descended a tamped down track, veering sideways towards the thicker foliage about it. A steely edge overcame the bondsman's voice as the path narrowed before us, drawing our mounts closer together.

'I knew those men back there, they are McGowans. They believe that our law should not bind them, since they have pledged fealty to the O'Rourke, and claim to have found themselves within our confines because they were waylaid by a Sassenach incursion. Yet they are more treacherous than a sack of snakes, for we have watched them for weeks. They do not report enemy sightings to us and do not join our musterings, nor those of our overlord. Today they learned that deceiving chieftains does not profit them. They have paid for their trespassing with many heads from their herd. For even the ones that they tried to hide from us were accounted for.'

'They shall have a hard time getting through the winter.'

The bondsman snorted, then resumed his lament.

'We should have slit their throats and taken all of their cattle. Yet one must tread lightly in these treacherous times, when the betrayal of the slightest underling could spell the undoing of the greatest lords of fair *Éirinn*. For the name we give these roving *túatha* is creaghts. They are our lifeblood, since they are always on the move outside of winter when they repair to the byres. It is the creaghts that enable us to resist the Sassenachs in the mountains.'

Nial fell silent for a few moments before he resumed his explanation.

'The creaghts are not only our strength but also our eyes and ears. Many a chieftain has been deposed when one of these discontented, roving *túatha* turned a blind eye to a Sassenach incursion. They are sometimes even known to betray their lord's whereabouts to the enemy. Our lord Mac-Glannagh therefore seeks to refrain from unnecessary acts of cruelty against them, choosing instead to always observe our laws. For obeying our laws is one certainty that his reign has afforded all Dartrymen, which has secured their loyalty in these perilous days.'

'And the Scottish gallowglasses?' I asked, 'do they also bow to the law?'

A loud sigh was heard from my companion, as he stooped sideways to avoid a low-hanging branch.

'The Scots bow to no one,' he hissed, 'except for that witch of Lady Dervila Bourke. Yet little is done to rein them in, for their axes have rescued us many a time on the field of battle. And given the sheriff's recent raids in the south, my lord MacGlannagh will need to hire even more mercenaries.'

'But that will be an unbearable strain on the land!' I cried, horrified at the prospect of the constable MacCabe bolstering his numbers.

'Indeed,' sighed Nial, 'it will be difficult for the chieftain to secure the loyalty of both tribesman and mercenary. Yet he has no choice, since the alternative does not bear contemplating. For but three years ago, a great pact was sealed with the enemy. Yet the MacGlannaghs did not hold to their terms, and our lord has long strayed from that treacherous agreement, since it is not favoured by his people.'

My jaw hung open in disbelief.

'You signed a treaty with the Sassanas?'

'Yes,' said Nial with a rueful look, Lord MacGlannagh signed it at the bidding of his overlord the O'Rourke, together with the other tribes of Connacht. It was meant to secure peace, and for a time we feigned acceptance of the habits and manners of our foes. Yet when their sheriff and his lieutenants rode through our lands and dealt out punishment and death in the name of the crown, the boot soon began to pinch. For a time we withstood these trespasses. Then the enemy killed the travelling son of our overlord the O'Rourke, while he journeyed home from abroad where he had been studying for the priesthood. All hell broke loose and Dartry rose up in rebellion with the O'Rourke of Breifne. The previous sheriff of Sligo was hunted down by Lord MacGlannagh and slain by his own hand, so that bards across Connacht still call Tadhg *Óg* the sheriff-slayer, whenever they sing his praises. Yet these songs are fast growing old, for the new sheriff of Sligo George Bingham is unlike any enemy that we have faced before. It is now accepted by all that Sassenachs defile the order of things. Bingham himself defies all manners and customs, for it is not unknown for him to strike at us outside of the fighting season.'

A look of fear crossed the bondsman's face, until he calmed down enough to resume talking to me.

'To our fortune, the sheriff of Sligo has not the means to sustain a lengthy winter siege. For that would surely place our lives in jeopardy. The byres would have to be emptied and all fodder borne with us into the heights. A life in the mountains during winter would be a living torment filled with the bite of frost and wolves. We would be hard put to it to feed ourselves and our heads of cattle.'

'But surely the Sassanas' raids dwindle during the winter?' I asked, unnerved by his words of foreboding.

'Hardly so, grey wolf, which is why we must now also maintain a permanent troop of mercenaries outside of the fighting season. You speak as one who has not strayed long from the refuge of Rosclogher. Yet ever since you Spaniards appeared, almost a half dozen raids have been thwarted along our southern borders. We have never known anything like it. Only three days ago did word reach Duncarbery of a new incursion into *An Ghráinseach*, when a ruthless force of troopers raided the creaghts' settlements. The constable Mac-Cabe was dispatched hence in all haste. For although they are unpopular, the gallowglass are fearsome warriors when they are summoned, who do not know fear of death and who will stand and fight to the last man. They are a wall of steel that is even known to stand up to the charge of cavalry. But what is that sound?'

We had almost reached the dense thicket that skirted the marshland, when his words were cut short by barks of mocking laughter and the trampling of heavy feet. As we brought our mounts to a standstill, two men burst through the trees to our right. They walked with a great swagger, kicking something resembling a football between them. Their heavy jackets and axes revealed them to be gallowglass warriors, with more of their number suddenly appearing behind them, marching with red raw calves ahead of their officers who rode huge cogs.

Although I could not yet see the whites of his eyes, the figure of Donal MacCabe upon his huge charger was unmistakeable by the axe and rifle which were strapped to his back, as his appearance filled my mouth with the dry taste of fear. As they ran ahead of the rest of their troop, the two leading Scots had a tussle over the object that they were booting ahead of them. A hefty swing from one's foot brought it rolling over towards the legs of our steeds. It appeared to be a blotched, reddish-black round object. I almost took it to be an oversized onion plucked from the ground, what with the scarlet tendrils at one of its ends.

Then to my horror I recognised chipped teeth, as I instantly made out a freshly dismembered human head, with stringy, muddied hair on one end and torn veins and a partly ripped spine on the other. When I turned to stare at the two gallowglasses, I saw that they had already gained upon it, appearing entirely ignorant to our presence as they kicked the head before them once more, leaving me stunned at the disregard with which they treated it. Behind them the gallowglass constable reined his mount in a few feet away, as his troop of Scots slowly encircled us and held their great axes before them. Nial beheld the Scots warily while he hissed quick instructions to me beneath his breath.

'Be careful what you say, for they are capable of anything.'

The arms and apparel of the mercenaries were caked with blood, while the severed heads of slain troopers bobbed upon the flanks of their mounts. The constable bristled with menace as he rode between them, with a huge mercenary following him upon a broad-backed cog. He was a sight both terrible and impressive, for his huge arms looked like they could wrench the head off a bull. Nial saluted the constable who did not appear to notice him, for MacCable's eyes were fixed on me.

When he finally broke his stare, I breathed a sigh of relief. The constable then summoned a thin specimen from among his party who was a short, bare-headed chaplain assigned to the gallowglass troop. Donal's fists were bunched tightly as they were rested upon his sides, while he barked at the tiny prelate who seemed to wilt before his gaze. When the small priest finally spoke, his Latin sounded rudimentary and heavily accentuated.

'Constable MacCabe has heard of thy mastery of the gun, grey wolf. He says his men would be glad to have thee among their number.'

Despite the unexpected praise which had been accorded to me, I was also mindful that I was bound to the chieftain's service.

''tis an honour to receive such an offer, yet I am now bound to the service of our lord Manglana.'

When my words were translated the constable scowled at me, causing the bondsman to twitch awkwardly in his saddle. Donal seemed unconcerned with the discomfort he had caused Nial, as he spurred his horse forwards and reined it in alongside me. Harsh words erupted from his fearsome face, which were heavy with contempt as he spoke in rasping syllables, causing flecks of spittle to strike my cheeks.

His effrontery shocked me, since it reminded me of the savage German landsknechts in the service of Spain. They also behaved as though they were a law unto themselves, making demands of their Spanish paymasters and entering bloody fights with their allies before and after battle with the heretic. My mind strayed from these memories when the small chaplain at MacCabe's back gestured wildly in my direction as he translated Donal's heated words.

'Thou shouldst choose thy loyalties wisely, grey wolf. 'tis a great honour to form part of Constable MacCabe's troop, and his offer shall not be made to you again.'

Nial flinched again when I replied.

''tis indeed a great shame that I am otherwise bound.'

After the small prelate translated my words, Donal grabbed me by the neck with a loud growl. I was stunned while he shook me hard, almost dropping me from my own mount as his prelate translated his words of anger.

'Constable MacCabe says that he answers to no man! He says that he is not the beggar in this land!'

The guard of grim gallowglasses drew in closely about us. They were all spattered with blood and grime, holding severed heads from the crown as if they were lanterns. My skin crawled at their approach, while the constable still shook me wildly. A sudden ring of blades was heard as Nial kicked his mount forward. In one deft motion his swords left their scabbards to cross themselves before the constable's throat like a pair of great scissor blades, with their ends rested upon MacCabe's shoulders. The shaking instantly stopped, and the following instants played out slowly while the ring of Scots stared at each other in surprise.

I dared not stir, while at my side the bondsman roared at the gallowglass constable, his face a mix of incredulity and outrage. His sudden gesture had been one born of desperation but also quick thinking, as the few dozen gallowglasses around us swiftly checked their step at his words. A sigh of relief left me at the momentary respite, although we were hopelessly outnumbered. In all the commotion, none of us noticed another approaching band of horsemen until a sharp whinny was heard, followed by a steely cry in crisp, flowing Latin.

'Hast thou not fought enough for one day, Donal Garve?'

We jerked our heads sideways and saw the riders trampling the soggy earth. Beneath the darkening sky overhead, black mud could still be seen upon their flanks from which there hung the severed heads of fallen enemies. Behind these mounted warriors we could also make out wounded men being dragged on crude litters built from staves and blankets. The foremost rider's black hair was swathed about his face, leaving me to sigh deeply as I recognised the tanist who called out to the gallowglass constable again.

'That man is our guest, friend Donal. Thou would not renege on our duty of hospitality?'

The constable shoved me away and sneered at Cathal, and his words were translated by his prelate.

'Greetings, little lord, I see that thou hast taken to painting your face like some tavern whore.'

The Scots were already sniggering and snorting at their master's slight. Cathal was silent for a few moments, then replied in a low voice.

'The will of Lord MacGlannagh will be obeyed.'

As he spoke, his highborn cavalrymen raised their spears above their heads, as they readied to charge down the gallowglasses if Cathal's words were ignored. At the sight of their movements, the constable drew away from the bondsman, with a dismissive wave in my direction. He bellowed his last insults as his small prelate scurried after him, translating his master's words loudly and defiantly.

'We grant thee the company of these foreign dandies, for we need not dirty our hands with men of Spain. They shall abandon us all at first spring, when we shall hold you to your wager.'

An awkward silence passed during which I feared that the two bands might still come to blows. Then MacCabe finally wheeled his mount away, calling out and gesturing to his men who followed him as he made in the direction of Duncarbery. When the band of rugged Scots was gone, Nial and I were motionless for a few moments. Our breathing was heavy, for we still could not believe that we had survived our encounter with the gallowglasses.

The air about us resounded with barking and lowing, as more of Cathal's band approached, accompanied by a pungent smell of horse sweat. They led at least twenty heads of black cattle by chords of sheep gut which were looped about the beasts' necks. Meanwhile their huge hounds bayed at them, keeping them along a straight path.

The tanist's face was barely visible to us and his hair was unruly, with the front of his saffron tunic spattered with hair and gore. His steaming mount came to a halt but a few feet away from us, as he greeted us in his unerring diction. I studied his furrowed features as his hair fell away from his face, with my unease at his disfigurement swiftly replaced by gratitude for his protection. Nial breathed a long sigh of relief.

'A timely appearance, my lord,' said the bondsman, as he slid his swords back into their sheaths.

Cathal raised his voice while his cattle streamed past us, as he told us of his raid.

'Aye, we hath relieved the O'Reillys of many heads. Our tribe should survive winter through the new year with full bellies.'

His words were not lost on me, for it had already been explained to me by the bondsman that the Irish considered winter to be the start of the year.

'Your raids never leave you empty handed, my lord Mac-Glannagh!' exclaimed the bondsman with a broad grin.

Yet his smile was not returned, as a dark frown fell across the unsightly face of the tanist.

'Thou speakest truth, *Dua Claimthe*. Yet we paid dearly for our raid, for it was a challenge to ambush even one of their creaghts! The O'Reillys were somehow aware of our coming, for every herd was shadowed by a huge presence of cavalrymen! In the end we had no choice but to split our force, so that the attention of our enemies was diverted, long enough for us to raid an unguarded herd.'

He was interrupted by low moans as horsemen led riderless horses past us, which in turn dragged dying and wounded cavalrymen behind them on makeshift litters made out of cloaks and spear-truncheons. The tanist spoke again in a lowered tone of voice.

'We made off swiftly with our gains, through less used passes which are known only to us. We had a night's advantage, yet the devils still caught up with us, so that it was a valiant effort to shake them off. For they were more persistent than gadflies, attacking again and again over uplands and vale, only withdrawing when we were finally deep within O'Rourke's territory. It seemeth that their cavorting with the Sassanas has rendered them a fearless and defiant foe, for over a third of my force is now perished or lost.'

Cathal frowned deeply.

'The landings of the Armada have led our enemies to increase their vigilance as well as their incursions into our territory. My raiding was hardly begun, when tidings reached me of a force of Sassanas raiding the *túatha* on our southern borders.'

'I did not know...' said the bondsman, while the tanist served him with a knowing nod.

'Indeed,' said Cathal, 'I rode there in all haste to extend my lord's protection to our people, only to find that Donal had reached the enemy before I did. His men are troublesome devils, but the Scots also fight like devils: the surviving herdsmen told us that Donal and his men overcame twice their number on the field, and none of the Sassenachs survived their onslaught.'

The tanist paused to goad his mount towards the trees ahead of us, then spoke to us again.

'Keep up, dear friends. We should not tarry beyond the marsh at this hour.'

We followed his lead, riding a few feet behind his large band of men. Nial and I rode astride him, with the tanist seeming content to share his mind with men who were not related to him by blood. His stare fell upon me, when he saw me adjusting the front of my tunic which the gallowglass constable had undone.

'Are thou well, grey wolf?'

'Frightened more than hurt,' I replied with a shrug, 'I was sure that our end was nigh.'

The tanist shook his head in disagreement.

'Do not suffer undue fear, for thou art a guest of the Mac-Glannagh. Donal's bark is louder than his bite. Although it does not mean that he cannot bite when he wants to.'

The bondsman grunted.

'Indeed he seems more obsessed with biting rather than considering what he bites.'

The tanist snorted in contempt.

'He feels the threat of the Spaniards as keenly as the enemy.'

'How so?' I asked, unsettled by this revelation.

Cathal chuckled darkly.

'The days of raiding and ambushing our enemies cannot prevail forever. Time will tell whether we have sealed our fate or preserved it by aiding Spanish stowaways. Yet if we are to have any hope of resisting our enemy, we must learn all that our Spanish allies have to teach us. For we must soon learn to engage the enemy on the open field. We must learn marksmanship and to fight like the Imperial troops of Spain. Nial has often recounted his experiences in Flanders to me, it is why we have him teaching fencing across the land. And I believe that the teaching which you provide to the chieftain must soon be imparted to the kerns.'

'Thou wouldst have them march in formation and fire rounds in turn?' I asked, surprised that a seasoned cattle rustler yearned to learn advanced battle tactics.

'It is of the essence that thou does this,' said Cathal, casting me a wide-eyed glance of urgency, 'for I feel that the time of reckoning is at hand, and that we must match the Sassenachs with their own arms or perish. The gallowglasses alone are no match for an organised force of Sassenachs that is geared to meet them: it is only a matter of time until an enemy army sweeps through these lands, just like it did in Munster. It is why we are grateful for Nial's instruction with the blade, yet we must learn the use of new arms and of field formations, although I fear that the assembly of freemen have not yet understood this. And the bards viciously reject all advancement. For they consider any modernising to be a threat to their position, just like the gallowglass constable.'

Cathal sighed aloud.

'Yet although I am the tribe's champion cattle raider - a post venerated since time immemorial - I know that over time my raids will no longer suffice to sustain us. Nor can we afford to keep incurring the loss of men which I have just suffered.'

'How many men perished in all?' asked Nial.

'Seven,' replied Cathal, as his mount made its way over the rocks buried in the mud beneath us, 'and as many wounded.'

'That is hard.'

The tanist sighed once more.

'It is what our people have been taught to accept. Each raid is glorified by the harpist and hymned by the bard.'

Nial grunted.

'Yet this is thy first raid as tanist, and thou hast rustled many heads. All glory should be accorded to thee.'

'That it should,' said the tanist with a rueful smile, 'yet do not wager against Donal also demanding a mention.'

XXI

ROSCLOGHER AND MULLAGHMORE, DARTRY, COUNTY LEITRIM

2 – 10 October 1588

U pon our return to Manglana's town, the tribesmen greeted us with great cheers as they pointed at the forty rustled cows. Cathal's reappearance was accompanied by the tolling of the abbey's church bell long after we had retired to his large cabin along the lake. As the wounded were led to the infirmary, a smith was ordered by the tanist to kill two cows with hammer blows to their heads. The cowflesh was then braised in its own hide before being cut and sent to Cathal's cabin. All throughout the soughing of the wind and the odd drizzle of rain, the hut was filled with the smell of cooked meat and the sound of song.

Manglana's own bard Fearghal also made an appearance during our feasting, with all revellers going silent at the sight of his hard stare and scarlet jacket. After his paean of tribute to the tanist was delivered, Cathal gifted him a large side of mutton which was hastily snatched up by the bard's servants. Thereafter the bard took his leave, and I was relieved to see the back of him after the dark stares which he had cast in my direction.

I banished the memory of his appearance by helping myself to a goblet of usquebaugh. Meanwhile Cathal's men howled their battle cries until late after dusk, with their mottled beards increasingly streaked with animal fat. Throughout their merrymaking, the tanist sat cross-legged at the edge of our number. He seemed oblivious to the din about him as he stared into the flames, with shadows flickering across his scarred features.

The following morning was a more sombre affair, when funeral rites were held for the men who had perished on the tanist's raid. Afterwards the town was filled with the strident wailing of the dead's relations and certain older women called keeners. These keeners beat their chests for hours while howling the virtues of the dead, and I later learned from Nial that many of them were in fact paid to do this by the families of the fallen. As I watched them wailing and beating their chests through the town, it occurred to me that the woe which they displayed was so convincing that their fee was in fact well earned.

The lake was possessed of a noontime glow when the chieftain himself rode into Rosclogher with his large escort of bluejackets. At the news of Manglana's return, the tanist ordered his men to lead their recent gains before the ringfort. It was with these prizes at his back that Cathal the Black greeted his lord, as he dismounted and raised his sword in salute. On his part Manglana rode alongside his tanist, before reaching out his hand and clutching Cathal's forearm in a tight grip of approval. Thereafter he ordered that some of the heads be slain and great fires lit across the greensward, which heralded another day-long feast. As I helped myself to yet another cutting of beef, I wondered whether life in Dartry did indeed consist solely of fighting, cattle-thieving and revelry.

My feasting was brought to a crude end when another display in marksmanship was requested of me by the rowdy tribesmen. The effigy of Elizabeth was brought out onto the green once more, and it took well over a score of shots to appease the crowd, until the shot-riddled head of the wooden Elizabeth was finally blown off its shoulders. After humouring the onlookers with my skill, I received countless slaps upon the back as my name was cheered, and my mazer refilled at least a dozen times before I could retire into the dusk.

As I stumbled off into the shadows, I could see the dignitaries seated at Manglana's long trestle table. The bard had pride of place at the chieftain's left shoulder, and the Lady Bourke was seated at her husband's right, wearing her usual impassive gaze. O'Ronanyne and Cathal also sat at their lord's table, yet my eyes were trained on the face of Muireann who occupied a seat alongside Dervila. Although the ollave still made no sign of acknowledging me, her red-headed son Lochlain cast me long stares from over her shoulder.

After reaching the lakeside, I collapsed onto the grass, breathing in the evening air and noting the quivering eels in the growing moonlight. The silence of dusk found me content in the company of my own thoughts and a full belly, basking in the protection of hosts who had armed, shod and clothed me. In those quiet moments, I felt a twinge of distress as I tried to remember Elsien's face, only to keep thinking of Muireann. After a time I abandoned the exercise, with my hand slipping down to the ampoule at my breast which contained the ring.

'Eufrasia,' I muttered to myself, 'who in hell are you?'

The days which followed bore even greater opportunity for solitary contemplation. For although I was still expected to instruct the chieftain and his men in marksmanship, the highborn freemen soon lost interest in me once they decided that I was of little relevance to their petty intrigues. This did not trouble me in the slightest, since I had enough to worry about without needing to bother myself with the schemes of the highborn Dartrymen, who were as proud as Spanish courtiers.

I beheld them with secret contempt whenever they strutted past me in their linen shirts. They wore plaited sleeves beneath their mantles and long cloaks, while they also wore sporting gloves and riding shoes of costly leather. Nial told me that in the evenings they often listened to the bard's odes before Manglana's hearth, when Fearghal would compare their cattle raids to the exploits of Hannibal and Scipio. Such comparisons were of course ridiculous, so that the bondsman and I laughed long and hard following his mention of this.

Meanwhile the other Spaniards in the infirmary regained their strength, with four of them often prowling around Manglana's town like a pack of reunited wolves. It was not long until they discovered mad Orla's daughters at the settlement's edge or started to cheat our hosts at dice. I rebuffed all their invitations to join in their mischief, choosing instead to seek refuge in Dartry's surrounding forests. Whenever the weather held, I would traverse the bog and travel through the woods, wandering far enough from the circle of marshland but never beyond the mountains which loomed south of the lake.

I was intrigued by the rugged, untamed beauty of the country of Dartry, by its expanse of coast-bound heights and its grassy flanks which sustained the large cattle herds that nourished the rebels. I often sighted wandering herdsmen, who rarely travelled alone and were always armed. These were people who needed no maps and lacked for nothing, who were largely devoted to their pastoral life. They were a far cry from those Spanish peasants who had long thrown their hoe to the ground and gone off in search of better fortunes in the filth-strewn cities of the Peninsula, in the hope that they might become petty noblemen and freed from work and tax.

When not wandering through the country, my time of leisure included visits to the Jesuit's household to leaf through his books. His library contained titles by Macchiavelli, Aquinas, Catiglione and Erasmus, as well as a few authors of antiquity like Virgil, Horace and Livy. O'Ronayne's servants always greeted me with civility and let me leaf through the pages undisturbed. I was amazed that the knowledge of these writers had reached such a far-flung corner of the world.

Yet in time I learned that knowledge was highly prized among the Dartrymen, with the Jesuit often spotted teaching the rudiments of Latin and scripture to noble sons beneath a great hazel beside the lake. Muireann was sometimes also seen teaching verse to gatherings of children, with her soft voice sounding like that of a siren.

Sundown would always find me making my way back towards the abbey's outhouse to await a game of chess with Nial. During this time, a clash of wooden swords called wasters was often heard from the greensward, where the bondsman drilled fresh-faced youths in the rudiments of sword-fighting. In my moments of solitude in the outhouse, I sometimes hazarded to pull the ring out of my bandolier, and hold it closely in my cupped hand, ready to hide it away at the first suspicious sound.

Its stone was dark at night, with its green sparkle dulled by the sun's descent. Yet in the nightly outline of the gem I could see myself at the prow of the ship, which transported me and Pieter to the land where all our dreams would be realised. So moved was I by the great fortune in my possession that I sometimes found myself stroking it with the edge of my forefinger.

A prize whose price shall fluctuate wildly, I thought to myself, *yet in a time of scarcity I could fetch a fortune for it in Antwerp or Venice, or perhaps Naples.*

It was a prize which also caused me much anguish, as I wrestled with my plan to abandon Dartry after winter. I felt my throat thicken at the thought that one would willingly abandon the offerings on the natives' tables where a place was always kept for strangers. In spite of the ring and the ambitions it could realize, I found that the Irish way of life was becoming increasingly endearing, despite the ongoing shadow of the Sassana threat.

Dartry was also a place where I was held in high esteem by townsfolk who never wanted for beef, and whose women were possessed of extreme beauty. Furthermore, I had found peace again for the first time in months, and with it something resembling contentment. My blissful serenity was due in the main to my ignorance of happenings beyond the borders of Dartry, and it was yet to dawn upon me that my emerald ring had come to occupy the thoughts of some very dangerous men. Indeed, had I known of the whirlwind of distress that Ascoli's ring was yet to unleash on my hosts, I would have cast it to the very bottom of the lake.

Manglana's soldiers did not doubt the threat of the Sassanas since they constantly behaved as if they were in a state of war. I often spotted bands of kerns gathered on the greensward, sharpening their skills with spear and blade. The extent of their training was combat at close quarters, which would be useful in an ambush. Yet they lacked any knowledge of pike and shot tactics, so that they could not counter a square of trained Sassanas on the open field. Manglana's highborn cavalrymen would not be of any help either, since the absence of stirrups at their feet kept them from being of any serious threat to a mounted trooper armed with a lance.

'They need more advanced tactics and weapons,' I sometimes mentioned to Nial, 'if they hope to fight the heretics on the plain.'

The bondsman would nod at me knowingly, but I did not know that he was sharing my concerns with the tanist Cathal who in turn raised them with Manglana himself. Eventually the chieftain referred to my concerns in person, while he persisted with his early morning attempts to master the rifle.

'Thou believest us to be poor fighters?' he asked me with one of his sideways glances.

'Hardly my Lord', I replied, 'thy men are amongst the bravest swords I have yet encountered. Their strength in battle would be without equal should they master the methods of Spain. For we live in days of great change Sire, which have not left the ways of war untouched. I have already recounted the great disaster which befell the Grand Armada, since the heretics built smaller ships which bore more guns and which could fly more swiftly over the waves. And verily do I tell thee, as your loyal guest, that if thy men shall not advance in their ways of battle, then they will themselves also meet with the Armada's fate.'

My host grunted at my words and stormed off with a chewed lip, yet my warning did not fall on deaf ears. For not long afterwards, the chieftain requested that I commence training his personal bodyguard in marksmanship, together with the force of kerns which was barracked in the ringfort. Much time was wasted on trying to improve the aim of men armed with only a handful of muskets, since their main weapons consisted of bows and crossbows. My frustration at this state of affairs was expressed loudly to myself amid a spate of dark blasphemy, which was overhead by the bondsman. Nial once more notified Cathal the Black of my frustrations, which in turn reached Manglana.

'Art thou insistent upon the use of the gun?' he rasped at me another morning, making me feel somewhat flattered that my opinion reached him so swiftly.

'The gun has changed war, Sire. Indeed, it is a device which has changed everything, not least of all my life. One cannot march in file without it, for its noise alone causes the stoutest of chargers to lose its footing.'

My insistence prompted the chieftain to invite me to ride west with him and his men on the following Monday, towards his chief castle near the village of Tullaghan. As we approached it, I was impressed by the large seat of power with high walls that dwarfed the tower house of Rosclogher, being possessed of a strong gate and large towers. The strategic importance of this keep was not lost on me, since it defended the road that bound the north and south of Ireland's western coast. Yet it was also granted access to the ocean, where Manglana and his allies could obtain access to goods that were officially denied to them by the English-held garrison towns.

The chieftain's party did not veer towards Duncarbery castle, since they were in great haste. After we rode past it, we proceeded towards the stretch of shore which fell within Manglana's dominion. Cathal led Manglana's highborn cavalry downhill towards a small and secret bow of land known only to the Dartrymen. Upon reaching this place I was surprised to see a small Scottish merchantman with struck sails anchored a rifle shot away from the shore beneath a greying sky.

The sight of the sea reminded me of my previous sufferings aboard the Armada's hospital ship, together with the subsequent shipwreck. I did my best to banish these memories as we reached a small inlet which reeked of stale seaweed and approached a score of armed men in billowing coats. I noticed that they were a band of sea dogs, who stood before their three rowing boats which had been hauled upon the sand.

At our appearance, the burliest among their number barked at his fellows who proceeded to lift four large chests out of the skiffs. The leader of these smugglers limped before us with a wicked grin on his face that was as coarse as a whetstone. I soon learned that he was a Scot, one of those daring merchants who secretly traded with the rebel chieftains by way of barter. He plied his lucrative trade free from tax, far from the eyes of bedels and bailiffs who cluttered the seaside towns.

Manglana used Latin to address the man in person and referred to him as 'Bailey'. After he bowed to Dartry's king, Bailey proceeded to offer Manglana a cup of wine, only to be surprised when the chieftain invited me to taste it in his stead. Despite the chill wind that blew over the Atlantic, my face was flushed and my heart warmed by the taste of the fine Gascoigne drop, with both Dartrymen and sailors laughing when I vigorously nodded my approval and held my empty cup out again.

A whole hogshead of the splendid drink was purchased for nine cowskins, then further bartering was conducted. The chieftain had not come to the meeting empty-handed, what with Cathal's horsemen having borne many goods from Dartry. Meanwhile the Scots had brought with them swords, crossbows and other arms, which went repaid with skins of all creatures ranging from the wolf to the hare, as well as candles and mantles which had been made by many a wife and child. The smugglers gleefully stowed away all these goods, yet they were clearly keen on one prize in particular, which Bailey asked after with a glint in his eye.

Manglana's men proceeded to hand wooden cages to the Scots that were filled with young pups, for Irish hounds were greatly desired outside Ireland for their huge size and strength. These princely gifts were further rewarded by the smugglers with costly goods that included a chest of queenly garments desired by the chieftain's wife, together with a bountiful supply of herbs and medicines which had been requested by O'Ronayne. Among these worthy gifts was a book on medicine which Manglana gave to Nial for safekeeping, for it was the costliest article which had swapped hands that day.

'Redmond will be delighted,' whispered the bondsman with a smile, as he wrapped the book in his mantle to protect it from the rain, 'for he has long wished to get his hands on this.'

Other large consignments consisted of sacks of salt and kegs of powder, for which Bailey received ample payment through the costly skins of the pine marten and the highly coveted dye plants of woad and madder, which would colour the clothes of wealthy nobles and aristocrats. Many jars of honey also changed hands, in exchange for the muskets and crossbows brought by the traders. At this point the chieftain requested my intervention, asking me to examine the weapons and to name a fair price for them. At his request the smugglers' faces paled, and their eyes were fixed upon me as if I were some harbinger of doom.

Since the defence of the tribe was crucial to protecting my own hide, I scrupulously inspected each of the dozen muskets, checking the straightness of their bores and the quality of their matchlocks. When I asked for their price, the payment quoted to me was higher than I had expected, when summing up the value of the other items which had been traded.

''tis a hefty fee thou askest for these weapons,' I said, fixing Bailey with a hard stare, which led him to slightly bare his teeth at me and shift uncomfortably from one leg to the other.

'Dear indeed is the price that I claim,' he said testily, 'yet it is not cheap to slip past English warships.'

'And yet,' I said, having expected his line of defence, 'thy price should fetch us rifles and not mere muskets.'

Bailey stiffened as though a pail of ice-cold water had just been emptied down his back. It took him a few moments to find his voice again.

'Thou speakest of prices as if thou payest them thyself, friend Spaniard. Yet thou art but a guest among men who I have known long before thou ever set foot in this land. They come to me freely, since few would dare cross the English crown to furnish rebels with arms. For to be caught dealing with outlaws means certain ruin, but to sell them arms spells certain death. The grey merchants from the towns might steal away into Dartry to furnish thy lord with cutlery and cloth. Yet 'tis old Bailey whose head shall be cut off by an axe blade, should my ship not escape the English fleet.'

It was certainly true that he dealt with the Dartrymen at great personal risk, yet it seemed to me that he had earned almost thrice the value of his goods from a people oppressed by war and who faced an uncertain winter. Things might have taken a turn for the worse, for Bailey was already casting fearful glances at his customers, who scowled back at him. So I thought to help Bailey out of his corner, since he knew that he had been found out by one who had travelled farther than any of the Manglanas.

'Indeed thou speakest truth, friend Scotsman. And thy dedication to Dartry's cause is to be commended. Yet wouldst thou not bear some gift of goodwill upon thy next return?

But mere trifles that might aid thy Irish partners in their Holy cause, while going some way to secure their future custom?'

His reluctance to provide an immediate reply was telling, for I had forced his hand. He eyed me warily, leaving me curious to discover the extent of his desire for Dartry's goods. At last he snarled a reply through gritted teeth, in the manner of all worthy merchants who feared a bad deal.

'And pray tell, friend Spaniard. What precisely would these trophies consist of?'

'But a few horns of the cow,' was my gentle reply, 'as many as thy hold can carry.'

Bailey's snarl turned into a smile and he laughed mockingly, all the while casting looks of disbelief at his fellows.

'Cow horns?' he asked, 'is that all? And pray tell, what would thou doest with these horns were I to bring them to thee?'

'Bear our powder in them, of course.'

'Bear your powder? And what of the wooden flasks we have brought ye?'

'They are not as secure against the damp,' I replied. 'Powder is expensive and spoils easily.'

The smuggler chuckled to himself, then left me marvelling at the bravery of his next words, which were proof of his own personal daring.

'Yet spoilt powder means a fatter purse for old Bailey and smugglers everywhere! Why should I meet with your request? Can ye not cut your horns from your own herds? I hear they boast more heads than there are in your protector's own army.'

'They are indeed many', I replied, 'and have horns that can bear both usquebaugh and ale. Yet I hear tell that the cows in the high places of your land are longer in the horn, and the sooner powder leaves the barrel and enters the horn, the lesser the chance of its spoiling. As for fattening thy purse through spoilage, know that these people already question the use of firearms, and that spoilage ruins not only their powder but also their confidence in the gun. Let not greed and short sightedness blind thee from a more lucrative trade.'

Bailey then paused from his chuckling, as he studied the rifle which hung from my shoulder. His voice lost its haughtiness when he spoke again.

'The MacGlannaghs have always been suspicious of the firearm. How dost thou think to persuade them of its worth?'

As soon as he said this, I pulled the rifle off my shoulder and took aim at a spiralling gull overhead, then fired at the sky. The Dartrymen cheered my steady aim, with the smugglers staring on in disbelief as a flapping mass of bloodied bird crashed into the sand but a few feet away from us. As the echo of the shot carried over the sea, the stock of my smoking rifle met the ground as I leant over it to press my point further.

'As thou can see, friend merchant, my skill has gone some way towards persuading them otherwise. Yet the quality of thy stock would seal their convictions. And do not perceive me as your foe, for thy daring has earned my admiration. Indeed, thy honesty amongst men of thy trade is unheard of. For I can see that thy barrels are mostly unspoilt, and that but a mere handful of thy matchlocks are rotted beyond repair. I admit that thou hath surprised me, for thou hast had a great opportunity to swindle these men, which thou hast not exploited.'

At my words Bailey's shoulders sagged in relief as his grin widened. His men also appeared relieved, only to frown again at my next words.

'Following the landings of the Spaniards, these men have acquired a greater understanding of firearms, so your lengths of slow match shall no longer be needed. If my lord's gallowglass mercenaries have use of the snaphance musket, then surely thou can bear us a consignment of them straight off the forges of thy land.'

'But this would entail greater risk...' protested the smuggler feebly, 'and the Sassenachs would learn of this trade...likely double their watch!'

'Greater risk means greater profit,' was my instant reply.

Bailey laughed at this, as did his men. Upon seeing that he had heeded my words, I was glad that I had refrained from telling him to avoid bearing us worn muskets picked up from retired soldiers, which were barely fit to be used as walking sticks. As a final means of securing his loyalty, I sought to open his eyes to the greater possibilities which he had as yet failed to understand.

'If the Manglanas succeed in mastering the rifles, the eyes of O'Rourke will also be drawn to thy trade, as will those of his other sub-kings beyond Dartry. And then those of their allies. If you heed my words and furnish us with the requested guns, you will soon find yourselves at the head of an armed fleet, instead of a solitary merchantman.'

Bailey swallowed hard, taking in the meaning of what I said, then turned to face the chieftain.

'And the lord MacGlannagh shall meet the full price of these arms?'

'Aye', replied the chieftain at once, 'payment will be honoured in full.'

Bailey nodded slowly, his mind already going through the contents of his next consignment when he spoke again.

'Then God willing, we shall meet again at winter's end.'

As the smugglers shuffled back towards their boats I stared after them with longing, tormented by the false hope that one of their number might invite me to leave with them. In truth, I knew that such a journey would bear as much risk for the smugglers as it would for me, if their ship were to be waylaid by the English navy. Still my heart was heavy as the Dartrymen's packhorses were loaded with the newly purchased goods, as I watched the small Scottish ship slowly disappear towards the horizon, bearing away the roguish traders who answered to no king.

During our return journey to Rosclogher, the chieftain beckoned to me to ride alongside him. He was impressed by my exchanges with the merchants, and grateful to have an ally who understood firearms. All the way back to the town he questioned me further on how I thought his army could be improved, and I readily met his questions with answers I had long thought of during my stay among the tribe.

When we returned to the banks of Lough Melvin, Manglana and Cathal immediately set about meeting my recommendations. Labourers were hired to bear rocks from a nearby quarry to build two small magazines within the ringfort, and their walls were padded with the ample cow hide available in the town to prevent dampness. At my instructions the chieftain's carpenters also constructed wooden skids on which the barrels of gunpowder were removed from the tower house and instead stored horizontally above ground, to further prevent any unnecessary spoilage.

Some of the aged townsfolk were also ordered to further grind down the newly purchased powder. My influence on the chieftain did not go unnoticed, yet although I had the sharp eye of a marksman, I had not yet understood the threats to my person which were being hatched among certain tribesmen. For although the days ahead were to enlighten me otherwise, I had not yet realised that there existed as many dangers within the tribe as there were without. So busy was I with re-arming and training the Dartrymen that I was left with precious little time in which to read anything beyond the dark stares of the gallowglasses, or the frosty silences of the bard Fearghal.

Following our encounter with Bailey, I discovered a sense of purpose on the training ground which had been lost to me for years. For the promise of the new rifles gave further relevance to training the Manglanas, if not just to trick the tribe into believing that I was entirely taken up by their cause and not bent on fleeing Dartry in spring. Meanwhile I learned as many things as I could which would ease my flight. I strained my ears whenever the tribesmen spoke, so that I was soon able to utter some salutations and phrases to some of the natives who smiled at my attempts and also struck up conversation.

My strength was already restored by the time the stitches on my head were removed, so it also seemed best to partake of the sparring sessions being conducted by Nial. Yet the bondsman rejected my request, instead proposing that we conduct our fencing away from the eyes of the common kerns.

'It will not do to tarnish the invincible aura which you have acquired,' he said.

An hour before dawn would find us riding within the vicinity of *Sliabh Aradh*, where Nial put me through my paces in the light of the rising sun. There was also another reason for these private meetings, for the bondsman asked me to teach him the use of the rifle in return for his training with the blade. Although he often made light of firearms in front of other men, in private he wanted to learn more about their use.

So during the mid-autumn evenings Nial would pick up the rifle and heed my instructions to load and fire it. The bondsman was a quick learner, yet his patience with the gun would at times wear thin whenever he lacked aim and dexterity. One morning he felt entirely frustrated, as he choked on gunsmoke and slammed the rifle's stock against the grass.

'It is a filthy weapon, the firearm!' he rasped, pulling his head away from his blackened fingers.

'But a deadly one', I whispered, taking the rifle back from him.

'Pah' he spat, 'I have had enough of the rifle to last me a lifetime, let alone the rest of the day. It has been well over three hours of shots going wide and the stench of rotting eggs. Let us fight in the manner that good tradition dictates.'

A hiss of drawn steel was heard as one of his swords was held before him, glinting in the wan sunlight. I looked up at the pale orb of light which crested the greying heavens above us.

'Indeed', I replied, 'for all its deadliness, a gun is worth nothing on a rainy day, save for the mighty blows of its stock.'

I gently balanced the priceless rifle upon some rocks to avoid laying its barrel on the dewy ground, then drew my Irish sword. Although he was a novice when it came to fire-arms, Nial made me look an absolute dunce when we exchanged thrusts and parries with our blades. It only took the bondsman a few moments to dispossess me of my weapon, although I was surprised to find that I was still able-bodied enough to counter some of his blows.

After an hour of duelling, which mainly consisted of my having to bend over and retrieve my sword from the ground, I eventually managed a lunge that all but caught Nial unawares. The edge of my blade would have split his chin open, had his gauntleted hand not snatched up its point.

'Steady on, Spaniard,' he exclaimed in surprise, 'we are wielding real swords not wooden wasters! And this is but sparring, remember? Save your cleaving of throats for the heretics!'

'My apologies!' I exclaimed, realising that I had been overcome by a heat of blood and had almost wounded him, 'although it seems impossible that I managed such a thrust.'

'Peace!' he laughed, pushing my blade away and taking a few steps back, 'you did well to attempt it, for you shall never get so close to *Dua Claimthe* again.'

'We shall see about that,' I grinned, moving my legs apart and raising my blade over my shoulder again, in the manner he had shown me.

As our next blows were traded, we saw a distant party of riders leaving the cover of forest about Manglana's town and travelling along the uneven plain below us. Our blades fell to our hips as we observed this body of riders and footmen who made their way east.

'Who are they?' I remarked, almost to myself.

Nial growled his reply as the fingers of his left hand passed over the scabs on his face and forehead.

'It is that hellwhore of the queen, doubtless playing at being the great hunter again.'

He spat on the ground in ill-concealed rage.

'Norman witch' he hissed, 'curse her and the filthy gallowglass mercenaries she brought to Dartry as part of her dowry. I shall never understand why she does not confine herself to Duncarbery. Although she must derive great satisfaction from irking the chieftain with her presence.'

'Witch?' I asked in shock, fearing that she might cast a spell or a malediction upon my person, if she had not done so already.

'She constantly dabbles in medicines, poisons and spells,' said Nial with a sneer. 'Little wonder that her husband is unable to restrain or control her. The conceited sow struts about his lands while he pays her a huge sum in maintenance. He is even building her a keep at *Tirconnel*, which is to be manned by the gallowglass.'

'Truly?' I asked.

'I'd give her a keep!' snarled the bondsman. 'Were it up to me I would have already locked her in a cell and flung the key into the lake.'

'Can O'Ronayne do nothing to stop her?' I asked, feeling disturbed by the bondsman's talk of her devilish pursuits, while recalling all the women which the Spanish Inquisition had burned as witches.

'Hardly,' replied Nial with a look of disappointment, 'for the Lady Bourke backs all of his initiatives and maintains his apothecary and library out of her own purse. All this is of course a great good, yet a greater peace would prevail if she remained in one place while the chieftain stayed in another. A greater calm prevails whenever she keeps away from our lord, like when she journeyed to her father's lands in the southwest for long stretches. Indeed they say that after her marriage to our lord she returned home for well over a year, before she was seen in these parts again. Yet she has of late taken to shadowing his frequent visits to Rosclogher, on the pretext of there being better hunting around here.'

I shielded my eyes with my hand to better view the hunting party, when I suddenly realised that it had come to a halt, with the figures at its head gesturing in our direction. When it advanced again, the foremost riders among the party turned right as their easterly course changed into a southerly direction.

'They're...they're heading towards us,' said Nial, echoing my thoughts.

As the gathering of riders and footmen grew larger, we made out the familiar sight of two women at the front of the large body of men. Dervila and Muireann did not tarry behind their male companions, nor did they ride with both legs dangling over their mount's flank, as was the custom of highborn women on the Continent who always rode side-saddle.

Their party's mounts consisted of light and gracile beasts, which resembled the courser except that they were slighter of build, and were referred to by the Irish as the *'hobynis,'* which I could only pronounce as 'hobby'. It was a swift, agile steed which was greatly favoured by the natives, since it excelled in the chase. I also noted that these Irish hobby horses were not gelded, being possessed of a great spring to their step and an excited twitching of their heads.

'Be careful what you say', hissed Nial to me beneath his breath, 'it is not healthy to incur the Lady Bourke's ill favour.'

'Have we not already incurred it?' I whispered back to him.

Muireann wore a band of linen under the chin that was also pinned to the top of her head, a fluttering wimple that declared her widowhood to all. The ollave's dress also consisted of a short saffron tunic and a thick woollen mantle wrapped about her shoulders, while Dartry's queen was trussed in a more elaborate costume, with a juppe - that stylish French descendant of the jupon - reaching down to mid-calf, which was in turn swathed in an open riding gown lined with marten fur. A velvet riding hood covered Lady Burke's scarlet locks, and she bore a wicked looking sparrowhawk upon a gloved wrist.

The bird's glare was not dissimilar to its mistress' hard stare, as Dervila studied me without betraying a single sentiment. As the chieftain's wife approached us, I could see that her band was flanked by a score of footmen who bore great staffs with which to beat the woods. They also strained at great leashes, to hold back sleek white hounds which were even bigger of limb than a colt.

As the baying, clinking force drew nearer, I returned my stare to the bondsman who had assumed a stoic expression. When the men were barely a few feet away from us, Dervila raised her free arm, bringing the progress of her party to a halt. She next advanced upon us with only the ollave riding alongside her, while a fierce group of gallowglasses followed them on foot.

At the approach of Manglana's queen I could not but marvel at her features, with her long yet attractive face possessed of a slender nose above lips which were tightly pursed between two dimples. Upon observing her more closely, I realised that her handsome features were very similar to those of women from the Low Countries. The bondsman had told me that she was not native to Dartry, hailing instead from a country to the southwest of Sligo.

Her people were not Gaels either, being descendants of those Normans who had invaded Ireland with Strongbow almost five hundred years earlier. After countless battles with the Irish, Strongbow's followers had themselves taken up the customs and tongue of the natives, becoming more Gaelic than the Gaels themselves. Many of these Anglo-Normans or 'Old English' also rebelled against the wave of 'New English' invaders, who had commenced their attempts to take the whole of Ireland during the reign of their king, Henry VIII. When she brought her mount to a halt before us, Dervila addressed us in fluent Latin.

'Thou wieldest that base weapon which slaughtered my son.'

Behind her the ollave said nothing and kept her eyes fixed on the ground, where her two great hounds Roe and Branan sat and awaited her next movements. Muireann looked as sombre and severe as always, although some colour had at least returned to her pallid face. When I looked back at Lady Dervila, I realised that we had still not replied to her. I also

noticed that she eyed the weapon in my hands almost wist-
fully until she spoke again.

'Perhaps thy base weapon might rid us of a terrible scourge,
one which has attacked both our herds and our villages. For
Dartry has of late been afflicted by a huge pack of wolves -
and a most evil one at that.'

She tilted her head slightly to one side, with her next remark sounded almost grudging.

'Indeed, the presence of a skilled marksman might help ensure that our errand is accomplished.'

A few moments of confused silence lingered at her words,
when at last the bondsman cleared his throat awkwardly and
spoke up hesitantly.

'Art thou requesting Juan to join thy hunting party, my
lady?'

At his words a devilish smile played upon Dervila's lips.

'Is thy companion ignorant of Latin, Ne Douorugh, that
he should have others speak to me in his stead? 'tis a shame
that we have fed and clothed these castaways, only for them
to stand still as statues when addressed by the wife of their
protector. Yet if he will not speak to me, then mayhap he will
shoot for me.'

Her words left me feeling embarrassed, so that I attempted
to stutter a reply before the bondsman raised his voice again.

'Then thou shalt forgive Juan, my lady, for he is indisposed.
Thy husband hath ordered that he is to devote himself solely
to training his soldiers.'

Dervila's lips curled into a scowl before she issued a low,
mocking laugh. A sudden beating of wings was also heard

from the hawk upon her arm, while her horse shifted its head from side to side.

'Of a certainty this training can wait, for mine is by far the more pressing task. My husband keeps enough men idle for them to survive another day without instruction. Yet the quarry I seek might only be slain through the hellish arts of thy companion. And we will all suffer if we do not at least show the túatha that we have at least attempted to protect them from the wolves. For I need not remind you, friend Ne Dourough, of the restless rumours that grow daily among them due to their sufferings caused by our struggle. And their patience with us hath worn very thin already, what with all the soldiers and mercenaries they have had to put up with.'

Her words were of little revelation to me, for during our nightly discourses Nial had already spoken of the scarcity of food amongst the tribesmen, given the great lengths to which the Sassanas had gone to in order to starve the Manglanas into submission. Inland trade from the towns had been all but cut off, with the stream of grey merchants and hawkers which once passed freely through Dartry being reduced to a trickle. This meant less goods at a greater price, which had taken its toll upon the tribesmen, who often had to provide lodging to the hated gallowglasses. This was a crippling burden, especially when one considered that they already had to provide for the upkeep of the chieftain's kerns.

'So tell me, revered fencing master,' said Dervila, with no attempt to disguise the contempt in her voice, 'will thy friend reject my invitation like he refused that of Constable Mac-Cabe?'

Her head fell back at our looks of surprise as she laughed aloud again. At my shoulder Nial stiffened with indignation, until he at last found his voice.

'I am bound to protect the Spaniard. What would thou have me recount to thy husband if any harm should befall him?'

'Oh,' responded Dartry's queen, dabbing at her tears of mirth with a kerchief which she whipped from her hawking glove, 'have no fear of that, *Dua Claimthe*, for I have men enough to guard thy precious charge. Spare me thy feeble excuses and consider my invitation to the Spaniard withdrawn.'

When she said this, I called out to her, suddenly concerned that she might ride off without us. For a day of hunting appealed to me more than another afternoon spent training the kerns. I also hoped to win Dervila's favour, to protect myself from the aggression of Constable MacCabe and his gallowglasses.

'Verily, my lady,' I gasped, 'thou speakest the truth of it. I should lend my skills to the service of this land, for I owe it much.'

'Ah' she replied with a grin, 'it seems our guest hath discovered his tongue. What of it then, *Dua Claimthe*? Thy charge hath accepted to partake of the hunt.'

The bondsman sighed in resignation and shrugged.

'I cannot speak on behalf of Juan, my Lady. Yet I must also join you, for I am pledged to protect him.'

'A fencing master to also join our party?' replied Dervila with a mischievous look of surprise, 'why with the best blade and the best shot in all of Dartry in our service, we shall be mocked by the whole land should we fail in the chase.'

She paused to smirk at us, then her face assumed an expression of deathly seriousness.

'I must return to lead my men on, for they are a large gathering who grow restless. Make haste and fetch your steeds. We have a long ride ahead, for we make for the great wood that borders Breifne O'Rourke.'

Lady Bourke kicked her piebald steed and rode away from us, as Muireann also wheeled her dapple mount about and made after the queen. As they rode off, a loud hiss of frustration was heard from Nial, He next turned on his heel and shouted at his horseboy Torcall, who ran up to us with our mounts in tow. The bondsman sheathed his swords and snatched up the reins of his horse, while barking further commands at Torcall. The horseboy bowed to his master and ran off like a man possessed towards the direction of Lough Melvin.

'Where is he off to?' I asked.

'I bid him to hasten to Rosclogher', replied Nial, amid the jangle of his two scabbards as he kicked his horse alongside mine, 'he is to inform the MacGlannagh of our whereabouts, since you will no longer make your meeting with the bluejackets. As I have already told you, grey wolf: in this land fighting men are not to be idly slighted!'

The bondsman sighed at my hapless attempts to climb my steed while clutching its left ear. He finally spurred his charger alongside me and hauled me from under the shoulder onto the back of my stallion. I gratefully grasped the destrier's mane, gasping as I climbed upon it and wrapped my legs about its back. When I took up the horse's reins, Nial seized me by the shoulder. I turned to face a deadly stare of such severity that it shocked me, since I had never seen it before.

'The lady Dervila,' snarled the bondsman, 'is a glib specimen, so weigh your words carefully before you utter them. You must say nothing of our lord's dalliances.'

'Of course not!' I exclaimed, taken aback by his strength, yet his gaze did not waver until I had wrested myself free of his grip.

Behind us the loud blast of a bugle was heard, and across the plain we could see Dervila's party resuming its eastwards journey.

'What fool's errand have you got us into, grey wolf?' whispered Nial.

'It is not healthy to incur the lady Burke's ill favour,' I replied, then struck the destrier's ribs with my heels.

Together we galloped off towards the distant band of riders, like a pair of pinnaces after a great fleet which ventured into unknown waters.

XXII

DARTRY, COUNTY LEITRIM

10 October 1588

We were soon trailing the hunting party, disturbed by the rustle of the sparse trees about us as a cold westerly howled across the plain. As we pressed on, the odd cry of bird and beast caused Nial and me to reach for the swords at our sides. The queen's party spent almost an hour journeying along the distant mountain walls to our right, working its way through trees and bushes while skirting the edge of bog and moorland until Dervila signalled a halt. When the men before us parted, we saw the chieftain's wife gesturing to me to approach her.

I hesitantly spurred my mount ahead, just as the bondsman's pursuit of me was cut off by a closing ring of horsemen. I fell in beside Manglana's queen, close enough to make out the sun's radiance on her face. The ends of the red hair beneath her headdress complimented the ageing beauty of her face, which was pronounced by high cheekbones that quivered whenever she spoke. Behind her I could see Muireann's stare still fixed on the ground. The ollave wore an impatient expression, as she waited for her mistress's latest distraction to subside so that they could proceed with the real business at hand.

'Ride with me, Spaniard,' said Lady Dervila, 'for the kingdom of Dartry boasts a wealth of good game, yet it is a starving pauper when it comes to good conversation.'

I bowed so low that my nostrils glanced past my horse's mane.

'It shall be an honour, my lady.'

She smiled the faintest of smiles and spurred her horse forward, with the great clank of scabbards and reins resumed as her party also made towards the distant copse. I found myself at the centre of the hunting party, soon realising that it numbered over two score. Its other members consisted of elderly highborn riders who held gilt bridles atop their stirrupless saddles. Each of them had a hawk perched upon their arms while lowly kerns ran about them with spears in hand.

As we covered the uneven ground towards the forest, I marvelled at the unlikely series of events which found me part of an Irish queen's company. Meanwhile Nial cast me wary glances as he rode at the back of our party, which served as a constant reminder to watch my words. His concerns were not ill-founded, for during the pursuit of our quarry Dervila proved a riding companion who was both inquisitive and possessed of a keen wit. I responded to her probing questions with care, while remembering that I was but an amusement to her.

'Thou art indeed learned in Latin, friend Spaniard,' commented the MacGlannagh's wife after a time, 'how doth a man of thy civility tolerate being a guest in the kingdom of Dartry?'

I was about to speak frankly to her, then hesitated as I cast a nervous glance at the huge Scottish mercenaries about her, fearing that they might share my words with the constable Donal MacCabe. Upon noticing my anxiety, Dervila produced a giggle so carefree that it sounded like a girl's, while casting me a look which was as shrewd as a vixen's.

'Art thou fearful Spaniard? Indeed thou should be, for not all have received thee with open arms. Many are those that feel threatened by your skills and your proximity to their master. Yet thou canst address me freely, for these apes who serve as my bodyguard do not have Latin ears.'

Her reading of my thoughts only served to further unnerve me, yet with a quick bow of the head I replied to her question. Muireann's eyes remained trained on the ground ahead of us while I spoke.

'Indeed your grace,' I said, 'the Scottish constable is a man who extends a peculiar courtesy to strangers.'

The queen closed her eyes and raised her brows in resignation.

'He is but a wild animal, one possessed of delusions of grandeur. Yet this is a wild place and he serves my ends. There are few in this land that would dare to cross him, wouldst thou agree?'

'That is a matter for thy determination, thy grace. Yet if my view of the matter is sought, I would say that one shouldst have a care when seeking the protection of wolves.'

My reply was met by a long sidelong glance, leaving me to wonder if I had provoked her displeasure.

'Be not too hasty to judge my decisions until thou hast weighted thy own,' she replied, 'for whose protection hast thou sought, if not that of wolves?'

She pressed her case when she saw the surprise on my face, almost as if she derived a strange pleasure from the unease which she caused me.

'Indeed MacCabe is a brute, he hardly attempts to hide it. Yet his ways scarcely differ from the manners employed by that whoring drunk of my husband.'

She cast a dark glance in the direction of the bondsman who rode with a frown at the back of our party, then raised her voice so that he too could hear her.

'Long may my lord husband parade thee around with him, while feigning to be a civilized man with an appreciation of Continental ways. Yet he is nothing more than a scurrilous, conniving rogue, who only learned Latin so that he could woo me when I was but a girl on the cusp of womanhood. Back in my younger days I stood by the window of my father's keep, admiring a rugged prince from a far-off land who had ridden long leagues to seek my hand. Yet he had hardly snared my affections and bedded me when the soft and gentle manners were swiftly replaced by his wild Gaelic ways. It is a wonder he can speak any Latin at all now, given that it is not useful for his drinking and wenching. For thou should know Spaniard, if indeed thou hast not learnt the truth of it already: my liege lord is a man of base pursuits, not possessed of the qualities to be expected from one in his position.'

After she spoke, she issued a howl of laughter which sounded as mocking and hollow as it was unexpected. It was evident that she bore a great disillusionment, since she felt betrayed by an old love which no longer existed. After she had recovered her composure, Dervila seemed to mull over her last words, until a sideways frown from Muireann seemed to prompt the queen to offer some defence of the MacGlannagh's person.

'He is indeed possessed of brutish ways, yet my husband has at least sought to always uphold the law. In this he has surpassed his elder brother, that feral, revolting creature who was king of Dartry before him.'

She barely restrained a shudder at her reference to the former chieftain of the Manglanas, and her lips curled bitterly when she referred to him again.

'Thou hast had the good fortune of never knowing our last chieftain, *An Faolchù*. For he exceeded even the Sassanas and the gallowglass constable for savagery. He raped the *túatha's* daughters and stole from them as he pleased, siring countless bastards and murdering any who dared oppose him. It was a great mercy, one granted by the Almighty, that his reign lasted only four years. Yet it was long enough for him to sow great misery and distress. Many are those who whisper that his spirit has reappeared in the form of the leader of the pack of wolves that we now seek. Perhaps today we shall discover the truth behind these rumours.'

I rode on, uncertain what to say, as an unusual silence overcame the leader of our party. While she kept silent, I noticed the rank smell of sweat on our chargers and the mercenaries about us. My ears were filled with the snort of the horses until a muffled sob was heard from the lady Dervila, and I was shocked to see her holding her face in one of her hands. When she pulled it away, I could see that it was flushed and streaked with tears, her voice almost breaking when she spoke again.

'To think what a great lord my Aengus would have made. He who was so bold and wise, yet who is now but a headless corpse beneath a lofty pile of rubble.'

Her pained expression turned into one of anger and loathing when she spoke again, while I did my best to hold her anguished glare.

'I can scarce believe that his place has been taken by that deformed pretender of Cathal the Black! There is so little justice in this world! Indeed I often wonder whether the rustling of cattle is all that our new tanist is good for! Outwardly he always feigns prudence, yet he is the most conniving weasel this side of the mountains, and a bastard whoreson accused of *fingal* at that!'

At her tirade I fumbled for a reply, finding myself unnerved by her revelations.

'I thought the Dartrymen did not consider any births illegitimate.'

'It appears that thou hast been quick to learn of the ways of Dartry,' she snapped, 'yet remember Spaniard, that I am not one of these Gaels who freely fornicate with each other. Mine is Anglo-Norman stock, which the Gaels refer to as the Old English. For certain, the latest breed of Englishmen in Ireland are also my enemies since the ways of Rome are revered by my people. Yet to us a man not born of lawfully wedded parents is held to be a bastard, regardless of what the Brehon law dictates.'

The tanist's parentage was obviously an old bone of contention, so I merely nodded to her while hoping that she did not learn the truth of my own origins.

'Anglo-Normans...from France?' I asked, while wondering if her education and refinement hailed from Spain's rival.

'Hardly so, Spaniard,' she instantly replied, 'for we Anglo-Normans were Flemings who once settled in the south of Wales.'

I smiled knowingly at her words, since her striking features reminded me of the women in the Low Countries.

'Flemish,' I whispered almost to myself, nodding my head slowly.

Dervila eyed me warily.

'It is the truth, Spaniard.'

I nodded my head and raised my hand.

'Indeed, I do not doubt it my lady. It is just that thy looks are familiar, since I have myself served in Flanders.'

She served me with a keen glance.

'Thou serveth Spain in the Low Countries?'

'Aye, my lady.'

'Do Spaniards bear affection for Flemings?'

Her words left me to cough uncomfortably, and I felt it appropriate to explain further.

'I knew a family in a village called Willebroek who treated me...who treated me with kindness.'

Dervila raised her brows at this revelation, while also noticing the stutter in my voice.

'Tell me more about this family.'

I nodded obligingly, thinking that it would be best for me to tell her the whole truth.

'I was barracked in Willebroek during the siege of Antwerp. It was a troublesome time and the Spanish army had long gone unpaid. One night my path crossed that of an old widower named Reynier, the village's miller. He was being beaten by two drunken Spaniards. They only let him be when I threatened to report them to our officers. He had a few cuts and bruises and had suffered a vicious kick in the thigh. So I helped him along to his house, leaving him in the care of his son and daughter. Their names were Maerten and Elsien. When I turned to walk away, his daughter ran over to me and told me that her father had invited me to sup with the family.'

Of a sudden, my mind was flooded with memories of the fresh-faced girl with a low fringe and a shy innocence. To a filthy soldier of Spain who had crawled out of the trench, Elsien had appeared the picture of sheer temptation. For she stood on the very cusp of womanhood, a stunning raw diamond unaware of its own beauty. I sighed deeply at the memory, and for a few moments I could not bring myself to speak further. After a few sudden breaths I regained my composure when the queen of Dartry spoke again.

'Thou had feelings for this woman?'

After all the sufferings I had endured during the past year, I hung my head and pressed my eyelids down with thumb and forefinger. I tried to stem the tears with my fingertips, then quickly brushed one away when it slid down my cheek. Manglana's wife appeared entirely taken aback by my display of emotion, so that it was some time until she spoke to me again.

'Peace friend Spaniard, I should not have enquired further. I see now that thou hast known great loss.'

With gritted teeth I nodded to my protector's wife. I suddenly noticed that Muireann had also fixed me with a stare of her own, which was quickly withdrawn when she saw me returning it. In that moment it occurred to me that both Dervila and Muireann were also strangers to Dartry and had also endured a recent crushing calamity. So taken was I by this realisation, that I did not notice that another tear had left my eye until it slid halfway down to the tip of my nose. When I swiftly wiped it away with a curse, Dervila served me with a stiff warning.

'Thy love for this woman must have run deep, Spaniard. Yet thou betrays weakness at thy peril in this hostile land.'

She leaned over towards me, whispering beneath her breath.

'I can prepare thee an ancient cure, should thou require it. 'tis but a marchpane concoction, yet one said to have healed broken hearts since beyond living memory. I have myself resorted to it after learning of the death of my son. I can vouch for its soothing properties.'

Her offer was tempting, for I had long wondered if I would ever be rid of the torment which I felt at the memory of Elsien, which no amount of killing had yet relieved. Yet the bondsman's warning returned to me then, as I recalled his reference to Dervila's witchcraft. I smiled back at Dartry's queen, thinking of the best way in which to rebuff her offer.

'I shall consider thy generous suggestion, my lady,' was my cautious reply, 'although verily do I confess that this pain I feel is all I have left of she who is gone forever. I would not readily dispense with it, despite the great woe it causes me, but I may in time request the use of thy potion.'

The chieftain's wife beheld me in stunned silence.

'I have not often met soldiers such as thee, Spaniard. May-hap thou shalt find some peace and companionship in Dar-try, during the time that thou are with us.'

I bowed my head to her, while wiping my eyes against the hanging sleeve of my tunic.

'That I shall my lady, for as long as I can steer clear of the Sassanas.'

'Aye the Sassenachs,' she replied, 'they are indeed a relent-less and hard-hearted enemy. Yet their evil may yet bear little fruit. They shall brook no agreement or compromise, being only bent on stamping out our ways and turning us into New English. They do not understand that it is not the way of this land's peoples to bend others to our will through force. For in the past, many have been accepted among our number with-out question, since it is our law to offer hospitality to aliens and travellers, even more so in these dark days. Yet although we are accepting of others, it does not mean that we are not also brave. We will not bow to atrocity and violence.'

At her words I twitched uncomfortably in my saddle, re-calling the treatment which I had been subjected to before my escape from Sligo. Upon noticing my unease, Dervila quickly sought to comfort me.

'Do not fear Spaniard, for thou shall always be safe in Dar-try. Indeed, thou hast more to fear from our feuds and tribal rivalries with the O'Reillys and our other neighbours than thou hast from the Sassenachs. Do not forget that we are buffered by the sea to the west and our overlord the O'Ro-urke to the east, who is the most powerful man in the whole of Connacht. Meanwhile the unassailable Irish cattle lords dominate the north, while the great mountain walls to the south also shield us from our enemies' passage.'

'Yet are these boundaries enough to fend off an army?' I asked, since the question had long occupied my thoughts during my private moments in the outhouse, while lying upon my pallet and toying with the ring. Dervila snorted defiantly.

'The closest thing to an army passed through this land but four years ago. Many squadrons of men raided Dartry under the command of a haughty young upstart, one Brian son of Teige. He was in league with the Sassenachs, who had appointed him as their sheriff of Sligo. His men slew many innocents among the *túatha*, carrying off many more heads than he had riders. Yet my husband and son instantly pursued him with as many men as they could muster. The young turn-coat thought that he had given them the slip when he fled to Breifne, yet the men of Dartry hounded him each step of the way with the mightly gallowglasses at their backs, until the sheriff finally turned to face them in the shadow of Beanna-bo. His troops were crushed by the onslaught of Dartry. Brian barely fled with his life, only to be captured and execut-ed three days later by our overlord the O'Rourke of Breifne, who preferred to slay one of his own kinsmen than betray my husband, who is his most loyal lieutenant.'

Her face was a mixture of pride and indignation when this tale was recounted, and her next words left me greatly reas-sured of my safety.

'The outcome might have been quite different, had our son Aengus not ridden ahead to summon a band of our allies in Breifne. Aengus was always possessed of a great foresight and natural leadership, I darest not think what shall befall us now that he is gone. Of course the victory was claimed by my uncouth husband, whose army returned to Dartry in triumph with all of the reclaimed heads of cattle. From that day on he earned himself the nickname of Sheriff-Slayer, which still strikes fear in Connachtmen and Sassenachs alike. His reputation offers us more protection than the mountainsides, for many fear to even pass along the borders of Dartry. In truth my husband's only achievements since defeating the last sheriff have been drinking and whoring. Yet many still believe that to enter his lands unbidden is as dangerous as plundering the young of the griffin, or to attack a lion in its own den.'

I nodded my head at her words, yet Manglana's wife seemed suddenly concerned that she had not allayed my fears.

'Has my tale troubled thee, Spaniard? It is only my husband's strength which has waned, yet the Dartrymen remain a fearsome prospect.'

'I do not question their strength,' I said, 'for it is the wickedness of the Sassanas which troubles me, since they are both ruthless and deceitful. Their sheriff George Bingham is learned in the methods of war, while their boundless greed is famous among all God-fearing peoples. I fear they shall not rest until they have broken your resistance.'

For a few moments Dervila seemed to have no reply. She flicked her reins across her steed's shoulders, spurring it after the ollave who still rode at the head of our party. I had become so engrossed in our debate that I hardly noticed our surrounds, which consisted of green pastures broken by hills and wild trees. Great rises could be seen to our right, with glimpses of the lake to our left visible through the foliage.

The dull clink of steel returned my attentions to the ugly gallowglasses who flanked us. For although they went on foot, their step never wavered, and they instantly took up a brisk jog whenever our mounts broke into a canter. Their presence disturbed me, so that I spurred my horse towards the chieftain's wife. After tackling another descent we proceeded over uneven plains and rumbled over the hillocks to our right, then descended into a tree littered vale where our progress was reduced to a trot. As we passed through the dells and shadows of the trees about us, Dervila's low voice reached my ears as she spoke to me over her shoulder.

'The land of Connacht is possessed of a spirit, a presence that cannot be killed. It charms all off their feet, I doubt whether it can ever be broken or subdued. Its people might be killed defending it, but its spirit cannot be conquered by man alone. This is what the invaders do not understand. They might burn its fields, rob its gifts, kill its people, live to a ripe old age upon its ground, but ultimately this same ground shall claim them. Change cannot be hastened among our people, as I have learned to my own great cost. Despite the invaders' worst efforts, the spirit of Connacht will never be mastered.'

'Great words indeed, my lady,' I smiled, feeling truly awed by them, 'ones which would not go amiss upon the lips of your poet bard.'

Dervila grinned as the slightest blush crept along her cheeks.

'I do not speak of the imagined, Spaniard. My own Anglo-Norman forefathers arrived in this land with hostile oars. They followed the banner of their great leader Strongbow and were filled with the resolve to conquer and subdue. Their aim was also to suppress the natives, yet this land's spirit seduced them until they became as Gaelic as the Gaels themselves in their manners and customs. The Sassenachs send their worst people against us, vile tosspots and scum who cannot imagine any customs being unlike those in their own land. But the more learned amongst them will also be seduced in time.'

She paused, staring in the direction of the ollave who rode ahead of us.

'And despite any denial on your part, I know that thou hast already been charmed by this land.'

It was my turn to blush as she grinned at me, for I knew that she spoke true.

We were barely a few feet away from the closest foliage, when the queen's dog handlers trudged away from our party in two groups. A half dozen of them walked right while the same number of them made towards our left. Their charges hopped up and down in excitement as the woods were approached, prompting their masters to desperately haul at their leashes as they continued to fan out. They had hardly reached the first cover of forest when the hounds' baying became ever more distant as they were released from their leashes.

There were heard great crashing sounds as the dogs' handlers commenced beating the brush with their heavy staffs, which would send wild beasts fleeing across our path. Meanwhile the ollave led our party deeper into the forest. Great crunching, crackling noises were produced by our progress, for the morning dew had long since dried and the forest floor was no longer soggy.

'A late start', muttered the queen alongside me.

Her steady voice betrayed a tinge of excitement, as we ducked beneath the lowest hanging branches.

'Yet with some luck,' she continued, 'we may claim the head of *An Faolchú*, should he cross our -'

Then her speech was broken by a loud trumpet blast which was issued by the beaters in the distance.

'They have started the drive,' exclaimed Manglana's wife, 'the wood's creatures will soon be heading towards us!'

My rifle was whisked off my shoulder and swiftly primed as I attempted not to fall off the English destrier. This balancing upon the horse was harder than the priming of the gun, for the ground had become more uneven. The dead leaves of autumn masked all ditches and furrows, which in turn left the party's mounts to stagger wildly. Dervila's attentions remained fixed on what lay ahead while she spoke to me.

'It appears that thou art no stranger to the hunt.'

She was instantly distracted by the loud snorts of a beast which bounded across our path, so swiftly that it was barely recognised as a deer. The moment it swept past us, a couple of arrows struck the trees along its path, when a loud bugle blast was heard once more. My eyes were trained on the head of our party, where I could see Muireann's face redden before her lips were released from the bugle's horn mouthpiece.

As the blast reverberated in our ears a loud hunting cry was heard, so that it was suddenly every man for himself. Dervila's steed sped after the ollave's as I spurred my horse on after her. The ride through the trees was both treacherous and uncomfortable, leaving me to lean against my charger's neck to avoid blows of the low-hanging boughs. So tortuous was my ducking and diving that I soon envied the smaller and sprightlier horses used by the Irish for the chase. It seemed like an eternity until my flight through the dells and the bursts of daylight came to an end.

The mounted Dartrymen had proved themselves both nimble and excellent horsemen, so that it took me a while to catch up with them. My indomitable mount was streaked in sweat by the end of it, with its flanks throbbing wildly as we regained sight of the hunting party. We found them dismounted and with their arms held at the ready, as they gently placed their satchels and gear upon the ground. When I climbed off my horse, I saw the bondsman approach me with a cautious gait.

'Did you tell her anything?' he asked nervously.

'Not a word,' I replied, holding his stare until he looked away, seemingly satisfied that I was telling him the truth.

'I am wearying of this fool's errand' he rasped with a broad frown.

'Why do they tarry?' I asked.

'Their quarry has been struck by two bolts, yet it remains on its feet and has fled where the horses cannot follow. It is a noble quarry: a great red stag, which is deadly despite its wounds. It is trapped at the end of a ditch beyond the trees, where its escape is also blocked by thicket. It might charge at any moment and will certainly do so if it is disturbed.'

As I understood the reason for their delay, I also realised from the distant, faint baying that the hounds were still too far away to be used to displace the quarry.

'Why can they not shoot it?'

'It is shielded from bowshot by a literal web of curved boughs that are entangled athwart it. If one wants a clear aim with the bow, then one has no choice but to step out before it.'

The danger of such an attempt was obvious, for it would take foolishness rather than bravery to take such a risk, especially since the flanks of the beast would be impossible to aim at. When the low muttering ahead of us slowly grew, I noticed that the other riders in our party were locked in a fierce debate with Dervila and Muireann. A band of kerns had gathered in front of them, casting nervous glances at the bickering nobles and then back towards the cleft in the trees, wherefrom there were heard the ragged breaths of the stag.

Eventually the chieftain's wife snatched a bow from one of the highborn riders who stood at her shoulder, while hissing at her retainers beneath her breath. Despite her wrath, one of the men stepped forward to seize her by the arm, then grabbed her bow and remonstrated wildly with her. A furious growl was heard from Dervila when at last she shoved him away, while I seized my moment and stepped towards her.

'Whatever is astir, my lady?' I asked, holding the rifle before me.

As she whirled towards me, the highborn Gaels around her appeared both fearful and curious.

'Keep thy voice down,' she hissed, 'for there is a worthy prize within those trees, but none of these cravens will dare earn it.'

'To refuse to risk one's life without good cause is hardly cowardice.'

Her eyes narrowed at my reply, while those about her who understood some Latin shifted uneasily from one leg to the other. They knew that it was not often that their lady met with open contradiction, and the lady Bourke's lip already trembled angrily when another voice was heard behind her.

'And what art thou proposing, Spaniard? That we abandon the noble beast to its suffering and return to the greensward to practice our aim?'

The natural beauty of Muireann's features became flushed when she spoke. I silently raised my hand towards her as a gesture to keep from stirring, then stepped aside from the gap in the trees wherefrom there was heard a sudden bellow. For a moment I froze to a standstill and the hair stood upon the back of my neck. Yet when no more noise was heard from the beast, I squeezed through the thick boughs alongside the cleft, making my way through them with as much silence as I could manage. As the path fell into a steep ditch, I just about kept my footing, hopeful that I might get a glimpse of the wounded stag.

I next spotted a pair of kerns from the hunting party, attempting to somehow bend their bows through the spaces in the trunks before them. At the sight of me they withdrew, as one gestured to a gap in the thick brush ahead of him. With soft footfalls I reached his side and stooped over his shoulder to spot the dim outline of our prey, which stood within a sort of tunnel made out of tree trunks and high grass.

I took in the scarlet splotches against the ground and tree roots, until my gaze came to rest upon the legs of the massive beast, which puffed up huge clouds of mist. A thicket at its back barred its escape while it stamped the ground angrily, reminding me of a cornered bull in a Spanish arena. As my vision became better accustomed to the poor light, I saw two arrows dangling from the deer's haunch and breast, as it struggled to keep on its feet. Its sharp antlers swayed from left to right before it, ready to slash at anything that stood in its path. It was bristling for one last charge and its eyes were wide with fear. It was a most splendid creature, and I swiftly surmised it to be an act of great nobility to relieve it of its suffering.

After noting a hole through the brush through which I could detect its shoulder, the bore of my rifle slid through a narrow space in the boughs ahead of me. My feet were spread apart as I braced myself for the kick of the rifle butt, with my eye fixed through the rifle's sights upon the beast's shoulder. The deer was less than half a musket shot ahead of me, with the ensuing blast followed by what sounded like the beating of a hundred birds's wings as they made towards the heavens.

When the stinking cloud had dissipated, a cry of joy was heard from a kern alongside me as he crashed towards the limp form of the deer which had crumpled onto a bed of dead leaves. Another cheer also rose as the kerns behind me slapped me on the back, while the other Dartrymen tore through the cleft in the trees led by Dervila and Muireann, to observe the felled creature in wonder. It had been a clean shot, straight through the heart. I was doubly glad that I had achieved the first kill of the hunt, while also showing the rifle to be a highly effective weapon.

At last, the beaters and their hounds reached us, as the quarry was strung up by its hind legs to the branches of an oak tree. A skene dagger was used to slit its throat open, which instantly commenced its bleeding as the hounds were led away. When our hunt was resumed, the chieftain's wife insisted that I ride alongside her, for she seemed impressed by my skill with the rifle. Along the way she asked me to slay a boar and a pheasant, which were both swiftly shot down. As the beaters in the distance scattered more wild animals, I shot down two more creatures, just as the ollave ahead of us took aim at them with her bow. As Muireann flashed me a furious stare I smiled back at her nonchalantly, while the lady Bourke told me off.

'Do not persist with frustrating her, Spaniard. The *ollamh* is not a woman to be lightly crossed.'

At her insistence I slung the rifle back on my shoulder while Manglana's wife addressed me again.

'Thy aim from horseback is most accomplished.'

'Beasts make clearer targets than men,' I replied with a shrug.

She nodded at my words.

'The rifle is a powerful weapon. In the past, women had little enough hope of defending themselves with swords. Now I fear that their safety will be further diminished with the advent of the firearm.'

Her words startled me, for after years of fighting I had obtained a different view, so that I spoke my mind fully.

'I disagree my lady. I have seen women brandish muskets and rifles upon the walls of besieged towns in the Low Countries, keeping depraved armies at bay. Anyone can learn the use of the firearm with time and commitment.'

For a few moments she returned a baffled expression. Yet before she had time to reply, the hawk perched upon her glove fluttered restlessly when the air was filled once more with the blasts of the bugle. Birds and beasts had again been roused by the hounds and the beaters, and our party dashed after them through the woods, straining at our reins as we twisted and turned beneath the boughs with both Scottish gallowglasses and Irish kerns sprinting after us.

Before long a hart, two boars and a small wolf were killed, with a half dozen hares also claimed by our party. The second pig was cornered by the kerns, and as it charged at them one of the footmen stepped forward to skewer it, just as its tusks glanced the leather jerkin of his fellow. To my amazement, this kern was not berated or punished for this when the highborn riders finally arrived at the scene, with this lowborn soldier also allowed to claim the beast for himself. This was a practice I had never seen before, since I had often witnessed footmen being openly told off for killing prey before their noble masters arrived to slay it themselves.

The smaller wolf proved far more elusive, with Muireann exhibiting impressive tracking skills until we finally hunted it down. Her talent with the bow left me astounded, for whenever a creature was in her sights her arrows struck true and mortally with almost every shot. When the hunt continued after a brief rest, more hares and pigs were coursed and skewered, and the odd badger was also slain by the ollave, to the tribesmen's great delight. Dervila seemed the keenest hunter of all, galloping after Muireann amid loud cries of excitement. The ollave often stooped over her mount to read tracks, sometimes dismounting to study the earth for spoor. Her ability to read signs of the prey's passage led us from one quarry to the next, an uncanny ability which I could not but remark on.

'Her skill is impressive.'

Lady Bourke nodded her head in agreement.

''Tis truly a gift of the second sight, Spaniard.'

'A gift which matches her talent with the bow,' I remarked.

'Among her many *other* skills,' said Dervila, 'for not through Gaelic tradition alone did my son consider her his equal. Muireann is a formidable woman, who is as comfortable in the hall of a chieftain as she is running with the wild kerns in the bush.'

She turned to face me with a rueful smile.

'Indeed thou art fortunate, for thou couldst not have fled the enemy with anyone more skilled in finding their way through the woods. Muireann knows many secret paths throughout this land, and has a memory for tree and leaf unlike any other. In the more peaceful days of yore, she travelled widely through the wilds with her father, who was both a revered bard and great man. The halls of Duncarbery and Rosclogher often rang to his verse, which made my husband's bard look like a petty rhymer.'

I barely restrained a chuckle at her reference to Fearghal. For he always bore himself with great authority and was considered by the tribemen to be only second in rank to the chieftain himself.

'Yet I thought that her father was the chieftain of a neighbouring tribe?'

Lady Bourke flashed me a gentle smile.

'He was a chieftain, of sorts,' she said, 'for after years of wandering, he finally accepted the gift of an estate and tower house from the MacSweeney along our northern borders. Such was the fame of her father's verse, that similar offers were also made by a host of other chieftains. Yet the elderly Gofraidh Mac an Bhaird was swift to swear fealty to MacSweeney, who he knew to be a true admirer of his talent and a renowned host of many bardic festivals.'

A frown appeared on Dervila's face before she spoke again.

'I remember when she was sent to us as a young girl, to be fostered by my husband and me. She was mocked by some as a rhymer's daughter, yet she had already learned things from her father which eclipsed the knowledge of Dartry's most learned. Her feats were not solely confined to verse, for she would ofttimes venture into the forests along Lough Melvin with my son and their bodyguards. Together they struck many hidden paths known only to her, returning with rich prizes of game. Those were indeed happier days, in which the *ollamh* did much to enhance her reputation among us. For it is a principle of old Irish law, that the more talents you have, the more noble you are considered to be.'

At Dervila's words, I could not but marvel at the many gifts which Muireann was blessed with, when at a gesture from the ollave our horses were reined to a halt. My eyes fell upon the shadowy figure of Muireann, who briefly alighted from her saddle to examine some prints in the earth. As I admired the slenderness of her figure while she knelt over the ground, I was startled to hear the voice of the chieftain's wife in my ear, which was reduced to a low whisper.

'Indeed, 'tis a shame that Cathal and Donal will soon start to fight for her hand, to claim those lands and swords which belonged to my son. True love is ever treated with disregard, whenever great power is so close at hand.'

Dervila smirked at me when I returned her stare, so that I suddenly realised that she already held firm conclusions about my feelings for the ollave. Before I could reply, Muireann had already returned to her saddle, and taking her lead we rushed down a decline which led us out of the great wood.

We suddenly found ourselves within a great plain, with a yet larger forest standing ahead of it.

By this time the sun was beyond noontime height, and a few clouds had also gathered. Yet there was still radiance in abundance, enough for us to make out a small cluster of huts in the distance. After we reached them, Lady Bourke rode ahead with the ollave in the company of their gallowglass bodyguards, to speak to the creaght which had settled along the plain. Dogs growled and strained at the leash while we waited, when Nial rode up beside me.

'Is the hunt to your liking, grey wolf?'

'It is long since I last partook of such a chase. Dartry is home to magnificent woods which are choked with game.'

A pained smile overcame him as he looked away with a sigh, seemingly staring into the belt of mountain peaks ahead of us which studded the sky.

'A truth that our enemies know only too well.'

After half an hour, Dervila and Muireann returned to our party, with the voice of Dartry's queen being overcome with excitement.

'The wolves stole off with a ewe at dawn,' gasped Dervila, 'a shepherd boy saw the carcass being dragged into the woods ahead.'

The riders about her instantly called out to each other in loud, excited voices, while the shepherd boy was summoned to lead us to the place where he had last sighted the pack. There Muireann found drops of dried blood upon a rock, and the hounds quickly took up its scent. The beaters were ordered to keep behind our party as we slashed our mount's withers and trotted towards the trees, with the footmen's leashed dogs causing a loud din ahead of us. Wind blew through the trees and scattered both our hair and our scent, thereby reducing any hints of our approach.

We had barely commenced our pursuit of the trail of dried blood through the forest, when one of the hounds led us to the remains of a sheep's carcass. Muireann was swift to point out the huge paw prints that were surrounded by smaller ones.

'*An Faolchù*,' hissed Dartry's queen at the sight of the tracks, 'so it was he that struck again. But now we are here, he'll not see another dawn.'

It was almost mid-afternoon and I knew that haste would be required if we were to find the lair of the beasts. We would need time to plan an attack on it, given the lethal craftiness of wolves when cornered. Once we had climbed back onto our mounts, we did not dismount again for long thereafter. Whenever the hounds lost the wolves' scent by small streams, Muireann was swift to spot signs left behind by our prey. She only had to slow her horse a few moments before she noticed a broken branch or some trampled clump of grass.

Our advance brought us closer to the mountainsides, until one of the dog handlers tripped over a rock, which allowed his hound to free its leash from his grip and bound towards the beginnings of a tree-cloaked hillside. After it vanished through the bushes, there were heard great snarls and scuffles, which lasted a few instants until they were followed by a high-pitched howl.

When we reached the dog, we were greeted by a strong stench from a hole in the ground, beneath a large rock which jutted out of the earth. The bones within it revealed it to be a lair, with the flown dog writhing upon the ground outside it with its throat slashed open. The hound's distraught handler instantly fell to his knees and fumbled for his knife, then used it to sever his charge's gullet to relieve it of any further misery. As I swiftly drew my rifle a ghostly figure was seen bounding off into the distance, as yet another loud bugle blast signalled the wolf sighting as the chase was resumed once more.

'*Scaoil na botháin!*' screeched Dervila, at which order the hounds were freed from their leashes.

I took aim and fired a shot which took out the hind leg of the straggler. The dogs instantly set upon it, tearing clumps out of the fanged wolf's coat as we galloped past, with each hunter intent on slaying the leader of the pack. As the bush thickened, the flight of the beasts was delayed, but those of us on horseback also found our progress through the growth impeded when we were overtaken by the fleet-footed kerns. These barefoot warriors raced ahead of us with their spears held aloft, crashing through the trees and slaying another three of the fleeing wolf pack.

When the undergrowth cleared, we bore down on the remaining scavengers whose pelts served as a shifting target, and which I missed twice amid loud curses. Yet over a dozen hounds raced ahead of our company, claiming three more wolves until only the leader of the pack was left. It was twice the size of its fallen fellows and covered ground twice as swiftly. Just as the hounds were about to close in on it, the imperious beast vanished through a bush and over yet another small stream, which left the dogs scrambling about after its scent. Our horses' canter slowed to an ungainly trot as they waded through the onrushing water, with the small river barely forded when the chieftain's wife reined her steed alongside mine with a cry.

'Ahead of thee, Spaniard!'

I stared up at the trees, where I could make out the face of the scarred brute standing beyond bowshot, having crested a tree-cloaked hillock before turning to bare its teeth at us. It was a large, hideous creature which was possessed of a single eye. The sight of its malicious glare momentarily overwhelmed me, until I swung the reloaded gun before me and took aim at its head.

I suddenly noticed a small puff of smoke in the corner of my eye, which came from the boughs of a distant oak behind the beast. In that instant I recalled those bygone days spent serving as a bodyguard to the Iron Duke in Flanders, when I shadowed him through enemy-held forests and trained my eyes for the least sign of danger. In that instant I immediately recognized the plume of smoke as one which rose from the priming pan of an assassin's rifle.

My rifle fell to the ground as my hands reached for my steed's mane, with my raised knee meeting its back as I hurled myself at the chieftain's wife. I barely grasped the end of her mantle as the roar of a gunshot filled our ears. When we crashed to the ground, a howl left my lips as the talons of Dervila's sparrowhawk tore at my face. I beat away the wretched bird with my fists, as it attacked me from the arm of its mistress. Other birds also screeched overhead as they abandoned their branches in alarm. Many hands hauled me to my feet as kerns seized me from both shoulders and arms, with Nial's face appearing behind them as he beheld me in horror.

'What have you done, grey wolf?'

Blades nicked my throat and face as I trembled in the grip of rough hands, with the kerns baring their teeth at me like maddened wolves. Behind them a loud whinny was heard amid the cracking of branches, as Dervila's mount kicked the air in pain while the chieftain's wife was dragged away from its twisting haunches. Blood spurted from the shot wound in the horse's hind leg as the kerns hurled me against a tree, shouting at me in their tongue.

'Cén bhrí atá leis seo? An bhfuil tú gealtach? Íocfaidh tú as an eachtrannach craiceáilte seo!'

I was too dazed to even talk when the ollave appeared, screaming at the men while she gestured at the distant cloud of smoke.

'Scoirfidh tú amadán duit agus faigh fear an ghunna!'

The grip of the kerns was instantly released at her cry, and at Muireann's order they backed away from me and ran towards the hillock to find the hidden assassin. Meanwhile Dervila's gallowglass guards finally caught up with their mistress. A look of amazement replaced their stoic expressions as they found her on her knees, weeping and wailing as she placed a trembling hand upon the muzzle of her mortally wounded horse. At Muireann's impassioned pleas she eventually allowed for it to be slaughtered. As I gazed at the hole in the mount's left hock, I could not help thinking that I had myself been the target of the mysterious marksman.

XXIII

ROSCLOGHER TO DUNCARBERY TO GRANGE, COUNTY LEITRIM

10-18 October 1588

We returned from the forest along Dartry's eastern border towards dusk. Upon entering Manglana's town there we were met by great cheers from the usual gathering of townsfolk, who marvelled at the prizes from the forest which the hunting party bore with it. Yet their queen was quick to vanish from view. For although she had managed the ride back unassisted, she had turned pale as a ghost following her tumble.

At first it was thought that the loss of Dervila's horse was the cause of her pallor, yet it was soon suspected that she might have suffered some injury from her fall. As soon as we reached the town, O'Ronayne was instantly summoned away from the annals he was scrawling on sheets of vellum, to come to Dervila's aid. He swiftly rushed to her side in the lakeside cabin of one of her retainers, where he spent close to half a day caring for his queenly patron.

I was myself preoccupied with my own injuries, for the hawk's scratches on my face bled freely, so that at times I could barely see anything upon our homeward ride. By the time the town was reached, my right forearm was red from wiping my bloodied face. The bondsman led me to the infirmary, where someone proceeded to rinse my face with water.

After the dried blood was wiped from my eyes and cheeks with a damp rag, a poultice with a distinct scent of honey was applied to my face. I sighed with relief when my sight was returned, and I could also make out one of the Jesuit's attendants. When I was about to touch my face, my wrist was snatched by Nial who stood at my shoulder.

'Do not touch it, grey wolf. The poultice will help your wounds to heal.'

After a fitful sleep I was told the next morning that I could return to the outhouse. I was relieved to be so swiftly freed from the infirmary, so that I was almost grateful for the rain and freezing wind outside while I trudged back towards the outhouse. I ignored the natives peering at me behind their curtains, although I was later to learn the true cause of their awe. That evening the bondsman told me about a stupid rumour which someone had started among the tribe, that I had attacked a wolf with my bare hands when my aim had failed me. My blood boiled in indignation when I learned of this, for there was no meaner slight to be cast upon a marksman than to question his aim.

Yet my host soon learned the truth of what had truly passed during the damned wolf chase, so that the following day I was brought before Manglana himself to recount my version of events in his hall.. The question which most piqued the chieftain's curiousity was how I had learned of the assassin's whereabouts. As I stood in front of the highborn freemen gathered in the hall, I told them of the days when I had been assigned to the bodyguard of the Duke of Alba. While I spoke, I could see that they had assumed that same reverential expression which I had last seen when telling them of the events of the Armada.

After listening to my explanation the chieftain ordered that his hall be vacated. When the last highborn freeman left the chamber, I was left standing before Manglana, his bard and the bondsman, while the hearth crackled alongside us. Once freed from the eyes of his retainers, Manglana's shoulders sagged as he stretched his legs out before him. His speech also flowed freely, as he asked me how I thought we could better safeguard his person.

'Mayhap thy concern for thy safety is overly zealous, sire,' I replied, 'for thy people spend all their time mastering fighting skills when not devising raids on thy enemies. Furthermore, thy closest retainers have sworn death on all Sassanas, and all are dependent on thee for their protection.'

In vain did I air these thoughts, for Manglana was not swayed by my arguments. He fixed me with a hard stare and spoke the words which at last prompted me to provide the advice which he sought.

'Imagine that I was your Iron Duke, Alba. What would thou suggest for his safety?'

My recommendations were followed to the letter. From that day on one of the chieftain's bluejackets was always em-

ployed to taste the meat prepared for him, or any other food
brought up from the kitchen in the tower house. Every building and cabin was searched by bodyguards before Manglana
entered it, including the abbey of Saint Mel. His household
kerns were also advised to shield his person whenever they
passed a high promontory within range of any missiles which
might be fired.

The immediate outcome of these measures was to cause rumours of conspiracy to infiltrate the tribe, so that the highborn freemen began to travel in large groups through the
town, casting nervous glances about them as they stepped
through the tamped down lanes. It bothered me to see such
suspicious behaviour taking over the townsfolk, since it somewhat reduced the carefree innocence that I had first observed
among them. I also questioned the influence I was having on
them.

After all, I was convinced that the hidden assassin during
the wolf hunt had me in his sights and not Dervila. I also suspected that the gallowglass Constable, Donal MacCabe, had
a hand in the whole ugly episode. My own convictions were
reinforced when Nial finally discovered his horseboy Torcall
two days after the wolf hunt, hidden behind a bale of hay in
the stables with a huge welt across his cheek. At first the boy
was too shaken to speak, so that it took all of the bondsman's
and my coaxing, together with a fair few horn of usquebaugh,
to finally loosen his tongue. He told us that after he had left
us in the company of Lady Bourke, he had hastened to the
ringfort to relay our message that we were to form part of the
wolf hunt.

After performing this duty, Torcall was looking forward to a day without many chores, when he was snatched up by one of the gallowglasses who had spotted him speaking to the kerns on the green. The boy was dragged off before the gallowglass constable, who had taken up comfortable lodgings in one of the larger cabins along the lake, which was owned by an unfortunate aristocrat.

A few savage blows from MacCabe's men soon had Torcall crying out more information than a town herald, which was when the gallowglass constable learned that Nial and I had been invited by Dervila to join in her wolf hunt. Torcall was next hurled out the hut after being warned not to breathe a word of anything which had befallen him. The Scottish redshanks had filled him with the fear of God, and I did not envy the horseboy for the treatment he had received in a hut crowded with deadly gallowglass warriors.

No sooner did Torcall share this tale with us than he fell to his knees and wept, begging us not to repeat anything he had said if we valued his life. Both Nial and I were swift to allay his fears, but we exchanged concerned glances as we patted him on the shoulder and served him with more drink. I also realised that the shot which broke the leg of Dervila's steed could have easily been fired using one of the snaphaunce muskets owned by the gallowglasses. In any event, it was clear that any suspicion which we raised about the redshanks could only do more harm than good, especially given Manglana's reliance on them for defence and the impossibility of proving that one of the constable's henchmen had fired the shot.

Although the attempt on Dervila's life had led Manglana to become more suspicious of his own retainers, the ollave's wariness around me seemed to have eased. I was not sure whether this was caused by my attempt to rescue Lady Bourke, or her learning of my previous association with the Duke of Alba. Yet her eyes were no longer averted from me whenever our paths crossed in the narrow corridors of the tower house at Rosclogher during my visits to the chieftain.

The lady Mac an Bhaird even went as far as to acknowledge me with a swiftly withdrawn stare. Yet she was as skittish as a deer if I attempted conversation, as she quickly vanished into the darkness of the keep. This behaviour left me feeling confused, for since my arrival in Rosclogher I had never traded a single word with the person most responsible for my escape from the Sassanas.

So my interaction with her was restricted to these fleeting nods of the head, or else occasional sightings of her along the banks of the lake, where she would teach the children of the *Feni* a number of history-poems by rote. As she spoke, her younger charges beheld her intently as if she encompassed their whole world, dutifully repeating the phrases she had taught them whilst she observed them patiently. Muireann would reward their efforts with a gentle smile before assuming a severe expression once more.

I was often a silent witness to these exchanges, for whenever the gallowglasses left Rosclogher I felt safe enough to wander down to the edge of the lake. Upon arriving there, I would amuse myself with the sight of the goings on along the water's edge. These included Muireann teaching her pupils, or the distant attempts of tribesmen upon their crafts who struck the water with three pronged spears, as they availed themselves of the last of the autumn fishing. At times they would wander past me after returning to land, holding up their spotted catches which were the colour of silver and gold.

One day I was surprised to find that I could understand snatches of the ollave's words and also the cries of the men on the boats. I was particularly pleased, since they were not Gaelic words which Nial sometimes translated for me during our evening conversations.

I have weapons and the ring, I thought to myself, *now all I need to flee Ireland is to learn the language and to wait until spring.*

Life had long taught me that such idyllic times of tranquillity were never likely to last forever, and the other Spaniards in the town soon made sure of that. Their time spent among the Dartrymen enabled them to recover their health, yet their idleness did not lead to much good. This was disappointing to me, for I had hoped that a peaceful coexistence might be achieved. After all, the shepherd boys from the Canary Islands joined the Irish in their trolling for trout in the lake, as keenly as if they were fishing in the rivers and streams of their own land.

Yet the others refused to integrate at all with their protectors, with most instead choosing to skulk sullenly about the town while searching for whores and mischief. At times I would reluctantly find myself among their company, when some complained that their beef was half cooked while others moaned about the weather. Their talk of their plans to return to Spain was quelled whenever a highborn tribesman came within earshot, only for their grumbling to resume when the native walked away, with further complaints being aired about the savage ways of the Irish which they were desperate to flee.

Whenever this ingratitude was shared with me, I quietly nodded my head to avoid any inevitable arguments. However, I could not help thinking that these same complaining Spaniards had reached Dartry less than two weeks earlier with stick-like limbs and large beseeching eyes. Most had been ailed by untreated wounds or were left dumbstruck from blows they had received on their journey north from all manner of heartless robbers. Which was why I was baffled by the ungrateful attitude of the surviving castaways, despite their being spared a grisly end by the protection which was extended to us by Manglana.

Indeed, Dartry had offered us all manner of treatment and assistance. For not only were we Spaniards fed and clothed, but our dignity had also been restored through the friendship extended to us by the tribesmen. Following their recovery, each Spaniard had also been escorted to the tower-house and greeted in the chieftain's hall. Their words were translated by Nial or the Jesuit to the highborn *Feni*, who always hungered for tidings of events beyond the borders of Dartry, regardless of whether they were borne by a cowherd or a newsboy.

When finding themselves alone before Manglana's assembly, the Spaniards were always timid and feigned cordial behavior. Which led the *derbfine* to regard them almost longingly when they spoke, as if wondering what their own lives would be like if they also hailed from Iberia. Yet I was not as easily taken in, for I knew from my time spent in the army that it would only be a matter of time before the Dartrymen began to loathe all Spaniards. After all, I had often heard the natives grumble about the arrogance and uncouth manners of the gallowglasses whenever the Scots passed through the town, yet this behaviour would inevitably prove to be small beer, when compared to the galling, blinding arrogance of the troops of Imperial Spain.

As expected, four of my fellow castaways quickly turned haughty and arrogant, the moment they were recovered from shock and fatigue. None returned any of their hosts' affections or interests, since they openly derided the Dartrymen or laughed at their ways. They were full of bravado when in the company of one another, strutting about the town as if they were in the backstreets of some port town or city again, trying to catch the eye of some female companion. As I quietly watched them, I surmised that such a band of tosspots would be fortunate to secure the attentions of a starving, toothless whore from the gutter, who might still request advance payment from them.

Yet among the Dartrymen, these Spaniards could scarce believe their luck. For some of the Irish lasses were astir at the sight of them, with the less bashful among them shamelessly fluttered their eyelids at the exotic southerners. On their part, the Spaniards met these glances with sly winks, which seemed enough to snare some of the witless, worshipping lasses. Eventually the Spaniards did not have to stray far from their squalid lodgings to seek out fresh prey, as at dusk their huts were already full of squeals and ragged breaths. One night the gambolling reached such heights that one of the huts collapsed, with its occupants scurrying to the remaining cabin which housed other Spaniards, amid loud screams and snorts of laughter.

I also felt sorry for these unfortunate maidens, for many of them were all but pushed towards the Spaniards by their parents and close relations. Most of these relatives were blinded by their belief in the deliverance that Spain could provide them. It therefore always proved a fruitful jaunt for the five unscrupulous castaways, whenever they strode through the huts during rainless evenings, all the while humming obscene airs. Although many waved and called out to them, the sole intention of the band of foreigners was to seek out and cavort with young women, few of whom could resist their advances. Sometimes, the four Spaniards would head over to the cabins of mad Orla, exchanging their remaining winnings of tallow candles and dried meats for trysts with the lunatic's daughters who were the resident whores of the town.

When they were not on the prowl, they were to be found in two derelict huts on the periphery of Manglana's town which fast became their dens of iniquity. There they cheated the natives at cards and dice, before squandering their winnings on usquebaugh and wine. On rare occasions one of the Spaniards would lose, which encouraged the Dartrymen to take up their game, although this often occurred due to the dice not being properly loaded, or there having been too many dog ears and creases on the end of cards.

Inevitably the natives received their wins with loud cries of relief and hefty pats on the back, which prompted their Catholic allies to cajole them into another game in which the Irish were swindled once more. On one occasion the offer to resume a game would be turned down by a Dartryman, who would demand that the stakes be paid. This request was always met with promises that were never honoured, which in time greatly distressed the townsfolk who honoured their verbal agreements as if they were written contracts.

This overall attitude did little to endear the castaways to their hosts, so that I knew that trouble would soon erupt. This was not long in coming, what with the Spaniards still having their way with those bolder, younger lasses who were swept away by their swarthy looks. Yet when the women finally also tired of the Spaniards, the general mood of the tribe quickly turned when the Spaniards began to force themselves upon some of the reluctant maidens.

One of them, a corpulent thug named Juande, even started to violate the women with blows. On another occasion he also attempted to have his way with a lass at sundown, causing her to flee across the green while she screamed her head off. Nial and I ceased from our sparring as she ran into the arms of the startled bondsman. As the burly Spaniard ran after her I stepped forward to check his pursuit. He barely dodged the full force of my right fist before we were tugging at each other's tunics and hair upon the grass, as our knees wildly struck out at each other's groins. Unfortunately our desperate tussle was the firebrand which sparked off a whole brawl across the green, with his fellow Spaniards getting into a fist fight with the Irish kerns from the ringfort who were alerted by Nial's cries.

The savage fracas was finally quelled by the appearance of the tanist Cathal the Black. Nial fetched me a poultice from the infirmary to apply to a swollen eye, as we made our way back to the outhouse near the abbey. Along the way I limped past the ollave and a group of other nobles, who all cast me lingering stares as I turned my eyes to the ground, flustered by my torn clothes and my dishevelled appearance. Although the scene we had caused greatly shamed me, it set me apart in the eyes of the natives from the callous band of Spaniards which they hosted. My good manners were also not lost upon the Gaels, which granted me privileges like the relative privacy of the outhouse, which were denied to my fellow countrymen.

Some knowledge of the Dartrymen's tongue also helped to further ingratiate me with the tribesmen. During the weeks I spent amongst the tribe, I always strove to drop Gaelic words into my conversation with the townsfolk at every opportunity, to their great joy. However my exalted position did not make putting up with the Spanish quartet's insolence any easier, and I sometimes wished that Manglana would throw them out of his kingdom. On one occasion they even greeted the bondsman with insults and jibes, while he was busy serving them with food. I was outraged by their rudeness and made towards them menacingly as Nial seized me by the arm with a smile.

'There is no need for that, grey wolf, I have endured worse. For I served in the Spanish Netherlands, remember? Besides, my Lord MacGlannagh has ordered that they be treated as honoured guests and should not be harmed.'

'You are too good to them,' I seethed, 'you should hurl them out of here.'

'Orders are orders,' he smiled, 'regardless of how we feel.'

His words did little to cool my rage, yet I nodded back at him ruefully, while knowing that Irishmen – like all other non-Spanish peoples – often met with much derision and scorn by their Spanish allies, who often referred to them as

'Irish beggars'. It made my blood boil to think that the scum were treated so well by the Dartrymen, and in time it was devilishly hard to restrain myself further. For the Spaniards soon turned their attentions from the natives to me, as they proceeded to harass me for money. Most of them seemed certain that I had been paid for teaching marksmanship to the chieftain's troops.

'I have not made half a *maravedí* worth spitting on!' I would shout at them.

Yet my protestations were of no avail, as they insulted me for being a miserly Jew. They also issued tirades of blasphemy within earshot of O'Ronayne, leaving the Jesuit to cross himself in disbelief as the colour drained from his face. Yet anything I said fell on deaf ears, with the fools refusing to accept that the Dartrymen only dealt in barter.

This attitude left me to seek to avoid the other Spaniards' company at all times. One day I caught sight of my reflection when walking along the banks of the lake and noticed that my bedraggled hair had become so long, that it also covered the slight bald patch on the crown of my head. I realised that my appearance was not dissimilar to that of an Irishman, and the cold autumn weather meant that the olive tinge was also leaving my skin, since recent weeks had left me looking a lot paler.

Eventually the behaviour of my fellow Iberians became so foul, that I thought I might soon have to hazard an escape in winter. A recent attack by Juande on a highborn woman had the chieftain's assembly swiftly gathering in the great hall at Rosclogher. A heated debate ensued as to whether the Spaniards should be kept any longer, and to my great annoyance the chieftain ordered that I also be present at the discussion. As always Nial stood at my side, translating most of what was said into Spanish, while the constable MacCabe went off on his usual rant. Although I felt uncomfortable because of the vicinity of the fierce gallowglasses, my spirits were raised by the presence of the tanist Cathal *Dubh* and the warmth of the best hearth in Rosclogher.

'Besides, it is too risky to keep them any longer,' protested Donal, 'the Sasseanchs will already be furious.'

The tanist Cathal *Dubh* shrugged, as he stood with a band of his noble retainers alongside the hearth.

'Our enemies may be as angry as they please, it is no concern of ours.'

Donal sneered at him with twisted lips.

'It will be our concern if Dublin turns its eye on us. Mark my words, Cathal *Dubh*, these Spaniards are more trouble than they are worth.'

Throughout their conversation the chieftain regarded them solemnly, with Dervila's seat vacant beside them. I was reminded of her by the red locks of Aengus's son Lochlain, who stood before his grandfather wearing a forlorn expression. My attention returned to the chieftain's face when at last he spoke.

'These Spaniards have caused no end of bother, yet something tells me that we will not regret harbouring them, that our kindness towards them shall eventually be repaid. We should keep them for as long as they wish to stay with us. Furthermore, our enemy will not venture forth before the fighting season commences, when they might prove most useful to us. What say you, grey wolf? Does the fighting ability of your comrades warrant their keeping?'

'These Spaniards must be shown a firm hand,' I replied, 'for with a leader they would also be trouble, but without one they are even worse behaved. Yet if it comes to a fight with the heretic, you will be hard pressed to see greater valour than these men will display, for hard fighting is in their blood.'

My response was debated at length, until a vote was also taken, in which it was narrowly decided not to banish the Spanish troublemakers. This was due in no small part to Cathal's strong backing of my words, in which he dismissed Donal as a dotard for wanting to dispense with the world's best fighting men who had landed upon the doorstep of Rosclogher.

'Furthermore', said the tanist, 'the mountain passes and high places will be treacherous, for they will be attacked by wolves and claimed by the frost.'

The resolve of the tribe to shelter the Spaniards was soon to be further tested by events happening outside and not just within Darty. One rainless afternoon I was sitting along the banks of the lake, observing Miler the harpist stringing a lyre when Nial approached us with an anxious bearing. The bondsman's mouth was awkwardly creased and he had a wild cast in his eyes. He breathed a sigh of relief when he spotted me along the water.

'The heavens be praised! There you are, grey wolf. I have looked for you everywhere.'

'Whatever is the matter?'

'A grey merchant from Sligo has brought the chieftain a message from the heretics. The enemy has requested a parley with our lord.'

My blood ran cold at the mention of the enemy's desire to meet with my protector. A swirl of thoughts and fears instantly clouded my mind as I stuttered in reply.

'A...parley?'

'Yes. The chieftain is to assemble a party that is to ride out and meet with the enemy on the Tuesday. He has asked you to attend. In disguise.'

Try as I might, it was nearly impossible to conceal my anxiety at the prospective meeting with the Sassanas. I feared that the hidden ring might finally be revealed to my host, which would dash all the trust and respect which I had earned from him.

'Why do they request a parley', I growled, 'when they raid the land at every opportunity?'

'Who can tell until we ride out to meet them?'

I fell silent, fearing that an excessive show of alarm on my part might raise suspicions with the bondsman.

'But are we to trust their word?'

Nial's scowl was as dark as a thundercloud.

'Never.'

He picked up my rifle from the ground and thrust it into my hands, serving me with a stare of great severity as my fingers closed about it.

'We have heard that the man leading the band of Sassanas is the sergeant Treasach Burke. He is the cur who marked you in the dungeons of Sligo, who gave you and Muireann the chase. Our scouts shall keep watch on his party the moment they leave the gates of their garrison town, and every care has been taken by our assembly when choosing the meeting place.'

'And what renders this meeting a concern of mine?'

'The rules of parley must be observed, but only insofar as our enemy has observed them. My Lord MacGlannagh has ordered that as soon as the white flag is lowered, or any treachery or brutality attempted, you must rid us of the renegade sergeant. For he is not only a cruel soldier but also a skilled tracker, who serves as a great boon to our enemy the sheriff.'

'Is the MacGlannagh to lead our party?'

Nial snorted loudly at my question.

'Our chieftain's life should not be risked for petty meetings with the agents of the enemy. And he has ordered Dervila and Muireann not to join it either, although they are travelling to Breifne to attend a bardic contest there, hosted by our overlord the O'Rourke. The *tánaiste* Cathal *Dubh* shall lead the party in his stead.'

The thought of this impending meeting greatly disturbed me, so that I almost considered fleeing Manglana's kingdom for the open country. Word of it swiftly spread across Manglana's town while the chieftain summoned a rising out. He sent fleet-footed runners across the land to call upon men from the wandering creaghts to join the party that was to meet with the English.

In the next two days, the sight of fully armed kerns appearing in the town became a common one, with a score of them being hosted along the lake within two days of the chieftain's summons. During one of our sparring sessions, I told the bondsman that it was a sizeable number which had appeared at such short notice. Nial's expression barely changed as he parried a sidewards thrust of my wooden waster, as easily as if he were swotting one of the midges along the lake's edge.

'It is common enough practice among us for Lord Mac-Glannagh to host an *oenach*, so long as it is just. Parleying for war or peace is viewed as a legally binding summons, which must be observed by all. Strength in numbers at a parley also serves to impress the strength of our lord upon the enemy.'

My grip on my sword pommel slackened when he also proceeded to tell me that strength in numbers was also required since parleys were known to be dishonoured by the Sassanas.

'One of the worst violations was carried out by an English earl only ten years ago,' said the bondsman, 'for he ambushed an Irish lord's war band while the latter was riding towards their agreed place of parley. It is for this reason that we must travel in force.'

Nial left Rosclogher with his horseboy at dawn the next morning to teach swordsmanship to a tuath in the east of Dartry. Yet his revelation rendered my sleep fitful for the remaining days, with my aim during my hours of target practice being worse than usual. When the fateful day of the encounter finally dawned, the number of kerns who had appeared to join the tanist's band had already doubled. A large band of warriors was also gathered at the door of the abbey of Saint Mel. These were the highborn cavalrymen, whose numbers had been swollen by the riders from Manglana's chief seat at Duncarbery.

After O'Ronayne delivered a mass to commemorate the feast of the evangelist, we readied to commence our march towards our meeting with the enemy. I trudged over to the outhouse to gather my rifle and other gear, secretly cursing the grey merchants from Sligo who had arranged for the parley to take place. In the doorway of my abode, I found a horseboy snoring with his head rested over his knees. He awoke with a start when I loudly cleared my throat, then he ran off to fetch me a steed from the stables.

Thereafter I rode towards the green where the tanist's men were gathered. When his whole force was assembled, Cathal raised his arm to the chieftain who had stood motionless with a small coterie of retainers and attendants before the town. This served as the signal for us to depart, with my mantle pulled closely over my face as we made off.

I was overcome by such a black mood that I barely acknowledged a wave from Muireann's son Lochlain. The grey sky was not an encouraging portent, with my spirits further dulled by my having to ride alongside Donal MacCabe and his troop of gallowglass mercenaries. They formed an iron rearguard to the tanist's force and swelled our number to over a hundred strong. Cathal also had a fifer and a drummer keeping his men in step. Before him a herald bore the coat of arms of Manglana's house, made up of two red lions upon a crisp, white banner.

The tanist himself was flanked by the Jesuit O'Ronayne and Echna, the tribe's revered Brehon judge. Our journey did not last two hours, for after reaching Duncarbery castle we kept to a beaten path which stretched along the coast from north to south. It was the closest thing to a main thoroughfare in Dartry, being the main passage between the territories of the powerful O'Donnels of Ulster and the O'Connors of Sligo.

After a time spent travelling with the high mountain range to our left and surrounded by billowing rushes and moorland, we arrived at a meeting place which was not far from where I had been shipwrecked. To our left the great rise of Arroo Mountain seemed to dominate the whole sky amid the beats of the drum and the shrill sounds from the fife. As the grass about us grew higher, our hair was soon ruffled by sea gales as we saw the distant grey periphery of the ocean.

I shuddered at the sight of the water, as I recalled the great suffering which had been experienced aboard the Santa María de Visión and the terrors which I had endured thereafter. The memory of the dungeons of Sligo left me wondering why I was heading in the direction of an enemy I had been both desperate and most fortunate to escape. Then the face of Treasach Burke reappeared in my mind, a vivid memory which stirred a great rage within me. I suddenly found myself greatly desirous for revenge, so that I dug my ankles into the flanks of Gilson's destrier. I was keen to put a ball through the head of the cur who had flogged and tormented me in the depths of Sligo castle.

We next forded a river and left the range of heights behind us, while ahead of us the flat-topped peak of Ben Bulben rose like the crest of a green wave which was about to collapse. Thereafter the road twisted past a cluster of hillocks, until we spotted Grange in the distance, with its the hive-shaped huts made of wicker and wood. The settlement marked the southernmost boundary of Manglana's kingdom. It was also the location agreed by both parties, given the ease with which they could each retreat back into the lands over which they held sway.

Being on the edge of Manglana's land was a double-edged sword for the inhabitants who dwelt in the village. For although there was much trade that could be afforded to travellers who passed through it, it also meant that visits from rebels and royalists alike were not uncommon, given the ever-shifting border of Dartry. Which in turn meant that a fair portion of what was earned had to be given up to whichever force decided to turn up in the town.

Due to this tortuous reality, the O'Hartes of Grange were ever quick to defend themselves, so that a force of kerns instantly appeared at our approach. At the sight of them Cathal *Dubh* rested his knee upon his mount's back, lifting himself above the riders that flanked him as he waved his hand and called a halt.

The men and mounts in our party were motionless as the tanist next called out to the foreign tribesmen before him. Thereafter there followed an uneasy wait until an elderly man appeared, whose long flowing beard revealed him to be someone of great import. He stepped through the bristling guards who had gathered in our path to exchange terse words with the tanist. Cathal finally dismounted as the chief of the settlement bowed low before him. While I observed these proceedings from my saddle, I noticed the Jesuit kicking his horse towards me. He reined his steed near mine and whispered to me with a severe expression.

'When we pass through the village, stay close to me.'

'Why?' I asked.

'Just do as I say,' he answered, with obvious irritation in his voice, while nervous laughter was heard from the tanist and the elder from Grange.

'What are they talking about?' I asked, nodding towards them.

255

'The tanist Cathal has assured O'Harte that we come in peace,' said O'Ronayne, 'and O'Harte has acknowledged the dominion of our lord MacGlannagh over these lands.'

I was later to learn that the O'Hartes had been given possession of Grange by the O'Connors of Sligo, and held onto it despite the troubles caused by the Sassanas in Connacht. The elderly O'Harte's salutation was but a formality, yet one that was necessary in order for us to pass through the town. As the men in the tanist's party prepared to follow Cathal, the Jesuit climbed off his steed, bidding me to do the same. I followed him closely as we entered the village.

We ignored the tribesmen who scowled at us through the doorways of their huts. As we followed their aged leader through the settlement, I made out a huge edifice which rose above the other dwellings about it. It was the largest building in Grange, and at the sight of it O'Ronayne suddenly grabbed me by the arm and slipped off into a narrow passageway.

Two rugged kerns scampered after us, having evidently shared a previous understanding with the Jesuit. I stumbled after O'Ronayne in silence, until we came to the large structure which had caught my attention. Upon leaving the huts at our backs, I could see that it was in fact built upon a tall base of rock which was a head above us. This indicated that the wooden building above it was a large granary, which had been erected upon a high stone base so as to protect its contents from rats and other vermin.

I remembered one of the tribesmen telling me at Rosclogher that the village of Grange got its name from *Grainseach*, which was the word for 'granary' in the Irish tongue. It was a building which had long since fallen into disrepair, for some of the wooden planks in its structure hung sideways like the broken ribs on a carcass. There was no grain within it, and it held a faint stink of rotting wood and excrement. I turned to the Jesuit with a look of confusion, while he beheld me with a hopeful smile.

'Why did you lead us here, priest?'

His curled forefinger straightened as he pointed above his head, and for a moment his eyes widened in wonder.

'Here you can commence your climb to the top. That shall serve as your vantage point.'

I turned back to stare at the building in shock. It was a large structure almost three storeys high, built of rotted planks of wood which had been nailed against vertical poles. I noted that a fall from the top of the structure might not be fatal, although it could well break one's limbs. With an inward curse, I turned back to the prelate and voiced my concern.

'That structure could not support a mouse, let alone a man. I would have more luck attempting to scale a thatched mud hut at Rosclogher.'

For a few moments O'Ronayne said nothing, although his lower lip trembled in outrage and his face assumed a violet hue. After finally regaining some composure, he managed a reply.

'Ne Dourough has told you of our Lord's orders. The roof of this granary is the only place of vantage in this vicinity. It is why Grange was proposed for this parley.'

With a loud curse of annoyance, I turned back towards the wretched building and stepped closer to its base of rock. I reached above me and pushed one of the poles, finding it to be sturdy enough for a likely climb. Behind me the two kerns had fallen to their knees and clasped each other's hands, and with a nod of gratitude I allowed them to give me a leg up. My fingers slipped through the spaces of the lowest planks overhead as I grasped the bottommost wood and hauled myself towards the roof. I was surprised by my agility throughout my climb, which reminded me of the days spent skirmishing in the service of Spain.

With each step up I tugged at the planks above me before I climbed them, with my rifle and my pack dangling wildly from my shoulders. As I glanced over my shoulder, the Jesuit appeared a lot smaller, yet my smugness at managing the ascent swiftly dissipated when the two kerns clambered ahead of me.

After the two Dartrymen reached the top of the structure before me, I ignored their outstretched hands and heaved myself onto the top of the granary. After collapsing upon one of the beams, I drew a deep breath before rising on all fours. The roof had a rickety appearance, with gaping holes through the rafters where the straw had not been replaced. Below us the figure of the Jesuit could be seen making his way back towards the tanist's party, which had already crossed the town and was assembling upon a plain at the southern side of the village.

To my right the distant outlines of islands could be made out, which reminded me of the lee in which the ships of the Armada had been berthed. A shudder ran through me as I recalled the fierce storm in which I had lost Maerten, when the three Spanish galleys were smashed against the beach. I averted my gaze from the sea and trained my eyes on the area beyond Cathal's party, feeling further discomfited when

I made out the distant silhouette of Sligo and the large, flat-topped hill behind it.

I returned my attention to proceedings below me, noting that the O'Hartes had already withdrawn back into their village. Meanwhile Cathal's kerns sat cross-legged upon the ground in small circles, stroking their beards and playing dice amid the odd argument and cry of laughter. The gallowglasses kept to themselves as they always did, while the cavalrymen dismounted and gathered about Cathal, who seemed to be intently listening to their words. I could see that O'Ronayne had already returned to the tanist's side, with the Jesuit casting wary glances in the direction of Sligo, along with Echna the *Brehon* judge.

I withstood the stench of the granary for close to an hour, until a sign of the enemy's advance was finally noted. Across the plain, one of the tanist's barefoot scouts was seen sprinting towards Cathal's men. His haste was so great that I barely managed to prime my rifle and swing the doghead about, when the boy blurted a snatch of breathless words at the cavalrymen, all the while pointing a shaking finger behind him.

The tanist instantly ordered the kerns to return to their feet, with their swords a quarter drawn and their spears held aloft. Meanwhile the horseboys among the tanist's band hurried towards the highborn with their steeds in tow. The gallowglass constable Donal MacCabe was already mounted, with his gallowglass footmen also back on their feet and their ugly axes held before them.

A loud bugle blast echoed in the distance as the obscure shadows of distant riders rapidly approached the tanist's men.

One of the kerns beside me gasped when the great host came into view. Great, white pennons quivered in the gale, with each of them bearing a red cross. Over fifty horsemen rumbled into full view, while I cursed myself for having partaken of the mad enterprise.

As if to further confirm their greater strength of arms, a square of infantry followed the cavalry, armed with shot and pike. Even the meanest footsoldier bore a breastplate and a steel helmet, with a stout sword belted to their hip. All of the Sassanas also had an iron shield strapped to their back, which bore the colours of Saint George. In the settlement below me, a few of the O'Hartes could be seen creeping out of their huts to catch a glimpse of the impressive and demoralising sight of the English force. At the sight of the approaching militia, a few of these tribesmen seized their faces in despair, while a few also hurried out of the village and struck the open country.

A great unease seized me when the foremost Sassana rode into view, with his helmet borne in his gauntleted hand. Treasach Burke grinned widely at Cathal's gathering, appearing none the worse for wear since our last encounter. His breastplate shone with a cold lustre when he reined in his steed and bowed before the tanist, who did not return the salutation.

My blood boiled at the sight of the renegade sergeant, as my heart battered my breast like a door knocker and anxious breathing seized me which released great puffs of mist. I did my best to stem the tell-tale breaths while I centred my sights on Burke's head. My forefinger hovered over the serpentine, itching to draw it back and fire the ball that would blow the sergeant's head off. Yet a white flag fluttered from the raised lance of one of his retainers, which left my finger wavering over the wheellock's trigger.

'Chuir mo Thiarna Mac Fhlannchaidh chugam freagra a thabhairt ar do thoghairm. Cad é atá á lorg agat, a nathair?'

Cathal spoke in a tone that was both harsh and stiff, while the sergeant observed him with a hateful grin. For although Irish was Burke's first language, its use had been outlawed by the English Crown in the parliament of Dublin, so that his utterance of it would have greatly displeased his heretical masters. Furthermore, many of the troopers in Sergeant Burke's phalanx were of English background, who probably found it hard enough to follow an Irish renegade without having to also listen to him speaking in the Irish vernacular.

Of course, none of the Irish rebels would learn or speak English, which meant that the impasse could only be countered through the use of Latin. It was Burke who first attempted it, and before long the faint voices of both the tanist and the renegade sergeant carried across the plain towards the village.

'Greetings, my lord MacGlannagh,' said Burke with a deep bow, 'thou hast my thanks for riding to our meeting. May I also congratulate thee on thy recent ascension to *tánaiste*.'

'The base compliments of a fawning serpent mean nothing to me,' replied Cathal tersely, 'what is the purpose of thy master's summons?'

The grin on Burke's face wavered slightly, with any hope that the meeting might be cordial being swiftly extinguished by the tanist's hostile reply.

''tis in relation to a request made by Sheriff George Bingham to thy master,' replied the sergeant. 'Is Lord MacGlannagh on his way to our meeting?'

So saying, he cocked his head sideways and peered past Cathal towards the village behind the Dartrymen.

'Or perhaps he takes refreshment in the village?'

Cathal snorted aloud.

'Speak to me, cur, as if thou were speaking to him. For thou art but a lowly sergeant, who is fortunate to be addressing me directly. Thy master lacketh the courtesy to at least send a high-ranking officer to treat with me, although your friend Lieutenant John Gilson hath done well not to show his face before me. For I would shred him to pieces after the foul outrage which he committed against my lord's son. Now share thy master's request or haste thee back to thy misbelieving owners forthwith.'

'Sheriff George Bingham demands that you surrender the Spaniards that you shelter.'

'What Spaniards?'

Burke shook his head as a cynical smile danced upon his lips, which sickened me to my stomach.

'Let us not quibble over what we both know to be true. After all, my lord, we each have our own spies. A little bird has told the sheriff of the Spaniards that thy lord harbours.'

Some of the troopers behind him sniggered, prompting Burke to smirk at them before returning his attention to the tribesmen.

'The orders from Dublin have been clear. No one is to aid and succour the enemies of the Crown, upon pain of death. It therefore follows, that by the Viceroy's decree, you are all dead men.'

A loud guffaw was heard from the constable, Donal Mac-Cabe, as he kicked his horse alongside the tanist's. Although he was ignorant in Latin, his short prelate translated the exchange to him. The moment the gallowglass' derisory laugh was heard, O'Ronayne roared aloud, unable to rein in his indignation.

'Except that we are not dead men!'

Burke stared askance at the Jesuit, his eyes widening as he raised a finger in correction.

'Not *yet*. One does ill to spurn the rightful law of the Sassenachs. Indeed, 'tis a fortunate opportunity for you to heed the sheriff's instruction, for it may well prove your last. You must give the Spaniards up to us dead or alive...'

'Thou darest to threaten -'

The Jesuit's next outburst was cut short when the tanist raised an outstretched palm to him. I hung on Burke's next words with bated breath, wary of how he would seek to undo the tribesmen's resolve.

'Indeed thou puts up a brave resistance, although one that will not be without its consequences. But you have something that the Viceroy in Dublin fears.'

O'Ronayne snorted.

'What could the Viceroy in Dublin possibly fear more, than the greed of his servants in Connacht?'

Peals of mocking laughter were heard from the Dartrymen at the Jesuit's words. For it had long been reported by Manglana's spies that the English Viceroy FitzWilliam in Dublin had strained relations with the sheriff of Sligo George Bingham, as well as the sheriff's elder brother Richard Bingham who was governor of Connacht. It was said that the Viceroy regarded the Bingham brothers as being a law unto themselves, and reports of their great brutality towards the Irish in defiance of his commands had further confirmed his suspicions.

This was not to mention FitzWilliam's reported great rage, upon learning that Richard and George Bingham had not surrendered all of the plunder from the Armada's wrecks to the Crown. The sniggers and chuckles from the Irishmen persisted while Burke shifted awkwardly in his saddle. Yet he did not betray the slightest annoyance while he waited for the sounds of mirth to subside, then addressed the tribesmen once more.

'With all the respect due to an outlaw, Lord Cathal: barefooted, warring cow rustlers should not joke about infighting among their English betters.'

The tanist fell silent at the jibe, while his highborn subalterns hurled all manner of abuse at the renegade, using insults and curse words that I had often heard in the infirmary from other invalids during my recovery. Their insults were next echoed by the kerns, with all manner of fist shaking and snarling taking place until Cathal rose in his stirrups and yelled at his men to be silent.

It was a timely intervention by the tanist, since I noticed that Burke's men had already drawn and primed their rifles. Yet the renegade sergeant did not so much as flinch as he appeared to bask in all the hate which was directed at him. The Dartrymen barely recovered their composure, when O'Ronayne's face turned scarlet while he shouted at the renegade from over the tanist's shoulder.

'Grovellor! Murderer! Lady Dervila Burke has bidden me to bear thee this message, that she spits on thy person and denies thee the use of thy family name!'

His words prompted Burke to engage in a laugh that was as distasteful as it was affected, sounding like the high-pitched whinny of a castrated hackney.

'Ah yes,' he finally replied, 'the Lady Dervila. I remember her when I was a boy attending my father's cows, riding haughtily past us. She never once afforded us a single glance or salutation. As always we bowed low to her before minding our cows which would be seized by the troops of her lord and father Seaán mac Oliver Bourke, curse his Papist heresy. I wonder how she fares these days, married as she is to an outlaw and a kinslayer.'

'Stay thy tongue, heretic!' roared the tanist, 'we shalt not hear thee sully the good name of our lord. He has never slain any kin! Nor hath thou any right to proclaim him an outlaw!'

'I speak nothing more than the truth,' snapped the sergeant, 'and all who follow him are lawbreakers. The ink on the Composition signed by his own hand is barely five years dry. He surrendered his lordship to the English Crown that regranted him his title.'

'That treaty was not worth the vellum it was scrawled upon!' howled O'Ronayne, 'for both parties had duties that your masters all too readily ignored! Your treaty sought to render us slaves in our own territory, for your sole desire is to rape our land and its people!'

''tis the price of civilisation,' replied Burke immediately.

''tis the price of butchery!' roared Cathal, who had finally lost his temper, 'as our lord's Brehon judge will attest, our laws afford one the right to disregard a fraudulent contract!'

'Verily, 'tis thus,' said Echna, who was mounted alongside the tanist's horse, and who had not so much as stirred until then.

The sergeant's head turned to face the Lady Judge before speaking up again.

'I will not be swayed by the words of a woman, less by ungodly lawyers that are known to be sworn enemies of the truth. All Brehons constantly deny the supremacy of the English queen, instead lending your learning to the service of tyranny. Thy master's agreement with the Binghams was written on vellum, in the best legal Latin. It is the MacGlannagh who ignored its terms. Any fraud that was committed sits at his door, not ours.'

As the meaning of his accusation sank in, Cathal's fierce kerns broke out into cries of rage again, while behind them the steel wall of the gallowglass stood almost motionless, with the Scots' axes held out before them and their feet defiantly set apart. The tanist's raised hand silenced the Dartrymen again, yet it was clear that a great anger had spread among both parties, which might have easily boiled over into a skirmish if the parley was not soon ended. As if also sensing this, Cathal *Dubh* raised his voice above the dwindling mutterings and half curses which lingered in the air.

'It appears that thy master's terms are to be ignored, cur. Haste ye back to Sligo like the base hound thou hast become.'

'Wait!' exclaimed Burke, with a hand raised towards Cathal, 'for thou hast not heard all that I have to tell thee.'

'Then speak swiftly, dog,' snarled the tanist, 'before this encounter ends in bloodshed!'

'As a gesture of good will,' replied the sergeant, 'the sheriff of Sligo requests that you hand over at least one Spaniard. Just one little Spaniard – he who goes by the name of Juan.'

My blood ran cold at his words, while my finger barely refrained from pulling the serpentine. From that distance I thought I made out O'Ronayne half turning towards my direction.

'I also hear tell that his aim is not poor,' said Burke.

There was less urgency in his voice, as the silence that followed betrayed the surprise of the Irish at his knowledge of recent events at Rosclogher. My finger fell upon the serpentine and quivered without control, as a great fear overcame me that the prize I concealed might be revealed. At last, the tanist finally spoke.

'Why this Spaniard in particular?'

'Less than a month ago, he killed one of my men in Sligo, after we granted him refuge. The casualty of our good charity was a kinsman of Sheriff Bingham, who greatly desires justice.'

'The men of your sheriff have robbed my lord of his son!' screamed O'Ronayne, as his face turned from red to purple, 'can he also render justice to us?!'

Burke cleared his throat awkwardly.

'Juan's excesses were not carried out in battle. He is a cold-blooded murderer and a danger to all men.'

I hissed aloud at these lies, when Cathal piped up indignantly in a voice that was thick with scorn.

'What does this Juan look like?'

'His nose is broken...'

'What use is that to us?!' barked O'Ronayne, so loudly that his horse stirred, 'nearly every whiskered man fits that description!'

A burst of laughter was heard from the highborn Dartrymen, which echoed among the standing kerns when its meaning was translated to them. Burke smiled wryly at the Jesuit's words, until he spoke again in a voice which was thick with sarcasm.

'His hairline has thinned about the forehead, and a shaggy mane of saltpetre hangs about his neck. His back is striped, and he bears the mark of the spider upon his left breast.'

I bit my lip while my arms slightly trembled, when yet another indignant cry was heard from O'Ronayne.

'And what shouldst thou do for thy crimes against your own people? Hand thyself over to us?'

Burke waved him off, with the slightest hint of annoyance in his voice.

'That is straying from the object of our discourse. We are here to discuss whether or not thou shalt heed the sheriff's request.'

'Why should we?' said Cathal, voicing the question on everyone's lips.

In reply, the troopers gathered behind the mounted renegade parted to allow a half dozen of their fellows through, who bore two trunks full of contents which glittered in the sunlight. As the boxes crashed upon the ground, I could tell that they were treasure-chests engraved with the Spanish imperial eagles. They had been stolen from the wrecked galleys of the Armada, and I later learned that they were filled with silver plate and crown pieces. Burke gestured towards the riches to his right.

'Because we offer thee generous terms. Because our offer shall only be made once and shall ease thy days through the harsh winter months ahead. Which winter months will be even harsher, if ye do not heed my words.'

Silence reigned at the sight of the chests, as the renegade seized on the tribe's dumbstruck awe.

'The sheriff offers thee one chest for the Spanish slayer Juan, and another for the other foreign misbelievers.'

When his last words reached my ears, it took all of my years of professional marksmanship to keep myself from touching the hair trigger. My rifle trembled in my hand as the gallowglass troop's short prelate translated Donal's exclamation with a slow nod, while beads of sweat prickled my brow.

'Thy reward for an outlaw is most generous.'

''tis so,' affirmed the sergeant, quickly eyeing the Scottish mercenary constable, 'and my master also pledges to furnish you with cows from his land through the winter. That thou may have soft flesh that is thick off the bone, unlike the stringy beef from the mangy cattle which loiter in these parts.'

The Jesuit instantly piped up without any hesitation.

'We reject your offer. We can have those spoils whenever we want. And your head too.'

Burke was silent for a few moments, being unable to muster a speedy riposte. Then he finally spoke again.

'Thou wouldst instead help the Spaniards, who laugh at you and call you Irish beggars?'

'At the least,' retorted O'Ronayne, 'we shall not be dogs that serve heretical murderers.'

'Thy insolence shall cost thy people dear,' snapped Burke, 'ye cannot prevail against us, and have already once spurned the chance to live in peace.'

A growl was heard from the tanist Cathal when he replied to the sergeant.

'A peace that requires us to live as thralls!'

'Happy is the thrall that knows his full dues,' snarled Burke, 'but be that as it may. Thou may seekest to appease your neighbours on occasion and not always counter them. Differences of faith may well endure, yet our number increases by the day while yours dwindles.'

'Thou speakest as one who has not heard of the Spanish force in the north!' replied Cathal.

Mocking laughter was heard from the renegade, which reached a pitch that made my skin crawl.

'Dost thou refer to Don Antonio de Leiva? Thou would do well to forget about him. Even now he finishes repairs to his ship and readies to sail his men to Spain.'

The tanist turned red in the face, and it took a few moments for him to recover enough composure to speak.

'And when was thou called upon to give us advice?'

'Since the harm you risk became greater,' replied Burke insistently. 'Know that the sheriff desires this man Juan in all haste, otherwise why would his offer be so extravagant? The Spaniard is dangerous, he is a seasoned killer. Thou would do well to beware of him.'

Silence lingered again at this warning, before Cathal once more defied the renegade.

'When did a dog learn to speak like its master?'

Behind him, the Jesuit gestured towards the direction of Sligo.

'Begone with all haste! Thy fears are not ours! Let thy master know that we are deeply insulted!'

'Thy responses shall be relayed, as if they came from thy master's own mouth. But be warned before I depart, that for every day that you do not respect the sheriff's orders, his vengeance shall be swifter and harsher.'

The voice of the tanist was thick with contempt.

'Since when were threats used in a generous bargain? Dost thou not seek to protect us with thy advice? Thou shouldst also warn the sheriff, that he should not send his lowliest servants into our lands to mock us. I am the right hand of Lord Tadhg *Óg* MacGlannagh, who is the first lieutenant to his brother the O'Rourke. Both of whom only answer to our liege lord Philip, the Catholic King of Spain.'

A few moments passed in which the renegade sneered openly.

'Then farewell sire, we shall see whether my words of warning are but empty threats. Permit me only to add that the Binghams have sent word to the queen's spymaster, Francis Walsingham. They have told him, that of the Spaniards who landed in Connacht, over a thousand were put to the sword.'

The number of slain Spaniards served as a chilling reminder of what would befall me if I fell into the enemy's hands. I squirmed awkwardly upon the granary's rooftop as I sought to ignore the mouldy smell that wafted towards us from inside it. Meanwhile the Dartrymen swiftly dismissed the renegade sergeant's jeers and proved themselves the most loyal of Spanish allies.

'Many hundreds of Spaniards still live,' declared Cathal haughtily, no longer feigning ignorance of our existence, 'and they are the best fighting men in the world.'

'Indeed, thy news is hollow as your new faith, traitor!' shouted O'Ronayne, 'since all men know that the sun does not set upon the Spanish Empire! In time, God's servant King Philip will avenge the lives of his slain subjects!'

'May your Spanish allies appear when your moment of need is greatest,' replied Burke with a sneer, 'although I fear that your trust in them is misplaced. For this is after all a rebel north, and it is already too late for thee, pock-face, although thou dost not yet know it. In any event, thou shalt soon be served with a reminder of the fate of those loyal to the king of Spain.'

The Dartrymen's hands fell to their sword pommels at these last words, which they had taken as a threat. The rifle stock was pressed against my shoulder as I studied the large gathering of troopers, bracing myself for a treacherous attack by the enemy. Yet Burke only beckoned to the soldiers before him, who immediately commenced to gather the contents of the chests into sacks which were slung over the backs of their pack horses. While this took place, the hair rose on the back of my neck when Sergeant Burke's head was raised towards me, and in that instant, I could have sworn that he was staring in my direction, as if he knew of my presence.

When the sacks on the pack horses were filled, a loud blast of a bugle was sounded as the enemy host prepared to depart from the plain. Perhaps due to the Sassanas' arrogance at being the larger force, or due to the carelessness of its bearer, their white flag was no longer caressed by the sea breeze, having instead been dropped and dragged across the turf. In the corner of my eye I noticed the tanist and the Jesuit turning towards the granary, while my threnody swiftly left my lips.

This day will the Lord deliver thee into mine hand;
and I will smite thee,
and take thy head from thee

Amid the great rustle of armour and scabbards, the sergeant flicked his reins across his mount's withers as he made to follow his men. My shoulder supported the rifle butt and my eye was strained against its sights, to ensure that Burke's bobbing head was trapped within them when the last words of the fateful psalm were uttered.

Then I swiftly pulled back the serpentine, producing a shower of sparks from the fool's gold as I braced myself for the kick of the gun. A faint tendril of smoke rose before me and long moments passed in which nothing else happened. In shock I pulled the trigger again, yet still nothing happened. I instantly recalled something similar happening to me years earlier, when my gun had been soaked while crossing the waters of a Flemish river.

'Holy host of the Madonna!'

My cursing was as desperate as it was loud as I fumbled to release another ampoule and shook its contents into the palm of my hand. As first feared, the powder was thick and moist in composition. The swearing beneath my breath instantly turned to blasphemy as I looked back at the plain and saw the sergeant thundering over a hilltop, with his bodyguard of troopers bunched tightly about him. When he had disappeared from view, a cry was immediately heard from the Jesuit towards my direction, which only added to my woes.

'What are you waiting for Spaniard ?!'

I was about to protest when a loud cry was heard from one of the tanist's riders, who realised that the enemy had not left us empty-handed. As the distant din of the troopers died away, Cathal dispatched two kerns to carefully approach a small chest which the enemy had left behind on the plain. The remainder of the Irish host slowly gathered about it as the kerns and I proceeded to climb down from atop the granary's rafters.

My black mood had not abated by the time we reached the ground and rejoined the tanist's party, who stared at the pair of kerns struggling to release the padlock which kept the iron chest shut. Their efforts met with little success, so that they stepped away from the box to allow the bristling figure of Donal MacCabe to get to it. With a hefty swing of his *lochaber* axe the lock was rent asunder. Then the chest's lid was kicked open by one of the kerns, with gasps of shock heard when fish were seen within it.

The tanist uttered an exclamation in Gaelic and ordered his kerns to empty the entire contents of the chest upon the grass. As the slippery creatures bobbled forth, a great stink of rotten salmon wafted out of the empty box, with our wonder turning into horror when a severed head was noticed at its base. Dark hair was curled about it like the tentacles of some wretched sea creature.

At Cathal's order one of the kerns grabbed the head from its crown and held it aloft, and as the face spun towards us the Jesuit howled in sorrow and fell to the ground, covering his face with his hands. Other cries of anguish and anger were heard along with O'Ronayne's sobs, when the extent of the Sassanas' mocking threat became clear. Ahead of us the tanist trembled once, yet this was not caused by the chill wind that passed over the plain, as we stared on in horror at the severed head of Aengus.

XXIV

DUNCARBERY TO ROSCLOGHER, ROSCLOGHER TO GLENADE VALLEY, COUNTY LEITRIM

18 - 22 October 1588

It was a forlorn party that returned to Duncarbery castle, where Manglana was said to be awaiting our tidings. The discovery of his son's head had lowered the spirits of the Dartrymen, although the stoic expressions of the Scots gallow-glasses marching in the rear remained unchanged. Before our northbound journey was resumed, Cathal *Dubh* had ordered that the severed head be returned to the strongbox which was born by two of the kerns. No mention was made of my failed attempt to shoot Burke, with a grim silence swathing our party like one of the brat mantles which were worn by the Dartrymen.

Yet I still cursed inwardly as I rode with the tanist and his cavalry in the van, the rifle bouncing against my back like the tapping finger of an accuser. I could not understand how my powder in the ampoules had become soaked, since it had come from the store I had fashioned in the ringfort on the morning before our departure. A great fear gnawed at me throughout our ride, that the whole of the powder provision might also be ruined. On occasion I turned my head suspiciously towards the Scottish gallowglasses, then looked away whenever Donal MacCabe was seen sneering in my direction.

I had no doubt that the Scottish constable had somehow learned why I had also travelled to Grange. There was also little doubt on my part, that he would soon be making light of my marksmanship, for I knew how threatened he felt by the presence of Spanish troops in his paymaster's kingdom. We travelled along a meandering path amid the murmuring of sea gales, for after our gruesome discovery Cathal did not want either drum or pipe to be played. Amid the odd, sinister sounds of the wind, I often looked over my shoulder, fearing that we might be pursued by the enemy. Yet apart from the grim features of the gallowglasses, all I could see was the ever-distant sight of the flat-topped Ben Bulben, flanked to its left by the Leitrim hills.

After almost an hour on the march, the sounds no longer bothered me. We proceeded through the ever-thickening cover of trees, which soon eclipsed any glimpse of the heights behind us. Our general mood did not lighten when we at last sighted the first huts of Duncarbery. The townsfolk's smiling faces turned to stares of concern as we disconsolately trudged through them towards the chief seat of Manglana's power.

It was a high-walled structure, with rows of slit windows as well as turrets and crenellations along its roof which was made of lead. A high-walled bawn surrounded it, which had a small barbican protecting its entrance. Most of the tanist's force retained their black mood long after Cathal and the Jesuit were summoned into the keep with a few of their close retainers, to brief their lord of the happenings at Grange. Although he was not invited, the constable MacCabe still joined them, while leaving his men to tramp around the town, where they bullied the tribesmen into offering them food and other refreshment.

The Sassanas' strongbox was borne by some of the tanist's kerns to the chieftain's hall. It was close to dusk when they reappeared outside the castle walls to summon me into the keep. They found me among a band of Dartrymen who sat cross-legged about a low fire, as I stared at the cloud-strewn sky overhead. I had mulled over my preparing and loading of my rifle for hours, while knowing that my aim would also be brought into question. It was therefore with leaden feet that I followed the kerns through the corrugated door of the keep. Once inside we climbed a ladder to the second floor and ascended the steps to the chieftain's hall.

The stronghold was almost twice the size of the tower house atop the crannog in Lough Melvin. Yet I barely noticed its designs as my eyes were kept on the ground, dreading each step as we approached my protector. When the doors of the hall were thrown open, I stepped before the raging hearth, feeling so much warmth that I hardly noticed when my mantle slipped off one of my shoulders. Manglana was seated upon his throne on the other side of the chamber, with his *feni* standing about him with hung heads and slumped shoulders. When he spoke it was with particular strain.

'Why does the enemy crave thee above the rest of thy coun-trymen? Our spies do not tell of any loss endured by the sher-iff's family in Sligo.'

At the chieftain's feet stood the strongbox with its dreaded trophy within it. So I chose my next words with great care as I sought to offer a half-truth which I had considered telling before riding to the parley.

'The Binghams also fought in the Spanish Netherlands, my lord,' I said slowly, 'my reputation as a marksman was known to them there. I once slew their kinsman during a forest raid.'

My story was only partly false. Fo my skill as a sharpshoot-er during skirmishes had indeed secured my infamy among Spain's enemies, so that the name 'Abelardo de Santiago' had become synonymous with 'the Lynx of Haarlem,' a nickname I had earned at the terrible siege of Haarlem after we had trapped William of Orange at the Manpad.

'They also knew me as Alba's bodyguard,' I added.

The chieftain observed me in his usual, passionless manner.

'And thou swearest, grey wolf, that there is nothing else I should know?'

I stood rooted to the spot, with the thought of the emerald ring burning a hole of guilt through my conscience.

'None, lord,' I managed.

He did not utter a word in reply, then nodded once to his bodyguards who escorted me out of the keep and back to the town. Although the meeting passed without incident, I felt that I was treading over thin ice thereafter. I cut a more forlorn figure than usual as we rode to Rosclogher the next morning. When I was reunited with Nial he listened attentively to my account of the misfiring rifle. Yet the tidings he shared with me did little to placate my concerns as we lay alongside each other in the outhouse of Saint Mel.

'The gallowglass constable,' he told me, 'clamoured long and hard at Duncarbery castle for the chieftain to give thee up to the enemy. He could not believe that such a rich offer by the Sassenachs had been passed up for the lives of Spaniards. He claimed that thou wouldst never have done the same for us.'

Nial also told me that the words of MacCabe had also sparked heated arguments among the chieftain's assembly, with Cathal and O'Ronayne hotly insisting that the tribe's Catholic allies not be surrendered to the enemy. I heard how Manglana had dismissed the pleas of the Scottish constable, when Cathal promptly reminded all present that I had rescued Lady Bourke from certain death, which ended all debate.

Yet the Sassanas were not silent for long thereafter. A day after Aengus's skull was reunited with his body, distressing news reached Rosclogher from across Dartry. Envoys of the tuatha appeared at different hours of the day, bearing various arrows which had landed in their village. Each of these shafts had sheets of vellum attached to them, which promised great rewards in return for any captured Spaniards, 'and chiefly Juan, that murderer and enemy of all God-fearing and honest men.'

Strict orders were issued by the chieftain that these offers of ransom be ignored, yet this did little to ease my distress. I was still concerned after the gallowglasses returned to Duncarbery castle, which allowed me to freely travel about Manglana's town. The enemy's desperate efforts had not waned since the meeting with Burke, and I dreaded how they might next attempt to snare me. For it was clear that the sheriff had not forgotten the trinket which I bore.

It had been days since I had seen the cause of all my woe, for solitude was a prize that was all too rare in Manglana's town. One morning Nial was summoned to the keep on the crannog, which seemed the opportune moment for me to study the cause of all our perils. As the ring was pulled out of my ampoule, I held it up to the wan morning light which streamed through the boards in the wall. The stone shone with an unearthly splendour in its golden casing, with a blurred reflection of my quivering lips seen in its green surface as I delivered a scolding.

'You troublesome little thing. I should cast you into the lake and be rid of you'.

I next regarded the scrawl along the inside of its golden band, wondering what the words might mean.

'Eufrasia,' I said, biting my lip and thinking hard, 'who is she?'

Such was the power of the thing I held aloft, that it seemed to assume animated qualities. For a moment it almost seemed to observe me in curious silence, while with the fingers of my other hand I opened the lowest of the twelve ampoules which were attached to my bandolier. Half of the powder within the wooden charge was emptied into my free palm, with the ring placed onto the small mound of black dust. I tightened my hand into a fist, leaving enough space within it for the powder and ring to be poured back into the wooden charge on the bandolier. As I reattached the charge to the cap that hung from the belt, I could not resist a self-satisfied smirk.

'You should be safe in there for the time being.'

The ring was barely slipped inside the charge when the fur curtain shielding the entrance was flung open with a fearsome ferocity. O'Ronayne breathed heavily when he stumbled inside, with his round face scarlet as he ran up and grabbed me by the tunic, hurling a whole jumble of words in my face. I pushed him away, feeling outraged at his having startled me.

'What is the matter, priest? Are you drunk?'

O'Ronayne rubbed his eyes while I gestured at him to calm down, until my hands were firmly planted over his mouth to stop his flow of gibberish and his stinking breath. I held on until his eyes seemed to be about to pop out of his head, with his speech slowing when I released my grip.

'A captain, grey wolf! A captain!'

'What captain?'

'A Spanish captain but a few leagues from here. He is being kept slave by a heartless man - we must rescue him!'

I studied him in bewilderment, while attempting to make sense of the news.

'We must rescue him?'

The Jesuit nodded at me fervently.

'We must!'

There followed an awkward silence in which I tried to ignore the prodding of my conscience. My mind scrambled for a reason which might sufficiently delay the Jesuit's plea.

'Should we not first notify the chieftain of your discovery?'

After serving me with a long stare, O'Ronayne nodded to me.

'Aye, we should alert the chieftain. Where is Nial? We must request an audience with Lord MacGlannagh immediately.'

When I told O'Ronayne that Nial had been summoned to the chieftain's hall, he instantly rushed out of our hut towards the lake. I ran out after him, urging him to postpone relaying his discovery until Nial returned. Yet the hard-headed mule of O'Ronayne ignored me throughout, as we proceeded to cross the lake and climb to the topmost floor of the Rosclogher tower-house. There we found Manglana's bodyguards barring our access. Yet O'Ronayne was not to be deterred, as he pleaded with the battle-scarred veterans to allow us inside the hall. At long last, one of the bluejackets was sent to interrupt the meeting of the assembly who allowed us to join them.

Upon our entry we were greeted by the dim outline of the tribe's highborn subalterns, as sunlight shone through the slit windows behind them. Manglana sat behind them with a scowl on his face, with the lady Burke seated to his left. Nial had told me that Dervila was never absent from military councils, due to the Scottish mercenaries which she had contributed to the chieftain's army. O'Ronayne and I were barely halfway across the straw strewn floor that the Jesuit fell to his knees and cried out to the exalted gathering.

'Fuair mé captaen Spáinneach mo thiarna! Gabhadh ag gabha é! caithfimid é a tharrtháil!'

His plaint was no sooner delivered, than the fearsome figure of Donal MacCabe stood forward, hotly replying to the Jesuit. I felt anxious that I could not understand the hostile Scot, yet Nial had already appeared at my shoulder to translate the exchange.

'It is bad enough that they come to us. But to seek them out? It is lunacy! We do not have the men to spare!'

'It is our Catholic duty!' replied O'Ronayne, appearing even more flustered than before, 'God shall not judge us kindly if we do not act!'

The constable appeared hesitant to pour scorn upon a man of the church. He instead turned to face Manglana, whose lips were pursed while he stared into space, grappling with the dilemma which had been presented to him. At last, the chieftain spoke up, while also staring at me.

'He might be an asset, perhaps even persuade De Leiva to join in our struggle.'

O'Ronayne was swift to seize on this remark.

'He is a captain in the Spanish navy my lord! His experience would be invaluable to our cause!'

'Invaluable?!' snorted MacCabe as he pointed a finger in my direction, 'as invaluable as the aid of this so-called sharp-shooter, who could not strike a lake with a pebble were he standing before it!'

Despite the fearsome reputation of the Scottish merce-nary, my blood seethed at his slur, while my fists throbbed in anger at my sides. The gallowglass served me with a sneer of contempt, as his wolfish eyes beheld me mockingly. While I struggled to bridle my rage, Manglana sat back in his throne and gently stroked the end of his lengthy beard. Donal and I were still glaring at one another when the chieftain asked the Jesuit another question.

'How many men would you need?'

The Jesuit raised his hands pleadingly.

'But a handful of fleet-footed wood-kerns my Lord. We will return with him upon the morrow.'

Manglana sighed wearily and leaned back in his seat as he considered the words of the Jesuit. Finally he spoke again, with Nial hesitating for a moment before he translated his lord's words to me.

'Fate does not smile on the hour of your captain's need, friend Redmond. For I need all of my troops to undertake a perilous journey east into Breifne. Our overlord the O'Rourke has summoned all sub-kings to him at Newtown, to share knowledge of our enemy's movements. I cannot spare any men for the roads are unsafe, and the Armada landings have caused our enemies to double their watch.'

I felt instantly relieved by the chieftain's reply, while O'Ronayne's head fell forward as if he had been dealt a blow to the stomach. It took him some moments to recover from his disappointment, until he rose to his feet to deliver another lament with the palms of his hands tightly held together.

'I entreat you to consider the man's plight my lord. He is a fellow believer who fights for the faith.'

Manglana sighed.

'I am tormented by the sufferings endured by all Spanish castaways outside my lands. But to risk my men for one of their number cannot be deemed wise.'

O'Ronayne's arms fell to his sides in resignation, so that I could not help feeling sorry for him. A sombre pout was worn by all of the highborn subalterns who were gathered in the assembly, which greatly contrasted with the broad grin on Donal MacCabe's face. Cathal *Dubh* was not at hand to offer support to his ally O'Ronayne, since he had been summoned away to the northern confines of Dartry, where a troop of Sassanas had recently been sighted.

In the event, the Jesuit found backing from an unlikely source. All throughout his pleas, Dervila had watched him like a hawk without stirring. Suddenly she stood up as her clarion voice reached our ears. Nial was as surprised by her intervention as everyone else, leaving me to shake him lightly by the arm until he translated her words.

'Where is the captain kept prisoner?'

'In Glenade valley, my lady,' replied O'Ronayne.

'And when did you last pass that way?'

'Upon the yesternoon, your grace.'

Dervila pursed her lips and squinted slightly, as I wondered what designs were going through her mind. I silently also hoped that there was nothing that she could do to overturn her husband's final decision. After a few moments of deliberation, in which she tapped her chin with a curled forefinger, her voice filled the hall as she delivered her thoughts.

'Indeed, the road is most unsafe. And the enemy goes to great lengths to capture our allies. But some tell of a mountain path which is unknown to most men.'

She paused to draw breath while I feared the worst, then spoke again.

'There is one who knows of this path, if not also of others, that would skirt most dangers. This person is bound to me, yet I am glad to lend you her service...on one condition.'

O'Ronayne's eyes lit up at her words, as he rose to his feet with outstretched arms.

'But speak the words, my lady! If it is within my power to grant it, it shall be thine!'

Dervila turned her head towards me with a furtive smile, which left me feeling like a mouse caught in the gaze of a night owl.

'I demand that this grey wolf trains me and my attendants in the wielding of the firearm. 'twould be but a small group of my choosing, that would not number more than five ladies in my retinue.'

I expected the subalterns around me to laugh, until I noticed that they listened to her in all seriousness.

'Why would a lady want to use a firearm?' asked the chieftain, 'guns are dirty and stink. You may as well learn the art of tanning for-'

I was amazed by the manner in which Dervila interrupted her husband, as her strident voice resounded across the hall while she gestured towards me.

'Until I saw him use his rifle, I thought all firearms to be filthy weapons. Loud but useless when compared to an arrow or spear. But I can now see how they shall evolve, how it shall serve women to learn the use of the musket. The rifle is but a glimpse of the future, a glimpse of a time where it shall be used by the lowliest churl.'

Donal growled his own protest when she said this, seemingly unnerved that I had won the favour of his strongest ally.

'But your grace! Whoever heard of a woman bearing a firearm?'

Nial spoke up in the vernacular, startling me and the members of the assembly. His face reddened when he next translated his words to me.

'I told them of the heretic Dutchwomen who brandished guns upon the walls of Haarlem. They were used against the Spaniards with deadly efficacy.'

Few knew of that episode better than I did, since I had won great honour during the siege of Haarlem. As I nodded back at Nial, the tribesmen ahead of us leant towards each other, while they whispered hurriedly in muffled tones. Dervila nodded at the bondsman, openly acknowledging of his remark.

'A most worthy contribution, *Dua Claimthe*. Indeed it appears that our enemies have been swift to master the use of these new arms. Our women will certainly be better protected if they can learn how to use the gun.'

A sudden streak of light through a loop window blinded my view, while Nial swiftly translated Dervila's next words to me.

'Will you honour my terms and help rescue your kinsman?'

I hesitated to reply to her for a few moments, when O'Ronayne spoke up.

'It sounds like a fair pact. What say you, grey wolf?'

I fell onto one knee, mistakenly hoping that my pledge in Latin would be the extent of my involvement in the Spanish captain's rescue.

'If it is thy wish, my lady, I shall verse thee in the use of the firearm.'

The queen's reply in the same tongue was immediate.

'If they can shoot half as well as thee, they will be safer when the men are away on their raids.'

O'Ronayne bowed gratefully to Dervila, who served her husband with a dark stare as she returned to her seat. Manglana appeared to ignore her as he addressed the Jesuit, with Nial translating their speech to me once more.

'I shall assign some of my bodyguards to your cause.'

The priest bowed his head deeply again.

'My thanks, sire. We should also be escorted by another grey wolf, perhaps Juan here. This would help the captain understand that we do not mean him harm.'

These words hit me like a thunderbolt while a frown formed on the chieftain's face.

'That will mean two days without any training in marksmanship.'

With a chuckle the Jesuit engaged in a flourishing bow, while I resisted the temptation to plant a kick in his backside.

'Ever generous lord! Forever mindful of your duty towards your Catholic fellows!'

Manglana turned to his wife who still glared at him.

'And who is this guide that you have proposed, woman?'

'Why, the ollave Mac an Bhaird, of course,' was her frosty reply.

O'Ronayne clapped his hands in glee.

'Most enlightened lady! Who else could lead us to him in safety?'

To my surprise, my heart leapt at this revelation, as my poison grail suddenly seemed less foul. Yet Dervila's tone turned severe at the Jesuit's expression of delight.

'Muireann shall accept the task of her own free will. After her last brush with death, I will not force her hand.'

A number of kerns crowded our skiff when we were ferried back to the town. Upon reaching the bank of Lough Melvin, they darted off in all directions in search of the ollave, who was known to frequently disappear to a secret location in Dartry. I received no word of our impending mission for the remainder of the day, with the kerns' errand all but forgotten until loud whinnies were heard outside the outhouse.

In that moment I was busy cleaning my rifle, when Nial appeared to tell me that Muireann had been found by the scouts and was in deep deliberation with Dervila in the tower-house of Rosclogher. At the first signs of dusk, messenger boys were ferried to the town from the crannog, bearing word to us that the ollave had accepted her queen's request. They also bore us the order to gather up our weapons and assemble before the agreed meeting place of the abbey.

After the curious episode at Grange, I had not let the bandolier or the rifle out of my sight, while also ensuring that they were not damaged in any way. They were hastily slung about my shoulders when I followed Torcall, who raised a blazing brand over his head as he escorted me towards Doire Mel. A cluster of lights danced before the abbey's door, and in the torchlight we could see that Manglana and his queen had crossed the lake and stood in the presence of their bodyguards, waiting to bid us farewell.

Cathal *Dubh* had not yet returned, yet the bard Fearghal stood alongside the chieftain with his harp held at his side. At Dervila's back I could make out the ever-present glint of the huge Lochaber axe of the gallowglass constable Donal MacCabe, whose gaze was as dark as the enfolding night. My anxiety also grew when the wind howled through the surrounding trees, while we were served with black pudding as a meal for our journey.

'It is humble yet wholesome fare,' whispered Nial, who had also appeared to bid us Godspeed, 'enough to last you two days.'

'Will you not be joining us?' I replied.

'Unfortunately, I have been summoned north to train a tuath,' he said, 'although you shall be in my thoughts.'

I barely grunted my thanks as I quietly envied his lot, while stuffing the food into my pack. My brat mantle was furled about my shoulders to ward off the chill, for my legs were already rigid with the cold that bit through my tresses as I turned to observe the men in whose company I was to travel. O'Ronayne stood in the doorway, dressed like any other tribesman in a white tunic and a shaggy brat mantle pulled around him. The Jesuit stared expectantly in the direction of the town, with a half dozen kerns gathered at his back. I had previously seen some of them in the ollave's company, and one of them passed through his fellows handing out strips of cloth.

He was a retainer of Muireann's late husband, one of the many leaderless warriors who had blindly followed the ollave's command ever since Aengus had perished. I took the rags that he offered me, then wrapped them about my sword hilt and powder charges to muffle their sounds on the march. The errand that lay ahead of us was one fraught with peril, and I had partaken of enough nightly missions in the past to know that silence would be our greatest ally.

The noise of the men died down when Muireann strode towards us. She was escorted by a dozen stony faced kerns in blue jackets, who bore a javelin in each hand as was their custom. At their belts hung the slender *skene* daggers which could be whipped out in the blink of an eye. The ollave was garbed in a plain tunic and cloak which fluttered wildly about her. She looked as keen as a hound on the scent, as her high cheekbones twitched beneath her swirl of chestnut hair. Her faithful wolfhounds Roe and Branan had been left in the keep, since the mission required stealth. Yet the absence of her hounds did not detract from her presence, and I marvelled at the sight of this woman who commanded such respect from men, being possessed of a dignity which only enhanced her natural beauty.

'She is indeed a daughter of kings,' whispered Nial in wonderment, 'all valour is hers.'

When I turned to look at him, I could see that his face was crinkled with emotion. Muireann appeared almost bothered by her impending errand, yet swiftly bowed to Manglana and his party who raised their arms to her in a silent salute. After turning her back on them, she strode away from the lake towards the surrounding trees and bog, with her band of kerns gathering about her like a pack of wolves. Each man knew their place without a word being uttered by the ollave, with our journey to be undertaken on foot.

'Godspeed, grey wolf,' whispered Nial, who stood at my shoulder.

I nodded to him, then fell in behind the kerns and tried to keep in step with O'Ronayne. As we approached the bog our path skirted the huts on the periphery of the town, where my fellow Spaniards had gathered to whore and gamble, despite the bad weather. A great cry was heard when they spotted us.

'Traipsing off with your wench again, Juanito? Better you than us, comrade! Let's hope the wolves find that captain before you do!'

O'Ronayne grunted angrily at their words, yet I ignored them as we hurried after the ollave and left the prying eyes of the town behind us. After stepping through the trees and mud, our gathering fell into a single file as we travelled over the rocks in the bog, using this hidden trail until the cover of trees was reached. The kerns paused to hurl their torches into the marsh, so that we were further concealed by the dark of night and barely able to see one another in the twilight.

Muireann instantly kept to an eastward track through the forest, which curved steadily upwards towards the mountain range ahead of us. As we drew closer to them the silence was broken by the odd howl of wolves. A great sense of foreboding was felt whenever the ollave stopped to study our surroundings, then led us further into the bush.

'Is she using a map?' I asked the Jesuit, unnerved by the ollave's pauses and wary of the dangers that lurked in the vast darkness in which we found ourselves.

I had also long worried about what landmarks I would use, when I would flee Dartry after the winter and return to Spain. For the thought had long gnawed at me in recent days, that if I was to keep the ring then I had to escape from my hosts as soon as I could.

'We Gaels have no use for such items, grey wolf,' snorted O'Ronayne, 'for we can find our way about our lands blindfolded'.

I silently prayed that he was as good as his word, when the Jesuit spoke again.

'Such charts would only assist our enemy, who has been seeking to map our lands for years. We have often ambushed their cartographers and spies, while they attempt to recreate our lands on vellum.'

I was disappointed to learn this since I realised that I would not be able to use a map to flee Manglana's kingdom. Yet within the next hour Muireann demonstrated that maps were of no use to her, as she led us around the dark outline of *Sliabh Aradh* which was shrouded in cloud, keeping to a grass track in its shadow. We held the ends of our mantles up to our noses as we travelled, so as not to produce any tell-tale puffs of mist as we breathed in the cold air.

The ollave struck a narrow path towards the lesser hills about it, which was for the most part barely wider than a man, yet in parts could only be crossed by walking sideways through it. Our path wound up and down the rolling hills until the woods cleared, when we next found ourselves passing beneath the cover of low stunted trees and bushes. The brisk step of our party slackened when the ground underfoot became muddier. As I regained my breath I briefly turned away from the kerns, then started in surprise when the Jesuit grabbed me by the shoulder and hauled me closer.

'Do not stray from the *ollamh's* lead, grey wolf. Each of her steps is chosen with precision, for there are countless pits, crevasses and bogs that do not easily meet the eye.'

Thereafter a spring returned to my step, since I was resolved not to trust the treacherous ground which we covered, and keen to keep close to our guide. Our journey largely passed without incident, until we started a descent which became increasingly filled with trees.

'We must soon retire for the night,' whispered O'Ronayne.

This was welcome news to me, since the sun had long descended from its lofty perch, as a grey cast had overcome the land about us. I knew that it would soon be so dark that we would not even be able to see our own hands before our faces. As we were about to enter the denser cover of trees, we froze to a standstill when the whinny of a horse was heard ahead of us. A rider was seen crashing through the growth, heading straight towards our party.

'A scout?' gasped O'Ronayne, for the rider's armour marked him out as a Sassana.

We were so stunned by the mounted man's appearance that at first no one stirred. Then the rider reined in his mount, being so close to us that I could make out his slackened jaw while he stared at us in amazement. Muireann was the first to recover her senses as she pulled her bow off her shoulder, instantly fitting an arrow to her bowstring and releasing it.

Yet the Sassana was swiftest to react, as he swung his shield out before him. It met the blow of the shaft which crashed through it, thereby sparing the rider a fatal wound. Upon blocking this missile, he spurred his horse which whirled back towards the direction it had come from. As the horse charged off, a couple of spears hurled by the kerns narrowly missed its hindquarters.

'Holy host of the Madonna!' I cursed, pulling my rifle butt against my shoulder.

I was desperate to stem the rider's flight since I wanted to atone for my failure to pick off the sergeant Burke from the granary in Grange. The curious incident of the damp ampoules had haunted me ever since the day of the parley, so that

I had spent most of the day checking my powder and charges. It was with a degree of renewed confidence that I slammed down the doghead, swiftly whispering my usual psalm as my sights centred upon the nape of the rider's neck.

The scout was crouched over his mount as he lifted his head over his shoulder, seemingly relieved by the distance he had put between us. He was barely a half dozen yards from the deep woods when I lightly tapped the serpentine, so as to ensure that the muzzle did not quiver and send my shot astray. The air was filled with smoke and a loud roar, with the horse ahead of us never slowing when its rider crashed to the ground.

I was left waving frantically at the stinking cloud from the rifle. My target lay twitching on the grass onto which he had fallen, although his mount was nowhere to be seen. I breathed a long sigh of relief as two of the kerns rushed off to inspect the body, yet I was alarmed by the ollave's outburst as her eyes fell on the gunsmoke that still billowed from the device in my right hand.

'Thou hast revealed our position to the enemy!' she snarled, 'I had him in my sights!'

She nodded her head at the arrow which was fitted to her bow, as the truth of her words struck me harder than the worst kick of a rifle butt. My ears still rang from the fatal gunshot, so that I knew that the sound would have carried far over the hills and glens. In the distance the blast of a bugle was heard, and the ollave scampered away towards the dead body, gesturing to us to follow her.

'God help us,' muttered O'Ronayne as he made after her, 'these hills will soon be filled with troopers.'

His packs bobbed upon his shoulders as I hurried after him, with the Dartrymen who picked through the dead rider's clothing being swift to rejoin us. By this time nightfall had set in, so that I could barely make out the figures about me, and I was certain that I would soon lose sight of them all and end up lost in the woods. The Jesuit was almost knocked over when I ran straight into his back, for our guide had come to a standstill as she surveyed the rises about us from left to right.

'We must press on,' gasped O'Ronayne, more to himself than to anyone else, 'we are too close to Lough Aganny.'

Our pace quickened as we hurried up and down the hillocks before us, and our blood ran cold when the howl of a wolf was followed by yet another bugle blast.

'God help us,' muttered the Jesuit, 'for the night shall not pass quietly.'

We had barely scaled the fourth rise since the shooting, when we heard the clink of armour and the thud of hooves to our left. The tribesmen exchanged nervous stares amid the nightly chirp of crickets.

'The night shall not pass quietly!' hissed O'Ronayne.

Muireann gestured ahead of us, towards a hedgerow of hollies and bushes around the bottom of the hill which we could barely make out in the faint light of the moon. We tripped over the grass and desperately clawed the ground as we charged towards the distant shrubbery, with any feeling of weariness instantly dispelled by a bugle blast behind us. The ollave was already far ahead of us when the first flickering torches came into view. Muireann snatched one last look over her shoulder as she hissed another command.

In my haste, my rifle strap slipped off my shoulder. It dangled from my forearm as we covered the last yards and hurled ourselves headlong into the trees, getting as far as we could within the trunks before we fell against one another in a throbbing, fearful mass. My head was thrown back upon the grass as a sweat streaked elbow was buried into my cheek, yet I dared not cry out or stir.

The kern who flung himself over me became as rigid as a corpse when a streak of lightning flashed across the sky. In the growing darkness I could barely make out O'Ronayne ahead of me, with the kerns slowly pulling their mantles over their heads as the first drops of rain began to fall. There were at least twenty flickering torches behind us, and as they drew closer towards us it was all I could do not to scream and bolt for the open countryside. It was a temptation that grew with the sound of the advancing horsemen who approached our hiding spot.

Another streak of lightning revealed their proximity, as well as the twisted scowl of Treasach Burke. The sergeant was crouched over his horse as he intently studied the ground before him. The sight of him brought back memories of the horrifying torture chamber in Sligo, which made the hair rise on my body like that of a cat held above a stream. My limbs tensed and my lips parted when the Sassanas started beating the leaves, as my hand fell onto my sword pommel. I would have issued a war cry and rushed at them had a hand not fallen over my mouth in that precise instant. As my cry was stifled, I restrained the urge to rise off the ground and die on my feet, rather than being stabbed in the bushes.

In those moments I remained still by mustering all of my courage, which had been forged in all the previous skirmishes I had fought in enemy held lands. A great restlessness within me was suppressed, while my ears became as keen as those of a new mother. The clink of poniards tapping against sword belts was heard as the troopers encircled us, like those great snakes in the Indies which coiled themselves about their prey before crushing the breath out of them.

Another flash of light revealed the shimmer of domed helmets, with the Sassanas drawing so close about us that I could smell their sweat on the wind. Their swords slid out of their scabbards when something seemed to attract their notice, as they stepped ever closer towards us.

'MacGlannagh Abu'!'

The distant cry was followed by the yell of another trooper. The horses whinnied as the surrounding riders wheeled their mounts around and galloped off into the distance as if after the devil himself. They were barely a few feet away from us when a low hiss was heard from Muireann, and I suddenly realised that the hand against my face belonged to her. We struggled back to our feet and tore off into the distance, desperate to get as far away from our pursuers as we could. We ran up another steeper rise, keeping to a winding path until we finally fell to our knees, coughing and panting with exertion. When he had regained his breath, the Jesuit echoed my thoughts.

'Treasach Burke? But how did he know?'

Muireann rose to her feet with bunched fists and bedraggled hair.

'There is treachery afoot,' she snarled, 'we must attempt another way.'

As we drew closer towards the crest of the mountain, the rain eventually dwindled. We were buffeted by a stiff breeze as we climbed a path which stretched leftwards. As the lower ground was left behind us my nerves became less frayed, although I dreaded the great silence that hung over us, which was only interrupted by thunderclaps. As we trudged past the scant foliage, advancing along the edge of a cliff to our right, my heart was beating ever faster. I struggled to keep up with the Dartrymen, while hoping that we had eluded the mounted troopers.

My Irish comrades were tireless walkers and marched on like ancient Romans. The remainder of our ascent passed without incident, except for the odd howl of a wolf which jangled our tattered nerves. At these sounds the kerns swiftly raised their javelins as I snatched up my ready primed rifle. Our wariness abated when Muireann finally signalled a halt, which I barely noticed despite the increased moonlight.

'We can rest here awhile, grey wolf,' said O'Ronayne, 'it seems that there is not much ground left to cover.'

We sought shelter from the rain under the cover of a row of crooked hollies. After we ate some of the food which we carried, I tried to ignore the painful blisters on my feet. I suddenly realised that one of the kerns in our number had vanished, then understood that his war cry had caused the diversion which allowed us to escape from Burke. The man's sacrifice astounded me as much as his stealth, and I quietly prayed that he had succeeded in fleeing the troopers. Meanwhile the kerns quietly drew sacks out from beneath their cloaks, which contained peat and dry sticks. Muireann knelt among the faggots and drew a small blade and flint from her pouch.

The other members of our band were already rolled up in their blankets, except for the appointed watchman who would exchange his post with his fellows each hour. I followed their lead and wrapped myself in my mantle, praying to God that the ollave's fire would grow despite the wind and banish the chill that made me shudder. Some black pudding and dried flesh cuttings were passed between us, as well as a mouthful of water from the skins.

I awoke hours later in a cold sweat, disturbed by memories of the chamber in Sligo that often haunted my dreams. The other men still slumbered about me, wrapped in sheepskins which were as black as our nightly surrounds. Before me a figure was bent over the flames, and a few muffled sobs made me realise that it was the ollave. I could have sworn that I heard her whisper the word 'Aengus', and for a moment she appeared so fragile and wracked by grief that even my own hardened heart was moved. With a low grunt I threw off my blanket, then rolled onto my side and crept towards the embers of the smokeless peat fire. It had been lit between two rocks so as to shield the flame from any watchers.

'Shall I take over?'

A rasp of steel was heard as her dagger was drawn from its sheath, with its point held a few inches away from my face.

'What dost thou seek?' she hissed, 'thou shouldst be asleep.'

Although we had barely spoken throughout our journey, I was overwhelmed by her sudden hostility.

'I cannot sleep.'

She pondered over my reply for a few moments.

'Why not?'

'I had nightmares.'

The ollave nodded slowly at my words.

'So it was thee that was whimpering. Thou should attempt slumber once more, for I have only just commenced my watch.'

'But alas, I cannot sleep, and would readily relieve you.'

My words seemed to catch her off guard, and she was speechless for a few moments before she turned back to face the fire.

'I shalt not abandon my post. Do as you please, grey wolf, yet keep thy voice down.'

Dead leaves rustled when I rose from the ground and sat back against an old trunk, a few feet away from her. I also kept myself at a safe distance from the fire, since the bandolier was slung across my breast, with the precious ring tucked away in one of its powder charges. A wooden click was heard as they knocked each other, a sound which did not go unnoticed by the ollave.

'Thou never strays far from thy bandolier.'

It was but a passing remark, yet one that filled me with guilt, at the thought of the ring hidden inside the ampoule.

'The enemy was sighted not long ago,' I replied feebly, as I removed the bandolier and placed it upon the ground.

Muireann stared at the flames of the low fire, with her arms wrapped beneath her cloak which was draped over her cross-legged figure. The rain had long subsided, and I noticed that her hair was not covered by the mantle as its brown ringlets fell over her shoulders. I was greatly intrigued by her presence, for it was the first time we were close together since we had first fled the men of Treasach Burke. Since there were many questions I wished to ask of her, I made another attempt at conversation.

'How much longer until we reach Glenade?'

'Not more than an hour's march.'

'It is a lot of bother for one Spaniard, is it not?' I said with a smile.

My remark was met with a deep frown of disapproval.

'Thou seemest reluctant to help thy own kinsman,' whispered Muireann.

'He is no kinsman to me,' I objected, 'but merely my countryman.'

'But thou serveth the same tribe, dost thou not?'

'Aye,' I replied, after some hesitation.

'We would never abandon an ally,' she said, looking back at the fire, ''less a fellow tribesman.'

I sighed.

'Then clearly thy tribe means much to thee.'

'Why would it not?' she snapped, turning once more to regard me suspiciously.

I realised that I had to weigh my response carefully to avoid seeming like a turncoat, although I was after all a deserter.

'Would thou be loyal to a tribe which had betrayed thee?'

Her eyes narrowed at my question.

'When did thy tribe betray thee?' she asked.

'I am not sure where to begin, my lady. I know that we often served our king against the heretic, risking both body and soul. Yet we never saw pay or good food for months, if not years on end. As if that were not bad enough, I was also betrayed by my own fellowship, four men who were meant to be closer to me than brothers.'

For a moment I hesitated, for the memory of their trespass still rankled with me, with their faces appearing to me all too vividly in the surrounding darkness. I trembled angrily at the thought of Gabri and Cristò, as well as Salva and Ramos who had condemned me to the oar of the Santa Maria de Visión.

'What did they do to thee?' asked the ollave, sounding keen to hear my account.

After a while I replied to her, suddenly feeling as if a great burden had been lifted off my shoulders.

'They slew someone dear to me. Destroyed our lives and our dreams with one spiteful act of greed.'

'Was it the Flemish woman?' asked Muireann suddenly, so that I was amazed that she still remembered my exchange with Manglana's wife.

'Aye, the Flemish woman. My late wife Elsien.'

I fought back the prick of tears, as I did whenever I thought about her. Muireann beheld me intently, then withdrew her stare and turned back to the fire.

'That would never happen here,' was all she said.

I cocked a cynical eyebrow at her in reply. Yet for a while neither of us spoke, with the long silence between us only interrupted by the odd crackle and hiss from the flames. Eventually the loud snores of a kern were also heard. With a low growl of annoyance, the ollave rose to her feet and walked over to the offender, kicking him soundly in the leg. The man rolled over with a loud grunt and whipped out his dagger, holding it before him. When he recognised the ollave, he slid his blade back into its sheath and lay down again, grumbling to himself as he returned to sleep.

'Is that why thou are reluctant to find thy fellow tribesman?' asked Muireann unexpectedly, as she returned to her seat on the grass alongside me.

'Nay,' I sighed, 'for what is done cannot now be undone. But this captain might be of the blood. Which would make him both haughty and proud.'

Muireann was silent for a few moments before she spoke again.

'What dost thou mean when thou sayest *of the blood?*'

'I mean that he will be an officer from a highborn family, who considers anyone unlike himself to be below him.'

She mulled over my appraisal before sharing her thoughts.

'You Spaniards are a strange people'.

'We are?'

'The chieftain speaks highly of you, as do the tanist Cathal and O'Ronayne. Yet all I can see are men who act for themselves, with little thought for others.'

'What is so strange about that?' I asked, in mock surprise.

'It reminds me of those renegades who abandon their rightful lords to join the enemy. Men who betray their own people. Men like the sergeant, Treasach Burke.'

Her inference left me bristling in annoyance, and I was swift to rebut it.

'I assure you that I have been anything but disloyal to my lords and people. I have stormed forts in the name of the king, I have looted and pillaged. I have crawled into foul mines and cut throats in the dark, carried out night raids on guarded trenches and stood in squares on the field of battle.

I did all this out of a desire to serve king and country, I never questioned my actions for years. Somehow I am still alive, for the Lord has cast His arms about me for over a quarter of a century. Thou wouldst not believe the twists and turns which have led me to this place, although I greatly fear that it shall be my last port of call.'

No sooner did I say these words than the ollave looked confused, then looked away again.

'Aengus was as happy as a child when he heard of the Spanish landings,' she whispered sadly, 'he said we should sacrifice our lives, if necessary, to rescue the soldiers of Spain. We travelled south to attend a bardic contest hosted by one of the *Ó Conchobhair*. We were meant to leave the day before you rescued me, yet we tarried when Aengus learned of the shipwrecked Spaniards. He said that it was our duty to help you.'

'And thou thinkest that he spoke in vain?'

Muireann was deep in thought as she picked up a stick and poked the fire with it.

'In truth I do not know what to think. The constable, Donal MacCabe, says that our hospitality shall not be repaid, that you Spaniards shall abandon us with first spring.'

I swallowed tightly at the prediction of the Scottish gallowglass, since I also suspected that he might be proved right. Then I awkwardly cleared my throat while doing my best to sound defiant.

'And what dost thou believe?'

Muireann shrugged.

'The chieftains have always hoped that the king of Spain will come to their rescue. But then theirs has always been a vain hope.'

'Why?'

'Because if the Spanish king wanted to help us, he would have already sent his soldiers here.'

When she said this, I recalled something Manglana once said, about being a subject of King Philip II.

'But surely it can only be a matter of time,' I said hesitantly, 'the king of Spain is your king too, is he not?'

'Perhaps. Yet he is a distant king, a king who has forgotten us. Who throws us some gold every now and then. And now that his troops are finally here, they shalt not even help us. They say that de Leiva has over a thousand men under his command, yet our spies have reported that he does all he can to set sail for Scotland. Nay, grey wolf, it will be the Gaels themselves who shall liberate Ireland. We must help ourselves, or no one else will.'

When she said this, it occurred to me that her people's fight was truly a worthy cause. For it was a struggle for survival, and not a battle like that of the Spanish Imperials in Flanders, whose only objective was to fill their king's coffers with taxes like the tenth penny. Yet I was suddenly concerned that the ollave might support MacCabe's claims in the chieftain's assembly, which would leave me at the mercy of the Sassanas. So I swiftly sought to defend Manglana's decision to offer us shelter and protection.

'No one shall fight as hard as you for your own land,' I said, trying not to sound confrontational, 'yet the Spaniards who you have harboured may yet prove worthy allies in your cause.'

The doubt in her voice only grew when I said this.

'Thou rescued my life, although I suspect it was because thou needed a guide. Yet thou hast never attempted to trick us nor use us for your own pleasures.'

I said nothing while she continued.

'But most of the other Spaniards in the town, they are not honourable men. They taunt our women and complain of the hospitality that we provide to them. Some even scoff at our ways and talk about fleeing to Scotland.'

'I agree that the men you refer to are not of the best quality, my lady. For they are rogues, cutthroats and gaolbirds.'

Her lower lip trembled when she beheld me again, her eyes like deep pools of amber in the firelight.

'So are you not all the same?'

It was a question that troubled me, so that when I replied to her my voice was possessed of a slight stutter.

'I-I have known honourable Spaniards if that is what you are asking.'

'Then why art thou so afraid of this captain?'

XXV

Glenade valley to Rosclogher, Dartry, County Leitrim

23 – 27 October 1588

I had no reply to Muireann's question, as I sat alongside her in awkward silence, staring at the glowing embers before us. The quiet between us was soon broken by a distant bugle blast, which was not loud enough to waken the slumbering kerns.

'What was that?' I asked, mindful of our recent escape from Burke's men.

'The renegade still seekest us,' said Muireann, 'yet he hath clearly lost our trail and ventured too far afield. It is a great risk he takes, travelling so far north.'

I stared out at the darkness beyond our windswept summit, which was rendered all the more ominous by the resumed howling of wolves.

'Fear not, grey wolf,' she said, with some concern in her voice, 'we are safe over here.'

I sighed aloud, then lay back upon the rocks for a few moments. After our escape from the sergeant, I had helped myself to too much usquebaugh to steady my nerves, so that I desperately needed to relieve myself. I excused myself and left the ollave's side, yet she did not reply. With a shrug I wandered off into the dark, suddenly relishing the prospect of being alone for a few moments, away from the band of Dartrymen.

The moon was full and cast a fair amount of radiance upon the rise. It allowed me to put a musket shot's distance between me and my travelling companions, as I made towards the lower ground on the western side of the promontory. Through force of habit, I walked as silently as I could manage, breathing in the keen, cold air until I found sufficient cover behind a sharp slope. Upon reaching it I raised the lower folds of my tunic and showered the grass before my feet. I issued a low sigh when this business was ended, then made to return to the Dartymen.

'Holy host!' I hissed, whisking out my dagger at the sight of the shadow that stood before me.

'Calm down, grey wolf,' whispered O'Ronayne, for my back was arched like a cat's and I was almost about to run him through, 'it is I. Lower your weapon.'

'Jesus wept,' I gasped, 'for a moment there I thought you were the devil of sergeant Burke himself.'

O'Ronayne grunted dismissively as I returned the blade to its sheath.

'What are you doing here, priest?' I said.

For a few moments the Jesuit said nothing, so that I felt anxious about the cause of his appearance.

'Grey wolf,' he finally managed, 'I wanted a word with you.'

'A word? About what?'

'I came...I came to warn you.'

'Oh?' I replied, feeling even more confused than before.

'The *ollamh*...the Lady Mac an Bhaird,' he rasped irritably, 'she is...she is fair...and among women she is rare, yes she is, but...'

'But what?' I replied, suddenly getting an inkling of what his unexpected visit might be about.

In the wan light of the moon, I could see him shaking his head once.

'But she's not for you,' he blurted.

I stifled a half chuckle and raised my eyebrows in disbelief, then snorted once before replying to him.

'Why of course she's not for me, Father,' I replied, 'I'm a grey wolf, remember? While she is the highborn widow of a prince. And besides, she's only recently bereaved and still in mourning.'

The Jesuit seemed instantly relieved by my reply as his shoulders sagged forward. In the darkness I could hear him breathing more easily, until he spoke again in a sheepish tone.

'Well then that is good, grey wolf. That is understood then. It is just that, among other things, she is...well, as you say she is recently widowed and you would do well not to overstep the mark with her.'

I almost pitied him then, as we stood a few feet away from each other, with the distant, high-pitched howls of wolves breaking the silence which reigned in the heights surrounding us.

'It is for your own protection, Juan,' he whispered at last, surprising me by using my first name, 'seeking any closeness with the ollave would present dangers to you that you -'

'In truth,' I told him with a raised hand, 'I only sought private conversation with her since I could not sleep. After all, we both barely fled the Sassanas with our lives. A bond was formed then which can never be lost.'

I did not feel overly convinced by my words when I uttered them, yet I was keen to end the discussion which had become tedious.

'Yes,' he said, 'I appreciate that. Yet there are already highborn tribesmen who see her as the key to further their own ambitions. They would not take kindly to an alien becoming close to her.'

'Verily,' I said in an exasperated tone, while realising the validity of his argument, 'I appreciate your warning and I thank you for it. The future of the tribe is linked to hers, whereas my future is wholly uncertain.'

'So you appreciate the situation?' he said.

'Perfectly,' I snapped, wishing that he would end the uncomfortable exchange.

'Very well,' he whispered, 'then I suppose we should return to...'

At the faint crunching sound behind him, I clamped a hand over his face and hurled myself onto him. We tumbled onto the hard ground beneath us, more loudly than I would have liked. We were barely sheltered by the rocky scarp to our right, yet the foolish whoreson priest tried to push me away.

I slid the edge of my hand off his nostrils so that he could breathe, while the edges of my lips brushed his ear.

'Do not stir,' I hissed, as he slowly refrained from his struggle, while he realised the potential gravity of what was afoot.

As I slightly raised my head, I could make out faint figures in the distance, the silhouettes of men who were crouched low as they made their way towards the slumbering Dartrymen. I counted eight, then thirteen ambushers who had stealthily fanned out along the edge of the summit where we had camped for the night. My unease only grew when I also made out the pointed ends of their morion helmets.

'Christ's bones,' I uttered, fully suspecting that there were other men in the darkness, 'they've tracked us.'

In that instant I immediately realised Burke's design, which was a deceptively simple one. After tracking us down, the sergeant had sent a Sassana galloping north to issue a bugle blast, which had lulled us into a false sense of security while the troopers ascended the rise.

Whoreson, I thought to myself, as I drew my hand away from O'Ronayne's face, leaving him to produce a hoarse whisper.

'That devil of Burke.'

'Yes, he tricked us,' I replied, then threw myself against the edge of the slope while pulling him after me.

The hair on the back of my neck was already standing on end, when a loud cry and scuffle was heard in the distance.

'Muireann!' gasped the Jesuit, making an attempt to rise before I pounced on him again and held him down.

'Be still,' I growled at him, with my hand muffling him again while he tried to bite it, 'we may be their only hope, fool.'

He relented once more while other cries were heard, followed by the chilling crack of a pistol and a clash of steel.

'God help us,' muttered O'Ronayne, as I withdrew my hand from his face, 'how many are there?'

'Twenty, I think. Maybe more.'

'By the devil,' he gasped, 'we must get help.'

'From where?' I hissed, rolling around to think as I bit my lip.

'What can we do,' he exclaimed, 'there's only two of us.'

'We must think,' I said, closing my eyes.

During my army years, the various *camaradas* which I formed part of had often attacked twice our number during raids, in which we disrupted our enemy through grenades or stealth. Yet Muireann's fire appeared to have grown bigger, so that Burke's men would spot us long before we were upon them.

I know they will kill the kerns when he sees me, I thought, *because I alone know what he's after. Why he has travelled so deep into enemy territory.*

I cursed myself for having left my rifle, priming flask and bandolier behind. I grudgingly accepted that the *skene* dagger was my only weapon, when suddenly an idea formed in my head.

'Are you armed?' I whispered.

O'Ronayne patted the sword at his left hip and he also drew a dagger from his belt. I nodded at him, then raised my head again and felt a lump in my throat as I made out a half dozen forms spreading away from the fire like fingers on a slow opening hand. They were most likely scouting the rest of the peak, so as to ensure that all of the ollave's band had been captured.

Or Burke has already realised that I'm missing, I thought with a low sigh.

When I raised my head again, I could see that two of them were making in our direction, with a third trooper walking to the other side of the summit.

'Can you use that sword?' I whispered.

'I wield anything that draws heretics' blood,' he growled.

'Good, for it might be a close thing.'

'Just say when,' replied O'Ronayne, instantly assigning command to me.

'Listen,' I said softly, 'I will circle round the right and take one. I'll not kill him outright, so that he disturbs his fellow. You must go around the left side and be ready to sneak upon the other from behind. You must be swift and strike his throat side swing. The throat and not the back of the neck - understand?'

'Let's go,' snapped the Jesuit, instantly rolling away from me.

I cursed his impetuousness, then kicked off my brogues so that I could walk barefoot. I quickly scurried on all fours like some nightly predator along the bottom of the scarp, counting till ten before then lowering myself even further and crawling along the rocks, ignoring the scraping and scratching against my limbs. I trained my eyes on the crouching figure who was almost at the edge of the ridge, beneath which I had only moments before been hidden away with the Jesuit. The usual fear pierced my stomach and played havoc with my insides, so that I hesitated for a moment. Yet I put the feeling out of my mind, while recalling the words which my former sergeant once snarled after beating me to the ground in Willebroek.

'You're a cold, heartless, talented killer. You've slain enough men for me to know that.'

I found a strange reassurance in the memory of Ramos. For although I would always hate the whoreson, I still held a grudging respect for his prowess in battle. Which was not to mention the truth of what he had said, for I had engaged in many ambushes involving stealth, in which I had crept up on an unsuspecting enemy dozens of times before. All too often it had been done with my legs quivering in agony after an infinitely long march - with lice burning my skin every step of the way - so that I was mad enough to attack anything by the end of it.

This is nothing, I thought to myself.

I quickly crawled over the craggy rocks, the *skene* dagger quietly released from its sheath as I advanced upon the trooper with his helmet barely visible against the twilit sky. The shadowy form of his fellow could be seen a few feet away. I slowly rose to my feet, when a loud roar in Latin was heard from the camp which slightly startled me.

'Where is the Spaniard?!'

As the captured kerns screamed their replies in Gaelic, I could already smell the fluttering brat mantle which the Sassana held tightly over his shoulders.

So much for outlawing the Irish dress, I thought to myself, then made out the back of the trooper's neck as I sprang at him.

The palm of my left hand was wrapped over his mouth as the point of my *skene* dagger was slammed between his neck and shoulder. I next kicked his calf so that he fell to one knee, while I slightly released my hold on his face and gave the *skene* dagger a twist, long enough for him to issue a low groan. The sound was loud enough to alert the dim figure before us.

With a low curse the other trooper whirled towards us and reached for his sword. I yanked my dagger free of the Sassana held in my grip, with his fingers already scraping at my face as I slashed his throat open. In the distance a woman's voice rose in protest, while another shape appeared in the dimness before me. The swish of O'Ronayne blade was heard, which was swiftly followed by a muffled thud as the second trooper fell to the ground. A series of sharp rasps were heard as the man held his severed gullet, which were fortunately drowned out by wolf howls as well as the yelling and cries from near Muireann's fire.

'The Spaniard, whore!' shouted Burke, 'and where is the priest?!'

I gritted my teeth as I resisted the impulse to flee back down the hill and leave the Dartrymen behind me. Yet it was not the honourable course, and I could not bring myself to lose Ascoli's ring so easily. Furthermore, despite my protestations with the Jesuit, the thought of abandoning Muireann to certain torment at the hands of Burke did not bear contemplation. I rifled through the clothes of the dead trooper at my feet, swiftly taking his sword as well as his bandolier, priming flask, scouring stick and pistol.

'Well armed, these bastards,' I whispered to myself, as the Jesuit called out to me.

'Grey wolf?'

'Keep your voice down!' I hissed back at him, 'and put on his helmet.'

I pulled the helmet of my own victim onto my head, then clutched my mantle closely about me as I hurried over towards the Jesuit and started searching the body of the trooper he had killed.

At least the priest is good in a fight, I thought to myself, as I took the very same items from his trooper that I had taken from mine.

'They've taken them prisoner,' gasped O'Ronayne.

'Yes,' I replied as further shouting was heard from the direction of our camp, 'we have no time to lose.'

'What do we do?' asked the Jesuit, and with the helmet on his head I almost mistook him for one of the troopers whom we had just assaulted.

'Walk ahead of me,' I said, while ramming a ball down the pistol with the stick, 'but first open the priming flasks and ampoules and hide them beneath your mantle. Approach the sergeant as if you were a trooper, I'll not be far behind you.'

'Just walk up to them?' asked O'Ronayne in disbelief.

'Yes,' I gasped, 'then fling the flasks and ampoules onto the embers and strike the troopers closest to you.'

'And what of the ollave?' he asked nervously.

'Leave that to me,' I said, 'just go.'

He was about to ask me something else, then nodded once and did as I said. I followed him at a distance, praying that the other troopers would take us to be their returning fellows. As O'Ronayne walked closer towards the kerns, I shuddered once upon noticing how Burke's force had overpowered the Dartrymen. I quickly counted ten more men in the sergeant's band, although one trooper lay near the flames with an arrow through his throat.

Muireann had at least taken down one of them, yet three of our kerns had been slain, with the others lying face down with the troopers' swordpoints nicking their necks. The ollave herself was held in the grip of a burly Sassana, who held a dagger to her throat while he yanked her hair back so that she looked up at Burke. On his part the sergeant yelled threats at her, while he stoked up the fire with the end of his sword blade.

'I'll sear both sides of thy face, hellwhore, until thou finally reveals their whereabouts. Did they accompany thee up this hillside?'

He really does like to burn people, I thought to myself, shuddering yet again as I noticed that he had laid his dagger alongside the fire.

Its blade was already rendered red hot by the flames which been fed and stoked up by the Sassanas to alert their comrades to our whereabouts. Meanwhile O'Ronayne trudged over towards the other troopers while I followed him with the pair of primed pistols held at the ready, all the while praying that the Jesuit would quicken his step. At any moment I feared that the growing fire would cause the other Sassanas to recognise him. In the event my fears proved unfounded, since the Jesuit had the sense to keep the helmet low over his head, with the cloak wrapped tightly enough around his body for no one to recognise him.

'Any sign of them?' shouted Burke as he turned to face O'Ronayne, while still poking at the embers.

'Nay,' replied the Jesuit, then threw off his cloak and shocked his observers by flinging both the priming flasks and all the bandoliers into the flames. The troopers stared at the fire in disbelief, while the Jesuit proceeded to raise his sword in the air and bring it down on the closest Sassana.

There was heard a cry of stunned disbelief from the man, while O'Ronayne whirled towards another trooper and ran him through the thigh with his sword point. In the meantime I had already picked my targets, with the burly trooper holding Muireann being the first to receive a ball in the face. I flung the smoking pistol away and held up the second one, taking out another Sassana who held down our most heavyset kern. As my second pistol was hurled over my shoulder, the dead trooper's sword was held out before me as I raced towards our stunned enemies. Most of them had already pushed away their Irish captives to get away from the flames.

'Go Santiago!' I yelled, overcome by a mad fury as I raced at a fleeing Sassana and hacked his throat open.

The first eruption from the fire had men screaming as it flung us onto the ground. A number of other detonations followed in swift succession, causing a disruption that I hoped might allow us some meaningful fightback. As I sprang back onto my feet the subsequent eruptions lit up the peak, so that it was suddenly easier to make out friend from foe. In the amber radiance I could make out a stunned Sassana who tottered before me in a daze. I was upon him in a heartbeat, slashing his gullet as I made out the dazed figure of Muireann upon the ground, too close to the conflict to be safe.

'No!' I cried, suddenly overwhelmed by fear.

I ran through another trooper, then kicked him off my blade and ran over towards her. As yet another explosion was heard from the fire, I turned to see its flames fanned by the wind towards my weapons. They were perilously close to my bandolier, and at the thought of the ring inside the ampoule I turned my back on the ollave and raced towards it. Meanwhile kerns called out to me as they wrestled with the sergeant's troopers, yet all went ignored until I had finally seized up the bandolier and hurled it over my neck and shoulder.

'Grey wolf!' cried O'Ronayne behind me, as he shoved a trooper away and pointed towards the cliff edge.

I made out Burke scurrying over towards the trembling figure of Muireann with a raised blade. It was a sight which left me shaking off my trance caused by the ring, as I ran towards him with my sword held before me once more. Yet the sergeant's blade was already held over the ollave, as he readied to mortally wound her. In that instant Muireann's eyes shot open, and with a gasp she rolled over backwards as Burke's sword thrust showered sparks against the rocks. A groan left my lips as she fell over the cliff edge, leaving me to roar in anguish as I raced towards the sergeant feeling overwhelmed by sorrow and rage.

'Elsien!' I howled at the night in stunned disbelief, as Burke peered over the precipice, 'Elsien!'

As I aimed a sword thrust at the sergeant's back, he whirled about and caught it against his blade. Amid the ring of steel, I bared my teeth at him as he stumbled away from me, with the slightest grin playing on his mauled lips.

'You've grown stronger, rabbit,' he chuckled, then proceeded to shove me away.

'I'm no rabbit,' I snarled at him in the quivering brightness, 'I'm a lynx!'

I aimed the blade at him again with an overhead swing, which would have dealt him a mortal blow had he not ducked at the last instant.

'Not yet, rabbit!' he yelled, as he turned and fled into the night.

I cursed inwardly as he made off, then fell onto one knee and stared over the precipice into the darkness.

'No,' I gasped, 'no, not again...'

'Grey wolf!' hissed a voice just beneath me, 'help me!'

I looked down in disbelief, then made out two fair hands clutching at a clump of roseroots. The ollave glared at me as she struggled to maintain her grip, with her feet dangling just over the edge. With a loud gasp, I immediately reached over and seized her wrist, hauling her up towards me until we were face to face.

'Thou called me Elsien,' she said quietly, staring at me in bafflement with her lower lip trembling.

Yet I could not reply, as an agonised howl behind us had her shove me aside and run over towards the fire.

'To me!' she screamed as she snatched up her bow, while I staggered back to my feet and hurried towards the desperate melee near the fire.

A savage clash was still raging around the camp. A trooper was about to drive his blade through a kern when I hacked at his knee, leaving him to collapse to blows of the Dartryman's spear butt. None of the eight kerns had yet perished, yet another trooper lay dead on the ground, with the fight hanging in the balance. Then two bolts from Muireann felled another pair of Burke's men, before the remaining nine troopers fled after their master, with another three struck down by the spears of the kerns, who instantly ran onto the dying men and cut off their heads with their sword blades.

O'Ronayne had enough presence of mind to order the kerns to resist chasing the fleeing enemy. As these men returned to the fire, we stared at each other in shock, gasping for breath while blood pounded our temples. While the battle frenzy among us subsided, the usual feeling of desolation and loss followed, as kerns quietly picked up their dead fellows and laid them alongside each other a few feet away from the flames. I walked over to Muireann and Redmond who observed these proceedings, then silently took the skin of mead offered to me by the Jesuit.

'You fought well, grey wolf,' muttered the Jesuit, between ragged breaths, as I swallowed a mouthful of his brew.

'We must not tarry,' said the ollave, 'for we have lost enough men. And who knowest for certain what other devils Burke may summon. We must lay our comrades to rest with haste, then gather our belongings and depart.'

'The wolves will find them,' sighed the Jesuit.

Muireann served him with a look of disbelief.

'And what wouldst thou have me do?' she snapped, 'remain here until Burke returneth? 'tis thy mission which has led us here, Father. This officer of thine had better be worth it.'

The height of the moon suggested that dawn was perhaps two hours away, so we instantly did as she instructed. O'Ronayne administered a blessing to the fallen warriors, then loudly promised that in coming days they would be returned to Rosclogher for burial. We collected our gear and weapons, as well as the arms of the dead troopers. Then we followed Muireann in grim silence as she led us downhill towards the cover of trees.

Our progress was largely without incident until the ground became muddier, and Muireann dropped to her knee to examine it as one of the kerns walked ahead of her. He had barely taken a couple of steps that he suddenly found himself up to his breast in the mire. The ollave instantly beckoned to the other kerns, one of whom removed his mantle and held its end out to the fellow who was up to his armpits in the sludge.

'Bog cotton,' remarked the Jesuit, as he bent over the mud and tore out a reddish-brown stem with a tuft of white bristles attached to the top end of it, 'he should have known better.'

The sinking kern held the mantle tightly as he was pulled out of the mud and dragged onto firmer ground. When Muireann rose to her feet again, her voice was low but firm, and swiftly translated to me by the Jesuit.

'Stay close, grey wolf. She asks that we walk in a single file and shadow her steps.'

We ventured forward, stopping whenever she drew her foot away from the mud or struck a different path. Throughout this part of our journey, no man dared to push on ahead of her as the little tufts of cotton grass often grew in clumps along our path. Our progress was immensely slow until the bog was finally crossed, when we once again reached hard ground. We next made swift progress downhill until we at last sighted Glenade. It appeared to us as a deep, cliff-walled space beneath us. A great lake within it was dotted with raindrops when at last we entered the valley. Eventually the sullen colour of our surrounds assumed some brightness as the sun rose in the sky.

After using Muireann's secret paths through the mountains, the Jesuit next took the lead. We followed him to a curious dwelling upon the edge of the great lake, which consisted of two huts of wattle and daub built alongside one another. The ring of hammer and anvil were heard from within the furthest dwelling which obviously contained a smithy. As we briskly broke cover I drew my rifle as I brought up the rear, peering about us for signs of the enemy until we hid behind the wall of the smithy.

O'Ronayne left us to knock on its door, which was opened by a bearded man of a thickset frame. After their first exchanges, the Jesuit was soon shouting angrily, as he unleashed an impassioned scolding. The blacksmith knocked the Jesuit to the ground amid words of anger, so that the furious kerns alongside me broke cover and rushed at O'Ronayne's aggressor. Within instants they had whisked him off the ground by his arms and legs, carrying him through his own household. Upon reaching the open forge within, they hurled the man upon it. The blacksmith howled as his back and legs were seared by flame, then sprang off the fire and tore out of the house.

The sight of iron smelted by timber made me momentarily recall the distant days of my childhood, when I had served as a smithy's apprentice along the Grand Harbour of Malta. My thoughts were next drawn to the bellows where a man sat upon a stool.

'Who are you?' he whispered, after a few moments.

The Spanish captain appeared to have been working the forge with all the industry of a Basque producing harnesses, yet his accent was Andalusian. As we gathered closely about him, I noted that he had the appearance of one worked half to death. He was lean and gaunt, and his body was streaked with sweat and grime. O'Ronayne bowed and addressed him in his fluent Spanish.

'As promised, captain, I have returned to escort you to sanctuary.'

A hoarse voice was heard which bristled with wounded pride.

'Does such a place exist in this cursed land?'

The captain's moustache was flanked by two months of thick bristle above his forked beard. He was also dressed in ferns and hay-bands, and his eyes gleamed with genuine curiousity when O'Ronayne introduced me as a fellow Spaniard.

'Why do you stare at me in that way,' he said, 'have we met before?'

While I looked at him, I somehow knew that I had run into him before, although I could not yet recall the time and place.

'I am of the same mind, but I cannot remember where our paths did cross.'

'What is your name?'

'Juan.'

The captain frowned at my reply.

'I meant that of your house.'

I cleared my throat awkwardly.

'De los Hospitalarios.'

'A bastard?' he exclaimed, unable to mask his sneer of contempt. Since I was not unfamiliar with this reaction, it was not difficult to contain my anger.

'Born of and raised by the Knights Hospitaller,' I said defiantly.

He shook his head slightly as he cleared his throat, with the haughtiness already detectable in his voice.

'That is most curious. My name is Francisco de Cuéllar, I was captain of the San Pedro.'

I bowed deeply before him.

'Greetings, Captain. I sailed with the Santa Maria de Visión.'

Before de Cuéllar could ask any further questions, the Jesuit hurried towards us with a blanket and gown.

'We cannot tarry, Captain, for only last night our enemies were sighted. We must leave now.'

De Cuéllar breathed a sigh of relief as he released the bellows and threw his hammer into the forge. The Jesuit frowned when I pointed at the captain's knees which were wrapped in blood encrusted bandages.

'He cannot walk.'

O'Ronayne was not to be deterred. At his orders a makeshift litter was swiftly assembled, as a blanket was secured to two spear shafts. Muireann led our party on as we bore the captain, with O'Ronayne whispering to me as he held one end of the captain's litter.

'He is as light as a feather.'

The blacksmith's wife cast us a dark look when we hurried out of the smithy, but the Jesuit shook his head while I warned him that she might give us up to the enemy.

'If they reveal that they housed a Spanish officer, they are as good as dead. Let us only hope that she is not a witch that casts a spell upon us.'

'Would she dare do that to envoys of Manglana?' I asked in surprise, 'is he not her lord?'

'That he is,' admitted O'Ronayne, 'yet many rents have been collected to support our fight with the enemy, and the tribesmen grow weary of war. Their allegiance to Lord Mac-Glannagh grows strained with each passing year of the ongoing conflict.'

The mention of the tribesmen's tested loyalty did little to ease my fears. Yet it did much to add a spring to my step, despite my great weariness from the previous night's march. We travelled close on Muireann's heels, with Captain de Cuéllar bouncing wildly upon his litter as we bore him away. Before long, the lake had vanished behind the trees that grew closely about us. Our progress was slowed by the branches in our path, as we pressed on towards the mountains. De Cuéllar eventually whispered to me from his stretcher, with his voice sounding more high-pitched and nasal every time he spoke to me.

'Riflemen are usually of the blood.'

'They are.'

'And that is your rifle?'

'Not this one.'

The captain's next words sounded doubtful.

'You said that you sailed on the Santa Maria?'

'Aye.'

When de Cuéllar made to speak again a distant crash of hooves was heard beyond the trees to our right, as my hand was forced over his mouth. Muireann turned to glare at us with a forefinger pressed to her lips and her eyes widened in terror. We collapsed to the ground as a troop of riders burst past our cover, barely a few feet away from our party. The Jesuit confirmed my worst fears when the sound of the horses became a distant rustle.

'More troopers.'

The ollave raised her head from the grass.

'Do not speak again unless it is absolutely necessary.'

When the captain's mouth was freed from my grip, he spoke up again, while O'Ronayne bent over towards him.

'Our guide has asked that we keep silent,' said the Jesuit.

To our surprise, the captain glared back at him.

'I am a captain in His Majesty's navy. I do not take orders from you.'

His words greatly irked me as I grabbed him by the scruff of the neck.

'Breathe one more word and we shall leave you behind. You may find that the heretics are not impressed by your rank.'

He pushed my arm away.

'Easy, friend Juan, I cannot breathe.'

I restrained the urge to let go of the blanket, yet he thankfully kept silent for long enough for me to calm down. Then he spoke again, causing me to flinch at the audacity of his request.

'You could at least tell me your true name.'

'I have already done that.'

His smirk was both cynical and indignant.

'Since when have bastards wielded such princely weapons? I do not believe you. Could you not make up a more plausible story?'

I averted my stare from him and did not bother replying, while de Cuéllar observed my fingers which were wrapped around the edge of the pole.

'One thing is certain,' he said, 'you are no officer.'

For a while we wordlessly glared at each other, until I returned my attentions to the path. The forest leaves were goldened by sun and darkened by shadow. They became sparser when we resumed our climb into the endless cluster of hills and mountains. When the top of the third hillock was crested, we lay the captain down on the heather and I fell to my knees feeling utterly winded.

De Cuéllar did not utter a word of thanks after he wolfed down the kerns' offerings of strips of dried cowflesh and black pudding. When the ollave proffered him a skin he fixed his eyes on her, and never drew them away until he had gulped down some water. When his thirst was slaked he returned the skin to the ground for the ollave to pick it up. As she bent over it I noticed that he observed her closely.

'A woman scout,' he declared with a mocking grin, 'dost thou also speak Latin?'

Muireann ignored him as she stood up and gave him her back.

'Huh, thought not,' he said, keeping to Latin, 'still, a pretty thing for a savage.'

The ollave's face turned beetroot red as her hand fell onto the pommel of the *skene* dagger at her waist. Upon noticing

her displeasure, the Jesuit quickly rose to his feet as he sought
to pour oil on troubled waters.

'The *ollamh* and I both speak Latin,' he quickly blurted out.

De Cuéllar pulled a face.

'Ollave? What is that? Dost thou mean whore?'

Muireann whipped out her dagger and seized the captain
by the neck, hurling him back upon the ground as she rested
her blade edge across his throat. De Cuéllar hardly helped his
cause as he aimed a punch at Muireann, which to his fortune
caught the Jesuit's chest as O'Ronayne desperately sought to
tear the two apart. On my part I hurled myself in front of
the advancing kerns with flailing hands and loud protests, as
I sought to spare de Cuéllar from their ire. For they were already gathered about him with gritted teeth and drawn daggers, intent on reducing him to cuttings of cow flesh.

'Peace! Peace my daughter!' howled O'Ronayne as he held
Muireann by her dagger arm, 'he is a stranger to our ways.'

Muireann ignored the Jesuit's pleas as she leant towards de
Cuéllar's face and buried her knee in his chest.

'Employ care when thou addresses the daughter of kings,'
she whispered, pushing down on her blade until a drop of
blood was seen on the captain's throat, 'thou art not the first
Spanish swine with poor manners who I have had to contend
with.'

De Cuéllar bared his gritted teeth and glared back at her,
while O'Ronayne grasped her wrist in both hands until his
knuckles whitened.

'Peace my daughter, peace.'

The ollave withdrew her blade and got off the captain with
a snort of disgust, then seated herself some distance away

from us. The kerns also stomped off after the ollave and sat down a few feet away from her, all the while muttering darkly to themselves. Meanwhile O'Ronayne told the captain off while I regained my breath.

'Muireann is no common wench like those you get following the Army of Flanders! And among my people an *ollamh* is to be accorded the utmost respect! She is after all a member of the *fili*!'

If de Cuéllar was impressed, he did not show it.

'Very well, but what is an ollave?'

'The *ollamh* is our tribe's bard of history and literature, who keeps alive the memory of our forefathers. Her role differs from that of the poet bard, who stirs men to battle by reminding them of past braveries.'

The captain snorted.

'I never cared much for rhymers.'

O'Ronayne sighed.

'To us it is not but pretty verse. Theirs is a craft which melds law with history and verse, a profession obtained through years of study.'

The captain made a show of listening intently before he cocked an eyebrow and attempted to look impressed.

'You do not say? Can they also juggle?'

The Jesuit sighed disappointedly and kept away from the captain until we resumed our march. More bogs were traversed and uphills left behind. To our left *Sliabh Aradh* towered above the rolling hills, and eventually we briefly paused from our trek to view the stretch of lake which lay beyond the cover of trees below us. For a few moments I stared on in admiration at the sight of the sky meeting the mountaintops, beyond the sheen of its furthest bank.

After a lengthy downpour, the clouds became scattered enough for us to detect the sun amid flecks of blue, which rose to almost noontime height when at last the marsh was reached. It was with great relief that I followed the ollave over the hidden path through the bog, for my arms burned after almost three hours spent carrying the captain's litter from the valley of Glenade. A glance in his direction revealed him to be scowling at the muddy ground which surrounded us.

'Where are you taking me?' he grunted, clearly not impressed by his surrounds.

'To a stronghold belonging to the king of this land,' gasped O'Ronayne over his shoulder, while he also struggled to keep hold of his end of the blanket.

'I see no stronghold,' muttered the captain, 'all I see is mud and dirt.'

'It is a ring of marshy ground,' I cut in swiftly, 'which shields the tribesmen from enemy attacks.'

'The only thing this miasma offers us,' snorted de Cuéllar, 'is the plague.'

For a moment I wondered what the tribesmen would make of his arrogance, and if we should have wasted so much effort to bring him to Dartry. My fears grew as we finally reached the green, where we saw skeins of smoke above the huts in the town. Word of our arrival had already reached the tower-house of Rosclogher, and the bondsman Nial was seen approaching us from beyond the ringfort with a dozen armed kerns at his back. When he reached us, we were relieved to finally lower the captain onto the ground. O'Ronayne extended an arm to de Cuéllar and helped him onto his less wounded leg, before we lifted him onto the back of a dapple mare which had been led to us by Torcall the horseboy.

'What is this place?' asked the captain, staring at the mud huts about us.

'You will be safe here, Captain,' replied O'Ronayne, before taking up the horse's bridle and leading it towards the infirmary at the banks of the lake.

Countless people were gathered along the main avenue through the town, although de Cuéllar barely turned his head towards them as we approached the infirmary. The Spaniards hosted in the village were nowhere to be seen. Upon reaching the hut along the riverbank, the kerns helped de Cuéllar off his horse. Yet the captain at first refused to enter the infirmary, feeling slighted by the lodging that was being afforded to him.

'What is this squalid abode?' he grunted, as the grimacing kerns dragged him to the sackcloth bed which I had previously occupied.

No sooner did he fling himself upon it than he was instantly asleep and snoring loudly. After one of the surgeons had applied a poultice to his wounded knees and bandaged them firmly, I followed O'Ronayne out of the hut. I was glad that the whole expedition was finally over, yet we found our way barred by a few dozen tribesmen who had heard rumour of the new invalid and had gathered in the doorway to catch sight of him.

Muireann and her kerns had long vanished, so the Jesuit sent me to fetch a guard of bluejackets from the ringfort while he remained behind to fend off those Dartrymen gathered in front of the infirmary's door. Hence the doorway of the infirmary was subsequently guarded like it had been upon my arrival in the town. I felt strangely threatened by the sight of so much enthusiasm at de Cuéllar's arrival, which by far eclipsed the excitement at my first appearance in Manglana's town. This was not to mention how disturbed I had been by the captain's behaviour after his rescue from Glenade valley. I had not expected such haughtiness from a desperate man who had been fortunate enough to be rescued by allies.

I therefore avoided approaching the infirmary in the days which followed. A great trepidation grew within me, since I feared that the other nobles might become as outraged by de Cuéllar as the ollave Muireann. These fears proved to be ill-founded, for as soon as Dervila heard of the captain's arrival, she travelled to Rosclogher with a great escort from Duncarbery castle. Upon arriving in Manglana's town, she shocked everyone by entering the cabin built out of rude boards to meet him. It was a good two hours before she left the captain's side. I feared the worst as I spied on the infirmary from the monastery's outhouse, since everyone knew of the spell cast on women by seamen. Which was not to mention that Dartry's queen endured a loveless marriage with Manglana.

In the days that followed she never left the keep of Rosclogher except to engage in long discourses with de Cuéllar. Her interest was also shared by the tanist Cathal upon his return to the town. He was so enthralled by the captain's tall tales that he often joined Dervila at de Cuéllar's bedside. This was an eventuality that was both incredible and unforeseen, when one considered that the queen of Dartry loathed the tanist and usually avoided him at every turn.

They were so taken by his tall tales of Lepanto and other famous sea battles, that other nobles soon joined them in the squalid hut of the infirmary, which they usually avoided like the plague. Young Lochlain was soon also spotted accompanying his grandmother when she crossed the water to pay the captain yet another visit, although his mother Muireann was evidently still reluctant to visit de Cuéllar. Few remarked on the ollave's absence, for the captain had caused such a stir in the town that even Manglana's return to Rosclogher three days later almost passed unnoticed.

The next day was summoned to the chieftain's tower house by Nial. After crossing the lake I was thankful for the warmth of the great hearth in the hall, since the morning air outside was very cold. Both Cathal and Muireann were among the highborn gathered in the hall, with the Dartrymen speaking in their own tongue for a time before using Latin for my benefit. O'Ronayne raised the subject of Treasach Burke, who had tracked us during our journey towards the valley of Glenade. At these words Manglana looked greatly dismayed.

'Then there can be no doubt, that it was indeed the renegade?'

'None at all, my lord,' replied O'Ronayne.

'What drove them so far into our lands?' exclaimed Cathal *Dubh* from the shadows, 'they know that to enter Dartry means certain death!'

'The enemy evidently knew of our mission,' said the ollave, 'not even the goatherds use the path I struck.'

The chieftain bit his lip in anger while his hands trembled upon the arm rests of his oaken throne.

'This is evil tidings indeed,' he said at last. 'Many heads are being turned by the taste of Saxon silver. We must double our vigilance among ourselves, for the danger of an enemy within is far greater than that without.'

'Woe to them if they are caught,' growled O'Ronayne, 'and may their souls bear a great torment forevermore.'

'Woe indeed,' sighed Manglana, 'yet greater woe should come to pass in the interim should my next words reach the ears of a renegade.'

Manglana's inference was not lost upon the tribesmen crowded before the dais. The steward Malachy ushered all present towards the door except for me, the bard Fearghal, the tanist Cathal *Dubh*, O'Ronayne, Muireann and Nial. Even the bluejackets were seen leaving the warmth of the hearth, when Manglana called out to a boy who was making towards the hall's doors.

'Never has a page left my side without command!' he bellowed at Lochlain, causing his grandson to stop dead in his tracks, 'thou shalt return to my side and learn kingship!'

When he resumed his place at the foot of the throne, his red-faced grandson resembled a young pup with its tail curled between its legs. The boy was not alone in turning crimson, for I felt almost embarrassed to find myself part of the chieftain's inner circle and the subject of many piercing glares from the departing tribesmen. Yet the subject of the chieftain's ensuing discussion was of greater concern to me, as well as the part which I might be expected to play in it. When the last freeman left the hall, we stared at each other nervously as

Manglana addressed us after according to us the freedom of speech.

'The O'Rourke threw a great feast in my honour,' said the chieftain, 'as he did for all sub-chiefs who render tribute to him. Our beeves were well received by him, and the troubles voiced by our allies are the same as ours.'

'All the signs of a cruel winter hath long been in evidence,' remarked the ollave drily.

'Winter hath always been a thorn that also pierces our enemy's side,' replied Manglana, 'yet the greatest danger lies in the tribesmen's resolve. Across the kingships, men groan beneath the weight of the tributes and rents which are claimed of them.'

'Often did Aengus speak of this,' said Cathal, as his scarred features became further creased with evident concern, 'I have myself raised these concerns among the assembly, only for them to be lightly dismissed.'

''tis treason to deny our lord his lawful due!' spat the bard in a fury, 'were the Brehon Echna here, she would confirm this!'

'Yet the Brehon Echna is at Duncarbery castle,' said Muireann quietly, 'although we hardly require her presence to confirm that which you say.'

'The Brehon law must be honoured,' said Cathal, 'yet in a time of war the popularity of our lord is paramount, in order to preserve that same Brehon law.'

'Peace!' bellowed the chieftain from his seat, 'peace friends! The tanist Cathal doth speak of times of war, and I counselled our allies that war is the cause of the dagger which hangs over us.'

'Indeed,' said O'Ronanye, 'the cost of our fight with the heretic has exacted a grave toll on thy subjects. What with all the mercenaries who have been recruited to defend thy rule, which is as just as it is pleasing to our Lord.'

'And that was my message to my overlord and fellow kings,' smiled the chieftain, 'that the men have been idle for too long. A great rising out shall be required when winter is over, to distract the slovenly grumblings of the *tuatha* during the fighting season.'

'Returning home to empty bellies shall not distract their minds for long,' insisted the tanist, 'yet may only serve to further fan the flames of sedition that we fear.'

'Hast thou not heard our Lord!' cried Fearghal, with his teeth bared in outrage, 'it is their duty and honour to rally to his banner!'

'Peace, friend Fearghal!' retorted the chieftain, almost cringing at the bard's persistent defence of his person, 'for 'tis the aim of all present to uphold my rule. Indeed, the words of Cathal *Dubh* strike at the very heart of the matter.'

The bard was taken aback by this tirade, which allowed Cathal to speak freely.

'The tribute we seek must be reduced. For what guarantee do we have that war shall return to these lands? For years now, the fighting season has only seen raids on cattle and enemy garrisons.'

Fearghal started at these words, while Manglana raised his hand again while nodding his understanding.

'Thy concern is warranted, Lord Cathal. Yet thou shouldst also know that many dignitaries were present at my meeting with the overlord. These included bishops from all over the land, as well as noblemen from the Pale who are allies in our struggle. Many are certain that the next fighting season will bring great conflict across the land. For the Sassenachs still hunger for our domains which would bring them great wealth. It is said that the very rivers will turn red, for this will be no battle for heads of cows, yet may well decide the fate of the whole of Connacht. Our own overlord will be battling for his own existence, so that the loyalty and resolve of all his subjects will be tested.'

His eyes widened as he made this revelation. For a time none spoke until the chieftain further divulged his strategy.

'The raids keep up the spirit of my army and help to ease the burden of sustaining the mercenaries. Yet war will stir our people and divert attention away from our daily burdens. Indeed, the next battle with the heretics may not come soon enough, so long as it is not also our last'.

'O-our last, sire?' asked Muireann, in a faltering voice.

'Perhaps,' replied Manglana, 'if the whole of the garrison in Dublin empties upon Connacht. Our spies tell us that our enemies are hiring men again, and that military exercises have resumed upon the training ground which are being overseen by the Saxon Viceroy himself. These preparations are unheard of at this time of the year. They can only mean a busy fighting season after the winter months are over.'

I could barely restrain a shiver at this revelation, and the fires in the hall seemed to spin about my head as I fully realised the fragile protection which was being afforded to me by the Dartrymen.

'How do we know that they will strike out at Connacht?' I blurted.

'Well asked, grey wolf,' was Manglana's instant reply, 'yet where else would the attentions of the enemy be diverted? Leinster has long been subdued, and Munster was crushed only recently. In the north the Ulster lords still have too much power, and presently do not cause the Saxons any bother. For O'Neill's head has been turned by a woman, and O'Donnell's son is kept hostage by the enemy in the dungeons of Dublin. Nay, Spaniard, Connacht will next be attacked, for the enemy has long desired to subdue us and claim our possessions. Yet the Sassenachs shall be hard put to it, for as the Anglo-Normans before them learned during their own war of conquest: it is in Connacht that the invasions of aliens are resisted.'

Manglana fell back upon his throne and sighed aloud, while staring at the crackling hearth.

'We must do all we can to assure ourselves of victory. It is not enough merely to repel the enemy, we must do all we can to drive them into the sea. For they shall never refrain from seeking to exploit our weaknesses. And yet a great opportunity is still available to us, which may yet turn the tide beyond our reckoning. For the overlord O'Rourke asked one errand of us, in which we have failed him. Our despatch to de Leiva has clearly fallen upon deaf ears, for we have heard that the Spanish vice-commander is still busy repairing his ship to set sail with it to Spain. At his command are companies numbering over two thousand men. If they join forces with us, we would have enough men not only to protect ourselves but to liberate the whole of Ireland from the Sassenach scourge.'

'But my Lord,' said Nial, 'what can be done to persuade this Spanish commander to our cause? We have already sent

a runner bearing our message to him, yet we did not even receive a reply to our invitation.'

'I have already considered this, *dóerfuidir*,' said Manglana,
'and it was my opinion, and that of our overlord, that a Spanish officer might lend an ear to a fellow officer. We now have
in our possession a Spanish captain who you have rescued at
great risk, and to whom I extend my protection at great risk
to my rule. The O'Rourke has asked that we send the Spanish Commander another letter, one written by this captain
whom you have rescued. It may greatly bolster our chances in
the impending struggle.'

'And who should request this of the captain, sire?' asked
Nial, 'for it appears that this affair must be conducted in all
haste.'

'Aye *dóerfuidir*,' replied the chieftain, as his eyes suddenly
fell on me, 'thou shouldst ready to send another runner today.
As for relaying my request to the captain: I believe that we
have a Spaniard amongst us who is in our debt.'

Following our meeting with Manglana, I descended the
steps of the keep and returning to a skiff which bore me and
the bondsman across the water. The sky overhead had turned
a dismal colour of grey, which greatly reflected my mood as I
trudged over towards the infirmary holding vellum and ink.
My skin crawled when the kerns stood aside to let me in, for a
faint smell of blood and urine still pervaded the hut. I already
knew that my meeting with the captain would be an awkward
affair at best, since I had avoided his presence ever since we
had carried him to Dartry. To my relief, he appeared to be
sleeping peacefully upon his litter. Yet no sooner did I step
towards him than his eyes shot open at my approach.

'Hospitalarios!'

I shuffled uneasily towards him, with his eyes narrowing when he saw the materials which I carried.

'What errand are you about, you double-dyed ruffian? Do you seek to enlist me to the chieftain's service?'

I coughed uncomfortably into my fist before I set about explaining to him the task which Manglana had requested of us. At my mention of de Leiva, the captain suddenly sat up in his bed like a hawk poised to swoop.

'You mean to say that de Leiva is garrisoned but a few miles from here? And commands a galleass bound for home? What are we waiting for? We must join him!'

He tried to get out of bed, momentarily putting his weight on one leg before he fell onto the ground. When I reached out a hand to help him up, he pushed it away and tried to crawl towards the doorway, yet his progress was slower than a snail's. The captain sighed in resignation, while one of the barber surgeons in the infirmary helped me to lift him back onto his litter.

'Christ's wounds!' swore de Cuéllar loudly, 'but for my wounded legs I would be halfway towards the ship already!'

'Hence it might be best to delay him?' I asked, while I attempted to pass the vellum and ink pot to the captain.

De Cuéllar gave me a long hard stare and cleared his throat.

'Hospitalarios, surely you are not serious. Do you really expect me to make suggestions to the vice-commander of the Spanish Armada?'

'It was Recalde who was vice-commander,' I objected, although I already knew that it would be of little avail.

'Do not insult me, Hospitalarios!' yelled de Cuéllar, suddenly turning purple in the face, and displaying a haughtiness which even exceeded my expectations, 'I was the captain of a ship! I know who was what! Recalde was the official second-in-command, yet he was nothing more than the admiral's lackey! We all know that de Leiva was to assume command in the admiral's absence!'

'That is true,' I said, in an attempt to placate him, 'and it is our hope that the worthy de Leiva may join our cause and liberate Ireland.'

'Liberate Ireland? With the help of these barefooted savages?'

I cringed at his slur, then raised my hand to him while looking over my shoulder, in an attempt to persuade him to lower his voice.

'This is a Holy Crusade that is being fought here, Captain. It is no different from our struggles against the heretic in Flanders or the infidel in North Africa - except that we have greater need of troops here, to help those natives who are on our side'.

'What?! Join forces with these lowly savages who do not know a sword from a goat? Who hurl javelins at mounted pistoleers before running off for the cover of trees?'

His voice was still loud, while he revealed his contempt towards me and his protectors. It was all I could do to remain calm, while attempting to make a last plea. For I could not contemplate the thought of returning to Manglana's hall empty handed, after the sufferings his men had endured to rescue de Cuéllar.

'Captain, please listen to me carefully. Without these men we would be hanging from the beams of an abandoned abbey along the coast. Furthermore, you will have a great opportunity to claim glory and plunder in equal measure, if you attempt to persuade de Leiva to join the Irish cause. Long have we heard Irish exiles in many a port town, repeating the old saying: he that shall England win, let him in Ireland begin. We are living proof of the disaster that was the Spanish Armada. Yet we have a golden opportunity to regain some honour. You could claim all praise for the creation of a formidable alliance, should you write but a few lines to the Commander'.

I did not think that I had uttered anything unreasonable, yet de Cuéllar's face turned scarlet as he snarled at me.

'You listen to me, Hospitalarios! The Commander takes orders and suggestions only from the king, and the king never once sanctioned an invasion of Ireland! All troops and supplies are his and must be returned to him to use as he sees fit! Our duty is to return to Spain at the first opportunity, which shall be my sole intention when I am back upon my feet! I do not take orders from anyone below my rank, less a bastard whoreson of a Knight Crusader! Now begone with your fool's errand, or I will have you sentenced to death the minute I return to Spain!'

XXVI

Rosclogher, Dartry, County Leitrim

28 October – 1 November 1588

De Cuéllar's steps grew surer in the following week, until he was able to hobble into the town unassisted. During his visits there, he sought to win the favour of the native women that crossed his path in a deep and crooning voice. His swarthy looks and confident bearing soon meant that dozens of women crowded about him whenever he appeared in the town, holding their hands out to hi, and requesting that he also predict their own future. De Cuéllar eventually became the subject of so much attention that for a while thereafter he did not leave the infirmary, except at dawn and sundown when most tribesmen had already retired to their homes.

After recovering the use of his legs, the captain did not take long to discover the unruly Spanish quartet who loitered upon the edge of the town. This troublesome foursome of Juande, Valso, Koldo and Enano had long avoided him after learning that he held an officer's rank. After telling them that they were to obey his every last order, the captain immediately dispatched them with the command that they bring him ale. It was soon also rumoured that they smuggled mad Orla's daughters to him in the dead of night. Yet word of these indulgences seemed to only fan greater passions and rumours about de Cuéllar among the tribe, which grew when his presence in the town became scarcer.

Upon learning that the captain was back on his feet, Manglana ordered that de Cuéllar be brought to his hall in the tower house of Rosclogher. The chieftain was very curious about the officer he protected, especially after he learned of Dervila's and Cathal's frequent visits to the infirmary. As de Cuéllar limped towards the water, a great gathering of women instantly clustered about the dozen blue jackets who formed a defensive ring around the captain.

Girls giggled at the front of the crowd with heather in their hair, while elderly crones smiled on behind them. On his part, the captain strode towards the lake with his chest puffed out as if he were some great leader like El Cid, basking in the attentions directed towards him as he waved and blew kisses to his admirers. Their number only grew as we made towards the jetty, and a high-pitched squeal was heard from one of the younger maidens when de Cuéllar seized her hand and planted his lips upon it.

'Is he Spanish or from Italy?' whispered Nial behind me.

The comely blonde damsel beheld de Cuéllar in awe as he released her hand. She was still staring on after the captain in disbelief when he boarded the ferry, where he snatched a flute from the boatman's belt. He next surprised us all by blowing a vivacious ditty upon the instrument until we reached the crannog. The women from the town were besotted by his tune and stared on at him adoringly from the bank of the lake. Nial chuckled at the sight.

'Before long he will have had his way with a few.'

'If nothing else,' I snorted, 'he certainly has got bearing.'

I was not in the best of moods, for I was not sure why Manglana had also ordered me to accompany the captain to the keep. After the iron door squealed shut behind us, we made our way up towards the chieftain's hall. De Cuéllar was washed and dressed in a white tunic and cloak, and proceeded to recount his misadventures when we entered the chieftain's hall. The captain was a specimen who was both charming and glib, who employed a frankness which was disarming to his listeners. There seemed to be no way to stop him from talking once he started, which only made those present more eager to listen to his stories. Unlike the Spaniards who had reached Dartry before him, de Cuéllar flashed his highborn audience a ready smile whenever he spoke, which seemed to completely win them over.

The grin never left the captain's face throughout his delivery, until Manglana thanked him for the letter which he had written to de Leiva. Upon hearing this both the captain and I stiffened, and in the corner of my eye I could tell that he had flashed me a dark stare. Manglana appeared to take this silence as the stoic acknowledgement of a soldier who had done his duty, so that the letter was not mentioned again. I breathed a long sigh of relief, wondering how angry de Cuéllar would become once he learned that I had forged his signature at the end of a letter which I had drafted myself. I had taken great care to scrawl it in the poor handwriting that was typical of a seaman, before handing it to Nial to give it to a runner.

Thereafter the captain continued to work a charm over the tribesmen, further revealing himself to be an engaging Andalusian storyteller. So great was the spell he cast over them with his words that most barely stirred when he interrupted the chieftain's bard time and again. A few of those present gasped at the captain's audacity, since Fearghal Ó Dálaigh was held to be a seer by the Dartrymen, who could foresee the future and cast spells on those who caused him displeasure. Yet despite the bard's outrage, de Cuéllar seemed none the worse for wear, and before long the bard abandoned the hall, muttering in protest. No one batted an eyelid at Fearghal's departure except for Muireann, who unsuccessfully attempted to prevent him from leaving.

Meanwhile the peacock of de Cuéllar was fast winning over his listeners. Dervila seemed utterly awed by him, as she asked the captain question after question about his experiences. In doing so she fanned a growing blaze, since de Cuéllar instantly proceeded to share his adventures from his young sailor days, which included episodes from distant lands like Africa.

'Africa!' cried the tribesmen, 'is it true that there is no rain or cold?'

'Why none at all!' he lied.

They shook their heads in disbelief at his reply, as if they had just heard a gospel truth. The Imperial might of Spain seemed to shine through the captain's every gesture and radiate from his every last remark. He was as close as they would come to the distant Madrid, where men in starched collars held the world in their hands, deciding the fate of an Empire on which the sun never set.

De Cuéllar milked their misconceptions for all they were worth, clearly conscious that he was the object of great fascination and wonder. When asked about the Armada's defeat, he instantly laid the blame at the feet of Admiral Medina-Sidonia. I thought that this was unfair, for despite his own misgivings and lack of experience, the admiral had dutifully led a mission which had been doomed from the start.

'A dunce!' cried de Cuéllar loudly. 'Even his own mother thought him unfit for command!'

Although I had also heard this last rumour, I found it no less outrageous. Yet when O'Ronayne translated it I could see Dervila laughing aloud as her eyes twinkled with amusement. The captain was also quick to gloat about his gallantry during the whole tragedy, assuming a sombre expression which I had not seen before.

'While the battle raged, one of the English ships offered us terms since they were impressed by our courage. Yet although we bled freely and our ship was half sunk, I shot the messenger, never once acknowledging the mercy of heretics.'

A hearty cheer was heard from the highborn freemen when the Jesuit translated these words. When the captain finally finished talking, the assembly crowded about him, asking him questions and calling out to him gleefully. De Cuéllar played along for the best part of half an hour, until he finally caught sight of the ollave in the corner of his eye.

'Hey pretty one!' he called out to her, 'are you still cross with me? Do you not have the heart to forgive a poor Spanish castaway?'

O'Ronayne was reluctant to translate these words, only for de Cuéllar to repeat them in Latin. A few nobles laughed at the captain's teasing while others grimaced angrily. Muireann turned scarlet while her jaw throbbed furiously, as she instantly followed Fearghal out of the hall. When she brushed past the captain, de Cuéllar was not deterred, and even displayed a good use of Latin.

'Come over here kitten, do not make it so hard! I shall treat thee well, thou should not fear otherwise. Women such as thee do not grow on trees.'

Muireann whirled about and advanced angrily upon him.

'I live only to honour the memory of my late husband, Captain! Look to the foolish whores in the town, for thy wiles are wasted on me.'

The highborn freemen about her gasped in shock, and for once de Cuéllar appeared lost for words. Yet when she turned away again, a great anger clouded his face. I stepped forward and grabbed his shoulder before he could make after her.

'What are you doing?' he growled, shaking me off.

'Do not raise your hands on her, Captain! These people do not beat their women, their laws and customs are different to ours!'

He glared at me for a while longer, until he regained some calm.

'Uncivilised brutes', he grunted, 'whoever heard of leaving women unbridled? Yet we find ourselves in a strange place, Juanito, where we must depend on the charity of Irish beggars and Jesuits.'

He chuckled at the form of Muireann as she vanished through the door.

'That one is trouble, Juanito,' he said, jerking his head in the ollave's direction, 'a feisty beggar and no mistake.'

After his first encounter with the assembly, O'Ronayne offered to host de Cuéllar in the abbey of Saint Mel. Although I found it strange that he had been offered the abbey, unlike me, I was also relieved that he would not be joining me in the outhouse. Later that evening we dined on trestle tables alongside the best hearth in Rosclogher. Both the bard and the ollave were conspicuous by their absence, but between mouthfuls of cowflesh ripped off the bone and washed back with large swigs of ale, de Cuéllar still found time to share his tall tales.

'I'll tell you of the time I cracked a Fleming's skull in Zutphen!' he announced cheerfully, to great cheers of delight.

'Not another one,' I whispered to the bondsman, who rolled his eyes.

Despite the captain's rantings translated by O'Ronayne, the evening was a pleasant one overall. Nial and I ate our fill of meat while our ears were graced by the sounds of a lute. Yet perturbed looks were noted when de Cuéllar demonstrated a command of Latin, while insisting that Muireann be beaten for her insolence towards him. I fixed my eyes on my plate while I cringed in shame.

'The Roman doctrine of *Bonus Paterfamilias* is not to be scoffed at!' he declared, 'it grants man his rightful place in society, wherefrom all order follows throughout a law-abiding society!'

'If only such doctrine were observed by the Gaels,' muttered Manglana, to some laughter from other diners, who quickly fell silent when they noticed Dervila glaring at her husband in disgust.

The queen next turned her attention to the captain, with the patient smile of one who sought to explain different local customs to an alien.

'Thou will be surprised to learn, Captain, that among the Irish women may address a man as they please. We have the same standing at law, which forbids thee to touch us against our will.'

'*Almost* the same standing,' said Manglana gently.

Dervila was swift to scoff at her husband.

'Were it not for the Salic law, regrettably introduced by my Norman forebears, we would also be allowed to become chieftains. But in truth women still serve as chieftains in Ireland. In the west, for example, *Gráinne Ó Máille* has effectively ruled each of her husbands' territories.'

The captain appeared shocked.

'Is this true?'

'Indeed, it is. We have a great tradition of female rulers, captain, ever since the days of the warrior queen Maeve.'

De Cuéllar appeared disturbed as he took this in.

'Art thou also a warrior, my lady?' he suddenly asked.

Dervila's sword rang from its scabbard when she rose from the bench on which she was seated. She stepped a few feet away from it while beckoning to him to approach her.

'Spar with me and find out!' she cried, then ordered a highborn freeman to give the captain his sword.

De Cuéllar snatched up the weapon, then tried not to laugh while he fended off Dervila's sword thrusts. Manglana chuckled at the sight of his wife attacking the Spaniard, with the blades ringing aloud as the captain held her off, until the point of her sword pricked his throat.

'Not bad my lady,' he gasped, before he engaged in a feint and struck her weapon from her grip.

The sword clattered to the ground at the feet of the chieftain's steward, Malachy, who did not show any sign of noticing it. Meanwhile Dervila's face reddened as the captain's sword point touched her breast.

'Who taught you to fence?' asked de Cuéllar, with a devilish grin.

'My father's fencing master. And I shall soon master firearms too.'

De Cuéllar smiled cynically.

'Truly, my lady?'

'Aye,' she replied, pushing his sword arm away, 'we are to be trained by a seasoned sharpshooter.'

I looked at the ground when she nodded her head in my direction, leaving the captain to guffaw as he returned his blade to the highborn Dartryman.

'My lady has great hopes.'

She nodded defiantly.

'It will happen.'

'I shall believe it when I see it.'

Dervila returned to her seat where she weighed up his words with a smile.

'Would you accept a challenge to shot by one of my ladies?'

He could not restrain a chuckle when he replied to her.

'Why but name the time and place.'

'Ten days after Christmas, when the heretics celebrate their own Christmas, according to their false calendar. That way we will not endure any interruption.'

I was at once concerned by the date she had mentioned, for it was just over a month away. Yet the captain swiftly replied to her before I could say anything.

'Accepted! And what shall we wager?'

Dervila smiled.

'Thou may discuss that with the ollave when thou hast asked for her forgiveness. She is upset by thy conduct towards her.'

Of course, the captain did no such thing, which did not go unnoticed by Manglana. The chieftain did not display great warmth towards de Cuéllar, since he had already been irked by the Spaniard's attitude towards his bard. The following day Nial told me that Fearghal was long in private conversation with Manglana after de Cuéllar left the keep.

Thereafter De Cuéllar was not invited back to the tower house in a hurry, although Manglana did order the townsfolk of Rosclogher to refrain from harassing the captain. De Cuéllar took advantage of this liberty to exert a greater influence over the Spanish castaways in the town. He gathered us all into a hut, where he ordered us all to renew our oaths to king and country, and to swear fealty to him until we rejoined with the army in Spain.

'Returning to Spain is our duty,' he growled, between one swig of a wineskin and another. 'We must keep our eyes and ears open and find a way to get back to de Leiva at the first opportunity.'

After serving us with this command, the captain's attentions also turned to the women and drink which were available to him in the town. He was soon seen striding about with the black-hearted Spanish quartet who shadowed his every footstep, while largely ignoring the other four castaways in the town. These consisted of myself, the two boys from the Canary Islands and a priggish Milanese noble adventurer named Luigi Dal Verme. This treatment from the captain did not bother me in the slightest, for I did not wish the Dartrymen to associate me with the uncivilised brutes in de Cuéllar's new *camarada*.

'You appear to be giving the captain and his friends a wide berth,' remarked Nial, during one of our early morning sparring sessions.

'I have long avoided the companionship of my countrymen,' I replied, hoping that he might change our topic of conversation.

'That is rare for a Spaniard,' replied the bondsman, as he rested upon his wooden waster, with its point buried in the grass at his feet.

'Need I remind you of the haughtiness of Spaniards?' I replied, 'you also served in Flanders, did you not?'

The bondsman held my stare a few instants, then smiled wryly.

'In Flanders I fought hard for your king,' he replied, 'yet the Spaniards laughed at me, and called me an Irish beggar.'

'Well then, there you have it,' I replied swiftly, 'and they will scorn anyone, be it friend or foe. I lost faith in their cause long ago, although most of Europe has been crushed beneath their heel. The Continent is still smoking from the suffering and destruction they have wrought, and I would have none of it anymore. I have no urge to return to Spain or its army.'

'Then you would rather stay with us?' remarked the bondsman, with a look of surprise.

'I would be free of the horrors of war,' I replied after a few moments, 'I would gladly leave behind all wars of religion, which only serve to profit the few.'

'Does such a place exist in this world?'

I stared in the direction of the mountain range behind us which ran westwards.

'The Indies,' I whispered, 'a New World which can be reached on the silver ships. A New World where a poor man might live as a king, free from war and oppression. They say that he who discovers *El Dorado* might even live like a god.'

When I turned back to face him, Nial's face was a picture of longing and regret.

'Indeed, you are fortunate Juan, to know of this place and to have the possibility of reaching it. However leaving Ireland will not be easy, filled as it is with wolves and bandits, as well as Sassanas on both land and sea. Speaking for myself, I would be tempted to venture to this place with you, were I not bound to the MacGlannaghs by law. For the existence of a *fuidir* is not without its drawbacks, although Aengus saved my life. In truth, I owe everything to this tribe.'

In that instant I pitied the bondsman and his lack of choices. I then also recalled that I still faced many huge challenges, until I might one day secure berths on one of the silver ships for me and Elsien's youngest brother Pieter. However, my resolve to one day reach the Indies was only strengthened in days that followed. For I was filled with great anxiety by the captain's shameless flirting with the queen of Dartry. Dervila's attentions seemed to never stray from him during the colder months of autumn, with the queen constantly drawn to the captain's company and his tall tales from across the sea. They were often seen riding together, with their peals of laughter carrying across the lake.

Before long his influence upon her could also be seen in the way she rode her hobby horse, despite her ability to ride as well as the ablest horseman in Dartry. For the captain often charmed her off her feet by comparing her to noblewomen from the Continent, while also insisting that she ride side-saddle like them. Although she never rode in this manner while on the hunt, she always obliged him by riding in this fashion during their rides together.

Despite my misgivings about this outrageous flirting, I had to admit that following the captain's arrival, Dervila was no longer the sombre, broken woman who had been robbed of her son. De Cuéllar more than compensated for the emptiness that Aengus' passing had left behind, although it did little to win over Muireann. Day after day, the expert charms of a seasoned seafarer such as de Cuéllar were utterly wasted on her, and his relentless pursuit of the town's gullible women did little to grow his standing in the ollave's eyes.

His behaviour only served to inspire the remaining Spaniards to engage in further womanising. Soon the dark mutterings of the fathers of poor misled damsels became loud complaints raised with Manglana himself. Just when it seemed like things could not get any worse, I was summoned before the chieftain to provide an explanation for the Spaniards' behaviour, which left me secretly cursing their existence as I stood alone and embarrassed before the assembly of freemen.

'Why this behaviour, grey wolf?' asked the chieftain, with a frown on his face, 'have I not treated thee and thy fellows with all humanity and courtesy? Dost thou want for anything?'

My lower lip trembled with indignation when the chieftain included me among the pack of wolves who had committed every possible misdemeanour under the sun after setting foot in Dartry. In that instant it was all I could do not to urge him to banish them to the mercy of the Sassanas, when a loud crash was heard as the hall's doors burst open.

There were muffled protests heard from the gathering of highborn Dartrymen, who parted before a half dozen gallowglass Scots. I shuddered when I saw MacCabe marching at the head of the dreaded mercenaries, his chest puffed with self-righteousness as his mail rustled about him. At his back his huge son Brogan shadowed his steps, with the giant Scotsman dragging two Spaniards behind him by their collars. My heart sank when I recognised the pair, for they were none other than fat Juande and the tiresome runt nicknamed Enano.

Since their recovery in the infirmary, this dishonourable duo had done much to sully the name of the Spaniards among the tribesmen. For they had caused more mischief among the women of the town than a pair of foxes in a chicken coop. So infamous had their misdeeds become, that most of the freemen glared at them suspiciously, and even the tanist Cathal - who always sought to defend all Spaniards - had grown tired of their antics. Yet the tanist was swift to defend the misbehaving pair.

'Release those men,' he said wearily in Latin, 'they have the chieftain's protection.'

Before Donal MacCabe could reply, his huge son flung the two wretches before Manglana's dais. Although they were renowned for their haughty airs and raucous laughter, the two Spaniards remained silent and did not stir, resembling lifeless corpses. As he stepped towards their limp forms, the gallowglass constable glowered at the questioning faces of the assembly, while his angry words were translated by his short prelate.

'These vermin were found forcing themselves upon two married women!'

'Thy men are not charged with minding the affairs of the tribe,' declared the tanist, 'our Lord MacGlannagh has ordered that these men be our guests for the duration of their stay in Dartry.'

'Yet thou must protect the tribesmen from these aliens,' retorted the constable, 'I have heard of their unruly misdeeds from Duncarbery castle!'

Manglana grimaced at the two Spaniards when he spoke.

'What wouldst thou have me do?'

'Our laws must be respected,' bellowed the gallowglass constable, 'they cannot freely commit acts for which we would punish our own kin.'

'Thou speakest as if thou were a judge,' said Manglana.

Donal snorted aloud.

'The town is defended by both kerns and mercenaries,' he cried, 'who are men capable of great violence. What becomes of our command if they decide to follow the ways of these aliens, who have their way with our women at every turn?'

'Thy men hardly require any lessons,' shouted Cathal, 'when it comes to attacking our daughters!'

The tanist's indignation was not lost upon anyone present. For it was true that Donal and his men were chiefly loathed by the tribesmen because of their violence and abuse of women, more than the heavy toll of feeding and housing the Scots. The constable had no reply as he glared back hatefully at the tanist, until the chieftain spoke again.

'Donal Garve speaks truth. Word of the unwanted advances of these aliens upon our women, regardless of their wishes, has also reached me of late.'

A lump formed in my throat at these words, since de Cuéllar's dalliances with the lady Dervila had not gone unnoticed, which rendered the position of all Spaniards quite precarious. For all his infidelities, Manglana was after all the chieftain, whose reputation was not to be slighted among his own people. It was especially not to be slighted by an officer under his own protection, who was often seen publicly cavorting with the lady Dervila. My fears only grew when the chieftain called out to the judge in his tribe.

'Revered Echna, there are none more learned than thee in our laws of Brehon. Wherefore I ask: do our same laws also bind strangers?'

The freemen parted to reveal a woman in a headdress with streaks of silver hair about her shoulders. Echna responded to her lord in clear but accented Latin.

'Among the pages of the *Senchus Mor*, Patrick our Saint hath declared that strangers may choose whichever Brehon they please to decide their case. Thus would it appear, my Lord, that they are indeed bound.'

'My thanks, my lady Judge,' replied Manglana, with a low nod.

He next ordered his steward to summon the other Spaniards. Meanwhile his bard seized upon the opportunity to deliver one of his recitals, which went some way to relieve the great unease which could be felt amongst the assembly. Throughout his utterance the two guilty Spaniards sat at Manglana's feet under the watchful stare of his blue jacketed bodyguards. They beheld the ground in grim silence until the loud voice of Captain de Cuéllar could be heard outside the hall. He strutted through the freemen with Valdo and Enano at his back, the very picture of arrogance. At the sight of the Iberians, Manglana stirred slightly upon his throne and addressed them in a terse, loud voice.

'From this day on, you shall abide by our laws for as long as you are our guests. Our offer to host you still stands, yet you must respect our ways and traditions.'

'Allies should not make demands of each other,' replied de Cuéllar as he stood defiantly before the chieftain, 'thou hast sworn fealty to our king, Philip of Spain, who has sent thy overlord both gold and arms to aid thee in thy struggles with our common enemy.'

An unbearable silence fell over the hall while I shifted uneasily from one leg to another, when a great roar was heard from across the hall.

'Ungrateful cur!' roared MacCabe, as his eyes bulged above his scarred cheeks, 'thou hast the gall to make demands of our lord?! After he had thee rescued from the Sassenachs?'

'Peace!' shouted the chieftain, as he rose to his feet with outstretched arms. 'There shall be no blood drawn amongst my allies in this hall!'

On his part de Cuéllar betrayed no alarm as he shifted his gaze from the Scots' raised axes towards Manglana who spoke again.

'Thy men were caught forcing themselves upon one of our women. A woman who is a wedded mother and did not seek their attentions. 'tis not the first time captain, but it must be the last.'

De Cuéllar engaged in a flourishing bow, then issued a declaration which echoed against the walls of the chamber.

'For as long as we are under your protection sire, I hereby swear that none of my men will touch the hair of another damsel without her leave. If my order is not obeyed, I shall report their trespass to the army.'

'Thou wouldst do well not to forget your own oath, captain,' replied Manglana, 'for my Brehon will dispense with swift justice if my order goes ignored.'

De Cuéllar somehow held the furious stare of the chieftain, as he rested his hands upon his hips.

'And I pray thee to tell me lord,' he replied, in a tone verging on the contemptuous, 'what this justice may consist of? To berate one's allies may be taken as barbarous, yet to inflict punishment upon the king's troops is an altogether different matter. Which flies into the face of his martial laws.'

The lines on Manglana's face quivered in the firelight as he nodded at the Brehon who raised her voice.

'Our law is clear on the subject of raped women. And particular emphasis is placed on the violation of a gentlewoman of marriageable age, where the acts on her person cause her to blush. The honour price of the victim would be fourteen cumhals, meaning fourteen heads of cattle or pieces of silver.'

'What dost thou speak of, woman?' retorted the captain, 'we are castaways, and have not the means to pay such fines!'

'Which makes our lord's pardon all the more generous,' replied Echna, before falling silent at the chieftain's nod.

'Yet of what value is this pardon,' persisted de Cuéllar, 'if we have not the means to meet the declared penalty?'

'Then thy men would do well to recall their means before beating one of my subjects,' growled Manglana, 'for the next Spaniard that takes a woman against her will shall be thrown to the creaghts, to mind cattle until his fine is paid.'

De Cuéllar finally fell silent upon hearing this, while the rest of us stood about in the unbearable silence which ensued. In those terse instants I could have kissed the knave who burst through the doors, with his words diverting attention from the standoff between Manglana and the captain.

'The lady Dervila awaits instruction in arms from the Spaniard named Juan.'

At this announcement, the captain whirled towards me and issued a roar which was as loud as a gunshot.

'Do not keep Dartry's queen waiting, man! We Spaniards must always honour our oaths!'

He was still shouting while I shoved my way through the freemen assembled in hall, feeling grateful to be free of the painful meeting. Ahead of me the skinny page hurried down steps and slipped down the rungs of the ladder, then darted through the corrugated steel door of the tower house. I drew a deep breath of air as I left the narrow confines of the keep, stepping onto the small stretch of brown earth before it.

We were met by the sight of a large canopy of skins which sheltered Manglana's wife, which had been erected beneath the iron-grey sky. Beneath it, Lady Dervila cast a striking figure in her scarlet kirtle, while being surrounded by her ladies-in-waiting and a score of tall gallowglasses. I kept my distance from the Scots while I bowed deeply to Dartry's queen as well as the noblest womenfolk in the tribe. As I returned to my feet I noticed that their gazes were keen and expectant, except for that of Muireann. The ollave stood at Dervila's right shoulder, with the air of someone who would have rather been anywhere else.

'Thou art late,' remarked Manglana's wife sternly, which left me to swiftly engage in another bow.

'I humbly beg thee to accept my deepest regrets, my lady. I would have been here at the agreed hour, were it not for an unforeseen summons to court by my lord protector.'

'More a dank hall than a kingly court,' remarked Dervila, 'although thy fair words and flattery are always welcome. Yet not as welcome as thy teaching, grey wolf, for the patience of my ladies to learn the use of the firearm is wearing thin. For a time, we wondered whether thou also shared the opinion of most of the freemen among the tribe.'

'And what might that opinion be, my lady?'

'That a woman should not take up the gun.'

'Never for an instant, my lady!' I cried, 'after all, it was Erasmus himself who said that it becomes ladies to have something that is diverting, to pass away their leisure hours! And many regard him as among the wisest men who ever lived.'

Dervila beheld me with a hint of amusement in her face.

'What is this? A cold-blooded killer who holds humanist views?'

'That is me,' I sighed, 'and it has cost me dear.'

Dervila traded a swift sideways glance with Muireann, whose eyes narrowed in thought as her queen spoke again.

'We shall discover whether thy teaching is solely used to while away our leisure hours. Yet we are grateful for your instruction, for was it not also Erasmus of Rotterdam who said that one should acquire the best knowledge first, and without delay, for it is the height of madness to learn what thou will later have to unlearn?'

A smile grew on my face at her familiarity with the great humanist's teachings, while the five women behind her stepped towards me. Yet the queen herself did not rise from her seat, as I realised that the Lady Bourke would not partake of my instruction but only observe it. Unlike her husband, she was not one to throw herself into situations for which she had little preparation, since she was more content to first bear witness and learn from the efforts of others. Meanwhile her ladies stood before me with incredulous expressions, scarcely believing that a Spanish marksman was about to provide them with instruction that was unavailable to most men.

'Art thou versed in the use of the hackbut?' I asked them.

'Nay,' snapped a lady-in-waiting named Saorla, while scowling at me, 'yet we know that the musket cannot pierce good armour. Not unless it is fired from a lesser distance than that used to throw a spear.'

A lump formed in my throat at her open questioning of firearms.

'That is not true, my lady. The musket is hardly inaccurate in the right hands.'

'Except that the rifle is more accurate from distance?'

I turned in surprise towards the seated figure of Dervila, who had issued the loud remark.

'That is also true my lady,' I responded, 'yet both musket and rifle are effective, if one learns the rudiments of marksmanship.'

'Yet we have only muskets,' groaned Saorla, casting doubt upon the purpose of the whole exercise.

'One should learn to walk before running,' I replied.

The lady-in-waiting's face turned crimson at my words. I served her with a dark stare as I raised my hand to the highest of my ampoules and unslung the rifle from my shoulder. I explained the use of the slow match to the women, telling them to watch for its flame at all times. Whenever looks of confusion appeared, Muireann piped up to correct my bad Latin, so that my explanations could proceed unhindered. One of the chieftain's sisters groaned with toil when I handed her the gun. At the sight of her discomfort, I summoned a knave and described a gun stand to him. I then ordered that he travel across the lake to the town and ask the local smith to fashion one, before bearing it to us. Once this gun stand was delivered to me, the women listened closely when I explained to them that they could rest the heavy musket upon it.

'But alas,' lamented Dervila behind us, 'will that not worsen our aim?'

'Hardly so, your grace,' I replied with a slight nod, 'for the gun stand was devised by my former master, the Iron Duke himself, to spare a jolt to the shoulder of his hardest veterans. Indeed, such a device only serves to render one's shot truer.'

'What a delightful contraption,' said Dervila, with an excited gleam in her eyes as she suddenly realised that even women of smaller stature could use the weapon.

'War is delightful to all but those who partake of it, my lady.'

No sooner did I say this, than I noticed the astonished stare on the queen of Dartry's face. I was about to pardon myself for any impudence when she spoke again.

'Ah, more wisdom from Erasmus. It is just incredible that we have a student of the humanities in our midst.'

I chuckled nervously.

'Hardly a student, my lady. Merely one who had the time and opportunity to read the work of great writers.'

The queen of Dartry did not reply as Saorla spoke up.

'What are we to do if we do not have a stand?'

'Then thou must rest it over thy shoulder.'

The women took turns to clamp an unlit cord, until I next showed them how to pour powder into the pan and muzzle. Behind us Dervila's eyes never even blinked while she took in every detail of the scene before her. Saorla frowned awkwardly when she jerked back the serpentine as I had taught her to do.

'It seems easy enough.'

Her dismissive words caused me to chuckle.

'To fire a gun is not the mark of a good musketeer. One's accuracy and speed of loading are of far greater importance.'

I took them through all of the loading steps, which included the all-important act of blowing off loose powder. The ladies-in-waiting proved keen students, who bit their lips as they lit coils of match at both ends before passing them through the jaws of the cock. They also took it in turns to draw the serpentine. One of them issued a low squeal when the jaws shot into the pan, releasing a small wisp of smoke, instants before the eventual blast which sent the weapon flying from her grip.

After some of her peers had fallen to their knees, I noticed Muireann was as taut as a bowstring, while I showed her how to assume a proper posture. She flinched when I pushed her back straight with my knuckles, her face clouded with confusion when I gently set her ankles apart with my foot.

'Thy legs must be wide apart. And soften thy posture, as if thou were holding the bow. If the gun were to fly from thy hands...'

Her bearing slackened, which allowed me to adjust her arms which were as hard as dried branches. With an awkward frown I grabbed her wrists hard and shook them.

'Loosen the arms up more, my lady. That is better.'

My lips were inches away from her cheek when I leaned towards her. Her eye flickered towards me but once when my instructions were whispered into her ear.

'Dost thou see those silver sights?'

'Aye.'

'Place thy target betwixt them. Then pull thy finger back onto the serpentine.'

My forefinger rested on hers as I used it to gently pull back the small, curved lever. The warmth of her slender hands was enough to distract me, so that the kick of the rifle also took me by surprise. Muireann flew back into my chest, bowling me over onto the grass. I felt flushed by embarrassment as I quickly rose to my knees alongside the ollave, who lay upon the ground with the smoking rifle still held in her grasp. Her eyes widened in surprise at the hand I held out to her, then she grasped it and rose to her feet. I felt the slightest prick of regret when she released her grip from my fingers. She walked away with a red tinge spread across her cheeks, while the other ladies made a poor attempt of stifling their chuckles.

In truth the other women hardly fared better, with two flying to the ground despite my best efforts to check their fall. Yet as often happened, their knowledge of how to hold the musket grew with their keenness to wield it. I soon found myself the subject of competing attentions as students snatched the gun from me with a set jaw, resolved to test their aim again and to also impress their queen.

Upon witnessing such a successful lesson, Dervila soon ordered that my tuition further progress at least thrice during the week, promising me as much powder as the charges on my bandolier could carry. I was overwhelmed by her generosity, for the value of gunpowder was so prohibitive that I rarely used it beyond the first training session. The means available to the queen of Dartry were quickly apparent, for in the second lesson we were supplied with more powder.

My students did not hesitate to put it to good use. They were so determined to prove themselves to their male observers, and by their third lesson two of the ladies even came close to firing a shot every minute. Lady Bourke was encouraged by the progress of her highborn attendants, so that she eventually decided to take to load the firearm herself. She was cheered on by the inevitable crowd of growing bystanders who gathered to take note of the women's efforts. When a few boys whooped at Saorla, the queen's lady-in-waiting turned and took aim at them, causing the young upstarts to scatter like a murder of crows.

The red-haired rosebud was as sightly to the eye as she was quick to anger, and she was also Manglana's sister. I therefore employed the greatest courtesy when addressing her, for she always stared at me sternly as if scrutinizing my every last word. When she did speak it was always in a curt fashion that left one feeling ill at ease, with her questions always implying a mistrust of the knowledge which I was imparting.

Whenever I replied to her, she raised her head and cast me a doubtful look, then turned her attentions on the next lady-in-waiting taking aim. She was also the quickest to learn what I taught her, proving even swifter than the ollave at mastering loading and firing. During our sixth lesson, Saorla even went as far as to raise a hand towards me when I offered her the rifle which had just been fired by the ollave.

'Are thou not to partake of the lesson?' I asked, surprised by the sight of her outstretched palm.

'What purpose is there for me to remain in attendance', she snapped, 'when I have proved my deftness with the gun time and again? What hast thou left to teach me further?'

For a moment, her words left me blinking back at her in amazement, while the slightest snigger from one of my other pupils reached my ears. A great annoyance seized me as I slammed the rifle butt to the ground, so that for a moment even the haughty queen of Dartry seemed disturbed by the look in my eye as I glared at her retainer.

'Thou thinkest that thou knowest all there is to know about the gun, because thou can hit a target in friendly territory in the company of thy fellows? I promise thee, that taking aim is a matter altogether different when thou finds thyself upon the battlefield with a troop of horsemen bearing down upon thee, readying to cut thee and thy comrades to pieces. Not even the Lord Himself can grant thee succour in such moments, when all that may aid thee is the steadiness of thy arm, as the ground quakes about thee and rainwater pours down your neck, with the shriek of the charging horses only growing louder in thy ears. Indeed in such moments, I swear to thee, that the alternative to missing thy target does not even bear contemplation.'

My tone was still vigorous, although greatly restrained, so that my pupils stared on in awe at me.

'Or else thou might find thyself in the branches of a tree, surrounded by mercenaries beating the bush to find and kill thy friends. It is during these moments that thou must refrain from thy prayers and trust your practiced eye and hand. For each inch too high or too low, too leftwards or too rightwards can mean the difference between life or death. It is during those times, with a branch creaking beneath thy feet and the salt of thy sweat burning your eye, that thy hand must be true.'

Saorla's face reddened as I delivered my final thoughts.

'I assure thee, that it is not talent alone which has rendered my aim what it is. Hours and days and months of practice have been of the essence. And even then, one may find that one's shot still fails him.'

'As it did at the village of *Grainseach?*'

Saorla's question left me tongue-tied for a few instants, as I regarded her in outrage and disbelief. I realised that evil tongues had been at work after the episode of the granary at

Grange. After taking a few deep breaths I at last recovered the composure to reply to her.

'Indeed thou speakest truth, for even a handpicked rifleman of the Iron Duke of Alba may find that his arms do not meet his needs, even after years of practicing with a similar weapon. Which only serves to further prove my point, as well as to condemn thee to training which thou finds to be of no use.'

With that I pushed the rifle into her hands and bid her to take aim at an enemy breast-plate for over a dozen times, until her eyes were red-raw and her cheeks black. Although this hardly seemed to temper her spirit, it did go some way to silencing her complaints, which permitted me to proceed with training the other women in relative peace. Despite the resistance which had been offered by Saorla, the remainder of my unlikely pupils exhibited a great enthusiasm to learn marksmanship. I was swept up by their excitement while I rediscovered my own fascination with the firearm. My fingers dancing about the charges on my bandolier as I sought to quickly pour powder into the rifle while explaining yet another shot.

It was almost dusk when I reached for the twelfth apostle on my belt, and as I sought to remove its cap with one hand, I clumsily let it fall upon the grass. In that same instant I realised to my great horror that the ring was kept inside it. A chunk of powder slid out of the charge as Muireann swooped down upon it. My knees buckled when she picked up the fallen ampoule and grabbed the small mound of black dust in her palm, clenching her fist tightly about it in the dying daylight as she raised it towards me.

I stared into her widened eyes as my palm was slowly opened before her, to let the ollave place her fist onto it. As she released the powder, I quickly grasped it to check for the ring, which led me to unwittingly squeeze Muireann's hand. Just when I expected her gaze to be swiftly withdrawn, she held my stare for a few instants longer while she briefly also clutched my hand, which all too clearly betrayed her sentiments.

Thereafter I cursed myself for dropping the ampoule, which might have cost me both my reputation among the tribe as well as the precious trinket for which I had already endured so much torment and suffering. Yet my annoyance quickly subsided when I recalled the ollave's all too fleeting desirous expression. It lingered long in my thoughts during the following days when all training of arms was abandoned, as every last tribesman was needed for the MacGlannaghs' preparations for winter.

This allowed me to sleep long after the crow of the cockerel, followed by afternoons wandering about the town and observing the Dartrymen busying themselves from day to night. Their tasks included carrying large bales of hay to be stored in thatched ricks, which were tied down securely in the event of storms. All of the harvest purchased from the grey merchants in the south was gathered until the barns were filled with barley and oats, as well as apples and turnips. The late autumn had brought with it more rain, which delayed the preparations for winter. Nial was relieved when the wet was finally ended, as he stretched his limbs upon the bed in the outhouse and exhaled wearily.

'It has been a great effort, grey wolf. Yet the storage of these goods shall protect them from the faeries, who shall soon appear to blast every plant with their breath and feast on nut and berry.'

The bondsman had not spoken too soon, for the next day was full of winds so violent that they even drowned out the distant howl of the wolves. Nightfall found me tightly huddled in my mantle, with the only sounds about me being the creak of the boardings. Meanwhile Nial whispered the significance of the upcoming feast, which was to mark the beginning of a period that he referred to as the darker half of the year.

'Since the first harvests were gathered abroad, grey wolf, the feast of Samhain hath marked the beginning of winter. For 'tis an old Gaelic word which means summer's end, and it also marks the start of a new year.'

'The start of the year?' I exclaimed, 'yet 'tis still October!'

''tis indeed the last night of October which marks the beginning of the feast,' said Nial, 'and a vigil to last until the first sunset of November. To us Gaels this marks the start of the new year.'

'That is most curious', I remarked gently, 'for since boyhood the first of November has always been celebrated as the day of All Saints.'

Nial chuckled at my observation.

'Aye, 'tis also celebrated in Dartry as the day of All Saints, followed by All Souls' Day on the second of November. Yet the feast of Samhain is not forgotten, while the elders in our tribe whisper that most of our rituals during the feast of All Saints hath been poached from this ancient tradition.'

An excited tone overcame the bondsman's voice, as he proceeded to explain that Samhain was a time when everything changed in Dartry. This was proved in coming days, although none among the tribe could have suspected the unfortunate turn of events which we were soon to discover. Nial also told me of the many candles which were lit during the nightly vigil between the months of October and November, that was conducted to honour the spirits of the dead.

During this time, the lowliest churl to the highest born among the tribe treaded lightly, for fear that they might extinguish a candlelight and cause a great lament. I shuddered upon learning that the tribesmen believed the air to be thick with the presence of spirits, since Nial claimed that the veil between our world and that of the dead was at its thinnest. Upon providing this explanation the bondsman fell silent, until I spoke again.

'Are you afraid, Nial?'

Nial did not instantly reply to me, but when he did his voice possessed a great calm which I found somewhat disturbing.

'We must take great care, but I do not fear death. It is only the living who cannot see all ends. I believe it is why we are afraid of the dead.'

The time finally came for the herders to lead their livestock down from the mountains, when they passed them through huge bonfires lit between town and marsh. A great low of cattle was heard when the creatures were forced through the flames, with the beasts soon followed by the tribesmen themselves who cheered aloud as they stepped through the blazing pyres. While I observed these proceedings with some amusement, I was surprised to feel a tug on my forearm. I turned to find the red-haired son of Muireann staring at me with a slight grin on his face. About him stood other boys of his age, who I had often spotted from a distance as they observed my training sessions with the rifle.

'What is it, lad?' I asked, feeling baffled by his sudden appearance.

'Thou shouldst follow us, grey wolf, for thou shouldst also pass through the fire. It shall purify thee from evil souls.'

For a moment I was almost about to reject his suggestion, when I realized that his stare had turned from one that was mischievous to one which was expectant. With a grunt I gestured to him to lead the way, since it cost me nothing to walk through the flames and to save him embarrassment in front of his peers. After all, the boy was the son of the woman who had helped me to reach safety. As we stepped through the flames, I was amused to see that O'Ronayne had also partaken of the ritual, and as he turned to greet Lochlain I stepped up to him and regarded him keenly.

'Surely you do not condone these pagan practices?' I asked him, with some indignation in my tone.

The Jesuit beheld me in surprise.

'And why should I not? I honour the ways of my people as strongly as I embrace the teachings of Rome!'

So saying, he turned on his heel and walked over to a small pile of bones. He next joined other tribesmen in picking up two handfuls of them and hurling them onto the fire. These bones were all that remained of the weaker heads of cattle which had been brought down from the mountains, only to have their skulls cracked open by the town's smith and their flesh salted for the coming season. The remaining livestock had been led to the larger cabins about the town which served as barns.

'Thou seemeth awed by our preparations, grey wolf.'

These words revealed the presence of the boy Lochlain behind me. He had been separated from his smaller company of friends as he sought me out alone along the edge of the green.

'It appears that thy folk fear a long winter' I replied.

'Thou speakest truth,' replied the boy with a look of dismay, 'for the portents are that the *Cailleach's* dominion of the year shall be strong and unwavering, and the elders fear that winter shall be both long and harsh.'

'Some things should not be spoken of openly, *mac an ri*' said a familiar voice.

We realised that Nial had stealthily approached us from the direction of the bonfires on the other side of the green. Lochlain's face became flushed at the soft rebuke, as he wordlessly scampered off towards the town. Nial watched the boy disappear, then gestured to some folk gathered about a small fire with goods and other provisions.

'Shall we join in the festivities, grey wolf? There shall be food and wine in abundance.'

As we wandered towards the growing ring of Dartrymen, I queried Lochlain's description of the impending winter.

'Who is the *Cailleach*?'

Nial grimaced.

'The boy should not be speaking of such things, for the church does not tolerate mention of them. The *Cailleach* is an ancient divination that lewd folk still believe, along with other accursed or peevish things of the most absurd nature.'

'Yet who is she?' I persisted, finding my curiosity stoked.

'An ancient Irish goddess: the winter hag who has dominion over all things during the dark half of the year. Yet make no more mention of her to O'Ronayne.'

I jerked my head in the direction of the Jesuit, who returned from the flames where he had last been seen hurling the bones of slain livestock onto the fire.

'He does not appear too concerned by celebrations of a pagan nature...'

'Lighting fires and candles is one thing, grey wolf,' replied the bondsman, as he slackened his pace and shook his finger at me in annoyance, 'yet I assure you that talk of other gods is an altogether different matter.'

The rest of the evening was spent feasting with the natives, filled as it was with drink and food but little laughter. For about the cooking fires there could be detected a sense of fear, and even mad Orla appeared sombre as I walked through the flames, while watching townsfolk lighting candles and carrying them to their huts to light their hearths.

Elders watched children who searched for apples in large wooden tubs which were filled with lakewater, and a few of the youths had been veiled in white, with their faces blackened to appear like the dead. Some also bore turnips that had been carved into lanterns. When the Jesuit was out of earshot I could hear men speaking in muffled tones, while Nial told me that they were busy discussing ways how to ward off spirits. After taking a swig of wine from a wooden mazer, he regarded the distant outline of the mountains which surrounded us.

'Already now the dead claim unharvested crops abroad, and shall feast on animals that strayed from the creaght.'

Later that night, a messenger was dispatched from the keep, who informed Nial that the lady Dervila had ordered us to join the festivities in the great hall of the Rosclogher tower house. O'Ronayne joined us as we made our way towards the ferry on the lake. I was delighted to return to the best hearth in Rosclogher, being also relieved to see that the queen's court did not include the gallowglasses who had journeyed to Duncarbery castle two days prior. Upon finding myself free of the presence of these vile Scottish mercenaries and my fellow Spaniards, I helped myself to more wine with Nial, while the nobles observed their vigil in a manner not dissimilar to the lowlier Irishmen out on the green.

Manglana helped himself to what men called the 'Samhain pig', which was fattened all autumn on acorns and finished to perfection on the stubble of crops. Meanwhile the highborn spoke in muffled tones and looked warily over their shoulders whenever the wind outside became too strident. A great howl of dismay was heard when a child accidentally extinguished a candle with her cloak, so that it occurred to me while I observed this behaviour that pagan tradition had indeed been abandoned in all but fact. For belief in wandering souls ran deep among the tribe, reminding me of the suspicions held by Italian peoples, which were mingled with their faith in a bond which was as unlikely as it was unholy.

An hour before dawn, Miler the harpist strummed his lyre softly, in honour of those tribesmen who had fallen during the year which was about to end. When he finished, all those present marvelled at the first rays of light which pierced the slit windows, as Dervila rose to her feet and addressed us in the vernacular, with the bondsman translating her words which echoed across the hall.

'I bid ye join me, to celebrate the light half of the year which has ended. The dark half begins today: a time of new beginnings and of great stirring.'

No sooner had she spoken these words, than she crossed the hall with her ladies at her back. Once they were through the door the noblemen followed her lead, leaving us to hurry after them. We made our way towards the lake, where three ferries bore the highborn to the Abbey of Saint Mel.

After crossing the lake and entering the abbey, we could make out the black garbed O'Ronayne readying to deliver the holy mass. During it I avoided sleep by training my eyes on the face of the ollave, who sat at the very front of the church alongside Dervila. In this way, most of the words spoken by the Jesuit went unnoticed, until he paused to refer to the spirits which had gripped the tribe's imagination the previous night.

The souls of the just are in the hand of God, and no torment shall touch them. They seemed, in the view of the foolish, to be dead; and their passing away was thought an affliction and their going forth from us, utter destruction. But they are in peace.

A great silence fell over the crowd, for in that hour they all held the steadfast belief that the dead had walked among us during the previous night. So we all gasped in shock when a great crash was heard behind us, and we turned in fright towards the sound. In the doorway, his hands still holding the doors, stood Donal MacCabe. His eyes were wide and his mouth agape, while he howled his distress at the altar.

The Constable seemed possessed of a wild, haunted cast, his usually fearless face etched with a terror which left us trembling with dread. An altercation ensued between him and the fast-reddening O'Ronayne, when a great intake of breath was heard at the constable's next words. Groans of dismay followed, and men beheld one another in dismay as the Scot's cries rang in our ears.

'Tá na Sasanaigh ag teacht! D'fhág a gceannaire Baile Átha Cliath agus arm dhá mhíle láidir i gceannas air!'

'What did he say?' I exclaimed, as I seized Nial by the shoulder while his face turned pale.

For a few moments the bondsman was speechless as his eyes widened with fear.

'The English Viceroy prepares to leave Dublin,' he whispered, 'he is to ride west at the head of two thousand strong. The minions of hell have been unleashed!'

Here ends A REBEL NORTH, *being the second part of*
THE SASSANA STONE PENTALOGY.

The third part is called HERO OF ROSCLOGHER,
*which recounts the great perils faced by Santiago
and his allies, when thousands of enemies are unleashed
upon Dartry by the Viceroy FitzWilliam.*

Thank you from all of us at Tearaway Press for reading
A Rebel North by James Vella-Bardon.

We've worked really hard to get this title published and we hope you've enjoyed this award-winning, critically acclaimed, bestselling read.

If you'd like to support James' work, you could post a review about *A Rebel North* on Amazon, Goodreads or elsewhere, if you get half a minute. Doesn't have to be anything too long, just pick a rating and then add a line or two about what you made of his novel. This will help alert other readers who may also be interested in James' work.

If you need a hand with this, just contact us at:

info@jamesvellabardon.com

And if you're interested in receiving the occasional email update about James' books, you can sign up to his mailing list on:

www.jamesvellabardon.com

All the best!

HISTORICAL NOTE

Most of this novel is based on recorded historical observations and events. I tried to take a 'journalistic' approach when preparing to write this story, so that I read as many different sources about 16th century Ireland as I could. I did this to obtain as objective and balanced a picture as possible of the world in which Santiago finds himself after surviving the Armada shipwrecks. Years of research were mostly spent in the Fisher Library at The University of Sydney, in which I ensured that I read every available source on the shelves.

To my mind 16th C Ireland makes for a phenomenal setting, because of the different clashing cultures involved in the epic historical events which took place in it. In famous novels like James Clavell's 'Shogun' or Bernard Cornwell's 'The Last Kingdom' you have two main cultures clashing, yet 16th C Ireland contained a few more than that.

So what was 16th C Ireland like? The accounts of certain 16th C English chroniclers might have you believe that 16th C Ireland was a wild wood filled with savages in dire need of civilisation. Yet various written records over the centuries show that late medieval Ireland was in fact a thriving land formed of many kingdoms, which is confirmed by the famous Irish writer Seán Ó Faoláin in his book 'The Great O'Neill' in which he states: *"there was a Gaelic people, not a Gaelic nation".* The Gaels consisted of many thriving tribes, at least until the Tudors -or Sassenachs - started to put the boot in as they attempted to reconquer Ireland in the 16th century.

The reason I say 'reconquer' is that after William the Conqueror took England in 1066, other Normans invaded Ireland during the 12th century under the command of Diarmait and Strongbow. After taking over large parts of the east and southeast of Ireland, the Norman advance was halted by a Gaelic counteroffensive which was not successful in driving out the invaders. The Norman families in Ireland came to be called the 'Old English' or the 'Anglo-Normans.' In time many of them also adopted Gaelic dress and customs which were later outlawed by the English crown through the Statutes of Kilkenny in 1366.

After England recovered some stability following the War of the Roses, the Sassenachs would have cast a wolfish eye on the Emerald Isle due to the huge commerce in timber which it presented. In his essay 'Land And People, c. 1600', R.A. Butlin remarks on the deciduous hardwoods which dominated Ireland, that included the *"oak, ash, hazel, holly, alder, willow, birch."* Yet there were other great fortunes to be made in Ireland, which were not consigned to the trade in timber alone. In her book 'The Making Of Ireland And Its Undoing 1200-1600', famous Irish nationalist and historian Alice Stopford Green observes that the post of English Viceroy in Dublin (who was the representative who ruled Ireland on behalf of the English crown) was highly sought after, so that after John Perrot was appointed Viceroy by Queen Elizabeth

I, his brother cried: "*now he shall be envied more than he ever was!*"

In her book Stopford Green provides detailed descriptions of the wealth which was derived from 16th C. Ireland, despite the years of warfare, even stating that: "*In 1586 President Bingham calculated the revenue from Connacht alone at 4000 pound over and above the ancient revenue and impost, besides a good sum in fines, and to these sums he added 2000 pound in preys and booties...this in a time of ruined trade, when the imposts of Galway had fallen to nothing and no wine any longer came there...*"

In their article 'Ireland in 1534', scholars D.B. Quinn and K.W. Nicholls remark upon Waterford harbour (the only port rivalling Dublin) being "*a principal outlet for Irish commerce in hides and cloth both to England and Europe, its merchants had connections in French ports, across the Irish sea in Bristol and traded with Spain, Portugal and the Atlantic islands.*" According to these academics, even the smaller seaside town of Sligo enjoyed "*a highly regarded export trade in herrings.*"

Historical records show that 16th C Ireland made a great profit off its catch from the sea that surrounded it, as well as its catch from the inland woods. So that "*the woods also produced furs such as squirrel and marten skins as well as goshawks for which Ireland was noted during the period. More troublesome inhabitants were the wolves that were still numerous and whose skins appeared in the Bristol trade.*"

In her book 'Anglo-Irish Trade in the 16th Century', Kathleen Longfield describes how Irish rebels traded hides with foreigners who provided them with iron, guns and powder. These hides consisted of a large number of wolf and deer pelts. For 16th C Ireland was known as 'wolf country' and the deer were not lacking either, for in 1589, the bard O'Hugin recounted in one of his poems how *"hunting dogs drove deer from the woods for the chieftain."* Birds of prey were also traded, since Longfield states that *"their excellence made them famous throughout Europe"* and included *"goshawks, falcons, two kids of tercels, merlions, sparhawks."* The Spanish nobility is said to have prized Irish Wolfhounds, with creatures native to Ireland being so in demand on the Continent that English state papers also refer to a request by the Portuguese Ambassador in England made in 1568, where he asked if he could buy *"horses, hawks and dogs yearly out of Ireland"* for his sovereign. Longfield specifies that the reputable horses in Ireland were of *"the lighter breed, or 'hobbies.'"*

Imports to 16th C Ireland did not solely include weapons. Quinn and Nicholls state that *"wine was a principal Irish import: obtained directly from France and Spain. Salt was needed for the fishery and domestic use, coming from France, Spain and Portugal in foreign ships or through...Bristol vessels. The third major import was iron."* They also state that *"much English cloth reached Ireland as well as a soaps, dyes, pottery and beans."*

Despite these great gains to be won by English gentry and adventurers, the Irish country beyond the Pale was a mysterious and threatening place to most people back in England. Seán Ó Faoláin states that to 16th C English contemporaries, Ireland seemed *"a world as strange as the Indies were to Columbus, nine tenths of it an unchartered Thibet and the O'Neills and O'Donnells and its chief princes as remote and unimaginable as the Great Khan."*

Ó Faoláin also adds that most Englishmen were scornful and contemptuous towards Ireland, since they *"could not conceive that behind outer ring of port-towns, behind the wild Irish woods and dark Irish bogs with their gleaming pools of water, there was another mode of life as valid, as honourable, as cultured as complex as their own...they saw nothing but 'savages', 'wild hares', 'beasts', 'vermin', 'churles', 'rascals', 'felons', 'slaves', either to be rooted out, civilised or exterminated."*

Butlin says of 16th C Ireland: *"there were very few roads inland, and journeys on horseback through the 'straits', passes and fastnesses were fraught with dangers, both from the enemy and the elements. Bridges were rare and rivers often had to be forded."* It was a landscape that would take some getting used to by the English, if indeed most of them ever got used to it at all.

Unlike the English gentry, the Irish chieftains lived in all sorts of different places. In his article 'Crannogs in Late Medieval Gaelic Ireland', Aidan O'Sullivan states that crannogs (ancient fortified dwellings constructed in a lake or marsh) were *"a classic and evocative feature of early Irish settlement landscape",* with Steven G. Ellis stating in 'Ireland in the age of the Tudors 1447-1603: English expansion and the end of Gaelic rule' that *"even nobles lived in cabins made of boughs of trees and covered with turf."* Yet although the lifestyle of these Irish chieftains might have seemed rough and ready, they ruled over sophisticated societies which contained very complex laws and traditions. The Brehon laws contained rules about the ownership of the slightest ounce of honey, and also assigned erics (fines) for every type of offence, with no incarceration ever served as punishment and capital punishment very rarely carried out. There were many layers in a

Gaelic society, with the members of each rank being able to claim different honour-prices in the event of a crime carried out against them. The Irish chieftains also valued their poet and history bards, and in his article 'The Irish language in the Early Modern Period', scholar Brian Ó Cluív states that even those sons of Irish cheftains raised in the English court *"sought to maintain professional poets."* There was also much resource and time devoted to learning in Gaelic societies, and in 1574 we have an account of an Irish school by an Englishman, a partial observer, whose purpose was the destruction of Irish culture to replace it by English obedience:

"Without any precepts or observation of congruity they speak Latin like a vulgar language, learned in their common schools of Leechcraft (medicine) and Law, whereat they begin children and hold on sixteen or twenty years, conning by rote the Aphorisms of Hippocrates and the Pandects of Justinian."

Stopford Green states that in 1570, when the English made return by breaking Irish schools and destroying their libraries, they still had to recognise the talents of the people: *"sharp-witted lovers of learning, capable of any study to which they bend themselves...loves of music, poetry and all kinds of learning."* Stopford Green also adds that *"as any independent Irish life survived, the scholar was the most honoured man in the community. The spell of its culture fell on every foreigner who came to make his home in the country – on Norman barons, French soldiers, English citizens of the towns and lords of the Pale."*

As for the language that was spoken, Brian Ó Cluív states that by mid-16th C spoken English in Ireland *"was in a state of almost total eclipse"* because *"the reformation brought about a unity of purpose between the Irish and the Old English and the Irish language became a symbol of the Catholic religion."*

Latin remained an important language, with Benignus Millett stating in his article 'Irish literature in Latin 1500-1700' that *"Latin was the language used by the Irish in correspondence and conversation with foreigners...the well-educated among the nobility, both Gaelic Irish and Old English, had Latin as well as Irish and English, and some of them also spoke French."* In his famous letter (which is fascinating and also available to read for free online), Captain Francisco de Cuéllar - a survivor of the Armada shipwrecks and a character in Santiago's Armada Saga - wrote that local people could converse with him in Latin. The impact of the Jesuits on learning in Ireland cannot be underestimated, with Millett writing that *"most towns had a school...in some places were Jesuit schools for Catholics."*

Besides upholding the craft of the bards, Quinn and Nicholls state that *"every territory had an official Brehon (judge) or brehons appointed by the lord who tried cases affecting his interest or those of the territory as a whole."* Bards and Brehons were held in such high regard that Quinn and Nichols add that in all the Irish regions, bards and Brehons (as well as clerics and chroniclers or men of letters) were exempt from *"the general rising-out, by which all able-bodied men were required to serve at the lord's command."*

Of course, this land of learning and thriving trade was set to enter one of its most tumultuous phases as the 16th C wore on, with the 'reconquering' Sassenachs from Tudor England first crushing Silken Thomas in the eastern region of Leinster, and then Desmond's two revolts in the southern region of Munster. At around the time the Armada's ships were wrecked upon the western coast of Ireland, the slow and insidious reconquest of the western region of Connacht had begun.

Yet it was not always through war that the English sought to unsettle the Irish chieftains. The English tried other means to bend the chieftains to their will, such as entering into pacts or treaties with them like 'Surrender and Regrant' (devised by the very Thomas Cromwell who is the protagonist of Hilary Mantel's *Wolf Hall*) or 'The Composition Of Connacht.' However, entering into these accords with the Sassenachs was not without consequence for the Irish chieftains, who soon found themselves having to acknowledge a foreign legal system of possession, inheritance, landlordism and other institutes which would drive his followers to furious protests.

This left a Gaelic chieftain caught between the old Gaelic Brehon laws and the new English code, rendering him a demoralised white blackbird in that he could no longer rely on his old friends who rejected him or his new English allies who suspected him. The chieftain was often left with no choice but to either compromise with the English again or else fight against them (which the Sassenachs would have considered a revolt, given that the said chieftain had already entered a pact with them).

This in turn meant that those Irish chieftains in Connacht that did not accept English rule - who included O'Rourke in Breifne and the MacGlannagh (MacClancy) in Dartry – all had to eventually change from being traditional Irish chieftains engaged in the odd border dispute with their neighbouring tribes, to instead become full blown warlords. In her book 'From Kings To Warlords: The Changing Political

Structure Of Gaelic Ireland In The Later Middle Ages', Katherine Simms states that: *"the aristocratic king's court had become the headquarters of a warlord, shorn of the trappings of royalty and utilising paid professionals to carry out key military and other functions."*

Yet this presented the chieftains with a problem. 16th Century travel writer Fynes Moryson said of the Irish: *"they dare note stand on a plain field but always fight upon bogs and passes of skirts of wood"* or also attacked the enemy if it beat a retreat. This does not mean that Irish soldiers were to be trifled with, for Moryson also adds that *"the Irish were swift and terrible executioners...never believing the enemy to be fully dead till they have cut off their heads."* There was obviously no love lost between the Irish and their English oppressors, with Moryson adding that when the Irish killed the constable of Limerick, they cut off his head *"and played football with it."*

Yet the Irish kerns could not stand up to the English troopers on the open field, which made the Gaelic chieftains' need for paid professional troops (i.e. mercenaries) inevitable. These Irish chieftains turned warlords hired gallowglass warriors, who were essentially mercenaries from Scotland. Quinn and Nicholls state that *"great lords had services of a permanent body of galloglass, quartered on their territory, while lesser lords hired gallowglass at need"*, while also adding that *"they received high wages...were quartered on the country and their pay and maintenance must have represented a heavy burden for the areas on which they were cessed and billeted."* Maintaining these troops must have been an awful burden for the local Irish populace, although the Scots' prowess in battle was beyond doubt. In fact, Sir Nicholas Malby, the English military governor of Connacht described the Scottish mercenaries as *"the only hope that any evil-disposed Irishry have to sustain them in their enterprises."* Irish lords would have found a surplus of Scottish mercenaries to be hired against payment, for in his article 'The Completion Of The Tudor Conquest And The Advance Of The Counter-Reformation 1571-1603', G.A. Hayes-MacCoy states that these Scots were *"driven to Ireland by political and economic pressure and apparently rising population in their homeland."*

As for the Sassenachs, their reported cruelty is present in academic articles by scholars of all nationalities. G.A. Hayes-McCoy states that *"to the Irish and Old English, the likes of Malby were arrogant, ruthless men whose system threatened a wide spectrum of society, from the learned class to the jurists, poets to musicians to the men of war...the likes of Malby were suspected of the same sadism like that of Humphrey Gilbert, who killed man, woman and child and terrorised Munster by exhibiting to people the heads of their dead fathers, brothers, children, kinsfolk and friends."*

So it is no surprise, due to these unspeakable torments, that the Irish would have also looked to Spain for salvation. Hayes-McCoy states that in 1570, the Irish sought to induce King Philip to make Don John of Austria king of Ireland, stating: *"if we had a king like other nations none would venture to attack us."*

They also railed against Queen Elizabeth I of England, who they called *"Elizabeth the pretensed queen of England, the she-tyrant who had deservedly lost her royal power by refusing to listen to Christ in the person of his vicar* (the Pope)."

And although is hard to find any records which provide much insight in the 16th C Gaelic Irishman's mind, one cannot but imagine the excitement and delight that many of the long-suffering tribes would have experienced upon learning of the Spaniards who landed in Ireland following the Armada shipwrecks. Stopford Green states that in 1586 the Viceroy in Dublin complained of the Irish and *"the inward affection that they have always borne to the Spaniard."*

In his book "The Elizabethan Conquest Of Ireland, The 1590s Crisis", John McGurk also describes the poor quality of English solider sent to serve in Ireland, who would never have endeared themselves by their behaviour to the local tribes or to their subordinates. McGurk states that English Captains in Ireland were often *"more inclined to dicing, wenching and the like...rather than spare a penny will suffer their soldiers to starve."*

McGurk's writing also reveals that the quality of Sassenach sent to fight in Ireland was inferior to his countryman sent to fight on the Continent, when he shares the accounts of an English soldier in Ireland who states *"others are gentlemen and worthy, yet fitter for the wards of the Low Countries and Brittany where quarters were in good villages rather than here on waste towns, bogs or wood."*

So the 16th C Ireland in which Santiago finds himself can be fairly described as once a place of great trade, culture and learning, which fast deteriorated into an interminable war zone filled with great suffering, mainly due to the religious differences as well as the insatiable greed which fuelled the endeavours of European colonists back then. Very few places in 16th C Ireland could have been considered safe. Which is a good segue to my final note which relates to the parley scene in this novel: some readers might think that the precautions taken by the MacGlannaghs during the parley chapter are excessive, however it was not unheard of for parleys to be dishonoured. After all, Hayes-McCoy and other historians state that the Earl of Essex treacherously attacked and captured the Irish lord Brian McPhelim during a parley in October 1574.

ACKNOWLEDGEMENTS

They say it takes a whole village to raise a child, I certainly experienced that while growing up in one of The Three Villages in Malta. Since then, my writing seems to have created a village of sorts, made up of fans around the world who are connected through their passion for historical thrillers and WiFi.

Thank you to Pierre Fenech and Anton Tagliaferro for never allowing me to consider giving up and for getting what I'm doing and what I'm about. Anton believed in the voice from the very first, thank you. And thanks to my wife Donna Madden for her understanding and the challenge of being married to and raising kids with someone who is often not around but tapping away madly at their desk. There are many others to thank, of course. Thank you Dery Sultana and Professor Stephen Gatt for your interest and unwavering support, as well as my friends the world famous tenor Joseph Calleja and actor Andrei Claude who encouraged and inspired me to keep on fighting. I'd also like to thank my parents Frank and Josanne for all their kind assistance, as well as anyone else I've forgotten to mention.

Lastly I'd like to thank all those patrons and fans of Sheriff who kept the faith and who were gracious enough to read my work again. I hope you've enjoyed this latest Santiago yarn.

ABOUT THE AUTHOR

James lives in Sydney with his young family and a maniacal cavoodle.

The recipient of a few international literary awards and nominations, he enjoys reading gritty thrillers filled with moral dilemmas and a real sense of danger.

www.jamesvellabardon.com

Made in the USA
Middletown, DE
24 January 2023

22711874R00246